Revenge of the Drowned Maiden

Copyright 2021 Cal Clement
All Rights Reserved

*The characters and events portrayed within are fictitious.
Any similarities to real persons, alive or dead is coincidental and not intended by the author.*

No part of this book may be reproduced or stored in a retrieval system or transmitted in any form or by any means, electronic, mechanical, photocopying, recording or otherwise without express written permission of the author.

ISBN-978-1-7376655-0-2

Cover Artist: Juan Padron
Printed in the United States of America

This book is dedicated to my best friend and biggest supporter, the love of my life and my greatest fan. My wife, Megan.

"We must free ourselves of the hope that the sea will ever rest. We must learn to sail in high winds."
- Aristotle Onassis

```
REVENGE OF THE DROWNED MAIDEN

         by Cal Clement
```

PART ONE
"RED SKY AT MORNING"

Chapter 1

Pirate Cove
28 Sept 1808
19 Degrees 36' N, 72 Degrees 59' W

The deck of the H.M.S. Valor shuddered under his feet. Tim, oblivious to the danger, remained focused on the pirate vessel lying in wait just inside the cove. When the Valor heaved Tim was thrown from his stance on the quarterdeck. The groan of wooden timbers against coral filled his ears as he tumbled along the deck, helpless to regain his footing. The Valor lurched sideways, and the groaning was replaced with sharp cracking as her hull was breached by rock. Another sudden heave of the deck slammed Tim flat onto his face, coarse wood grain bit at his cheeks. A sailor approached to assist Tim back to his feet. The sound of cannon shot impacting the Valor preluded a blast of wooden shrapnel that pelted the sailor all along his side and in his neck. The sailor dropped to his knees, inches from Tim's face, blood pouring from his wounds. The man fell forward on top of Tim. Blood gushed from the sailor's wounds and soaked into Tim's shirt, covering his face and neck.

Tim pushed the wounded man off him. Rolling to one side, he tried to get his hands underneath his torso to push himself up. Another cannon shot thundered through the air, its report echoing around the cove and mixing itself with the impact. The Valor shuddered again with the impact while screams pierced through the gathering smoke. Every way Tim looked was a scene from hell. Deck timbers were shattered, lines snapped and recoiled from their tension while wounded sailors fled across the ship, desperate to escape the onslaught. Tim rolled to his back as another round impacted against the larboard rail sending more death dealing shards whizzing through the air just above him. A section of yard dangled limply above, suspended only by the sail it was supposed to be supporting. Smoke was building around the ship as Tim finally regained his feet. He took a step toward the seaward rail, intent on throwing himself overboard to escape his newfound hell. The impact of another cannon shot slammed him back onto the deck, smashing his chin into the unforgiving wooden planks.

His vision blurred, pain shot through his jawline and up into his scalp. He reached an arm out and clawed his way forward, crawling toward the rail that lay in front of him like a beacon of salvation. The sound of tearing canvas was almost inaudible amid the screams of the wounded and the echoing reports of cannon fire. The yard slammed onto Valor's deck thundered, reverberating the hull of the ship like a bell. Tim craned his neck through shooting pain to see where the yard had fallen. A mess of twisted wood, torn canvas and mangled lines lay about the deck. Sailors stumbled and crawled to escape the carnage through blinding smoke and flames. A moment passed without a cannon report, Tim strained to hear while he anticipated the next shot. It didn't come.

"They're reloading! Quickly now, get off the ship!" he cried through the smoke. The only answer that met his ears was the groaning death song of a doomed ship and her crew. Tim shoved himself to his feet and stumbled his way forward, his shoes scraped over the deck until he reached the bulwark. In a desperate lurch he threw himself over the rail, expecting to fall freely down to the water below. His efforts were rewarded by his right shoulder slamming onto the exposed hull of the listing ship. Confusion and fear gripped Tim as he rolled down the side of the vessel, slapping into the water as it frothed over the coral reef. The coolness of the salty sea gripped Tim, squeezing the air in his chest out in a forceful rush. The flow of the water's movement paused momentarily and then began to reverse itself, dragging his body beneath the sea surface.

Tim struggled in vain against the force of the water. He slammed into the top of the jagged sharp reef which opened deep gashes with every contact. Pain shot through him. Over and over, the water lifted him slightly just to push his body back onto the bed of knives. His hands, knees and shoulders were ripped to ribbons. In a moment of clarity, between the pummeling of the bobbing sea, Tim realized if he did not get away from the reef, he would be thrashed to death by the formation beneath him. As his body hit again under the force of a rolling swell, he grabbed onto the coral formation sending fiery pangs of pain streaking up his arms. In a desperate bid to survive, Tim pushed off from the razor coral with his feet pulling wildly with his arms until his face broke through the water's surface. He gasped in, expecting a lungful of air only to be choked by thick smoke. Pressing through his gagging cough, Tim wheeled his arms in frantic strokes, clawing at the sea while kicking his feet. Another swell came and he could feel its pull as the rise gave way and fell back again. He gritted his teeth, expecting the searing tear of his flesh as it met the jagged formations below. But the swell returned and no contact with the coral was felt. Tim realized as he continued stroking his way toward the outer shore of the cove what the pirate crew had known all along. The coral formation obscured the entrance to the cove, but only on the western edge. In his haste to confront them, he hadn't taken into consideration that the clever pirates could have been baiting him into a trap.

Shouts and cheers floated through the cove, meeting Tim's ears and burning deep into his psyche. He had been thoroughly bested. Perhaps, he thought, hanging Mr. Cobb had been a mistake. Cobb was insufferable and an inconvenient obstacle to what Tim needed to accomplish, but he would have likely seen through this rudimentary tactic the pirates had employed. Tim's feet touched onto gravel beneath him as he reached the outer edge of the cove opening. After a few more strokes his hands began to brush into the smooth rocks beneath him as well. Tim rolled to his back, floating in the shallow water, and looking up toward the starry night sky. What had been a terrible dilemma a day ago was now catastrophic. He sucked in the coolness of the night, unhindered by smoke this far away from Valor's wreckage. In a month he would be due to report his progress before a meeting of The Order. Representatives from Great Britain and the East India Company would be present as would several American investors and plantation owners. His task had been to create a stable route with which to smuggle captured slaves from Africa to the American south, thereby enriching both the East India Company who would provide transport and security and continue the legacy of cheap labor for agriculture throughout the southern states.

Tim's body floated along, drifting farther from the mouth of the cove until the back of his head pushed onto a narrow corridor of sand that lined the bottom edge of sheer rock guarding the coast. Tim pulled himself up to stand, gasping several times at the pain shooting through his knees with every movement. Under starlight and a slight moon, he could see just enough to follow along the sandy stretch until the high rock face gave way to sloping grassy hills. Fumbling his steps through the dim light, Tim gathered his thoughts for the future. He'd had no idea what had become of Geor Alton, the Crown's governor of Jamaica. After his ship the Georgia Spirit had been blown to bits by the pirate crew, he had witnessed as they plucked the fat oaf from the water. If the Governor was alive, he was a liability. He must either be recovered or silenced, permanently. Along with everyone he had come into contact with. Including the crew of brigands that had just undone everything he had spent the last year putting into place.

The night breeze dried Tim's shirt and caused his skin to tighten with goosebumps. The chill combined with pain from his wounds and a woozy weakness he felt from blood loss. He longed to stoke a fire in a wood stove, crawl into a plush bed and sleep away his woes. His knees throbbed with burning, stinging pain from every step. His hands were gashed and swollen, both palms cut deep in several places so that gripping anything would be impossible. Blood oozed from his knees and shins with every step. He could taste it in his mouth from the jarring impact of his jaw onto the Valor's deck. His nose and brow had suffered cuts, though Tim didn't remember if it was from the Valor or the coral. He trudged onward, slogging his spent legs through their fatigue and the sand that tried to swallow his feet with every step. Progress was slow, but eventually he could no longer hear the victorious cheering of the pirates. Tim was doubtful they would come looking, but leery to remain near the shore past daylight. If the pirates came looking and found him, his best hope would be for a swift end.

Revenge of the Drowned Maiden

Gereau Plantation
20 Nov 1808
Near Port-au-Prince, Haiti

Lewis Edgefield was waiting for the strike to land. His wrists were suspended above his head by shackles chained to a tall wooden frame. His head was spinning and heavy, he felt sick. That morning he had been introduced to his new surroundings and his new form of laboring, cutting cane. All day in the Haitian sun he had toiled hacking and hauling sugar cane with only a scarce drink of water. The field boss was an especially cruel man who seemed to take a great deal of pleasure in Lewis' misery. The process was grueling, cane was cut with a machete, then bundled and hauled to a rutty road where the field boss took stock as it was loaded onto carts to be hauled to the boiling houses in Port-au-Prince. It was there in the shade of a looming tree line where workers could catch only a brief respite from the blazing Caribbean sun, get a ladle full of water from a large cask where the field boss made his evaluations of how much to load onto each cart. This is where Lewis' trouble with the field boss began. When the sun had reached high into the sky, Lewis was denied any more water by the man who simply told him to, "Work faster and then we shall see." Lewis, angered by the cruel denial, did just that. He worked as fast as he could, bringing back another armload of cane ahead of the others. He drew knowing looks from the experienced slaves around him. Again, he was denied water and Lewis had to bite his lip to avoid saying something he would be made to regret. When he turned to make his way back to the looming front of cane opposite of where the carts were loaded, his limbs felt as though he were dragging them through sand. In a sudden wave, his head felt woozy and the humid air around him felt as if it was crushing him into the ground. His dizziness increased until he could no longer keep his feet beneath him and for Lewis, as the ground rose up to meet his collapsing body, the world went dark.

When Lewis awoke, he was being lifted and chained to the wooden frame. He was familiar with the apparatus, there was a similar implement on the plantation he had come from. He had seen others who had endured the torture of whip lashes from a field boss, but this was the first time he had been bound to one of the wooden frames himself. His eyes rolled uncontrollably while his head dangled. His feet were barely able to touch the ground leaving most of his weight supported only by his wrists. His breath only came in labored wheezing jaunts, sending a dagger of pain through his stretched ribs. He did not know how long he had been unconscious, but the sky was dark, and he was surrounded by the flickering light of a pair of hissing torches mounted to the pillars of the frame around him. Gathered in a semi-circle to his front were the slaves he had toiled with in the field earlier, each one displaying a dreadful grimace. He knew that in moments his back flesh would be ripped by the searing kiss of a whip, likely until the master's arm grew weary. Lewis squeezed his eyes shut, biting at his lower lip in anticipation of the pain he had heard described a hundred times over but never felt himself.

He thought of the night he had been taken from his parents and wondered where they were now. He remembered the day he first witnessed his father endure lashes and how his mother had soothed him, trying to shield his young eyes.

"This will teach you boy. There's no layabouts in my cane field, the next time it will be a noose for you!" the voice behind Lewis taunted. A crack broke the evening as the field boss reared back with his long leather whip sending a lightning bolt of adrenaline through Lewis' veins. He bit his lower lip, squeezing his eyes shut and bracing for the slicing jolt of pain. He waited for a long moment, gasping as the anticipation became too much and he realized he had been holding his breath in. The noise of a scuffle behind him broke out.

"Drop it," a woman's voice said from behind him.

"What is this?" the field boss' voice demanded, off balance.

"Judgment day is here, slave master. Time to pay the piper," a different voice from Lewis' front replied.

Lewis opened his eyes to see a line of armed men and women, black and white, approaching through the crowd of his fellow slaves. The gathered slaves parted to allow their passage until the line all congregated directly in front of the wooden frame he was suspended on.

"Swing that whip and I'll take your arm," the woman from behind him said. "Chibs, get him down."

A burly white man, with a bald head and thick graying beard stepped in front of Lewis, looking at him with a kind smile. "Aye Captain," he turned to the others, "Give me a hand here. I don't think his legs will hold once I get these damned shackles loose." Two of the other armed strangers quickly moved in, putting their shoulders under Lewis' arms. Chibs released Lewis' wrists from the shackles above and, in a rush of relief, he could feel blood returning to his arms and unrestrained breath into his chest.

"What are you doing? Who do you think…" the field boss demanded before his voice was cut short. Lewis craned his neck to try and see what was occurring when the men holding him turned and eased him onto the ground. Lewis' eyes widened; awe struck by the sight he beheld. A beautiful young woman was wrapping the skinny end of the field boss' whip around his neck. Torchlight glimmered from her light brown skin, shining in bright contrast of the white blouse she wore. "Remember me?" she asked, tugging on the whip to cinch it tight around his neck. Her eyes held a cold fury for the whimpering man she now drug along the ground toward the wooden frame. Without a moment's pause or hesitation, she tossed the handle end from the whip up over the cross frame.

"You two." She gestured to the men who had helped Lewis down, "Heave away and tie it off. We've more work to do." The two men snapped into action, pulling at the whip until the field boss' feet lifted off the ground. He kicked wildly, clawing his hands at the whip wrapped tightly around his neck. He bucked his body in a vain attempt to free himself, each movement losing strength, moment after moment until his arms dropped and he hung limp. Lewis stared into the man's face, the bulging eyes seemed to be looking right back into his own. The clattering sound of two large chests being dropped onto the ground broke his gaze on the dead man's face. Chibs, the man who had called the woman his captain wrested one of the torches off the wooden frame and held it high, standing between the two large wood chests. He lifted the lid on one and upended it, spilling an assortment of weapons from inside. Muskets, swords, pistols, daggers and tomahawks all tumbled onto the matted grass at his feet.

"Captain Lilith, Master of the Drowned Maiden, has ordered us to raid the estate house up the hill. We'll be leaving none alive and nothing will be standing when we set sail at dawn. If you want to collect your wages, now is the time. Anyone who joins is welcome aboard, otherwise, take your leave and stay out of the way." Chibs spoke over the crowd of slaves as they looked amongst each other with bewilderment. Several stepped away, fading into the night to make their escape as the armed men passed around weapons. Lewis looked up with a hunger in his heart to join when he saw the girl captain's glance linger on him for a moment. She approached and crouched next to him, holding a curved longsword in one hand and a pistol in another.

"You stay here, we will be back for you, and I'll see you to safety. You have my word," her eyes met his and reassured him as she smiled. Then she stood and turned without speaking another word, strutting away into the darkness with her crew and a slew of freshly armed slaves following.

Lewis was left alone, at the edge of a ring of light from the single torch left on the wooden frame where his former field boss hung, swaying slightly from the night's breeze. It had been a day since he had been packed off from his parents. Sold or loaned, he didn't know which, he was sent here to harvest cane. Now he was watching the contorted face of a man who had delighted in his toils sway in flickering firelight. A chill ran up his spine despite the muggy heat in the night air. Lewis drew his knees in close to his chest and rubbed at his tender wrists, thankful they had been relieved from the burden of hanging his bodyweight. A shot cut through the night, followed by another and then a long silence. A bright fire erupted through the darkness, sending shadows from the trees lining the road to the estate home dancing across Lewis' vision. Intermittent screams and cries floated to his ears, each seemed to end abruptly either punctuated by a gunshot or simply fading into the thickness of the night.

The fire grew as the moments he spent waiting alone drug on and Lewis watched with anticipation as the estate was consumed in a growing inferno. Orange and yellow flashes lit high into the darkness, glazing at his eyes until he had to squint to make out the silhouetted figures descending the road. As they approached, Lewis could make out the pair in front as the burly Chibs and, at his side, the girl captain. She shot a glance and a smile his way as they walked on, she turned to the armed gang following her, "Bring this one along. If he can't walk, carry him." Two of the larger armed men scurried up to Lewis, lifting his arms up over their necks. Without a word they hoisted him along, following as their captain led the way down the dark road. Her strides were flanked by another woman on one side and Chibs on the other. Each was carrying a crackling torch in one hand and wielding a pistol in the other.

The night grew cool and cane fields gave way to towering trees that hugged each side of the road. Lewis tried to keep pace with the men bearing his weight across their shoulders. His legs ached and exhaustion from strain began to take its hold. His head drooped, bobbing with every step. His shoulders and neck burned from the tension of his weight. The coolness of the night was soon lost as their pace quickened. Above, the night sky was fading into deep shades of a growing dawn. The gathering light seemed to accelerate their pace further. Sweat beaded along Lewis' brow, dripping into his eyes and falling onto the dirt road.

"Here it is," the woman next to the captain said, pointing to a narrow path ahead leading off into the thick forest. The column came to a momentary stop where the path diverged from the road and Lewis relished a chance to rest his legs. His heart sank as the torchlight shimmered up the trail and he could see the path led up a steep grade into darkness. The captain, looked back over the faces in the column of followers.

"Any of you who don't wish to come aboard, part from us here. Any who do are welcome to come along, as free men and women," she turned to the men assisting Lewis, "How is he?"

"Can't say he'll make it on his own Cap'n, I think I'll have to carry him," one of them replied.

"Whatever it takes. Trade him off if you have to, but I gave him my word we'd bring him and we're running out of time," she said.

"I've got him, lead on Captain," he answered hoisting Lewis onto his back.

The trio leading filed off the road and up the steep windy path. Darkness closed in around Lewis as the canopy of forest choked out the early glow from above. His weary eyes strained to see the ground ahead and Lewis wondered in amazement at how the man carrying him was so sure footed. The pitch of the path steepened and soon the head of the column ascended out of the thick forest and back into the early glow of pre-dawn. Beneath him, Lewis could feel the man carrying him quicken his pace. A breeze washed over them both carrying coolness and the distinct smell of the sea. They crested a grassy ridge overlooking a broad bay. Golden fingers of daylight stretched high into the sky, fading all but the brightest of stars into the recesses of a deep violet. Lewis perked up his head as the man carrying him began his way down the seaside slope of the grassy ridge. He looked out over the gentle rippling of the bay and in the dim morning light he could make out a ship. Tall masts stood bare in the steady breeze, swaying only slightly with the water's motion. As the light grew, Lewis's sight caught the motion of a banner hanging over the ship's stern. Billowing behind the imposing vessel, a black flag adorned with a skull and trident at its center and a chain along its bottom edge with a broken link in the middle.

Ritten Plantation
7 Feb 1809
Southwest of Charleston, S. Carolina

"Cotton, sugarcane and tobacco Mr. Walters. Do you know what these things all have in common?" Clyde Ritten stared into glowing coals at the foot of the fireplace. The room was an ornate study in Clyde's estate house, high ceilings trimmed with intricate crown molding towered above the expanse. Three walls of the study were lined with tall, dark wooden bookcases packed with leather-bound volumes. Above them were massive, painted portraits of Clyde's ancestry. Stern faced scholars, accomplished officers, and gentlemen alike, they all looked down in perpetual scorns immortalized by skillful brush strokes. On the wall opposite the fireplace, an array of windows towered from waist level and stretched high toward the ceiling. The scene displayed through the humidity fogged glass was a distorted view of a rocky stretch of Carolina coast. Overcast skies, spitting intermittent rains through the chill of the February evening cast an ominously dim gray through the windows. Clyde turned from the fireplace to face his guests, zeroing his glare in on Rory Walters. "Well?" Clyde demanded.

"These are all crops you harvest, Mr. Ritten." Walters responded in an even tone, his eyes unmoving from Clyde's glare.

"Me? Harvest? No, Mr. Walters. That's what we have Negroes for. Even if I felt inclined to harvest my own crops, which I don't, it would be impossible. No son, these are all crops that require a significant amount of labor on hand. Labor that you and Mr. Sladen committed to us. A ship every three months was what you promised if my memory serves me correctly. We saw no ship in September and now the ship expected in December is two months late. Just what are we supposed to make of this?" Clyde's tone iced over, and Rory could feel all eyes in the room turn onto him.

"I have not heard from Tim in months Sir. I have no idea what to make of these recent developments, he was supposed to be aboard the Gazelle with December's shipment." Rory's flat toned answer caused a flicker in Clyde's eyes that sent a shiver through his ribs.

"And yet here you stand in front of us, doing nothing to rectify our losses. If no shipment is delivered before this year's harvest season, every man in this room stands to lose considerably," the flash intensified, "Including you, Rory. Though it will not be gold or crops you pay with." A tense moment lingered over the room and Rory shifted on his feet slightly, darting his eyes to the onlooking faces of the other men in the room.

"We have received very disturbing reports Mr. Walters. A slave revolt in Jamaica, pirate ships engaging the Royal fleet and now another missing ship," one of the seated men interjected. "I'm sure you can understand why we would be growing anxious. Our question is, what are you doing, or going to do, to fix this?" His drawl belied an artificially friendly tone that strained to mask growing frustration.

"I can recruit some men and…" Rory started to

reply, shifting his gaze between Clyde and the man who just spoke.

"No. No, I've lost enough on men recruited by Mr. Sladen and yourself. I have purchased a brigantine and hired a crew to man her. You, Mr. Walters, will accompany the crew to Kingston. You will investigate what has unfolded there and report back to us here when you deliver every head we are owed." Clyde snapped.

"But, the revolt Sir, if the slaves have risen up…"

"Then they will be easy to find. Won't they?"

"Yes, Sir. Yes they will." Rory replied, feeling the weight of a collective stare on him.

"I should warn you, not to attempt to flea your responsibility here. My crew will bring you back to me, dead if necessary and do not come back to us empty handed young man." Clyde turned back to face the smoldering remains in his fireplace. "You will find the brigantine is expecting your arrival. They are harbored in Charleston; she's called the Southern Song and it will be a fitting ship for you. Now leave us."

Rory stood in awkward silence for a moment. He had not come prepared for such a journey and his reluctance to embark on it now was only surpassed by a dreadful fear of the consequences of refusing. His mouth hung open, unable to form a response. Clyde was expecting him to produce results where Tim Sladen had failed. Rory turned and made his way toward the door, his eyes catching on the scornful glare from a large portrait of a hard-faced man in a red coat and ornate hat. The image bore a striking resemblance to Clyde, including the perpetual scowl. When he reached the door, Rory turned back and scanned over the faces of the seated men to see that each was still fixed on him as he left.

The hallway was just as obscenely decorated as the rest of Clyde's home. Mounted swords and portraits filled the spaces of wall in between intricate sconces holding the light of low burning candles. The end of the hallway opened into an atrium lined with artwork from Europe and Asia with a grand chandelier hanging high above and a broad red carpet with gold fringe leading him to the front entrance. Unlike when he had arrived, there was no house servant to fetch his coat or usher him out the door. He found his hat and coat unceremoniously piled on a table beside the doorway and when he opened the door, he could see his horse still tied to a hitch rail. The chilled air quickly relieved Rory from the heat he had felt inside and before he mounted his horse, he could feel its icy grip on his fingers and face.

Rain drizzled through the gusts of a cold northeast wind and right into Rory's face as he rode. The road stretched out before him, green hills and trees on one side and the foreboding Atlantic on his right. Waves came in more and more forcefully as he rode, and the wind seemed only to grow in strength as he rode toward Charleston. As the dreary daylight faded from the overcast sky Rory's chill grew to an intense shiver. His toes and fingers stung from cold and merely holding onto his reins became difficult. The lights of Charleston were a welcome sight on the horizon, appearing just as Rory was beginning to fear he would never reach his destination. Smoke rose from stove pipes and chimneys scattered through the town, filling the cold air with the aroma of wood smoke and cooking food. Every breath Rory let out trailed a frozen vapor cloud behind him as his horse sauntered past the first few buildings.

The inn looked inviting. Its windows were fogged from the contrasting heat inside against the cold saturated glass panes. Rory stabled his horse in a large barn next to the establishment and entered. Inside he found a raucous group huddled around a large wood stove drinking ales and conversing loudly. The inn keeper approached him and after a brief exchange Rory managed to secure a room for the night. He was given a hefty plate of stewed meat and vegetables along with a couple of bread rolls and a deep mug of dark ale. The inn keeper left to fix up a room for him while Rory sat at the edge of the group, listening to their conversation as he wolfed down the hot meal.

"There must be something foul at play. They were due here in October. The ship that was supposed to meet and escort her in witnessed the whole damn thing. They were overtaken by a frigate class ship, flying a black banner," a bald man exclaimed over the gathered. His incredible statement met with a series of smart glances and rolled eyes.

"How the hell would you know anything about it, old man? They probably took their cargoes and sold them elsewhere. Their captain is the real pirate," a young man shot in reply, drinking deeply from his mug after he spoke.

"I know because my brother-in-law was the first mate of the escort vessel. He's a true man and a damn fine sailor, he's got no reason to make up tales," the bald man said, gritting his jaw.

"Well, if he's not a liar then he's a coward. They were charged to bring her into port, and they watched her be taken like a group of lily holding schoolgirls. Does your sister know she married a schoolgirl?" the younger man snarled setting his mug on a table.

"Cool your tongues! Any man who starts a fight in my inn will find himself without a roof or warmth for the night!" the innkeeper injected as he descended the staircase to the common room. "Any man who would cross swords with a crew under a black banner is a foolhardy soul, if you ask me."

"What would you know of it?" the young man sneered, "You cook slop and change bed linens."

"Think you know a thing or two young man? As a matter for you to think on, I sailed on the U.S.S Alliance during the war. We saw our share of actions son and I promise you, when a ship approaches under a black banner every wet behind the ears little sod like you starts thinking of hearth and home real quick. You'd be more likely to wet the deck from your trousers than with another man's blood," the innkeeper shot back, causing an awkward silence to fall across the room. The young blowhard slunk back into his seat, turning his attention back to his meal.

"What were they hauling? That ship that got taken?" another man asked the bald one, breaking the silence.

"From what I'm told. Sugar," the bald man replied. Rory's attention was turning back to his plate of food when the innkeeper joined the conversation again.

"I wouldn't doubt they were taken by pirates. I've

heard tales in this very room of the sort. A frigate ship, sailing under a black banner with an awful horned skull and a trident. I had a guest here about a year ago. He was a deserter from the Royal Navy. He said they had been chasing down an East India ship that had been taken in a mutiny. The buggers led them in a circle around a spit of land just east of Eleuthera and ambushed them with heated shot from the beach. That poor kid said he escaped the burning ship by the flap of a bird's wing before she went down. He swam to shore and was four days before he was rescued by a passing smuggler." All eyes were glued to the innkeeper's grave expression, framed between his lengthy red chops. "I wouldn't doubt the merchant ship you were talking about was taken by them. What did you say her name was?"

"I didn't. But my brother-in-law told me her name, Carolina something…" his voice trailed off as he searched for the name within the recesses of his memory.

"Carolina Shepherd." Rory said before clearing his mouth with a long drink of ale. Everyone sitting around the wood stove turned their attention to him.

"He speaks. Yes, I think that was it. How did you know that son?" the bald man asked.

"It happens I have been tasked to find that vessel. Find her and recover lost goods." Rory replied, wiping ale from his lip with his shirt sleeve.

"Tasked by who? She was loaded with sugar; seems folks around here would be just as glad she didn't make it. Good reason to drive their price higher," another man asked.

"Interested parties. She was bound for Britain after making port here with a load of local goods. That's lost income for your folks around here," Rory said.

"So, you're a pirate hunter then? My hat is off to you boy. Be sure to settle your bill before you put to sea," the innkeeper said, drawing a chuckle from a few of the patrons.

"I'll do that." Rory said, standing to leave.

"Good luck to you son. You're a braver man than I," the bald man nearest the stove called after Rory as he stepped his way up the stairs. Rory hardly took note of the goodwill message, his thoughts lay with the fearsome mental picture his mind had conjured of barbaric pirates torturing and murdering the entire crew of the Shepherd. The troubles that lay ahead kept him restless long into the cold winter night while wind howled outside.

Offices of the Admiralty
7 Feb 1809
London, United Kingdoms

Low hanging clouds gripped the London skyline as Admiral Alistair Torren's carriage pulled in front of the Admiralty building. The early morning chill of February was playing havoc on the aging officer's gout-stricken legs and feet, nevertheless he was dressed immaculately in a formal uniform complete with powdered wig and an ornate bicorne hat. The cobbled roads were still puddled with sleet from the night before. When the carriage door opened a blast of fresh, cold morning air wafted in. Though his legs and feet pained him in the cold, Admiral Torren was not about to let a complaint slip to the ears of his aide. He stepped out into the pre-dawn and the icy chill wrapped his legs. Turning to his aide, a young lieutenant named Jackson Thatcher, he fought the grimace his face wanted to make.

"It's early enough, lad. Be a charm and bring me the reports after you've made up some tea. I think I'll walk in the courtyard for a spell. Fresh air is good for the lungs, and it reminds me of when I was a younger man, at sea," he said with a smirk.

"Yes, Sir," the lieutenant replied in snappy military formality.

The long corridors of the Admiralty were always dark in the early hours when Alistair first arrived. He made it habit to be into his affairs before the sun shone its face onto London. His heel clicks echoed through the dark corridors as he strode toward his office. The final stretch saw him up a broad hallway flanked by a bank of tall windows to his left looking out into a massive courtyard and a wall of portraits on his right, a large grandfather clock ticking away the seconds mixed with the clicks of his steps until he reached his office door. Opening it, he was greeted by the dark outer room where his aide's desk stood, crossing the small outer room he entered the door to his inner office. Grand in size and decor, his office was kept a degree below sweltering. Alistair, stood in the dark office for a moment, as a fleeting thought crept into his mind. He shook off the nuisance and lit the lamp on his desk, rubbing his hands together over the glass to shake the cold edge held by the morning. Then he turned, abruptly, as if he were forcing himself to do so before he got too comfortable and proceeded out of the office, across the hall and into the courtyard through a set of glass French doors.

Cold air smacked his face and lungs as Alistair briskly set his course. He walked clockwise in a circuit around the outer perimeter of the court. In the center, a series of statues was flanked on either end by bronze warship sculptures. On the west end of the courtyard a large oak stood with bare branches and on the east lay a large rectangular reflection pool, which had long frozen over in the cold winter. Vapor trails followed along as his breath froze in the cold morning and with each lap he quickened his gait, twisting his face freely from the pain in his feet and legs without witnesses. Beneath his heavy cloak and uniform coat and the wool bicorne, Alistair began to perspire slightly on his third circuit around the large courtyard. When Lieutenant Thatcher arrived at the doors of the courtyard with a tray of tea and biscuits in one hand and a stack of letters and messages in the other, Alistair raised a solitary finger.

"One more Lieutenant, take those into my desk and have a fire going when I get in," he said in a slight huff.

"Yes, Sir," the lieutenant replied quickly turning to continue their daily routine. On his last half of his last lap, Alistair's legs finally felt some relief from the pangs of pain rising through the soles of his feet and into his knees. He slowed slightly as he neared the set of doors and stood with his hands on his hips looking over the peaceful serenity within. He eyed the statues of admirals and generals from long forgotten battles and traced his gaze over to the bronze frigate on the west end under the towering oak tree. "Damn it Grimes. Where in the bloody world are you?" he said aloud, lifting another cloud of vapor from his mouth before he turned and headed back into his office.

Inside the fire was roaring to life as Lieutenant Thatcher coaxed it with a bellows.

"That will do Lieutenant. Let's have the morning reports." Alistair said, shucking his cloak and hat and hanging his uniform coat onto the back of his chair. This routine was clockwork every morning, the early arrival, tea, and reports after a four circuit walk through the courtyard. Routine and uniformity were Admiral Torren's standbys, discipline and reserve was his trademark. Many of the statelier characters in London, at court and elsewhere, thought of him as a peculiar man. But in the Royal Navy he was revered. His seamanship and battle strategy were legendary but what was spoken of him the most was his approachable demeanor and humility. It was often said by sailors, "A drop of Nelson's blood wouldn't do us any harm," but a far more honest and rarer expression went, "Admiral Torren? I'd sail with him to the ends of the earth." And it was meant wholeheartedly by all whose lips it left.

Lieutenant Thatcher stood at the end of the desk opposite the fireplace and began sorting through a stack of letters and dispatches. He began with dispatches from the admirals and commanding captains in port, working his way through detailed accounts of ship supplies and daily occurrences.

"Captain Sharwood aboard the Dawn Fire has

requested a detachment of marines to assist in a press gang, he is severely undermanned and due to put to sea next week." Lieutenant Thatcher rattled, mostly eliciting no further reactions from Alistair than a head nod or a grunt. "This dispatch is from the governor in St. Kitts, apparently he sent a request to Governor Alton in Jamaica for additional sea power to deal with smugglers. He says his request went unanswered and he has heard reports from merchantmen that there was some kind of revolt on the island."

"What? A revolt?" the admiral looked quizzically at the young lieutenant.

"Yes, Sir. That is what his message says." Lieutenant Thatcher replied, as he paused reading the dispatches.

"How could that be? Our Caribbean fleet is headquartered in Kingston and the garrison at Fort Charles is more than sufficient to put down any unrest." Alistair said, thinking aloud.

"Perhaps there was a revolt, and it was put down, maybe the governor just could not spare the aid, Sir." Thatcher suggested.

"No. I've known Elliot Sharpe, the commanding admiral of the fleet there, since we were midshipmen, just boys. If there was a call for aid, he would answer. That is vexing, we shall come back to that later, I need to think on it. On to the next, lad." Alistair grumbled while leaning forward in his chair and rubbing the bridge of his nose.

The lieutenant went a shade past his normal pale while reading the next letter after he broke its seal. His eyes traced along the words written on the parchment and then began flitting back and forth between the admiral and the letter.

"Well? What is it?" Alistair prodded when he noticed the cadence of their back and forth had been broken by a long awkward silence.

"Sir, it is a dispatch from the garrison commander in Barbados, Colonel Wellworth. He is requesting additional troops and ships to reinforce his colony and citing mixed reports from merchantmen that Kingston has fallen to either a slave revolt or an invasion of pirates." Lieutenant Thatcher rambled, stuttering over words as he tried to get them out. "Sir, he is saying the Caribbean fleet is reported lost. Sunk in Kingston harbor."

"What? Let me see that!" Alistair stood, reaching for the letter. He drew a pair of spectacles from his breast pocket and held them in place while scanning the pleading words of Colonel Wellworth. As he read each sentence Alistair could feel a rush of blood to his face and a tingling through his fingers. The colonel's language left nothing to interpretation, it was a plea for aid amid the growing certainty that a grave and growing threat was present in the Caribbean.

"Damn it all to hell. Sharpe. Grimes. Damn it." Alistair uttered in a lapse of his trademark reserve. He snapped his attention back to his aide to find the lieutenant's face twisted in an expression of fear and confusion. "Not to worry, lad. We'll sort this mess. Get that fire out and let's get ourselves up to the admiral of the Navy's office, he should be in by now." Alistair said with a grim expression.

"Admiral B-Becker, Sir?" the lieutenant uttered, his confusion replaced with a look of displeasure and hopelessness.

"Lord Admiral Becker, young man, and be sure to address him properly. Better make sure your uniform is in sorts as well, you know how he gets with junior officers." Alistair replied with a slight grin.

"Aye, Sir." Thatcher replied, hurrying out to his desk to check himself over.

Alistair fumbled for a moment over the letter before pulling on his uniform coat and tucking the parchment into an inside breast pocket. Admiral Becker was an unpleasant man at best. Though he was higher in station, both socially and in billet, Lord Admiral Becker was younger and far less experienced at sea than Alistair and delivering bad news would be an unpleasant task. Attempting to steer the decisions the man made as a result of the bad news would be almost unbearable. Alistair considered a hasty retirement for a passing second, then shifted his thoughts to the task at hand. He looked over to the huffing fire in the fireplace that Lieutenant Thatcher had neglected to douse. Alistair cracked a smile at the young officer's fluster. He picked up a pitcher of water from a wash basin in the corner and poured it onto the fire, sending steam and smoke spewing upward.

The walk up to Admiral Becker's office was a more urgent pace than Alistair's typical purposeful stride. He and Lieutenant Thatcher made their way around the corridors on the perimeter of the grand courtyard and ascended a set of marble lined stairs with ornate columns and a pair of Royal Marines guarding the base step. The two sentries snapped to attention as Admiral Torren and Lieutenant Thatcher passed, crisply easing back to a position of formal rest when the pair were both behind their view and in the stairs. At the top of the stairs two tall, dark wooden doors were flanked by armor suits and standing Union Jack flags. Alistair paused for a moment just outside the doors and took a deep breath as if he were about to plunge himself into the depths of the briny waters of the English Channel. He raised a fist and knocked loudly with three deliberate thumps on the doors.

"Enter," a muffled voice inside spoke. Alistair smiled as Lieutenant Thatcher fumbled opening the door.

"Good morning, Lord Admiral. I have urgent news from the Caribbean." Admiral Torren announced as he entered the enormous office. The wall where he had entered through double doors was lined with flags from each of the historic kingdoms that now formed the United Kingdoms. The room was warm, though not as warm as Alistair would prefer. Along both walls to his sides were tall cases, some contained books and charts while others encased glass enclosures holding ornate weapons or intricate gifts he had received from the Royal family. At the far end of the room, behind an imposing desk at the foot of a tall array of windows overlooking the courtyard below sat a razor thin man dressed in civilian manner. He wore a powdered wig which spilled over his angled shoulders onto a black velvet coat with silver trim and buttons. His white blouse appeared to be silk and protruded slightly from the coat sleeves.

"A miserable cold day today, Admiral Torren, of course you would add to my displeasure on such a morning. What is this?" Becker grumbled and gestured to the lieutenant at Alistair's side. Alistair glanced over and saw Lieutenant Thatcher had donned his hat and was rendering a formal salute. "Do you mean to mock me this morning Admiral? Or is it just your aide who cannot grasp the delicate intricacies of an informal meeting?"

"My apologies Admiral." Lieutenant Thatcher fumbled and stammered through a reply while abruptly removing his hat.

"Well, I suppose you won't even give me the dignity of returning your salute now? Never mind addressing me by my proper station! Alistair, what is the meaning of this?" Becker's growling began to escalate as he shifted in his chair, leaning forward.

"Please Lord Admiral, forgive the ignorance of my aide. I will correct him in due time, but I have become aware of a far more pressing matter." Alistair answered, pushing through the man's arrogant tone to get to a productive note.

"More pressing? There was a day when he would have been flogged Alistair. Flogged and locked in stocks. Now what is it that you had to interrupt my morning with, what could possibly be so pressing?" Becker seethed, easing back in his chair and crossing a leg over one knee.

"Lord Admiral, there are two separate reports of some kind of upheaval in Kingston. One of them from the garrison commander in Barbados." Alistair started.

"So, send word to Elliot, find out the true nature of things, Alistair, really? Must I be troubled with such trivial matters?"

"The report from Barbados also indicates that the

Caribbean fleet is lost. A slave uprising or a pirate incursion has taken Kingston and sunk the fleet at harbor." Alistair said, raising his tone slightly.

Becker bolted upright in his chair. Placing both hands on the surface of his desk with his palms down and fingers outstretched.

"What in the bloody name of Mary do you mean the Caribbean fleet is lost? How could such a thing happen? Have you not received regular dispatches from Admiral Sharpe?" Becker snapped, hissing his words.

"I've communicated to you clearly over the last month that it has been some time since I last received a letter from Admiral Sharpe. Lord Admiral, we must act now to investigate and rectify this situation. If we have lost Kingston, likely the whole island of Jamaica will follow and the effect of that will weaken the empire significantly in a theater where we are in direct competition with not only Bonaparte but also the Americans." Alistair responded, evening his tone.

"Yes, yes. Right you are. Losing Jamaica would be catastrophic." Becker said in a softening tone as he stood and walked around to the front of his desk. "There are sensitive matters at hand here. Matters you are not privy to Alistair. I need a man I can trust to handle this."

"We are quite short of commanders Lord, between the channel fleet's blockade of Brest and trade enforcement off the coast of Africa and the strait of Gibraltar. Our northern fleet could spare a flag ship and we have a few in port we could reassign." Admiral Torren replied, fearing the answer that would come next.

"If we are short of commanders, then you will go yourself Admiral Torren. I trust that you still possess the capacity, yes?" Becker sneered with a taunting smirk.

"In fact, I do, Lord Admiral. I was just telling the lieutenant here this morning, it's about time I went back to sea. Land life does not agree with me. Nor the company it offers." Alistair retorted, turning to make his exit with Lieutenant Thatcher in tow.

Chapter 2

'Boston Autumn'
7 Feb 1809
19 Degrees 56' N, 72 Degrees 54' W

A thick fog encapsulated the merchant vessel adding to John Tarley's anxiety about being up in the highest reaches of the rigging. From his place along the spar of the top sail, he could scarcely make out the shape of the deck below. The air seemed so thick with the fog that it almost muffled the sound of calls. He worked his way along the sail yard, tying line in the manner the experienced top men had shown him, trying to maintain his footing and balance as he hurriedly went about each task. John had set out from England for the new world two years ago. When his high hopes for gainful employment and apprenticeship under a tradesman looked grim, he signed on to the crew of the next merchant vessel headed for warmer ports. The 'Boston Autumn' was far from the grand warships of the Royal Navy he had daydreamed about as a boy, but the square-rigged brigantine offered him an escape from the bleak outlook of being unemployed. His first cruise aboard saw him in the warm Caribbean, delivering merchandise in the Haitian port of Tortuga. Then, in an unannounced departure from what the crew had been discussing over meals, they made sail around the island toward Port-au-Prince. The detour took them a week out of their way and had them transporting a hold full of slaves back north to America. On their voyage away from Port-au-Prince, while skirting the northwest point of Haiti, they had come into some of the thickest fog anyone on the crew had ever seen.

"Reef Sail! All hands on deck, stand by to loose anchor!" came a call from below. John couldn't make out the deck through the gray haze, but from the gravelly voice he could tell it was the foul-tempered first mate. John scooted himself back across the sail yard to begin the process of pulling up sheet and tying off.

"Damn you kid, get your ass off the spar and walk along the line. I don't want to take all damn day," the sailor next to him growled.

"Ok, hold on. I'll try." John answered, fighting against fear and hesitation.

"Come on, come on. Let's get to it!" another sailor behind the first shouted, "The fog won't last forever, and I've got a warm hammock waiting!"

John rose to his feet, balancing himself precariously on a line strung along the yard. He gripped a stay line that ran from the mast out to the end of the yard so tight his fingers strained and the fibers of the course rope bit into his hands. He shuffled his feet along to the far end of the yard and with a sigh of relief straddled the wooden spar again between his knees.

"Un-sheet the top sail!" the grizzled first mate called, signaling the sailors below to loose the lines holding the bottom corners of the canvas taut. John started working his section of canvas with a fervor, fearing any delay on his part would further rouse his peers' ire against him. A loud rumble echoed through the dense haze, followed by a sheer whistling noise that grew in intensity until John's ears rang with a sizzling whiz that cut the air around him. Men below on deck began shouting back and forth and John looked up to see the sailors alongside him on the yard hurry toward the mast in a panic. Another loud rumble preceded a louder shrieking whistle that felt so close it sucked the air from John's lungs.

"It's coming off the stern! There's a ship out there, I can see her outline!" a voice cried across the deck. John's eyes bolted over the stern of the Boston Autumn desperately searching the fog for any sign of a vessel. Only hazy hues of gray and white hung over the gentle sea swells. "Hands, tie off those sheets, fly topsail and main. Ready on the yard!" the first mate shouted up. Another rumble sent a chill racing through John's blood as he realized what was occurring. The following whistle screamed so loud several of the sailors along the yard clamped their hands over their ears. The shrill cry ended with a roar of impact into the main mast followed by a blood curdling cracking of wood and a hail of shards flying through the air. John fought to maintain his grip on the line as the yard shuddered beneath him and his torso slammed onto the wood shaft supporting his weight.

"It's going over!" a voice below screamed amid the sound of screaming sailors and snapping stay lines. John looked up in horror into the foggy haze as the silhouette of mast and sail loomed, tipping in his direction. The violent crash stripped his hands from the line and an impact dragged him mercilessly from his perch on the yard. For a moment he felt a falling sensation, as if he were a stone dropped into a well. His vision swirled between the gray fog and the dark form of the deck, then he could see water rushing up to him. He impacted the water's surface in an unceremonious slap, catching him on his side and expelling the air that remained in his lungs. Salty seawater flooded his nose and filled his mouth as the shock of impact wore off. He looked up at the surface to see a web of lines and sailcloth bobbing along atop the swells. John kicked and pulled at the water, climbing with no handholds toward air. His side and leg still ached from the stinging impact moments ago, but that pain was all but forgotten for the terrible burning in his throat and lungs. He felt his chest spasming, crying out for air where there was none. Another pull of his arms brought him closer as his vision began to fade and strength left his arms with each contraction of his heart. Finally, his face broke through the surface long enough for John to suck in a lungful of air. He could feel the tangle of line around him, one running across his shoulder and behind his head. He wheezed in another deep breath, looking at the water around him and up to the Boston Autumn. Above on the deck he could hear a voice screaming

"Men overboard! Get a lifeline out!"

The line that had been floating limply around John's shoulders tugged at his shirt a bit. He twisted his neck to look and see what caused the movement, assuming it was another sailor swimming to where he was struggling to keep his face out of the water. Another jerk from the line sent a jolt through John's blood. He had been warned of something like this and now it was happening. The line started moving in the water and in another instant, it was zipping by him. John flapped and pushed his arms in a vain attempt to get away from the line as he heard a sailor above shout down, "Get away from that! The mast is dragging it down!" A swirl of water and bubbles drowned out the last of the sailor's voice as John felt the rope bite hard across his shoulder, propelling him downward with crushing force. He thrashed against the course rope, attempting a scream that only came out in a torrent of bubbles and garbled sound. The rope slid and tore across his shoulder, biting flesh away as it ground its way to the depths. John gave a desperate push against the rope, which bit into his hand as he pushed at it with every bit of strength he could muster and to his relief it slid down his collar and off his shoulder.

John was left dazed, far deeper than his first plunge beneath the surface and already starving for a breath of air. He kicked and pulled, focusing his eyes above him. The burning sensation returned to his chest and spread its fiery fingers through his shoulders and into his back. His legs ached from exertion and his head spun from the rapid succession of events that had just taken place. His arms felt weaker with every pull and John began to notice the terrible pain moving his left arm caused to shoot up through his damaged shoulder and into his jaw. He kicked with a fury, feeling his consciousness beginning to fade. The water's surface broke around his head and he gasped in a breath of air, immediately letting out a scream with everything he could muster.

"Help!" he cried, panting, and wheezing for breath. He looked around in the water for the next offending item that would try to drown him. A head popped over the rail and John could hear more yelling on deck above. He sucked in delicious breath, floating his face just above the surface. A thin rope splashed into the water surface next to where John floated and he could see a group of sailors standing at the rail on deck, waving him to grab hold. John wrapped his tender fingers around the lifeline and gripped it as best he could while his shipmates heaved him to the side. A rope ladder was lowered to the surface and John grabbed onto the bottom rung. Summoning what strength he could, he made his way to the rail, step by arduous step. Above him, shouted encouragements were mixed with the first mate's commands.

"Come on John! Just a few more steps!" a sailor called down.

"All hands! Arm yourselves! They're drawing near lads!" the growling shouts from the first mate echoed.

As John reached the rail, he was greeted by a slew of arms to pull him aboard. He fell onto his back, heaving breath into his lungs and feeling at the solid wooden deck beneath him, thankful to be above the waterline. A thunderous roar sent another whizzing shriek through the air, just over the deck.

"They aren't losing interest boys. Arm your damn selves and get ready, we won't be striking our colors today!" the captain shouted as he flung his cabin door open to come onto the quarterdeck. John looked up through his bleary, bloodshot eyes. He was barely able to make out the captain's form, but he knew the voice well enough. When his footsteps drew near, John could make out detail much better. The captain's face was flushed, and he stooped down to help John to his feet. The smell of alcohol was overpowering.

"Get up boy. Arm yourself! If they see us laying about the deck like a bunch of slack jawed landsmen they'll think us all cowards. Is that what you want?" The captain slurred.

"No Sir." Was the only response John could muster as he rose to his feet and a sailor shoved an antique looking saber into his hands.

"Come with me then, boy. We'll find out what sort of mettle you have today!" the captain growled loud enough for the whole ship to hear.

The fog was still so thick visibility only extended a few yards past the rail on each side. To the stern, a dark form was taking shape as it drew nearer with every passing moment. Muffled shouts and jeers floated in from the assaulting craft, taunting the merchant crew. John followed the first mate and captain to the bulwark over the stern as they surveyed the approaching vessel.

"They warned us about this in port. Why in God's name didn't I listen?" the captain griped over his shoulder to the first mate.

"We'll be fine Sir. Likely they'll just take some of our dry goods and we'll be off. There's no real pirates anymore."

"Did you not hear the barkeep we spoke to? There is a pirate crew in these waters, targeting ships hauling slaves! And what are we holding below deck? Honestly man! Are you that dense?" the captain scolded, drawing a grave look from his salty first mate.

The shadow of the approaching vessel became more pronounced through the fog, while taunts and insults continued to float in through the ghostly haze. As the ship drew nearer, detail became clearer and caused John's heart to sink. Along the starboard rail of the assaulting ship was a line of armed men and women, hurling insults and waving an assortment of edged weapons. Most of them were black with only a few white men scattered throughout the crew.

"It's them." John said, his shoulders sinking.

"Aye, it looks that way." The captain replied, "No use giving up before it's over though boy. If they take you, don't let them take you alive. No telling what they will do to you then."

A fireplug of a man, one of the few white men on deck of the approaching ship, pulled himself up to stand on the rail. He had a thick beard with a shock of gray running from his lower lip down. At his waist he wore a wide leather belt holding an array of pistols across his belly and a sword on each hip.

"Heave to and let's get to it you cowards! Don't make us chase you all damned day!" the bearded man called.

"Piss off!" the first mate shouted in reply and let fly

with his pistol. The Autumn's crew let loose an uproar of shouts and insults. The bearded man, unmoved by the pistol shot, looked back to his ship's quarterdeck like he was searching for some sign of approval. John's gaze traced back to where the bearded man was looking and then his eyes were caught with a sight that ran a jolt of ice through his veins. Hanging in the slight breeze above their pursuer's stern was a massive black flag. In the center of the field sat a fiendish looking skull with awful, twisted horns protruding from its head over a canted trident and along the bottom ran a chain with one broken link at the center.

"Captain..." the first mate said.

"I see it." The captain replied in a low tone. He turned from the rear of his ship and fumbled to check his pistol with shaking hands. "Two points to larboard. Run out the guns."

"Captain, they'll be on us before..." the first mate began to object.

"I know exactly what is about to happen! I said two points larboard and run out the damn guns! NOW DO IT!" the captain interrupted, yelling as he gradually began to lose his composure. John could see hesitation across the deck of the Autumn. Confused looks were being exchanged among the crew while their leaders bickered back and forth. The moment for action passed and a musket shot tore into the bulwark next to the captain silencing his quarrel with the first mate.

John dove for cover as gunfire sliced through the air above his head. The misty fog seemed to crowd in around the deck as he crawled to peer over the ship's wooden rail. A voice from the pirate ship cried out

"NO QUARTER!" hailing a thunderous roar of shouts and cheers from the pirate crew. All around him on the deck of the Boston Autumn, John saw fear plaguing the face of every man he looked at. The captain, finding some inner pool of resolute defiance shouted at his crew, "Is this how you boys want to go? Cowering to some brigand band of thieves? Not me!" He stood, drawing his saber in one hand and grabbing hold of a stay line with the other. "You'll find no easy target here you…" His rant ended abruptly with the report of a single shot followed by a hollow thud against the deck as his lifeless body collapsed. John could see a gaping entry wound above the captain's right eye, oozing his life blood out onto the wooden deck. Shouts and taunts from the deck of the pirate ship only grew in intensity. Looking along the Boston Autumn's larboard rail, John watched one by one as lines with grapple hooks careened over and then were pulled tight, biting into the railing as they were pulled in alongside the pirates.

Fort Charles - Kingston, Jamaica
8 Feb 1809

Lieutenant Robert Trenton stood atop the parapet of Fort Charles, overlooking Kingston's harbor. He spent the waning hours of the day the same way he had for months. Splitting his attention between scanning the seaward horizon and scouring the Jamaican hills for sign of the next threat. He and a company of soldiers had returned to Kingston from a sortie to hunt bandits in the countryside months ago to find a state of bedlam and slaughter. Fort Charles contained the remnants of a massacre. The heavy doors of the gateway remained intact as did the walls, so Robert and his men concluded that the attack had to have come from within. The captain of the guard lay slumped over his desk, dead from a dagger wound in his back. Soldiers were found scattered throughout the fort, from rampart posts to the barracks below, all dead. The only sign of a struggle were the bodies they found within the remains of the barracks, which had been burned to the ground. The governor's mansion had been ransacked and the governor himself was missing. The front grounds of the governor's estate had been the scene of a grizzly battle with both Royal Marines and some unidentified civilian corpses littering the steps and gardens. Robert, a lieutenant at twenty years of age, was now the garrison commander of Fort Charles and the only governing voice of authority to Kingston. The weeks that followed his return were tumultuous as he fought to repair the damage to the fort and earn the trust of the citizens of Kingston.

News of the turmoil in Kingston had spread over the island of Jamaica like a wildfire, bringing brigands and bandits to regularly threaten the precarious order Robert and his men had established. The harbor was all but impassable. Two warships had been sunk in the navigable stretch of water leading to the harbor. He had sent a dispatch aboard a merchant sloop to the garrison commander in Nassau but received no reply. Visiting with the townsfolk had netted him little to piece together the events that had occurred. It had been some sort of insurrection. A coup that left the fort full of dead soldiers, two sunken ships in the harbor and a missing, presumably dead, Governor Alton. Adding to the chaos were regular attacks from bandits seeking to capitalize on Kingston's misfortune.

Smoke trails rose from stovepipes and chimneys scattered through Kingston. The sea was moving with a slight chop outside the harbor under a steady northwest wind. The skies were clear, and Robert took in the radiant sunset like a child in an art gallery. Orange and pink streaked the horizon, fading into deeper shades of red and purple as the warmth of the sun slipped away. The steady clink of a hammer and anvil echoed through town letting everyone know there was a blacksmith still hard at his trade. While the evening light faded, Robert grappled with a feeling of being utterly and helplessly alone. His eyes shifted out to sea, scouring the horizon once more, hoping to see an approaching sail bringing relief. He bit his lip, fighting the urge to scream out in frustration.

Robert turned from the parapet, stepping onto a flight of wooden stairs that led to the ground level of the fort's interior. A makeshift barracks had been erected since the siege from a set of canvas field tents. The stables had burned along with the old barracks, so their horses roamed the compound's inner grounds. The Fort's magazine and armory had been left intact, still well stocked with only a few muskets missing. As Robert made his way past the barracks tent the wooden gate was opened for a returning patrol. He caught the eye of the patrol leader who hurried over to report his findings to the young officer.

"Good evening, Lieutenant. All seems well in town, nothing unusual to report Sir." Sergeant Brooks reported, falling in step with Robert as he continued to the garrison commander's quarters.

"Any arrests?" Robert asked, bracing for some form of ill news.

"No Sir. It was quiet all through town." The sergeant answered.

"I thought you said there was nothing unusual Sergeant." Robert said with a quick smirk. "The market?"

"Almost barren Sir." Came another quick answer.

"They're still afraid. Maybe that's good. Fewer people on the streets means less trouble and fewer dead the next time the bandits hit. Good work Sergeant, that will be all." Robert said, dismissing him as he entered the commander's quarters.

The dim light did little to improve Robert's outlook and he found himself sitting at the desk in the outer office where they had discovered the body of the garrison's previous commander. In the faint flickering glow put off by a candle he stared at the same bloodstained maps that had been sitting on the desk when they pulled the captain from the chair he now sat in. Grudgingly, he pulled open a side drawer and removed a leather logbook to write his daily entry. Ink had just begun to bleed into the fibers of the parchment when Robert's mind trailed off. He hadn't finished the word under quill, but a thought struck him and carried his mind elsewhere. He remembered a patrol he had led last August. The garrison commander had assigned him to accompany an American man who was dealing with a slave uprising. Small scale revolts were not uncommon, and it was not the first time Robert had been tasked with restoring order. It was not uncommon for the sortie to be aided by a landowner either. But what stood out to Robert then and what was causing his quill to create an ink puddle on his log entry now was the mounted reinforcements the American had at his disposal that morning. Robert had seen the man in the garrison commander's office before, even at the governor's mansion once. At the time, he had just presumed the man was a wealthy American who was carving out a piece of Jamaica's favorable sugarcane lands for himself. But now it seemed too coincidental to ignore.

Robert put his quill down. The flickering candlelight danced in the drafty office space adjacent to his living quarters sending shadows dancing on the walls. He pushed his chair back, muddling through his thoughts. His suspicions aligned for a moment, and he could clearly see the opportunity and ability of the American to carry out an attack against the governing authority of Kingston. What eluded him was any clear motive the American would have. Robert stood from his chair and paced around the room several times. Finally, with weary eyes and a tired mind full of fragmented thoughts, he retired to his quarters for another fitful night of sleep.

Haitian Inland
29 Sept 1808

The sand had given way to knee high grass as the dawn broke and Tim slogged his way uphill from the beach. His hands and knees were still shredded from

the coral and oozing blood. The first lights of morning
stung his eyes as he crested a hill overlooking the
coast. He looked back. The gently rolling waves
capped in white, washed up onto the beach he had just
spent the night traversing. A column of smoke from
the wreckage of the Valor rose into the western sky.
Tim slumped down to sit on the grassy hill. His knees,
hands and feet all stung with a hot pain from every
movement. A wound on his side from the coral was
not very long but it had created a deep, ragged cut that
seemed to engulf his entire torso in flaming pain. He
took a moment to evaluate his situation. He was
injured. His clothes were in tatters, his shoes falling
apart. He hadn't eaten since the day before and had no
fresh water. If the pirates came searching, he had no
weapon to defend himself. His situation seemed
hopeless until he tried to muscle himself back up to
stand, then a wave of lightheaded nausea overtook
him, and his hopes of survival seemed impossible. He
crumpled back into the grass, feeling consciousness
beginning to slip from his fingers like a wet line. As the
ground beneath rose to meet him, Tim clamped his
jaw. Anger and resolve overtook his spell of nausea
and he forced himself back to his feet. He turned to
face northward. The sun shining on him brought
warmth. His aching joints and throbbing feet nagged
for him to lay back in the grass and rest, but he knew
that to lay down would be to give in to a slow death. If
the pirates pursued and caught him, he would die. If
he did not find civilization and get treatment for his
wounds, he would die. If he did not get clean water
and food, he would die.

Every step brought pain. It would spike into his blistered feet and shoot up through the shreds of flesh in his shins to his tattered knees. Through the stinging and aching of his wounds he could feel as blood slowly escaped flesh. Though his hands had begun to congeal in an attempt to begin the healing process, every time he moved was like opening the wounds afresh. The laceration he had sustained on his side just below his ribs had covered all his shirt beneath it and much of his trouser leg in blood. Squeezing his hand to the wound brought waves of pain to his side, from armpit to hip bone and to his aching hand. But when he relieved pressure from the wound, the flow of blood increased to a magnitude Tim knew he would not long survive. He trudged his way down the north side of the hill away from the coast.

The rising sun soon awoke an oppressive, muggy heat that only exacerbated his misery. His mouth and throat burned for lack of water and his lips were soon chapped to cracking flesh as he huffed and wheezed through them. Every step became a labor of sheer will against certain death. Waves of nausea washed over him if he tried to quicken his pace and maintaining his balance became another struggle he seemed to be slowly losing. Sun exposure began to sting his bare skin turning it red. He trudged his way inland toward a tree line that seemed impossibly far across a stretch of high grass that waved along under a hot whisper of breeze and brought no relief. Morning had given way to the crushing heat of midday when Tim came upon a rutted road bordered by two broad ditches with pools of stagnant water. A sudden rush of relief overcame him as he hobbled the last steps to the ditch. Painfully, he lowered himself to prone and reached a cupped hand into the warm water. Raising it to his face, he sucked the water from his hand repeating the action several times. His parched lips and throat felt instant relief from the gritty water tinged with blood from his own wounded hand. Handful after handful he sucked in the murky liquid until his stomach began to twist into knots from the sudden rush of fluid.

Tim rolled to his back, sending a web of ache up his spine and down his side. The sun beat down onto his face. His head pounded. He closed his eyes and relished the gritty wetness under his shoulders. Nausea rose within him again and he quickly had to roll back over to retch out the muddy water he had drank. Every wave of convulsion tensed his entire body, sending pain from each wound searing through his nerves in an unbearable symphony of misery. After he had expelled the contents of his stomach and heaved with no further result another spell of dizziness encompassed him. He tried to muscle through it and pushed a hand against the ground to lift himself to his knees. The earth beneath him seemed to shift back and forth as if he were on a ship at sea again. He managed to rise to his feet and stood. Taking a deep breath, his senses seemed to clear for a moment and his balance restored. He committed to the battle of step after step, each one bringing a dizzy rush from deep within up into his head. He crossed the road in a few steps and looked into the water within the next ditch. His next step seemed to miss, and he had to catch himself as the earth seemed to sway again. His vision blurred slightly, and Tim blinked his eyes hard, squinting in an attempt to correct the doubled and tripled account he was registering. His next step buckled beneath him, and the water of the ditch rushed up as he crumpled onto the ground.

Mud pressed into Tim's face, caking over his eyes while the dirty water of the ditch filled his ears and nose. He reached out, clawing himself up from the slimy grit that now covered him. His wounds burned from contact with the muddy grime. As he pulled himself up from the pooled water, he could feel the last tendrils of strength leaving him, replaced by fatigue and nausea. Exhausted, but free from the mud of the ditch, Tim rolled onto his back. His eyes drifted up to the piercing blue sky as thin, wisps of white cloud floated away high above him. His mind drifted. The events leading him to this muddy ditch, covered in wounds and barely clinging to life, played through his mind in fragments. His tobacco farm had failed, and his debts forced him to take up a profession he had long ago walked away from. At one point, Tim had been a soldier. To satisfy his debts, he had been taken into the employ of Mr. Clyde Ritten, a wealthy plantation owner in South Carolina. The terms had been simple enough. Secure labor for the Ritten plantation and slave market near Charleston. Every slave he successfully delivered to the plantation would eliminate fifteen dollars of his debt to Clyde. For every slave he brought to market, he would net a third share. One share went to Tim, another to Clyde and the third share belonged to a collective organization called "The Order". Clyde had explained The Order to Tim only in murky detail, alluding that its members stretched from wealthy plantation owners of the south to opulent businessmen in the north and even extended to powerful elites in the old world. Tim had been introduced to scarce few members of The Order. His position with them was tenuous and his good standing was only assured by continued success.

The unraveling of his carefully plotted network began with the inept Jamaican governor, Lord Geor Alton. Governor Alton was pompous, condescending and above all, weak. Tim had selected the governor as his partner in the Caribbean to facilitate the transfer of African slaves from East India Company ships to American merchant vessels. The governor had assured Tim that he could run adequate interference with the Royal Navy as well as keep prying eyes from looking into the prison camp Tim established near a cove along Jamaica's eastern coast. The governor had massively overstated his abilities. In the following months, Tim's prison camp had been discovered, two ships carrying his human cargo had been raided and a massive payment due to The Order had been seized by a crew of pirates.

The sun burned his eyes and little relief came from closing them. Long through the Haitian afternoon he drifted in and out of consciousness, waking momentarily to attempt lifting his head to look around only to slip back into the abyss of tormented sleep. His flesh baked in the sun and on his last awakening during daylight, Tim knew that another day of exposure to it would be his death. When he came to again the sun was drifting low on the western horizon.

The breeze had shifted from an occasional hot puff from the southwest interior of the island to a stiff southern wind that carried the cool of the sea along with it. Reds and pinks lit high into the sky as the first visible stars began to show their light. Tim slumped back into the dirt, too weak to lift his head for more than a few seconds at a time. He slipped into another dreamless drift.

When he awoke again it was to a light dancing in front of his eyes. A man's voice seemed to echo into his ears, though Tim could not distinguish who was speaking through eyes he could only barely force open. The light grew in intensity and Tim knew it must be a lantern or torch held by pirates who had finally tracked him down to finish his misery. Tim closed his eyes and grit his jaw in anticipation of a sudden cold kiss of a sword point or the fiery impact of a pistol shot. What came next was a curious shock as Tim felt a large, rough hand lay gently onto his chest.

"Esta Vivo!" a voice said.

"Papa, quien es?" a smaller voice asked, it sounded like a young woman.

"No conozco a nadie, pero necesita nuestra ayuda." The deeper voice owning the hand replied.

Tim had no idea what was being said. He recognized Spanish but could not understand it. The voices continued their exchange and Tim was grateful they seemed to mean him no harm. A horse nickered nearby, and Tim felt shooting pangs of pain as the huge rough hands picked him up. Tim let out a groan as he could feel the man's shoulder under his chest.

"Sé que duele amigo, pero estoy tratando de

ayudar." The deep voice said in a gentle tone. Tim tried to summon a response as the man eased him down onto rough boards that jostled slightly under Tim's weight. The Spanish voices continued their exchange and Tim heard the slap of reigns. The boards beneath him jostled suddenly, sending bolts of pain ricocheting through his entire body. Tim struggled to lift his eyelids, desperately wanting to see any detail of what was going on around him. He managed to focus his vision enough to see that he was riding in the bed of a small wagon. The night sky splayed out above him with blurry starlight scattered through the darkness. Another jostle of the wagon smacked the back of Tim's head onto the rough boards beneath and his surroundings faded away from his awareness.

'North Wind'
21 Feb 1809
London, England

The morning tide had risen and was on its way back out to sea as Admiral Alistair Torren strode his way down the pier. The damp wooden boards gave a hollow thud beneath his heels that seemed instantly suffocated by the dense fog that had set in. A step behind and to his flank Lieutenant Thatcher had to work at keeping up with the salty old admiral.

"Provisions have all been loaded and accounted for Sir. As well as your personal effects, just as you instructed." Lieutenant Thatcher huffed as he sidestepped a suspicious looking board on the pier.

"Very well Lieutenant, and the fleet, the fleet is

ready as well?" Alistair asked without so much as looking over his shoulder.

"Yes Sir. The Dawn Fire has finished their refit and took on the last supplies and a new press from the fishing fleet last night. We will be joined in the channel by Commodore Tilley on H.M.S Steadfast along with the squadron he commands." Thatcher paused for a second, recalling the other ship names, "The Taurus, ahm, Destiny, Longsword and the Surprise."

"Don't be ridiculous the Surprise went down with all hands off the coast of France years ago Lieutenant. Try again," the admiral gruffed.

"Apologies Sir, the Ambush. H.M.S Ambush, she's a sloop, seventy-eight hands. She will make for a fine scout ship to screen for the fleet." Lieutenant Thatcher corrected himself, offering more information in hopes of redeeming the mistake.

"I suppose you will be advising me on how to command my fleet now lieutenant?" the admiral quipped with a smile the younger officer could not see.

"No, Sir, no I only meant to..." Lieutenant Thatcher bumbled.

"You only meant to make yourself sound useful. I get it lad. But we are going to sea. Something you have yet to experience in your career. Sea life is not garrison, son. Give me the information I need, no more, no less. Don't interject your damned opinions until you have useful experience informing that hat holder on your shoulders. Keep your mouth shut and don't embarrass me or I'll have you keeled, understand?" the admiral interrupted without losing a beat in his gait.

"Yes Sir." Lieutenant Thatcher replied with a

sheepish tone. Keeling was only something he had heard of. Differing versions were still practiced in the King's Navy, but not in the same manner as during the admiral's days as a captain decades ago.

Their procession to the end of the pier was met by a line of marines standing statue still along with a drummer beating steady roll. As Admiral Torren passed in front of them the drummer ceased as the marines simultaneously rendered their salute. The admiral returned their gesture in sharp precision without missing a beat off his pace. With Lieutenant Thatcher close behind, he climbed into the longboat that waited to take them out to the flagship.

As the sailors brought the longboat away from the pier, Admiral Torren began to feel the pangs of his age. The cramped seating in the small landing boat allowed no one the luxury of stretching out their legs, not even a high-ranking officer like himself. He looked over the faces of the sailors pulling at the oars. They were young. Fresh faced and in decent health.

"You boys fresh from the press?" the admiral asked, to none of them in particular.

"Yes," answered one of the rowers, he had fiery red hair and a face full of freckles.

"You mean yes SIR!" a petty officer snapped at the red-haired youth.

"Yes, yes Sir. My apologies." The young man stuttered, blushing at his error.

"It'll be the cat that teaches you, you keep that up!" the petty officer scathed.

"It's quite alright lad." Admiral Torren interjected, before turning to the petty officer. "He's a landsman still, but I'm sure you'll get him rigged right. Remember petty officer, patience is a trait of good leaders."

"Aye Sir." The petty officer responded in his graveled voice.

"Patience is a trait of good leaders lads, but, unfortunately, not a luxury we have at the moment. Heave to, we must get underway at once." The admiral spoke aloud over the longboat crew again. Their pace quickened, each man at the oars pulling with his whole strength to speed the shuttle along.

The fog seemed impenetrable as the longboat glided along through the calm briny sea. As the oarsmen pulled the craft closer a dark silhouette became visible in the misty close fog. H.M.S North Wind stood ahead of them, a formidable sight to behold. A second-rate ship of the line, she had two gun decks each carrying eighteen guns. The bottom battery on each side consisted of twenty-four pounder cannons while the upper battery consisted of eighteen pounders. On her weather deck were another six guns to each side, these were nine pounders that could be rearranged on deck to provide chaser guns for the bow or stern. As detail revealed itself through the haze the admiral smiled to himself. She was a magnificent ship, in impeccable condition. He looked over at Lieutenant Thatcher sitting beside him. His eyes were wide with awe.

"She'll do, I guess." Admiral Torren said, jesting at the young officer.

"She's a floating fortress Sir!" Lieutenant Thatcher replied.

"She was Lord Admiral Nelson's flag, when he

commanded the channel fleet. I imagine she will do fine for us. We may even manage to get her some battle scarring." Admiral Torren quipped, smiling.

"Scarring?" Lieutenant Thatcher began to inquire.

"Wait, see that? Her lady on the bow?" the admiral interrupted. He pointed to the intricately detailed carving of a beautiful woman under the bow stem of the ship. As they drew nearer, more detail became clear. She was unlike any lady on the prow of any other ship in the Royal Navy, with a flawless chiseled face pointing out toward the seas ahead. The carved woman wore a representation of an officer's jacket, with a healthy portion protruding from the top.

"She is quite revealed Sir. It is…" the lieutenant's voice trailed.

"Spectacular. She is spectacular son." The admiral said, smirking at his junior officer while he marveled at the wooden figure. "Get an eyeful lad. It'll be some time before you catch sight of a beautiful woman again. Crawling up over the bow for a peek is a good way to wind up swimming."

Drums erupted from the deck of North Wind and a cannon fired off the opposite side, rendering the ship's welcome to the admiral. Lanyards were lowered and promptly attached by the oarsmen and in minutes the longboat was being hauled up the side by a crew of sailors turning the capstan. Admiral Torren's knees and hips ached, but he managed to stand as they neared level with the weather deck. Captain Orwell Landreth stood at the bulwark rail, ready to greet the admiral's arrival.

"Good morning, Admiral and welcome aboard Sir."

The captain greeted him with a cheery smile.

"Dispense with the pleasantries Captain. Get this damn longboat aboard and let's get underway, I want full sheets before I set foot into my cabin." Admiral Torren said in a flat tone. "We haven't any time to lose."

Sailing under the direct command of an admiral was often a boon to junior officers. They ate well and often invited subordinate officers to dine with them sharing their personal food stocks and liquor. Admiral Torren had no intentions of such formalities on this voyage and meant to make that clear as early as possible. He would push the boundaries of strenuous sailing and aggressively engage with any who stood in his path.

Captain Landreth showed the admiral into the great cabin with the deck beginning to shift with motion from the sails. It was a large cabin and well-furnished even for flagship standards. An immense desk sat at the rear of the cabin, with a plush padded chair behind it. The row of windows along the fantail were close to three feet tall and beneath them sat a row of oak cabinets that doubled as a bench seat. In the corner a small wood stove was already stoked with a healthy fire warming the cabin. A felted map table sat against the wall next to the door leading into the cabin and a large painting depicting a line ship delivering its broadside during the battle of Trafalgar.

"I do hope this is satisfactory Sir." Captain Landreth said in a hopeful voice.

"This will do nicely. Once we rendezvous with the rest of the fleet, make all haste for Nassau."

Chapter 3

'Drowned Maiden'
7 Feb 1809
19 Degrees 56' N, 72 Degrees 54' W

Lilith's cutlass rang out as the steel collided with a defender's sword. Trina, the pirate who had introduced Lilith to the hard ways of sea life, dashed close to her Captain's side and drove a longsword into the defender's chest. The battle on deck of the Boston Autumn had devolved from a pitched fight into a one-sided slaughter. Wounded and dead lay about the deck, gun smoke swirled in the slight breeze of the foggy morning. Looking around, Lilith could see the resistance to her crew was hanging by a meager thread. Toward the quarterdeck, Chibs let fly with a pistol from one hand dropping a sailor who was sprinting to flee overboard. With Trina at her side, Lilith raced for the stern. As she climbed a short set of steps up the aft castle the cabin door flew open. Trina swiftly seized the man who had opened the door, placing her sword at his throat and forcing his back against the wooden bulkhead of the aft castle. The line holding the Boston Autumn's colors snapped on impact from Lilith's sword, dropping their stars and stripes banner to float through the breeze to the briny water below. Lilith stood on the rail, hoisting her sword in one hand, and holding a stay line in the other. "The ship is ours!" she screamed out over the deck. Cheers erupted from the deck of the Drowned Maiden and the Boston Autumn while the few remaining defenders lowered their weapons and raised their hands in surrender.

"Where is the captain?" Chibs shouted wielding another pistol over several of the surrendering men.

"The captain is already dead. He was the first man you shot." The reply came from the man Trina held at sword point against by the cabin door.

"And who would you be?" Chibs asked, drawing near Trina's shoulder.

"I'm the first mate. Tolliver Bellamy." Tolliver answered in a quivering voice.

Lilith walked down the steps of the aft castle, shooting a look across to the deck of the Maiden where William Pike stood near the helm, watching the events unfold.

"You have cargo on board that lives and breathes. For your sake I hope they all still do. Where are they?" Chibs pressed through gritted teeth.

"B-below deck, in the hold. There's near thirty of them." Tolliver stuttered, his face turning redder by the second, his eyes flitting back and forth between the crew of pirates in front of him.

"Take him below Chibs, he can unlock the prisoners and set them free himself. Let them do as they want with him when he has finished." Lilith said as she walked toward the cabin door.

"I won't do it!" Tolliver sneered, pressing against the blade Trina had trained against his neck. "You'll set them free over my dead body."

Lilith stopped in her footsteps looking at the defiant first mate and then to Trina.

"I can grant his wish." Trina said without looking away from the seething anger written on Tolliver's face.

"No. No, I have a better idea." Lilith replied, stepping in and motioning Trina to the side. "He refuses to watch his prisoners be freed. He would rather die than watch them leave without their chains." She turned to Chibs, "Get some line. Bind them to the masts, make sure this one can see everything."

"Aye Captain." Chibs replied, quickly setting to his task.

Lilith walked back to the rail nearest the Drowned Maiden and called over to William.

"Will, send over a few more to search the hold. Have the starboard battery make ready and run out the guns."

"Captain, possibly there's a better…" William began to protest.

"Just do it!" Trina shouted over interrupting him.

A moment of pause passed, and William's voice floated through the air, repeating Lilith's orders. Lilith clenched her jaw. Will had objected to engaging the merchant ship. Even though they had watched as their hold was filled with slaves bound for America, he protested. Restraint was the word he used. Lilith should restrain the crew and herself. *Not while they are dragging mothers from their children,* she thought. Watching as Will passed her orders to the gun crews below deck on the Maiden.

"Captain. This one is saying he wants to join us." A voice caught Lilith's attention over her shoulder. She turned to see it was Jilhal, an African woman the Drowned Maiden had taken on when they plundered the East India ship Gazelle. She was holding a sailor by his shredded shirt. He had a ragged wound over his collarbone and looked like he had died twice already in as many hours.

"Not today sailor. But I will spare you from the fate of your crew. You will be a parrot for the Boston Autumn." Lilith said, motioning Jilhal over to the opposite rail. Lilith put a boot up onto the rail and leaned against her knee, looking over to the flotsam scattered in the sea.

"There's some planks and a barrel down there. Can you swim?" she asked the man Jilhal had hauled over.

"Well yes, but…" Lilith didn't wait for him to finish. She motioned to Jilhal who promptly hit him in the belly causing him to double over. When he was bent at the waist, holding his lower belly from the impact of being hit, Jilhal gave him a swift kick to the ribs sending him flailing over the rail and slapping into the water below. Lilith looked down at the man as his head bobbed back up over the surface.

"You'll find land less than a mile due south." Lilith called down to the man who looked like a drowned rat, she pointed her arm out to show him which way to go, "You swim for the shore and then you can head east. Less than a day's walk will find you in Tortuga. You tell every man with ears. If the Drowned Maiden crosses their path while they carry human cargo, you are the last man I will leave alive. Do you think you can manage that?"

"What choice do I have?" he called back up. Lilith smirked a little and looked over at one of her crew that was binding the other survivors to a mast. She gave him a wave over and took a pistol the pirate had tucked into his belt. Cocking the hammer back she leaned back over the rail and aimed at the man treading water below.

"We could let it be a surprise for the next crew just as easily." Lilith said wrapping her finger loosely around the pistol's trigger.

"No, no I'll go. I'll swim for land and carry your message." The man replied in a rush quickly paddling away from the ship.

Lilith watched as the man she let live swam southward into the misty fog bank. She wondered if he could make the swim to shore with his wounded shoulder.

"They're all bound, Captain. The first mate has a front row seat." Chibs said as the swimmer faded into the gray haze. Lilith turned to see Chibs, half giddy from the fight and the prospect of releasing the Boston Autumn's prisoners, his eyes flitting back and forth between Lilith and Jilhal.

"Very well Chibs. Would you see to it that his prisoners are set free then? Take Jilhal, she can help." Lilith said putting her hand on the African woman's shoulder.

"Aye Captain." Chibs said in his graveled voice, a broad smile spreading across his face. Lilith caught his smile and smiled herself, narrowing her eyes as she glanced back at Chibs. The old sea dog he was, Lilith knew he fancied Jilhal. As daring and tough as her quartermaster was, he was still a shy bird when it came to interacting with the beautiful African woman. Jilhal, who had been widowed aboard the Gazelle, was the mother of Omibwe, who was a determined young man about Lilith's age. Though he had lost his leg from a wound he incurred while being taken captive in Africa, Omibwe had proved himself a capable helmsman and eager member of the crew. Lilith followed Jilhal and Chibs back to the weather hatch, passing by the survivors bound to each mast along the way. The tied-up sailors either averted their stares or looked with pleading eyes hoping to change the fate they suspected but could not be sure of. She stopped at the main mast, next to where the first mate, Tolliver, was bound. His position afforded him a clear view of the path from weather hatch to the gangplank, where the freed men and women would board the Drowned Maiden and escape the grisly future the Boston Autumn's crew had been ferrying them to. Lilith crouched to make eye contact, a foot away from the defiant slaver.

"I won't watch it. You wench of a fish wife, you think yourself a captain? You won't break me girl." Tolliver seethed as he tugged his arms against the ropes holding him.

"Oh, you'll watch." Lilith said, pausing slightly and leaning against her cutlass which was digging its point into the deck at the furious man's feet. "I'll be sure you see every one of them off this tub and then you will be the fish wife."

"Not a chance, wench." Tolliver shouted, spitting as he finished his words and clamping his eyes closed in a defiant gesture. Lilith wiped her cheek, clenching her jaw as her temper flared. One of Lilith's crew, Renly, a marine who had come aboard with William after their battle with the Valor, saw the exchange and quickly stepped over kicking Tolliver square in his chin. The impact rocked his head back against the mast behind him with a resounding thump.

"That's my captain, you worthless barnacle sucking coward." Renly hissed.

"Coward?" Tolliver objected through broken teeth and dribbling blood.

"If you'd had any mettle, you'd have died fighting." Renly said, stepping away as Lilith raised her hand toward him.

"Hold his head Renly. We don't want him to miss the show." Lilith said taking a knee next to Tolliver and pulling her sword up from the deck.

Tolliver writhed his head side to side as Renly took hold beneath his chin and at his hairline. Lilith took her cutlass in both hands, one at the handle and the other a few inches from the point. She pulled the leading edge of the point up to Tolliver's left eye and dug the point in just below his brow, sending a bright red oozing of blood down his face and the sword blade. Tolliver screamed and heaved against the ropes binding him, kicking his feet and slamming his heels into the wooden deck. Tracing a semi-circle Lilith slowly cut underneath the eyebrow until the lid dangled by a thread on the outside corner. She grabbed the eyelid and snapped it away, freeing it from his face and leaving his eye exposed to the world. Lilith mused for a moment at the naked eye, giving him a broad grin before she started on the other side. Tolliver tensed again under Renly's grip, kicking his legs and huffing ragged breaths through gritted fragments of teeth. Lilith flipped the other bloody eyelid over her shoulder after she finished, giving Tolliver a scornful stare. Behind her, she could hear as Chibs and Jilhal ushered the freed prisoners out of the weather hatch and to the gangplank.

"You will watch. Just as I said you would. You will watch as I give them back their freedom and dignity and you will watch as the sea swallows yours." Lilith said almost in a whisper while her eyes remain locked onto his. She turned to look at the procession of slaves leaving their captivity. Lilith's eyes caught the face of a woman about the same age as her mother had been, before Lilith had escaped her fate. The pirate captain fought back tears, failing as her vision glossed over in a blurry mess.

"You alright Cap'n?" Renly asked.

"Fit to sail. See to it the crew strips everything of value from her." She turned and raised her sword point up to Tolliver's throat, "Any goods they have won't be of much use on the bottom."

"Aye Cap'n, we'll have her stripped to the bones then." Renly replied and quickly turned to get to his task.

Lilith lingered in front of the disgraced crew for a moment before slowly walking back to the Boston

Autumn's cabin. Inside was dark and smelled of tobacco smoke, giving Lilith a passing thought of Chibs out on the deck. Chibs often smoked a pipe and Lilith had grown fond of the familiar scent. As her eyes adjusted to the darkness Lilith continued into the cabin, taking note of some books scattered on a desk along the side wall. Lilith flipped open the cover of the book sitting closest to the edge. Its pages were filled with sailing log entries. She set the log to the side and opened another book, an envelope sealed with a spot of black wax fell out of its pages. Lilith picked up the envelope and flipped through the pages of the book. She could only read a few words, something she had been working on with William, but none of the words on this book's pages looked familiar. As a group of her crew entered the cabin to begin hauling away anything of value Lilith tucked the pair of books and sealed envelope under her arm.

"Leave nothing." She said giving the two pirates an approving nod as she exited the cabin.

Lilith made her way across the gangplank in between her crew hauling away whatever valuables they discovered in the hold. Crossing to the deck of the Drowned Maiden she was greeted by a stern-faced William Pike, a lieutenant in the Royal Navy brought aboard the Drowned Maiden after a series of treacheries had befallen his command the previous fall.

"Captain, is it necessary to sink their vessel? We have already freed their prisoners." William said, matching Lilith's gait as she walked toward her cabin.

"It is necessary Will. If I leave them alive, they will just return to port and try again. You know this is true." Lilith answered without so much as looking over to Will.

"But if we were to..." Will began.

"No Lieutenant. The Boston Autumn drowns today, and I won't hear any more about it. Have the guns run down to the waterline and notify me when the crew is finished with her." Lilith said with an edge creeping into her tone.

"Yes Captain. Right away." Will replied, sinking back from Lilith as she entered her cabin and closed the door behind her.

Inside her cabin, Lilith could still hear the muffled shouts and calls of the crew outside. Hollow thuds reverberated through the ship from gun crews below preparing their cannons to execute her orders. Lilith leaned her back against the cabin door and slid down against the door onto her bottom. Closing her eyes, she could see the face of her mother. The night before her escape. She had pleaded with her, begged her mother to find a way to leave the horrible conditions of their life on the plantation. Tears formed in her tightly closed eyes as Lilith wrestled with the memories and pangs of guilt crept in. When she returned to the plantation, with a crew at her back, she had hoped to find her mother. She had hoped to free all the slaves from that horrid place. But on her return to the fields of her youth, Lilith had discovered that her mother had been hung the morning after her escape. Lilith had refused to fall prey to the evil wills of the depraved man who had in fact been her biological father. Her escape had left him dead, by her own hand on a washroom floor covered in blood and soapy water.

When she had returned, months later, to find that the slave masters had taken their vengeance out on her mother, Lilith burned the estate to the ground. She left none of the masters alive. But the reality of her mother being gone still lingered, haunting her in surprise moments of shock or nostalgia.

The dark cabin walls seemed to be closing in when a knock came at the door at her back.

"Captain. Gun crews are all ready and we've loaded everything we can carry. Ready to watch these bastards drown?" Trina's voice carried through the heavy wooden door.

Lilith wiped her face, drawing herself up to stand she pulled open the cabin door. Trina popped her head in.

"We found silver coin in her hold as well as salt pork and kegs of good dark ale Cap'n. Twenty-eight freed captives. I'm not sure I would've sent that boy swimming off to spread your legend. But I won't fault you for it, girl." Trina rambled, oblivious to Lilith's distress until their eyes locked. "What's wrong love?"

"My mother, Trina. I see her everywhere. Sometimes it is Jilhal's face, sometimes others. But every time it happens, I just can't control it, I become a mess." Lilith said through a deep sigh, relieved to bare her emotional toll to her friend and mentor.

"Captain. You've held onto this since the raid? We talked of this. You had to know the chances of finding her alive were remote." Trina said placing her hand on the back of Lilith's neck and hugging her close. "We're going out on deck, Captain. You're going to sink those bastards and we will sail away watching them slip below the waves. You must focus on the horizon ahead."

"I know. I had held on to some hope she would still be there." Lilith said lifting from Trina's shoulder, "We should go now. I don't want to linger here longer than we must."

Lilith and Trina stepped out on deck as Chibs was bellowing orders up into the rigging. Lilith walked over to the propped open weather hatch to find William, dutifully standing by at the foot of the stairs waiting to relay orders to the gun crews. She looked up at Chibs as the Maiden's sails unfurled in the wind and were pulled taut by line handlers.

"Ready when you are Cap'n!" Chibs hollered over, his smile beamed behind a puff of pipe smoke that rolled behind him as he walked. Lilith looked down to Will's grave expression.

"Open fire Will." She said with a flat stare.

"Aye Captain." He turned to the gun line, "Starboard battery! Fire!"

Crow's Nest Inn
8 Feb 1809
Charleston, S. Carolina

Rory awoke to the sound of a blackbird outside the window of his room. The sun had yet to rise but a pre-dawn glow emanated from below a ceiling of thick gray clouds. The squawk sounded, and then a moment of silence, a whistle of wind rattled the windowpane and then another squawk. Rory sat up and rubbed the sleep from his eyes. Looking out the window he grumbled to himself about the weather. The Charleston street below was a sloppy mess of mud and rain puddles. The squawk of the crow sounded again as the wind whistled. A chill rose up Rory's spine as he scrambled from the bed to dress. Opening the door, he was greeted by a rush of warmth from the open common room of the inn. At the base of the stairs an old woman was cooking breakfast on the large wood stove, filling the room with the aroma of frying eggs, bacon and coffee. Rory descended the wooden staircase and caught a glimpse of the sailors he'd been listening to the previous evening. They sat at a table in the corner, wolfing down their plates of food. Rory caught one of them shooting a sideways glance at him then looking back to the others with a smile.

"It's the famed pirate hunter boys!" he raised his voice loud enough for Rory to hear, "Watch yourself out there lubber. She's a ripe day for putting to sea, don't fall in or you're like to catch your death if you don't drown first."

"I'll try to keep that in mind." Rory said while sitting down at a table across the room. The old woman put a plate loaded with a generous serving in front of him and poured the steaming coffee into a mug for him.

"What ship are you bound to pirate hunter?" the man called across the room.

"Southern Song, she's a brigantine recently purchased by Mr. Clyde Ritten." Rory answered. The men at the table shared in a quick look among themselves. They turned to one sailor at the table as he pushed away his plate with an irritated huff.

"That'll be my ship you're talking about. We weren't

expecting you until tomorrow at the soonest. God damnit. Hunting pirates? The captain didn't say a damn thing about any of that." He huffed.

"You are part of the crew then?" Rory asked.

"I am. Not sure how much longer that will last," the sailor growled as he stood up from his seat. "Once you've finished your food, I'll show you down to the ship."

"What's the captain like? Is it an experienced crew?" Rory asked between bites.

"The captain is an insufferable dullard and a drunk to boot. The crew are just about as green as you will be by this afternoon. But the mate is the worst kind of awful. You'll see." He sat down in a seat next to Rory, drawing in close as he finished his rant. Rory's appetite faded when the sailor offered a broad smile of gapped and rotten teeth behind a scraggly unkempt beard.

"We'll go now." Rory stood offering a nod of thanks to the old woman at the wood stove.

"Right. Less in your stomach to toss up when we hit the rollers. You are a sharp one, I'll give you that." The sailor hooted slapping the table as he stood with Rory.

The two men left the warmth of the inn for the muddy tangle of Charleston. A cold, steady rain needled its way through the bleak skies, it was driven harder by gusting winds that seemed to slice through Rory's coat and chilled him immediately. The sailor, seemingly impervious to the wind or cold strutted his way up the road paying no mind to the puddles of pooled rain.

"What's your name mister? I didn't catch it at the inn. My apologies, I had my eye on hot food and a warm bed and a woman on my mind." The sailor's words seemed growled as much as they did spoken.

"My name is Rory Walters. And yours?" Rory replied in a shout as the wind gusts picked up.

"My mother named me Edward. But the crew all calls me dog breath or dog, among some other things. I'll let you figure that out for yourself." Dog grumbled through the wind gusts.

They turned a corner and made their way up a narrow corridor flanked by trade shops. At the end of the road a long pier stretched out into the harbor. The wooden hulls of small ships bobbed in the choppy water, their bare masts dancing back and forth through the driving rain. Near the end of the pier where the water deepened larger vessels were moored alongside the rain slicked wooden structure. Dog sauntered along the slick planks without missing a step.

"There she is. Take her in Rory, your new home!" the sailor jeered at him, unbothered by the frigid rain dripping off his face and beard.

Rory looked over the ship in bewilderment and alarm. Sitting at the pier, she seemed to be listing to one side. Her rigging was a disorganized mess of line in as poor a condition as her hull which showed signs of rot and slipshod repairs never fully completed. The small window arrangement over the fantail had several places boarded where a pane of glass once stood, and a smell of rotted food and refuse wafted through the wind bringing a gagging cough up into Rory's throat. Dog slapped him hard on the back, laughing so hard he doubled over.

"That wouldn't be the first time she got that reaction

from an introduction! Come on, the disappointment doesn't end there." Dog said through a deep belly laugh before ambling up the gangplank and onto the deck. Rory followed, disbelieving what he saw. Dog hadn't exaggerated the poor condition of the Southern Song, broken planks left holes in her deck. Line was scattered in haphazard fashion along both rails. Dog turned to the cabin door, which had been left slightly ajar. He knocked loudly while opening the door the rest of the way spilling the gray daylight into the cabin and revealing a chaotic mess that made the weather deck look orderly.

"Captain?" Dog called into the recess of the cabin, "Captain I've found our passenger."

Rory could smell a vile odor coming from inside that his nose told him was a mixture of rum, wine, poor hygiene and spoiled food.

"What? Who is it? Who is there?" a voice shot out from within the cabin.

"Captain, it's Dog. I've found our passenger, he's here now." Dog repeated.

Rory could see the form of the captain stand up from where he had been sleeping on the floor. His wine-stained shirt was ill fitting and did not cover a portion of his belly that protruded from the bottom. His trousers were undone at the waist and had a large dark spot covering his crotch and a large portion of both thighs.

"Dog." The captain grumbled.

"Yes Captain?" Dog replied.

"I've pissed myself again. Get us under sail before I set to the tavern again." The captain fumed kicking an overturned chair.

"Yes Captain. Likely that won't make a damn bit of difference, but we'll get her out to sea." Dog shot back, pulling the door shut as the captain threw an empty bottle at him. Glass shattered against the back of the door as Dog pulled it closed.

"Never mind the captain right now, he'll make a better introduction once we're underway. It's the mate that runs this tub anyhow." Dog said with a grotesque half smile of crooked yellow teeth, he leaned down and opened the weather hatch. "Alright you sods! Up and at em! I want tacks and main, cast off line and out to sea with you greasy pigs! Let's go!"

From within the bowels of the ship the crew came up on deck. They were a haggard looking arrangement, Rory noticed, even the younger sailors seemed to be in poor condition. *A ragged ship, a drunk captain, a misfit crew on a dangerous task. Of course.* Rory thought as he caught himself grimacing while he watched the crew make Southern Song ready to depart. Sailors yelled back and forth at each other through the gusting wind and driving rain. The experienced crewmen seemed to grow very short of patience with the younger hands, and quickly. A young man heaving on a line to trim the main yard into the wind lost his footing on the rain-soaked planks. The young sailor slipped and fell flat onto his back, still holding onto the rope he was dragged for a length up the deck before letting go. The sail yard swung loose in the gusting wind, the sail above flapping and half unfurled.

"Whoa! What in seven hells?" Dog cried out in his growling voice, he pointed to a sailor nearby, "You there, secure that line. Hands aloft, hold fast! We'll get her secured!"

The sailors on deck scrambled through the driving rain to remedy the dangerous situation. Dog ambled over to the deck-dragged sailor and assisted him to his feet.

"You ought to know better than trying to man a line by yourself in winds like this! Next time, put some shot in your pocket boy." He growled, slapping the young man over the top of his brow. The sailor turned and pitched himself back into the work of getting the ship underway as Dog walked by to the helm where Rory stood failing to mask his disgust.

"That mate you spoke of. The worst kind of awful?" Rory asked raising his brow.

"Aye. If you ask them, that is. I consider myself to have a nice rosy disposition," Dog replied with his twisted, rotten smile, "When I'm on land, at least."

Rory shuddered as a chill ran through him. His wool coat was soaked through, and the winds seemed to cut right into his flesh, prickling him with goosebumps. After more yelling on deck and enough curses from Dog to condemn a small village, the sails were set and lines cast away. The Southern Song pulled away from the pier and angled slowly out of the harbor. As she passed the out of the sheltered waters, the steady gentle rock escalated into a pitched heave. Rory compensated well at first. For the first hour he was able to stay upright just by bending his knees with the motion of the deck. Dog seemed to forget Rory was there, not even throwing a glance his way. The old sailor seemed consumed by what was occurring on deck as well as watching the man at the helm and switching his gaze between the sails aloft and the waves ahead.

The pitching of the decks beneath his feet seemed to grow more intense until Rory eventually could not keep himself steady without taking a step with each heave of the deck. To make matters worse, the angle of the wind and sail was causing the deck to roll side to side as well. As the waves grew in size a shuddering impact of sea against the bow was added to the repeating symphony of motion. Rory looked high up at the tip of the mast and a wave of nauseating dizziness washed over him. He grabbed onto a stay line at the larboard rail and looked over to the murky blue waves capped in white as they slid along Southern Song's hull. His stomach tightened and another wave of motion almost dropped him from his feet.

"Let fly the topsails fore and main! She's a stout one today but this old songbird can make her way!" Dog shouted to the top men and riggers on deck.

Rory looked up again, watching as the experienced men in the rigging crawled and climbed effortlessly through the perpetual motion completing their tasks. As wind filled the top sails and the sheets were drawn taut the motion on deck compounded. Rory looked to the opposite rail, seeing only gray sky for a moment and then the horizon passed upward, and briny blue waves dominated his view. The repetitive shudder of the bow hitting against the next wave broke into the rhythm of Rory's footsteps to keep himself up right. His right foot slipped out from under him as a wave of nausea combined with his tightening stomach. He managed to keep himself upright, barely, by his grip on the stay line in his left hand. Seeing his new passenger's plight, Dog walked over through the pitch of the deck and put his arm around Rory's shoulders. Pulling him in close Dog gave him a big smile with those horrid teeth and shouted over the wind, "Don't feel embarrassed, we were all once babes at the teat. Should I get you a nice warm bottle of milk and a blanket?" he cackled squeezing Rory in close. The odor of Dog's breath hit Rory's nostrils, eliciting an immediate gag that Rory fought. As Dog released him another pitch of the deck combined with a shudder of the bow breaking a wave and Rory could fight against it no longer. He threw his face over the side and released the contents of his stomach in a painful contracting retch, followed by another and another. As his breakfast left him, Rory remembered Dog's words from earlier in the day. "Less in your stomach to toss up when we hit the rollers."

"Welcome aboard the Southern Song!" Dog's voice cried out amid a roar of laughter from the crew as Rory heaved his breakfast overboard.

Ortega's
1 Oct 1808
Near Tortuga, Haiti

Darkness had enveloped Tim's mind. Hazy dreams from his youth, the smells and sounds of Georgia and South Carolina haunted him as he slept. At one point he awoke to dim lamplight and an excruciating pain in his side, voices speaking rapid Spanish and the smell of blood and rum. He had drifted away before he could piece together what was occurring or where he was. Taken to a time in his past when wounds were not his concern. He saw the farmhouse where he grew up, his mother's face with a welcoming smile as she did the washing and a stern scowl from his father sitting in his chair on the front porch. Images changed, rearranging around him and he was again floating on a wooden deck section with sharks in a feeding frenzy around him, snatching corpses from the surface while he waited to be next. The surprise and agony on Admiral Sharpe's face as he had pulled the trigger of his pistol, sending the ball that killed him into the man's uniformed chest.

Piercing light stung Tim's eyes through his eyelids. He struggled to open them. His right eye opened just slightly to glaring light that forced him to shut it. A fire crackled at the far end of the room he was in, and Tim could hear someone moving, pots and pans clattering. He became aware of the smell next. It smelled glorious. Like spiced meat and coffee mixed with the aroma of baking bread. Outside he could hear a chicken clucking away steadily. He shifted a little and noticed the bed he was laying in. It was a straw mattress, but the padding beneath his head felt soft and forgiving, like feather. His shirt had been removed. Tim felt drenched and hot at the same time. Sweat pooled on his chest and dripped down the sides of his face. He felt thirst like he had never experienced before. Tim opened his mouth, trying to speak. Only a dry cracking sound emitted from his throat. He struggled to lift his head only to wince at the throbbing pain the effort induced between his temples. Tim sucked ragged breath between his cracking dry lips and forced his eyes to open. The room was unassuming, rough wooden plank walls and floors. A round rug in the center of the room and sunlight pouring in on him from a window with no curtains. The wall opposite from the bed he lay in had a door which was open slightly, though he could not see well enough to make out detail in the adjacent room. Next to the door was a stool with a wash basin and pitcher.

Water! Tim's eyes locked onto the pitcher, and he felt an urgent need to drink. He tried to lift himself to sit up but was stopped by the fiery pangs of pain in his side. He pulled his hand up to his side to feel his wound and was surprised to find tightly wound bandages around his midsection. Wiggling his fingers, he found that his hands too were wrapped covering the palms that had been shredded by coral. Pushing up on an elbow, Tim managed to painfully bring himself to a sitting position. His head felt heavy, and the room seemed to spin from the exertion of the movement, but he paused only for a moment before continuing his quest for water. Twisting on the bed, Tim swung his feet, which he could see were wrapped in the same type of bandages as his hands and ribs, down to the floor. His strength was feeble, and the movement caused his head to spin again. Tim took another rasping deep breath before attempting to push himself up onto his feet. He managed to lift his butt from the mattress and put most of his weight onto his legs, sending sharp pangs of pain shooting through his feet and up his shins into both knees. His head throbbed and spun and as he tried to stand up the pain in his ribs flared and felt as if it would burn through his wrapped bandages. His butt plunked back onto the mattress. Another deep breath wheezed through his parched throat. The room seemed to spin. The sunlight pouring in seemed unbearably hot and bright.

Another attempt to push himself onto his feet yielded success and Tim managed to breathe through the shooting pains in his feet and legs. His ribs were throbbing now too but none of that mattered to Tim. All he was focused on was the pitcher holding water by the door. He took a step, almost crying out from the excruciating pain in his feet. The effort renewed his sweating, which only made him want more for the water inside the pitcher. A second step and then a third and he was almost in reach of the pitcher. He lifted his foot to take another step and the room felt like it spun. His head got heavy and started throbbing harder almost forcing his eyes shut. A forced final step brought the pitcher of sweet liquid into his grasp. He leaned his weight onto the stool and lifted the pitcher to drink. Liquid hit his lips and flooded his mouth. It quenched his throat, and he could feel it running into his belly. He took a deep drink before lowering the pitcher, he sucked in a deep breath sending a twang of pain shooting through his ribs and then lifted the pitcher to drink again. The water had a sharp aroma of being mixed with alcohol, but Tim ignored it and swallowed gulp after gulp until the pitcher yielded only drops. Satisfied, he turned and hobbled his way back toward the mattress.

The floor seemed to pitch beneath the painful steps

of his feet. Tim reached his arms out hoping to catch himself from falling. The floor rushed up greeting him with an unforgiving thud as he collapsed. Pain burned in his ribs and his knees and feet ached from the effort and the impact. His head throbbed and his ears rang but outside the door he could hear footsteps approaching. The door swung open and suddenly Tim's only view of the room was dominated by the face of a beautiful Spanish woman. Her eyes were dark jewels, and her silky black hair framed a stunning complexion. Her lips were full and her teeth brilliant in Tim's view. She was speaking to him, but he could not understand. He felt his strength failing but fought against unconsciousness not wanting to miss the view he had found. The woman stood up after speaking to him for a moment and hurried from the room. Tim picked up his head to marvel at her figure and could see that the bandages around his ribs had a growing circle of dark red. His vision blurred and his head sunk back to the floor with darkness closing in again.

Ritten Plantation
22 Feb 1809
Southwest of Charleston S. Carolina

Clyde remained at his desk in the study while his guests filed in. These same men had been here while he issued the directive to the mercenary he employed, Rory Walters. A letter had arrived in the morning necessitating further consultation among the invested parties. Clyde had never been a man to allow decision by committee, but the constraints of what had been formed hampered any one of them from trampling roughshod over another. Something Clyde intended to change. The Order was both an establishment for the conservation of certain social and economic norms in the Americas and Europe and a consortium to multiply their buying power for slaves.

His guests pulled up their seats, some lighting pipes while others helped themselves to Clyde's liquor. He sat back in his padded high back chair, fidgeting with an envelope that sat on his desk with a broken red wax seal. Clyde looked around the room at the sullen faces. Some of them were neighbors of his, while others came from much further away.

"Gentlemen, I understand the abruptness I have summoned you all here with and I do apologize. I hope those of you returning to Europe will not be delayed unduly for an additional meeting. I would not waste your time or mine, so I will be abrupt. I received a very troubling report just this morning from a spy we have in the Caribbean." Clyde broke the ice and then paused to gauge the reaction.

"A spy? I did not know we employed spies Mr. Ritten. Where is this spy?" demanded Tallum Wilmers, a wealthy merchant ship owner from Georgia.

"You did not know, because it is not necessary for you to know Sir. The construct we have established here benefits us all to the degree that no one of us can completely take over the network. My end is the security of this endeavor…"

"Which you are utterly failing at!" Philip Devereaux, their French representative scolded.

"I understand we have had some setbacks. But the

message I have received today contains a report from a man I employ in Nassau. He has included an exact copy of a message that was sent to the offices of the Admiralty in London." Clyde replied, his tone growing colder.

"Well. What did the report say?" Tallum pressed.

"The report says there was a revolt in Kingston." Clyde began.

"This is not new information, we have already received this report!" Philip interrupted.

"We have. But this is a report that was sent to London, to the admirals of the Royal Navy. Do you understand the implication here Philip or must I spell it out for you?" Clyde snapped, standing up behind his desk. "A report like this will be enough for Britain to send a large fleet to the Caribbean and that will bring our shipping to a halt."

"I thought you said the Brits would be with us." One of the plantation owners piped in.

"I said we have the backing of some Brits. Some very prominent and powerful. But if this news makes it over there and is somehow connected to our operation, I fear we won't have any help where they are concerned. No. We must deal with this situation ourselves." Clyde stood as he talked walking out from behind the desk. "Rory is on his way to get the situation in Jamaica contained, to whatever extent it can be. But I am afraid there may be loose ends elsewhere that need to be cleaned up."

Several of the attending guests exchanged confused looks as Clyde walked around behind the chairs where they sat. Clyde passed behind them looking over their shoulders.

"What on earth do you bloody mean? Loose ends?" asked Darren Blackwell, the emissary who had ferried communications between The Order and the lords in ownership of the East India Trading Company.

"Humorous you should be asking, Darren. I'm talking about you." Clyde said, producing a dagger from the back of his waistband. In a swift motion Clyde grabbed Darren's forehead, wrenching his head back over the top edge of the chair and plunged the point of the dagger into the Brit's throat. Darren flailed his arms and kicked his legs as the blade penetrated further and further into his neck, unable to writhe himself free under Clyde's lock on his head. After a few moments of ghastly death throes Darren's body sat limp, blood running from his throat and pooling on the chair and floor in front of him.

"This is madness!" Philip blurted as he rose from his seat with a horrified look on his face.

"These are mad times, Philip." Clyde replied, wiping his dagger blade with a kerchief he pulled from his jacket pocket. "But unfortunately, you happen to fall into the 'loose end' category as well."

"How dare you! I brought you into this, how could you…" Philip objected, backing his way toward the study door.

"You know too much." Clyde sneered drawing close to the Frenchman as he backed away. "You are the last avenue of information escaping us to Europe and we cannot afford their interference any longer. I'm sorry my friend." Clyde lunged himself at the retreating man, sinking the dagger to its hilt in his chest. Clyde continued pushing Philip until his back thudded into the wall between two large bookcases. "It's nothing personal Philip. Don't take it that way. It's just business."

Clyde held the man in place against the wall until he sagged to the floor under collapsing legs. He turned to an array of shocked and disgusted looks from the men now standing around him in the study.

"Well, now that unpleasantness is behind us. Shall we get to work? There is business at hand that needs to be discussed." Clyde smoothed down the front of his jacket and paced over behind his desk.

"You've just killed our connections to the East India Company and the French. How do you expect we will conduct our endeavor now?" Tallum said with a deliberate note of caution.

"We will have to make our own way. In this room we collectively hold more wealth and assets than anywhere in the south. Can we not blaze our own path? Or would you rather rely on the old powers of Europe to secure your destinies?" Clyde retorted sitting back into his seat. "Tallum, I need you to purchase us three vessels and crews to go along with them. Two need to be in fair shape and with large holds and one needs to be fast, very fast, a sloop should do. Mr. Harrison, I need you to send a formal letter of protest to the Senate of the United States, you are upset with the British Navy pressing men from your ships into their service." He paused and then held his hands out, addressing the whole group, "We will set forth our own expedition to retrieve as many slaves as possible. Hopefully, Congress will do the job of interfering with the Royal Navy for us." Clyde finished giving his instructions and settled his eyes back onto the corpse in the chair to his front. "Let us not forget gentlemen. We are in this together, let no one man among us be a liability to the rest, lest he suffer the consequences."

Every eye in the room had settled on the twisted pale face of the dead Brit. Clyde leaned into his high-backed chair, propping his hand beneath his chin. The men left in the room were all American plantation owners and merchants, slave owners and brokers. Their collective fortunes were well enough to take on the task at hand and each stood to lose far more by doing nothing. Crops would go unharvested, ships would go unloaded and unfilled, markets would go vacant and in the matter of two seasons their labor forces would be stretched to the breaking point. Sladen had failed. Walters would likely fail as well. *I'll do it my damn self.* Clyde resolved to himself silently.

"That will be all gentlemen. If I should be needing anything more, I will send word. Depending on how quickly we can hire men and crew ships, I intend to set out for the Caribbean within a month's time. We will recoup our losses, all of us." Clyde announced with a modest grin.

"And Mr. Walters? Has he not gone to do exactly what you now intend to?" one of the market brokers asked.

"I believe Mr. Walters will be somewhat successful on his journey, until he faces the navy fleet that is undoubtedly already on its way. The message we received from our man in Nassau went out weeks ago." Clyde replied in a calm, even tone.

"Who is this man you have in Nassau? Shouldn't we be sharing this sort of information?" Tallum asked.

"I think it best for all involved if I kept that one to myself. Ah, for now gentlemen. He is a dear old friend of mine and it would pain me to expose his disposition as my informant. Please, you'll have to trust me on this matter. In due time, I promise." Clyde answered, soothing their curiosity. "Now, if you will. I must ask that we part ways for now. There is much to do."

Clyde stood strutting his way to the study door without giving the fresh corpses so much as a wayward glance. He opened the door and proceeded down the large, windowed hallway at a brisk pace. Showing his guests to the front door, he bid them all safe and fair travels. As his house servants closed the ornate front double doors, he beckoned two of them to him.

"In my study, you will find that I've made another mess. It was unavoidable, really. Dump them in the hog pen and be sure the blood is cleaned off my floor." Clyde explained as if he were asking them to clean up a few party dishes. Each servant shared a knowing glance with the other.

"Yes, Sir." They replied before hurrying off to handle their new task.

Clyde turned in the atrium and ascended one side of a wrapping staircase to the landing above. He made his way through another broad hallway and entered a door flanked by two antique suits of armor. Inside the room was meticulously designed in similar fashion to his study. The hardwood floor accented dark hardwood cases surrounding the rooms perimeter. Leather bound volumes stuffed each shelf. Above them were rare pieces of artwork, though in this room there were no portraits. Proud depictions of military victories, figures on horseback hacking and slashing at their enemies, ships at sea unleashing hellfire in massive broadsides. Interspersed between them were painted maps from regions all around the world, Europe, India, Africa and America. Standing in front of the array of windows a large, dark wood wardrobe with bright brass fixtures dominated the room. Clyde slowly walked to the wardrobe and opened its doors. His bright red military uniform hung in the center. Clyde pulled the coat out holding it up for inspection. It had been twenty years since he had taken it off. He placed the uniform coat back onto its hanger in the wardrobe and reached into the far corner. He pulled out a broad leather belt with a scabbarded sword and pistol in it. Withdrawing the sword, he held it up to the window light looking at the blade gleaming in its reflected rays. Replacing the sword into the scabbard he then drew out the pistol. Years lying dormant had aged its fixtures, but he cocked the hammer, eyed the flint and squeezed the trigger to watch the hammer send a satisfying shower of sparks down into the pan. *These will do nicely. They've never failed me before.*

Chapter 4

19 Degrees 56' N, 72 Degrees 54' W
7 Feb 1809

John's limbs were numb from exhaustion and chill before he escaped the horrid view of the pirates taking the Boston Autumn. His shoulder that had been bit by the rope earlier ached and throbbed to the point he could barely move it. John put all his concentration and effort into floating on his back and kicking his legs only occasionally reaching his good arm up over his head to drag at the water. The foggy grayness closed around him hugging tight to the murky sea and soon he became disoriented. He was kicking a steady beat, trying to float along and keep his face out of the water. John's stomach knotted with the possibility of not making landfall. He contemplated just letting himself slip under the waves and drop into the depths below. He kicked along, deciding if he kept swimming until he couldn't then the resolution of his dilemma would present itself.

Off in the distance a thunderous roar erupted. John

could feel the concussive waves vibrate through the water and penetrate his flesh. Voices cheering filtered through the mist. Far in the distance, but he could still hear them and that sent a chill running down his spine. With renewed vigor, John kicked his feet in a steady rhythm, mixing in an arm stroke more frequently and pulling harder when he did. The sound of the cannons had alerted him that he was traveling in a general southward direction, the shoreline would not be much farther. Echoes of cracking timbers and shouting voices floated through the haze in an eerie death song. John swam with a heavy heart and a knotting stomach as he listened to the men who had been his crew drown aboard the ship that had been his home.

John's heels touched into rough gravel the same time as his head. For a moment he lay in the shallow water, breathing in relief, thankful he had found solid ground. He sat up, looking around at his hazy surroundings. The shoreline was all but indistinguishable to him with only a feint shadow of a dark form rising from the water in front of him. He sloshed his feet through the shallows. It seemed to keep stretching out in front of him, drawing him further along as the shoreline withdrew away from him. To John's relief, the shoreline appeared through the mist, revealing a narrow, graveled beach at the base of a steep grassy hill overhung by a canopy of trees. He slogged his way off the gravel and onto the grass. John dropped to his knees. He was overcome with exhaustion. His legs burned from the swim; his shoulder ached from its ragged rope burn. He looked up to the sky, which had brightened from the sun but showed no signs of relenting its blanket of haze. He closed his eyes, thanking God for his safe deliverance from the fate his crew had suffered. A moment of realization hit John and he realized he could no longer hear the screams of the crew or groans of the ship as she slowly sunk. John twisted himself around, plunking his back down onto the grassy hillside. His breaths came in rapid jaunts, increasingly more ragged as the reality of what had occurred set in.

Everyone he had spent the last months with was dead. The man who had woken him up for watch that morning. The salty old sailor who had been cursing at him for being sheepish aloft. The captain. All dead. The pirates had been tying the crew to the masts when John thought he could somehow barter his way off the ship. A tidal wave of guilt and regret washed over him. His mind ached from the flurry of events of the morning now overwhelming his thoughts. The sound of the waves lapping at the shore met his ears over his racing heart. The pirate woman had told him Tortuga was to the east.

"She wants me to warn the seafarers of Tortuga." John said aloud after regaining his breath. "I'll be telling the tale to all who will hear it. Lord help me, I will find a ship and crew willing to take up arms against them. Those bastards."

John began walking, though his legs were clumsy from exhaustion and shock he made his way along the shoreline where the gravel met the grass. As the day wore on, sunlight eventually broke its way through the fog. He was thankful for the clearing visibility and warmth the sun offered. Looking over his shoulder,

John feared he would see the awful black banner from the pirates returning to use him as gunnery practice. He quickly scanned the clearing sea horizon every few minutes, convincing himself that this errand the lady pirate had sent him on was some sick game they were playing. He quickened his pace. Slogging along in soaked shoes with his ragged trousers rubbing his thighs raw. The grass of the hillside was slick from the moisture of the foggy morning, the gravel beach was just as bad. He stepped along, making progress as quickly as his tired legs would allow, slogging and slipping between stones of the shore and the wet grasses just above them.

The sun burned high into its mid-day arc causing the coolness of the morning to recede under a muggy heat. The sight of a distant sail out at sea ahead of him gave a split-second pang of panic until he realized he must be nearing Tortuga. He stopped for a moment scouring the distant ship for any sign of that black banner and its dreadful horned skull. John heard a horse nicker nearby. He shifted his eyes to the hillside

"What are you doing down there?" a voice called down from above. "What are you? Some kind of bandit running from justice?"

"No. No my ship went down off the coast." John shouted back through his dry cracking voice. He looked around for the source of the challenge unsuccessfully.

"Over here mon ami. On the road" the voice called again, in a much friendlier tone. "I heard cannons this morning as I was leaving. That was you, yes?"

John could see the face of a mustachioed man ahead

of him, peeking just over some grass. "Yes. Well, the cannon fire wasn't ours. There were pirates, Sir. They've killed the crew I sailed with. Sunk our ship as well."

"Tsk tsk. Ah, it's not good. Dangerous profession to be a smuggler these days, no?" the man replied with a sideways grin.

"We were no smuggling crew Sir. I was manning an American merchant ship bound for Charleston with trade goods." John replied, unsure of what the man was getting at.

"Yes, right and a hold full of Negroes. Am I right?" the man said grinning wider.

"Well. Yes, but what does that have to do with it? They've killed my entire crew!" John snapped, growing angry and suspicious of the man and his heavy French accent.

"Your captain must not have heard of the angry girl pirate. She takes revenge for her people; it's said she sunk a British Navy ship just last year. Come up here you poor bastard, let me give you a ride into town. You can tell me about these evil pirates!" the man called waving him up.

John staggered his way up the short slope, sliding on the grass and losing his footing several times before stumbling onto a well-worn road. Only thirty feet up the hill, John's face reddened as he thought about slipping on the grass and rocks all day, if he had climbed the hill only thirty feet, he would have found his walk much easier. The man sat on the bench seat of a wagon drawn by two mules. The back of the wagon was loaded with barrels. John made his way up beside the wagon.

"How far into town?" he asked the man, who was leaning back on one elbow to take in the sight of the half drowned young sailor.

"Far enough you would rather ride than walk. But that is your decision mon ami, it makes no difference to me." The man replied giving John's shoes a look.

"Sir. I have no money to pay you." John said, hoping the man did not change his offer.

"I'm going the same way whether you pay me or not. It makes no difference, but good conversation is payment enough. Come on, you can tell me of your troubles this morning that left you looking like a beached fish, eh?" he replied, waving John up to take the seat next to him.

"How did you know we were hauling slaves?" John asked with a suspicious look as he plotted his seat next to the finely dressed Frenchman.

"I did not. I suspected. But this is so? You were hauling slaves?" he said, feigning surprise.

"We were. It was not a popular decision either. The captain had heard the rumors of pirates. But I suppose greed got the better of him. All of us really." John sulked remembering the look of the captain's face as his lifeblood had drained out onto the deck. It had gone pale, taken on a hollow look like John hadn't ever seen before.

"I will get you into town. From there, as they say, you are on your own. I would recommend you look for passage off the island right away. Haiti is not a place to linger these days. Especially for an American trying to smuggle slaves away. The plantation owners here are likely to hang you or put you to work in their fields. I'm not sure which would be worse." The man said, giving the mules a slap with the reigns.

"I'll manage." John replied, trying to get a sense of the man.

"The docks are always looking for strong backs. Usually, the same color you were trying to smuggle away. But you might find a ship that will pay to be unloaded, maybe you could even barter passage." The man said, giving John a sideways glance.

The wagon jostled and bounced its way along as the rutted road wound toward Tortuga. Without slipping along on the rocks of the shore or sliding on the grassy hillside John's clothed dried and his discomfort revolved solely around the ragged rope burn along his shoulder. The afternoon sun was warm and a breeze blowing from the east announced their proximity to Tortuga as John's nose could detect woodsmoke and the emanating scents of cooking meat. When the horizon revealed Tortuga's buildings and its harbor John was filled with relief. Soon he would be in the company of seagoing men, to spread his warning to all who would hear it.

'North Wind'
28 Feb 1809
45 Degrees 31' N, 23 Degrees 55' W

The roll of the sea pitched and heaved the heavy line ship North Wind as her namesake gusted cold torrents over her deck. The sea was cold and the winds bitter. Sailors wore every scrap of clothing available and working the rigging as a top man was a torturous sentence, four hours of freezing winds intermixed with sea spray and sporadic rains. The cold hampered more than the men up in the rigging, as Admiral Alistair Torren's arthritis and gout all seemed exasperated in the foul weather. His daily routine of walking, though, had yet to be broken by the week at sea. When he rose, he rose early, four bells on the dot. He would have his steward, Lieutenant Thatcher, stoke the fire in the wood stove in his cabin to a near unbearable heat, then dress and have a tea. While he was having his tea, he would hear the report from Lieutenant Thatcher on the fleet's condition. Which sails were visible on which ship, their current heading and speed along with the wind condition and any changes which occurred during the admiral's rest. Then the admiral would don his heavy boat cloak and bicorne hat and step out onto the weather deck. Every morning the admiral would walk over to the helm, without uttering a word to the helmsman he would have a look at the heading and then look aloft to the sails. If they were satisfactory the helmsman would receive a slight pat on the shoulder before the admiral stepped off onto his routine walk about the deck. On the occasion things were not to the admiral's liking he would have Lieutenant Thatcher summon the officer of the watch. The admiral corrected things with a subtle comment followed by a nod.

"The tops look slack to my eye, Lieutenant." He would say, in a hushed tone not to give shame or embarrass anyone. Alistair understood a well-treated leader then treats his people well. Well treated people perform better out of trustworthiness and desire to reciprocate. Floggings and an occasional dressing down have their place, but it is an extreme measure not to be entered lightly.

The admiral would pound out six laps around the deck of the ship, increasing the speed of his gait with each revolution regardless of sea conditions. Sailors and officers alike would marvel as the admiral jaunted around the rail to the bow where he would climb the forecastle stairs to tap the handle of his ornate cane on the base of the bowsprit then continue along the rail back to the quarterdeck. When he passed the helm, the admiral would then take lively steps up the stairs to climb the aft castle where he would tap the rail on North Wind's stern. Upon completing his walk, the admiral would remain on deck for an hour, either observing the helm or standing an informal post up on the bow. Lieutenant Thatcher was always dutifully at his side and ready to produce the admiral's looking glass if so requested. After lingering for an hour on deck the admiral would retire to his cabin and summon the ship's captain. He would receive the same exact report given earlier by Lieutenant Thatcher and then either address some deficiency he noted on his walk or dismiss him entirely.

On this particular morning the admiral had found a young midshipman, nestled in a pile of coiled line on the bow, fast asleep. Alistair tapped the boy with the business end of his cane, springing the young man into alertness and a state of panic.

"Easy there, easy young man. What's your name son?" the admiral inquired, raising an inquisitive brow as he asked.

"M-M-Midshipman Brant, sir. Elliot Brant." The young officer stuttered.

"Brant." The admiral gave a long pause, "Your father is captain of the Bayonet?"

"Yes, Sir." Midshipman Brant answered quickly.

"Well, lad. Best not be sleeping on your watch. It sets a dreadful example to the lads and I would hate for you to meet with the end of a cat o' nine when the captain catches wind of it. You're an officer aboard the damned admiral's flagship! Act the part son." The admiral scolded.

"Yes, Sir. It won't happen again Sir." Brant replied lowering the brow of his hat slightly.

"Your father was perhaps one of the finest gunnery officers I have had the pleasure to command. He gained his captaincy under Elliot Sharpe's command aboard the Endurance. When we get to the Caribbean, perhaps you would like to meet your namesake and learn whose honor you carry with you every day at sea son." The admiral softened his tone.

"I would like that, Sir. Very much." Brant replied.

"Well. Keep to your task. I do no favors for de-rated midshipmen." Alistair said, stepping off on his walk without another word.

On the bow the sea spray was cold but scant with the wind at their backs blowing it away. Admiral Torren stood silently staring out at the swells ahead of them. Occasionally he would tramp his cane on the deck as he mulled through his thoughts as if he were striking something from the record in his mind.

"Damn. Damn it all to hell!" he said aloud in a

frustrated growl.

"Sir? Is everything quite alright?" Lieutenant Thatcher said over his shoulder.

"No, Lieutenant. This entire errand is foul and everything about it." The admiral grumbled, biting his teeth into his lower lip slightly after speaking. "Elliot is too fine a tactician and too good a man to go this long without some communique. I've known the man for decades and his command as well. The Caribbean fleet was mine before he assumed that role and they are not a bunch of hapless landsmen. Whatever evil has befallen the fleet will be no matter for amateurs."

"Perhaps things aren't as disastrous as they seem Sir? Maybe Admiral Sharpe has everything well in hand by now?" the lieutenant replied, hoping it was true.

"I didn't get where I am by trusting for better outcomes in the world young man. We must assume the fleet is lost. Once we pass Bermuda, we should expect enemy contact on any given day." The admiral growled, tamping his cane as he spoke. "I don't know if it's the Americans, Napoleon, or pirates and it makes no difference. Whatever the foe we must meet them head on."

"Yes Sir. I am sure the fleet is up to the task Sir."

"I have no doubts in that regard lad. We have the finest ships and the best commanders I could hope for. I just pray that will be enough." Admiral Torren said, lowering his gaze from the horizon down to the wooden rail in front of him. "That will be all for now Lieutenant. I'll retire to my cabin. Please pay the captain my compliments and inform him to kindly report to my quarters."

The admiral turned and with his trademark brisk pace walked back toward his cabin. He paused at the cabin door, looking around the deck with a kind, gentle disposition. *Whatever lies ahead of us, I hope I have the mettle to spare these lads too high a price.* He offered the helmsman a grin and a nod when the young sailor looked back at him. "Well done lad, she's running along nicely." Then entered the cabin.

Inside the cabin door, Admiral Torren was greeted by a wave of heat emanating from the stove. The smell of the cabin was as familiar and welcoming to Alistair as the fresh sea air on his morning walks. Scents of timber and salt pork, leather and tobacco smoke lingered throughout the quarters. For years he had made his home in cabins aboard ships just like this one, the better part of his life had been spent at sea. *That blubbering ass thinks it is some type of punishment to send me to sea, ha! Send a fish to water and a war horse to war! Give a drunk a drink and give me my ship, offices and land life were cruel punishments compared to a life spent at sea.* Internally, the admiral had cheered when Admiral Becker had insisted he lead the fleet to the Caribbean. It was no secret that Becker despised conditions at sea. He had grown accustomed to the accoutrements of land life as well as frequent visits to the royal court and all the grandiose pomp and circumstance involved there. Being of noble birth still had its advantages, one of them being preferential treatment in military life and promotions. Admiral Becker despised life at sea, but had precious little real experience aboard ship, none of it in combat. *Give me a pitching deck and the spray on my face, let that bugger take all the offices and court visits he likes, this is the life for me.*

The admiral's attitude and internal dialog did little to help his ailing knees and stiff back. Every morning on rising it was a battle to loosen his joint and drive the aching from his feet and ankles. Afternoons were spent reviewing logs and inventories and instructing lessons on seamanship and command to Lieutenant Thatcher. At the admiral's insistence Lieutenant Thatcher had begun filling in on rotation as an officer of the watch. "To shake the garrison from you lad, it's just the thing to make you a real sailor," he told the young officer.

Ortega's
4 October 1808
Near Tortuga, Haiti

A beautiful face greeted Tim as he awoke. Dark brilliant eyes and full lips, soft copper skin and brilliant white teeth. The Spanish woman said something he could not understand. Tim tried to smile but he could only grimace through the burning pain in his ribs. He felt a tugging sensation at the bandages around his torso. The woman was changing the dressing on his wounds. Tim tried to reach his hands down to help only to have the woman gently brush them away. She spoke again in Spanish; it was soothing and beautiful in his ears, though he could not understand any of it. As his beautiful caregiver changed the bandages, Tim lolled in a dreamy half sleep. His eyelids were heavy, but he did not want to miss a moment of the woman's company. His head rolled sideways as the woman stood to wash his torso with a cloth and warm water from the basin. Tim's eyes opened wide, and an awakening jolt ran through his blood when a man in the room came into his sight. He was sitting in a chair next to the window looking back at Tim. He was enormous with broad shoulders and imposing arms. Tim guessed when the behemoth stood he would be a full head taller than himself. His face was bordered by a full beard that did little to hold in the friendly smile beneath. His skin was a deeper copper bronze than the woman's and he looked older, weathered. He spoke something to Tim, again in Spanish. Then the giant man pulled his chair close to Tim's bedside and he spoke again.

"English? You speak English?" he asked through a heavy accent.

"Yes." Tim managed.

"How do you feel Englishman?" the man asked as the woman started applying new bandages to Tim's ribs.

"I'm an American." Tim replied, struggling to speak through the shooting pains in his torso.

"Of course, you are. Defiant, is this the word? You refuse to die. You should be dead amigo." The man said, gesturing toward Tim's ribs and knees. "These are serious. And your belly, we thought the flesh had gone bad. But mija here, she has been cleaning your wounds and keeping fresh bandages on them. She thinks you will live, you must thank her, she saved your life."

"Thank you," Tim offered the woman with the beautiful smile in his feeble voice.

"Lay still," the man said as Tim tried to sit up, "Your wound won't heal if you keep moving."

"How long have I been here?" Tim asked in a raspy whisper.

"Five days amigo. You slept through all of it, except when you got up to drink the pitcher." The man said with a huge grin, "She mixed it with rum to clean your wound. If you wanted a drink my friend, you should have just asked."

"I was just thirsty, for water. I'm thirsty now." Tim replied.

The man motioned to the woman, and she made quick work of bringing a large cup of cool water. This time there was no alcohol smell, just cool clear water that quenched Tim's mouth and throat. Tim drank deeply savoring every bit that ran through his mouth.

"Not too quickly amigo." The man warned as Tim drained the cup.

Almost immediately Tim could feel his stomach knot as it tried to absorb the rush of water he had just consumed. Coupled with the pain in his ribs and knees it sent a grimace across his face.

"Where am I?" Tim asked as his guts churned.

"You are in my home. We found you along the road and I thought you were dead. You were covered in blood and mud in the ditch my friend." The man said, scooting his chair close and leaning over Tim as he spoke. "Before I tell you anymore, you need to tell me what happened to you. What is an American doing wandering the countryside of Haiti while torn to ribbons?"

"I am a tobacco merchant." Tim lied between ragged

breaths.

"But how does a tobacco merchant come to be in the middle of nowhere, left for dead?" the man said in a hushed tone while leaning even closer.

"I was aboard a ship." Tim struggled to speak, taking ragged shallow breaths after every couple words. "We were sailing from Jamaica to return home. Pirates pursued and sank the ship. I survived."

"Ha! Barely! Another day in the sun and you would be dead my friend! I suppose you want to know more about me?" the man smiled again. Tim nodded slowly.

"I was a sailor once. Ages ago. But, I fell in love with her mother in port," he said gesturing to the beautiful girl as she walked out of the room. "The rest is history my friend. I work for the shipwright in Tortuga, and we raise a few vegetables in a garden. It's a simple life, but we have everything we need."

Tim smiled at the satisfaction in the man's voice, "Your name Sir?"

"Tomas Ortega, at your service my friend. And yours?" Tomas replied.

"Tim Sladen." The answer came in weak and raspy.

"Well, Tim. You need to rest. When you are strong enough, we will talk more. I want to hear about these pirates you speak of. I will be off at the shipyard tomorrow, but if you need anything my daughter Emilia will look after you." Tomas said, lifting his large frame off the chair and left the room, pulling a small curtain across the door frame. In the failing light of evening, Tim strained to hear as Tomas and Emilia spoke out in the front of the home. He couldn't understand their words but hoped to somehow sense their tone. Tim feared for a moment that Tomas would change his hospitable demeanor and seek to end his burdensome guest with a blade or pistol. Listening to their voices calmed his fears. These were good people. Fatigue set into his brain like a thick fog, and Tim fell into a deep, dreamless sleep.

'Drowned Maiden'
7 Feb 1809
19 Degrees 56' N, 72 Degrees 54' W

Will had watched through the gun ports as the damage their broadside had done to the Boston Autumn opened her hull at the waterline. By the time he had made his way to the weather deck the ship was already listing heavily onto her larboard side. Screams from the crew wafted in through fog as the outline of their sinking ship disappeared into mist closing in around the Drowned Maiden's stern. His stomach knotted, thinking of the sailors slowly being pulled under the surface. They had been transporting slaves and Will had agreed to those terms when he joined the girl captain's crew. Still, as the last shouts of the sailors faded under the briny surface and were lost to the fog, Will felt a sickness clawing at his innards.

His duties aboard the Drowned Maiden kept him busy. In the past few months, he had made a motley band of escaped slaves and the remains of a pirate crew into an efficient sailing team. Despite a language and culture barrier, he had also managed to instruct the gun crews below deck and after many repetitive drills, both dry runs and live fire, they had become a deadly force to be reckoned with. Will believed that the gun batteries aboard the Maiden were perhaps the fastest he had ever seen. Their wholehearted dedication sprung up from a desire to please the captain, a powerful force aboard any ship. But aboard the ship that set someone free from a future of bondage, no other commander could hope for that sort of loyalty. The chests of gold that had been ransacked away from the Gazelle lay below in the hold, not far from the pirate crew's solitary prisoner. Geor Alton had at one time been the governor of the King's colony of Jamaica. His arrogance and greed had led him into a devolving situation that currently found him in a filthy cell in the bowels of a pirate ship.

Lilith had originally intended to hang him in 'pirate cove' as she named it, where they had sunk H.M.S. Valor. The change of heart had come at Will's urging. He could prove useful at some point. Will was beginning to believe that Lilith was growing tired of both the governor and himself. Every opportunity he had, Will encouraged restraint. There was a fine line between the righteous mission of freeing those who had been unlawfully taken and committing atrocities in the name of retribution. It fell on deaf ears. Lilith would exact her vengeance, freeing slave by slave and sinking ship by ship. The raid executed against a plantation near Port-au-Prince had taken Will off guard and caused a growing rift between the ex-naval officer and his young new captain. The pirate quartermaster, Chibs, seemed in Will's mind to be the most reasonable man aboard the ship. Will dared not speak to Trina about any of his concerns, nor even to the men who had come aboard with him as it seemed their loyalties had been taken by the beautiful young pirate as well.

Lamenting on the stern, Will didn't hear Lilith as she approached. A poke in his rib sent his blood racing and he turned to see the broad, beautiful smile of Lilith.

"Are you mad that we sunk them Lieutenant?" she had never stopped using his rank.

"No. Not mad I suppose. What are we to become if we are no better than they? What is worse Lilith? A slaver or a murderer?" Will's heart pounded into his temples as the words rolled out of his mouth.

"Suppose I let them go, Lieutenant. What would they do as soon as they return to port?" Lilith retorted, her smile fading as she spoke.

"I don't presume..." Will began.

"I'll tell you exactly what they would do. They would return to port, load heavier guns and more, shot along with another hold full of slaves before trying again! Fear is a weapon, Will. When ships depart with slaves and never return, crews in port will start thinking really hard before taking on humans as cargo." Lilith said looking up at the side of Will's face as he stared back out over the foggy seas.

"Right you are Captain. But do the ends justify the means?" Will pondered aloud.

Lilith rolled her eyes, "Whatever that means. I've told you before, Will, you are a welcomed member of the crew. But I will not hold you to my service if it is more than you can stomach."

"I will stay the course with you, Captain. If you will put up with my moral objections, from time to time."

Will sighed as he spoke, feeling a slight relief.

"Better go see to our prisoner, Lieutenant. Trina and I have a plan that could prove him useful to us after all these months. If he will cooperate." Lilith said, raising an eyebrow at him.

"What is it?" Will asked.

"Go slop some water on him and make sure he's covered himself. We'll meet you below and have a talk with the two of you." Lilith insisted, gesturing toward the weather hatch.

"Very well." Will said, starting toward the stairs down to the weather deck.

"Oh, Will." Lilith said as his foot hit the top stair.

"Yes?"

"Have you still got your officer coat?" she asked.

"Well, yes Captain, I do. It's in foul condition though." He answered, growing more confused.

"We will have to mend and clean it as best we can." Lilith said, before raising her gaze aloft to the breaking clouds. "Go get the good governor suitable for a visit. We'll be down soon."

Will forced a smile as he took slow and deliberate steps down the stairs onto the weather deck. Whatever Lilith and Trina had planned would involve him and Governor Alton. Will pondered what scheme he was about to be part of as he descended below the weather deck, passing the gun deck where he rounded his way to the stairs that would take him to the lower hold. Damp, musky and dark air greeted him as he stepped off the last stair. Will hoisted a lantern that hung on a pillar near the stairs and made his way up the corridor to the cell where Geor Alton was kept. The smell intensified from an uncomfortable waft to a putrid stench. Will pulled his blouse up to cover his nose and mouth while he raised the lantern to shine its light into the cramped quarters the governor occupied.

"I have news for you governor." Will said, his words muffled through the fabric covering his face.

Geor looked up at him, shielding his eyes from the light and squinting. "What is it?"

"Today, you're getting a visit from the captain. I'm here to get you presentable." Will informed, fighting a gag as he spoke.

"Am I not suitable for the Negro girl you serve lieutenant?" Alton gruffed, waving his hand at Will.

"No, Governor. In fact, I wouldn't be down here unless I was asked to be." Will retorted, coughing into his sleeve. His eyes watered and his throat burned from the odor of excrement and unwashed body in cramped quarters.

"Why haven't they killed me yet? It's not as if they aren't working at it, slowly and painfully. Just take me up on deck and dump me to the sharks. Walk the plank as it were. I only see a meal every other day and what is served is slop hardly fit to feed hogs. What in the bloody hell are they waiting for?" Geor snapped, shouting at Will.

"I believe, Sir, they have kept you alive so that they may use you at some point." Will answered, knowing it wouldn't sit well with the pompous old man.

"Use me? For ransom? That is the only thing they will get from me." Geor sneered. "I'll die before I help them with anything."

"All the same, Governor. The captain is on her way,

so, time for a wash up." Will said, lowering his hand away from his face. He reached for a pail of water along the deck and sloshed it onto the governor where he sat. Shock and anger played across the man's face as he wiped his scraggly whiskered face.

"Hardly a bath at all." Geor complained.

"Aye, and it did little to improve the smell." Will jeered before coughing hard into his sleeve yet again. "She may skin my back for it, but I think it best you come up on deck Governor. I can't stand this stench."

"If I can get properly cleaned up. I'll go." Geor said, lifting his nose into the air.

Will retrieved a key from his trouser pocket and opened the cell door. "I can't promise any finery Governor, but we'll get you cleaned up. I'd suggest you temper your tongue when you speak with the captain as well. She has a propensity for violence."

"I can be nothing if not civil." Geor said, lifting himself to his feet and trudging on stiff legs out of the cell. Will couldn't help but feel pity for the man. His soiled sailcloth trousers were far too large, and he held them up with one hand, his appearance was dirty and disheveled. A man who had once wanted for nothing in life was now lower than a common beggar on the streets of Kingston. His weight had dropped considerably since being taken aboard the Maiden, but he still carried an excess. Shirtless and shoe less he shuffled along the corridor ahead of Will toward the light of the stairway. Trina's silhouette walked down the steps into view as Will and Geor made their way toward the light.

"How is the good governor today?" she called

toward them.

"Struggling and ripe." Will replied, "It would be best for Lilith to speak with us all up on deck."

"She thought so as well. Everything is ready, hurry along now, Governor." Trina said, covering her mouth and nose as the governor approached. "I think you'll find her offer more than fair."

Will was the last of the three to step above deck. He was greeted by a large gathering of the crew standing shoulder to shoulder with Lilith and Chibs. They were all staring at him, Will felt a nervous tinge creep through his veins. It felt like the mutiny aboard the Endurance all over again. Lieutenant Shelton, the only officer to come aboard the Drowned Maiden with Will was standing along the starboard rail, his back facing the gathering.

"The Maiden demands a service from you." Lilith spoke loudly, so everyone on deck would hear.

"What is it you want from me?" Geor huffed. Will could see that despite his long stay in horrid condition, his pride was still wounded by being spoken to in such a manner.

"Governor Alton. You will sign and deliver to the governor of Nassau a letter of marque authorizing the Drowned Maiden and her crew to sink, burn or take prize any vessel transporting slaves. The slave trade has in fact been abolished by both the British and the Americans," Chibs said, shooting a look over to Will.

"That only applies to ships under the King's governance you fool." Geor snorted, sticking his nose into the air.

"It makes no difference. You will draft the letter and

sign it and you will deliver a copy of it to the governor of Nassau. After that, we will leave you ashore somewhere safe and you will be free of worry where we are concerned." Lilith snapped.

"And if I don't?" Geor stuck his nose higher, daring the young captain to do her worst.

"Oh, but you will. I have all the time I need to convince you." Lilith snapped, then looking over to Chibs, "Give him a bath quartermaster. See to it his disposition improves."

"Aye Captain." Chibs said taking a big step forward and motioning to two of the crew near the governor.

Two large pirates shoved the governor down to the deck with savage force. The governor had no more than begun to roll onto his side when one of the pirates put a foot on his shoulder while the other took a length of line and tied it around the governor's ankles. Will traced the length of line with his eyes and saw it led up to the rigging running along the mainsail yard. He turned toward Lilith.

"Are you going to keelhaul him? He won't survive it!" Will said, trying not to sound desperate to stop whatever was about to occur.

"I appreciate the suggestion Lieutenant, and I'll keep that in mind for later. But today the governor is just going for a little dip, until he comes around to my way of thinking." Lilith said, walking to the rail to watch as Geor was hoisted off the deck and swung out over the water. The sunlight had broken through the clouds and cast a glorious glow over the water. Even in the winter months the warmth of the sun made the waters of the Caribbean look inviting.

"Lilith, a letter of marque won't do for you what you think it will. Often times those privateers are still hung as pirates, especially if they take a ship flying the King's colors." Will objected, trying to change Lilith's course.

"I'm no fool Lieutenant. It won't stop the French or the Americans from coming after us. But a letter of marque in hand means we are right and legal in the eyes of the Brits. One less enemy to be wary of." Lilith said, looking over her shoulder at Will before focusing back on the governor hanging over the sea. "Drop him!" She called to the crew holding the line.

The governor wailed as gravity took him. His arms flailed, helpless to stop the descent. A resounding smack sounded along the surface and the only indicator of the governor was a torrent of bubbles rising out of the deep where the line holding him met the water. Will watched as the line trailed off the main yard from the movement of the ship. Below the surface, Governor Alton would be helpless to surface himself as the ship drug him by his feet. Long moments drug by and the column of bubbles floating up dissipated.

"Lilith, he is no use to you dead." Will urged.

She turned and shot him a look, "Haul him up."

The line crew hauled at the rope, heaving grip by grip until Geor Alton's soaked figure broke above the surface. The crew hauling the line continued until Geor dangled just feet below the main yard. Lilith gave Will an amused smile over her shoulder before taunting the governor.

"Feel like writing me a letter yet?" Lilith shouted.

Geor wiped his face with trembling hands craning his neck to try and look at Lilith as she yelled. His pasty skin was pink and red where he had slapped into the water moments before. Lilith looked back at Will almost searching for some reaction from him. "Drop him again."

The line went slack and Geor plummeted back into the brine with a loud slapping splash. Pirates all along the deck laughed and shouted taunts the governor could not hear. Lilith's eyes remained locked on Will.

"I wonder about you Lieutenant. I have since the minute you set foot on this ship." She said, "When the fleet arrives, will you betray us? Will you turn on me and this crew?"

"Lilith, I've only intended to do what is right…"

"Captain!" Lilith snapped.

"Captain, you're right. I have only wanted to do what is right, not betray my country." Will finished, leering his eyes toward the water's surface as the column of bubbles began to disappear again.

"You haven't Will. We sunk a ship full of slavers and the ships that mutinied against you. But Lieutenant, having two mutinies against you, you are really worried that you are the traitor?" Lilith said, cocking her head sideways a little and wrinkling her nose. "Are you sure they're really worth your loyalty Will?"

Will dropped his gaze to the deck, her words stung like a saber plunged into his flesh. He had pondered these very thoughts among himself, but to hear them come from the young captain made them sting all the more.

"Hoist him." Lilith said to the line crew. A few

grumbled at the strain to lift him from the water again but in moments the governor reappeared out of the sea.

"Ok, Ok, I'll do it! I'll write your damn bloody letter! Just bring me back aboard, for the love of God!"

Chapter 5

'Southern Song'
14 Feb 1809
31 Degrees 19' N, 76 Degrees 17' W

Rory's face lay along the wooden rail after he had been sick over the side. The raining had ceased but the Southern Song was still being tossed about by winds and heavy seas. The cool spray of the sea brought him comfort for a moment until the heavy pitching of the ship registered in his brain again and vertigo took over. Three days sailing had done little to calm his raging nausea and the sea seemed like a relentless tormentor. She was both beautiful and cruel. Softly spraying his face while he ailed and harshly threatening to drown him when he leaned too far over the rail. The wooden rail along the ship's perimeter had been his best friend for the past four days. He clung to it as the ship heaved in a never-ending pattern of up and down while simultaneously rocking side to side. Any food he consumed was only held down momentarily before being violently ejected while he held on for dear life to the wooden rail.

Dog and the rest of the crew seemed impervious to the effects of Southern Song's unceasing movement. The salty old seamen only complained about the rains and the foods. Rory looked on them enviously, hoping that he would possess their strength and fortitude and gain the better of his sea sickness. He had just finished heaving the last of his stomach contents over the rail when Dog's hand slammed down onto the sea spray-soaked wood next to his head.

"You'd do well to gather yourself boy. The battle of it is in the mind." Dog grumbled while looking down on Rory with bloodshot eyes.

"Have you been drinking?" Rory asked, feeling a wave of vertigo rising up into his stomach.

"Of course I have. A nip of rum might do you some good as well." Dog screeched a laugh, digging a small glass bottle from his trouser pocket and pulling the cork with his ragged teeth. "Here's to the sea and the Southern Song!"

Rory let fly with another retch over the rail, yielding little more than dry convulsions of his abdomen. He collapsed back to the deck and wiped his mouth with a sleeve. "What exactly do you suggest Dog? I can't walk more than a few steps without losing my composure. What would you have me do to cure this ailment?"

"Well. It's up into the rigging with you son. I'd have you climb the ratlines to the crow's nest. Nothing brings the deck into perspective like tossing around up top. It's all in your head boy, once you beat that, you've got her licked."

Rory eyed the old sailor, wondering if he was the

butt of another jest to the benefit of the rest of Dog's crew. Since leaving port hardly an hour had passed without some comment or question regarding his seaworthiness. Dog looked down on him with a grin of gapped and rotten teeth. Another heave of the deck sent a spray of misty seawater onto Rory's neck. *What have I got to lose?* Rory looked up, tracing his eyes along the towering mast reaching high above the brigantine's deck. Rigging lines crisscrossed angles between the deck and different levels of the mast, running through blocks and along the yards. Some were meant for trimming and angling the sails while others were set to brace the towering masts against the constant force of wind and sea.

"Lead on Dog." Rory managed.

The sailor was off in an instant, lurching his way along the rail toward the ratlines. His swagger seemed to grow with the presence of other seafarers on deck and Rory noticed a distinct edge in Dog's voice that was absent when the salted man spoke to him. Pausing for a moment to allow Rory to catch up, Dog gave him a stern look when they got to the base of the ratlines along the larboard rail.

"Mind your feet when we go aloft. Only one free limb at a time. You keep one in contact for the ship and two for yourself boy. You hear?" Dog gruffed through his scraggly beard.

"I can manage that." Rory replied.

"You'd do well to remember that. If you fall, it's either the hard deck or the cold sea for you and if you miss the lifeline the first time, there's not a chance in hell we'd get you before she becomes your grave boy."

He spit over the rail before grabbing hold of the ratline and vaulting himself up.

Rory followed suit on the forward side of the ratlines, pausing for a moment to look down to the sea as he stood on the rail.

"That won't do boy! No use looking down, we're headed up!" Dog's voice was cut by wind whistling through the lines in front of them.

Rory's gaze lingered for a moment on the dark swells of sea below and he lifted his eyes, forcing himself to look up. A jolt of adrenaline spiked through his blood as Rory watched Dog climb the first few rungs and then look back down to him. Rory clamped his hands onto the rigging and took his first step up, then brought his other foot up to the rung with the first. He repeated this process with his hands and then alternated moving one hand and one foot so that they were all staggered onto a different rung of the rigging. Dog climbed ahead just a step above as they made their way up the web of rope. When they reached the point where the ratlines intersected with the main mast a small wooden platform sat at the top of the rigging they climbed. Rory adjusted his hands and made an awkward mess of climbing off the rat line and onto the platform. There was no room for a missed step, the planks below their feet offered a scant foot and half to stand with no barrier against a long drop to the deck below. To their sides the mainsail yard stretched out beyond where the deck rail fenced in the ship below. Out there on the far ends of the limb, sailors taking in sail would be working directly over the water.

"Onward we go boy. Don't get too comfortable."

Dog's grinding voice offered no comfort.

"Of course." Rory replied looking upward as Dog began climbing the rope ladder that led directly up the mast to where the top sails could be handled.

Again, hand over hand and foot after foot, Rory followed Dog aloft until they reached the top sail yard. This level had no wooden platform, only an intersecting yard secured by ropes and iron fittings. The side-to-side motion that had plagued Rory's mind and wracked his guts into knots was exaggerated up at this level. When his waist was at the same level as the yard, Rory swung a leg out and carefully hugging the mast, climbed on to straddle the top sail yard as he saw Dog do a moment before.

"That's it, now you keep those legs under you and you lock the insides of your knees to the yard boy. Hold to this brace line and we'll have us a little sailing lesson." Dog shouted through the whipping winds.

"Up here?" Rory asked, not believing what he was hearing.

"Where else? Now the wood you have your arse on right now is the topsail yard. We passed the main sail yard on our way up. The yard suspends sail and lines as well as sailors from time to time, either by their butt sitting on it just like ours are right now, or by their necks if you catch my drift." Dog proceeded with his lesson. "Above us is the top gallant or sometimes called gallant. I'm not going to drag you up that high because the rains have stopped, and I think the boys below would take it hard to have your piss raining down on them when they just got dry. Larger ships have a fourth sail upwards of that and those are called royals. This old bird wouldn't handle a fourth and we just don't need it with our size anyhow."

Rory looked where Dog indicated with each different explanation and then caught himself peering downward. The deck of the ship seemed like a distant patch of wood in the never-ending stretch of rolling swells surrounding them. The sway of the mast teetered back and forth, and they would cross from being above water for a second then pass over the deck to back over water. Rory's head swooned as he suddenly became cognizant of the constant motion again.

"Hey, boy! Are you paying attention? I'm not up here for my benefit!" Dog snapped Rory back into focus. "Now like I was saying, the yard we're sitting on is on the main mast. Forward is the forward mast. Some bigger ships have three, then they would call theirs aft, main and forward. Or sometimes main, mizzen and forward. It all varies and some changes whether you're on a navy ship or not."

Dog's voice seemed to rattle on, and Rory did his best to pay attention. He named lines and pulleys, correcting himself several times when he mixed up their names. The side-to-side motion stuttered for a second as a wind shift caught the sails which sent Rory onto his belly, hugging tight to the yard beneath him.

"Damn your coward's soul boy! Didn't I tell you to keep hold of the brace line, now sit up!" Dog shouted, his face going red.

Rory clamped his grip onto the brace line running just above the yard and fought through his hesitation back up to sit.

"If you go onto your belly on this bastard in rough seas without something to brace yourself against, you'll wind up hanging beneath the damn yard, suspended by those skinny arms of yours. You won't last but a few minutes before taking a quick trip down to the water, or worse, you'll be another stain on the deck. Hold onto the damn brace line." Dog's voice returned to his normal growl. "We can reef these sails from on deck with their lines, but someone has to come up and secure them, foul weather or not. It's a dangerous job and I've seen more than a few sailors lose their footing this high up. It's not pretty."

Rory nodded, hearing Dog's words of caution. His only thoughts revolved around making their way back to the deck and relative safety.

"Dog, let's go back down. I've had enough for today." Rory shouted through the whipping wind.

"Aye, we'll go back. Just keep yer head on boy. Now, as I was saying…" Dog continued his lesson, ignoring Rory's request. The winds bit at his exposed skin, prickling at his ears and cheeks and numbing his fingers until they felt painfully cold and sluggish. Shouted voices echoed up from the deck below. Rory looked down onto the figures as they moved around on deck. Dog was continuing his explanation of some sailing procedure. Rory's mind danced between trying to listen through the searing cold wind and his desire to climb down to the deck. The relative warmth of the cramped berthing below deck seemed a distant luxury. Rory thought back to the warm inn with its soft beds and delicious prepared meals. It seemed a wonder to him that sailors would leave such lovely accommodations for conditions like these. Dog seemed to be finishing his lesson, or maybe had lost his patience.

"Now on the way below, don't get in a rush boy. We want to take her slow and steady, all the way down. You rush and you just may find yourself traveling to the deck a whole lot faster than you bargained for." He crowed, leaning closer to Rory. The sailor's breath cut through the wind, permeating Rory's nostrils and snapping his mind back to the task at hand.

Dog scooted himself with expert precision to the mast and rotated onto the rope ladder. Step by step, he descended while Rory attempted the same maneuver. Rory got his first foot onto a rung and clasped the accompanying vertical rope it was attached to in one hand. As the ship heaved and rolled, he released the stay line with his other hand and grabbed onto the other side of the rope ladder. When Rory pulled his remaining leg from the yard the motion of the ship in the opposite direction seemed more abrupt than it had previously. Rory's other foot missed the ladder rung he had intended to place it on. A jolt of lightning ran through his veins as his hands locked onto the ladder anticipating the need to arrest him from a fall. His foot found the rung and a sigh of relief left him. He closed his eyes for a moment, gathering his shattered wits. Step by step, he followed Dog through the web of lines and rigging to the weather deck. By the time his feet hit solid deck again, his stomach had released its knots of tension. The pitching, rolling and heaving of the deck was still noticeable, but after the exaggerated motions high above in the rigging the deck seemed tolerable.

Rory began to realize what Dog had done.

"Thank you, Dog." Rory said as the sailor walked toward the helm.

"For what? I may need you up there when we sail into a blustering storm. You'll be cursing my hide then." Dog grunted over his shoulder through his jagged smile.

United States Capitol Building
Washington D.C.
6 March 1809

John Gaillard gloomed at his desk over a letter received by one of his most affluent constituents. The letter spelled out in detail several instances of British press ganging against his merchant fleet. Outside his office window the Washington morning reflected his mood, gray and foreboding. The eastern horizon, which should have been lit by a glorious early spring sunrise, was marred by a dark bank of clouds promising more cold weather. John's office was sparsely lit by columns of gray light from the windows and the lamp which cast a circle of hazy yellow light from its soot-stained globe and threw its own set of shadows along the reaching walls of the South Carolina Senator's office. The letter on his desk represented only the most recent in a stack of complaints his office had received about the press-ganging activities of the British Navy. Though John suspected the British interdiction of slave trafficking vessels had far more to do with the complaints than a few sailors being forced from their employ. Parliament had abolished the legal slave trade and in the eyes of the British Government it was illegal for any vessel flying their colors to participate or assist in those endeavors. This halted the free flow of slaves from Africa through East India Company vessels as well as the Dutch Africa Company or any ship that held charter or letter of marque from either nation or hoped to in the future. The American Congress followed suit the following year, much to the dismay of southerners and the agricultural complex they relied on. Smugglers still found a way, but the regular, lawful trade of slaves from overseas was over. For the present time at least.

War throughout Europe was a double-edged sword for the American economy. Ship builders in Boston profited from Napoleon's appetite for American built warships, while cash crop merchants played a deadly game of cat and mouse in their trans-Atlantic shuttle to sell American goods. Not only had ships been stripped of their crewmen mid voyage, but there were also several merchant fleet owners claiming that their vessels and cargo had been taken as prize by the British. *How soon everyone forgets.* John's roots in America were deep, he was a proud American and a proud southerner. But he had been educated in England at his father's insistence. *We barely scraped our way through the last war with Britain and now the war hawks want to have at it again.*

A knock at the door interrupted John's brooding.

"Come in." John spoke as he rose from his seat

behind the desk. Eli Kincaid, John's aide and the son of his neighboring plantation owner in South Carolina, entered.

"Sir, you asked for me to inform you before the next session convened." Eli's voice was as feeble and weak as his stature.

"Thank you, Eli, I will be along." John gruffed, looking back down to his desktop and shuffling the letter beneath some other articles.

"Sir. I thought I might inform you that there seems to be discussion amongst the other senators." Eli stuttered out. "They are drafting some resolutions to employ privateers against the British from the sound of it. Just what I pieced together from hearing talk, Sir."

John went still for a moment. He quelled a flush of anger that welled deep in his belly and leaned against the surface of his desk on extended fingertips. "What else have you heard boy?"

"Many members in both the house and senate have received letters protesting actions of the British, Sir. Press ganging crews, interdicting American slave ships and taking merchant vessels bound for France as prizes for the crown Sir." Eli reported in his sheepish tone, dropping a timid nod with every few words.

"They mean to have a war and by god, it will be had. Best to get in front of it then." John muttered.

"Pardon Sir?" Eli asked, craning his neck upwards as if he missed some important instruction.

"Nothing. It's nothing son. I'll be along, thank you." John replied with a dismissive wave.

Gathering his effects, John pulled his suit jacket on and tucked a leather case under his arm. He exited his office and proceeded along the wide hallways of the capitol building. Members of the 11th Congress were still filing through the hall toward their respective chambers. As John entered the senate chambers he was inundated in a wave of noise. Chattering conversations throughout the large room melded into a disorderly array of words floating and wafting through his ears. It was an overwhelming sensation each time he entered. Members and their aides all vying for each other's attention, side conversations mixed with the exchanging of pleasantries and an occasional outburst of laughter or disagreement. John despised the disorder. Once the gavel fell and roll call began, he could begin to gather himself, he longed for the tranquility in his quiet office.

"Napoleon is master of Europe! We would be foolish not to press our issues with the British now!"

John clenched his jaw as he heard the exclamation float in behind him as he took his seat. *How soon everyone forgets.*

Several sharp clacks sounded from the dais as the presiding officer called the body to order, ushering a hush over the room.

"Order, order, order." George Clinton, the presiding officer announced while tapping his gavel. "This session of the eleventh congress will now commence."

A well-dressed man seated near the dais stood to be recognized.

"The president recognizes the gentleman senator from the commonwealth of Massachusetts to take the floor."

The senator stood next to his desk while placing his

finger down onto a parchment sitting on its surface. "I have here a letter from one of my constituents, the latest in a succession of many, pleading that we, the representative voices of this nation deal with the abhorrent and aggressive intrusions of the British against our seafaring vessels. Both near our own coastlines and abroad. The embargo act of the previous congress has done nothing to quell these hostilities and I believe it is time we take action! I move that this body must immediately deliver an ultimatum to the crown and demand he cease these attacks at once." The senator's words were drowned in a wave of vocal agreements and dissents.

The gavel sounded again as Clinton tried to hush the outbursts, "Do I have a second?"

"I second the motion!" a voice from the back of the room carried through the echoing snaps of the gavel.

"Very well then, we will open the floor for debate." Clinton grumbled leering over the room through squinted eyes. John took a deep breath and rose to his feet, feeling a hot rush flood over him as the eyes of senators all over the room drew to him. "The president recognizes the distinguished gentleman senator from the state of South Carolina."

"A good morning to my fellow senators. I have lived my life gratefully in this nation, which God saw fit to grace us with by his will and his mercy. He delivered us from the yoke of a foreign sovereign and has seen fit to guide us in the endeavor of self-governance unto our own greater good. I have also seen the might of the British military, firsthand. I too have been inundated with letters demanding action against the evil dealings of our former oppressor. But I would implore this body to seek reason and ask yourselves, are we up to the task of another war with the mightiest military in the world? Napoleon is Britain's enemy, of this there can be no doubt, but is he also America's friend? I still have my questions in that regard. I heard it said as I entered these chambers that now is the time to press Britain, while they contend with waging war against France. Gentlemen, he may have sold us Louisiana, but that does not make Napoleon our ally. France has yet to acknowledge American neutrality and still likely counts their assistance to us during the revolution as partiality toward their nation over others. I for one must object to the idea of sending any ultimatum, declaration or otherwise to present before the governing authority of Britain. This nation has suffered already from the feeble attempt of the last congress and its preposterous embargo act."

"You voted for it!" a voice shouted from across the room.

"He was schooled in London! His loyalist father would have us still paying the crown our taxes!" another shout chimed in. The gavel snapped repetitively as more shouts echoed through the chambers. John returned to his seat with a flushed face and beaded sweat gathering at his collar, satisfied that he had spoken his part for peace.

"Order, order. We will have order in the chambers! The president recognizes the gentleman senator from the state of New York…" Clinton huffed in a loud voice as another senator rose from his seat. "We will have an orderly debate."

'North Wind'
12 Mar 1809
37 Degrees 16' N, 50 Degrees 10' W

Sunshine broke through the gaps of heavy cloud formations casting down columns of golden sunlight onto the rolling sea. The winds had held steady from the north and Admiral Alistair Torren's fleet was making very good progress crossing the Atlantic. Alistair stood on the bow of North Wind enjoying the beauty of the morning. The breeze at his back still carried brisk tones but had lost its bitter skin biting chill. His walk that morning had been pleasant and yielded him the opportunity to greet several of the deck hands and a wide-awake Midshipman Brant, diligently standing his post as deck officer.

"How much longer do you suppose until we reach the Caribbean Sir?" Lieutenant Thatcher asked.

"Another week, lad, perhaps a week and a half. Nassau will be our first port of call. I mean to speak with the Governor and the garrison commander there. We should be able to resupply in a day's time, maybe two at the most and then we will bend every sail toward Kingston." The admiral replied, covering a slight irritation. Some moments in life were precious things, the breaking of several weeks of overcast weather being one of them. Times like this needed mindful presence and a satisfaction in focusing on the sea immediately ahead without unnecessary strife being paid to what lie beyond the horizon. Youth, ambition and exuberance hardly appreciate times like these.

"Is it possible Kingston has been retaken Sir? Could this all be for naught?" Lieutenant Thatcher continued, confirming to the admiral that he would be denied the opportunity to bask in the beauty that lay before him in peace.

"It is entirely possible Lieutenant. But securing Kingston against whatever foes have come against it is only part of our task. We must learn the fate of the fleet and either come to their aid or eliminate whatever forces are responsible for their demise, depending on the circumstances. Whatever the case or cause, I think it should likely be a trying endeavor. Admiral Sharpe is one of the greatest tacticians I have ever had the pleasure to work alongside, if he has fallen to an enemy, they will be formidable." The admiral said, clenching his jaw at the possibilities he faced. His tone was quick, cutting. But the moment of tranquility was gone, now his focus lie far ahead and there would be no undoing it. "Tell the signalman I want the fleet in a tighter formation and find out when the Ambush was last spotted, I've been on deck for at least two hours and haven't heard her spotted yet."

"Aye Sir." The lieutenant said turning to his tasks.

Alistair remained on the forecastle, observing the golden columns shining down in spots on the sea ahead, making the waves seem to dance under its brilliant light. Screening vessels could often go hours, sometimes even days without being spotted by the fleet. But heading into so many unknowns, it made his blood tinge cold when he thought of the sloop being engaged by some enemy without the support of the fleet. A sloop in open water is a nimble and dangerous adversary, which usually nominated them as the preferred vessel to scout ahead and screen the fleet movements. But they were lightly armed and could withstand very little damage before being crippled. Alistair tapped the end of his cane on the deck. Under usual circumstances he would allow his junior officers far more leeway than he currently was, but the unknowns were too murky, the possibilities too dire to take any unnecessary risks. Scrunching his brows to a frown Alistair turned and looked over the deck of North Wind, pondering whether old age was making him too conservative. Young officers tended to be more brash, to a fault oftentimes. The old warhorses were more cautious creatures, sometimes allowing caution to get the better of opportunity. Balance between aggressive action and defensive posture was the critical component that set many captains in the fleet apart, vaulting them on to higher commands. Alistair shook off the notion and returned his eyes to the horizon.

High above in the North Wind's rigging, a sailor called down to the deck officer, "Sail on the horizon, sloop. Looks to be the Ambush Sir." Midshipman Brant called back his compliments and turned to the helm to notate the sighting in his log. Alistair smiled remembering the morning a few weeks prior when he had caught the young officer nodded off on a coiled pile of line. It was a poorly kept secret among the crew, the admiral was slow to anger and as lenient an officer as they had ever seen. Somehow, the ship was running as clean and orderly as it ever had. And fewer discipline issues. Feeling his legs beginning to tighten the admiral proceeded back toward his cabin, paying the deck officer compliments along the way.

"She's running along finely young man, if this wind keeps on as it is toward noon fly the royals and signal the fleet to do the same if you will." Alistair said, gritting as his knees began to throb from his extended stay on deck.

"Aye Sir. Fly the royals if the wind holds and have the fleet carry on as well." Midshipman Brant answered with a crisply rendered salute.

"Very well then." Admiral Torren replied rendering a return salute as he passed into his cabin.

Inside the heat of his large cabin, Alistair removed his cloak and uniform coat. He hung them on a rack attached to the bulkhead. The small wood stove gave off tremendous heat and soon the chill in his fingers and nose dissipated. Lieutenant Thatcher hurried to pour a cup of dark tea before slathering a salted pork steak with spiced mustard next to a pair of fried eggs. The lieutenant deposited the admiral's plate of breakfast onto the desk as Alistair sat down.

"My favorite breakfast. No biscuits?" Alistair looked around the setting as he raised the cup of tea to his mouth for the first hot sip.

"What we had remaining are too far gone Sir. Full of weevils and gone to mold as is the cheese in your stores." The lieutenant informed him.

"Ah, every voyage gets to that point eventually. Do tell me, am I also running low of spirits?" Alistair inquired further.

"You still have several bottles of good whiskey and one brandy left Sir." Lieutenant Thatcher answered with a slight grimace.

"Very well. That should do until we arrive in Nassau, another week by my reckoning. When we arrive, you will scour that town for decent whiskey and brandies. If I am forced to drink rum while we are in the Caribbean, I'll have you flogged and keelhauled so that you may share in my pain." Alistair chuckled as he mopped yolk with a fork full of pork and took a bite.

"If I could make an inquiry Admiral." Lieutenant Thatcher replied, pausing at the admiral's side for a moment.

"What is it lad?" Alistair looked up from his plate with thick raised brows.

"I've heard several of the lads on board talk of keelhauling. I thought it was closer to fable than fact, is that actually a prescribed punishment Sir?" his tone permeated with concern and brought a wry smile to Alistair's face.

"I was jesting young man. Rarely would I have a man flogged, even if it were the prescribed punishment set forth in the articles. Never for failing his commander in creature comforts. Do you really think so lowly of me Lieutenant?" Alistair prodded while continuing to eat his breakfast.

"No, Sir. No not at all. My question was more in regards of keelhauling. I have heard several descriptions…"

"And you're concerned for the welfare of the lads. Is that it?" Alistair interrupted.

"Well. You are a lenient commander Sir. I am not as concerned for our fleet or crew. But, I have heard several descriptions, I am interested in the truth behind the lore Sir." Lieutenant Thatcher said.

"The academic in you will be your undoing. Sometimes the unspoken fear of a subject is enough to keep the lads in line Lieutenant. But, since I can see your curiosity won't be satiated by a few grumblings from an old man, I'll indulge you." Alistair finished his last bite and had a sip of tea while pushing his plate away. "On an extreme occasion, one must be punished in a manner that a simple flogging just won't do. A display so grotesque it makes hanging a man seem like a mercy. Keelhauling has been around the maritime profession since the days of old, in the age when piracy was a true threat to British naval supremacy. Likewise, it is a punishment reserved for pirates and mutineers and other foul doings in league with those offenses. Typically, in those early days, a man would be strung up by his hands and feet in the rigging to a line that had been fished underneath the hull of a ship." The Admiral paused slightly having another sip at his tea. "He would then be hauled beneath the ship, dragging along her keel, either cross ways from larboard rail down under and up the starboard side, or, if the captain is particularly cruel, from stem to stern as it were. If it had been a sufficient length of time since the vessel's hull was cleaned, the recipient would be ripped to shreds by barnacles whilst also held underwater and being slammed against the hull repeatedly. It's a ghastly business. Men get so ripped to ribbons they can't be recognized, half drowned and blubbering for their mothers and God. Awful stuff lad. But not to worry, if you can't find my preferred liquor,

I'll only have you drug through the drink once. And cross wise, since you do so well with breakfast." Alistair jeered at the lieutenant with another grin.

"How very kind of you Sir." The lieutenant replied, chuckling at his commander's teasing.

"I jest Lieutenant, but I honestly cannot think of an instance where I would feel right about subjecting someone to such a barbarous fate. Even a mutineer is deserving of some manner of dignity, we are all human beings. But why, might I ask, are you so bloody interested in such things?" Alistair pressed, locking his gaze onto the lieutenant.

"Well. It may be improper for me to inform Sir. But, at dinner in the captain's cabin the other night, he threatened to keelhaul his steward for some spilled wine. I thought it to be in jest at first, but the entire cabin fell silent." Thatcher seemed hesitant, but too loyal to the Admiral not to air the truth of the matter.

"Well then." Alistair's face began to flush with a tinge of anger. "Fetch me the captain at once. I'll have the matter of it settled before noon."

"Yes Sir." The lieutenant snapped to and turned to retrieve the ship's captain.

"Lieutenant Thatcher." Alistair said as the lieutenant reached for the door.

"Sir?"

"You do understand that I would never flog or keelhaul a man over a bit of liquor, right? I understand my jest was in terrible taste." Alistair said in a somber note.

"Of course not Sir. Never crossed my mind that you would." Lieutenant Thatcher could see the admiral was flustered.

"Very well, let's have the captain up here then. He and I will have a talk." Alistair dismissed the young officer and turned to look out over the fantail.

Fort Charles - Kingston, Jamaica
20 Feb 1809

They came in the night. Lieutenant Trenton was ripped from sleep by the reports of gunfire and alarm bells from the ramparts. Moonlight cast an eerie glow through the main courtyard of Fort Charles and as the lieutenant scrambled from his quarters with sword and pistol in hand a harrowing shriek cut through the air. Lieutenant Trenton turned toward the scream just in time to watch one of his soldiers fall from the top of the wall. Flashing gunfire erupted from atop the wall. Flickering torchlight interspersed the pale moonlit courtyard but the lieutenant couldn't make out how many attackers were moving against his men along the wall top. Another volley of gunfire rained down, sending the soldiers below scrambling for cover.

"We have to make it up onto the wall!" Lieutenant Trenton yelled, grabbing and shoving every soldier in sight toward the staircase closest to them. He ran with a group of four men toward the stairs.

Across the fort, another exchange of gunfire sounded, followed by clashes of steel. Shouted battle cries and screams of pain echoed from every corner of Fort Charles and Lieutenant Trenton felt as if every step was being dogged by an invisible molasses dragging at him. He lunged up the first two steps under the shimmering light of a torch above the stairs as gunshots impacted above him. Robert froze for a moment as debris falling from the impacts peppered his face.

"They've taken the ramparts!" a soldier shouted out at the top of the stairs.

"Keep moving! Go!" Robert screamed as he charged up the stairs.

A soldier in front of him stumbled Robert's feet entangled into the man's legs as he tumbled onto the steps. The side railing along the stair kept Lieutenant Trenton from falling completely down onto the steps. Robert's weight crunched his ribs into the rail, and he braced himself with his sword hand, using the hilt to push himself back to standing. The soldiers ahead lurched forward and out of Lieutenant Trenton's sight as he pressed onward up the steps after regaining his footing. Below in the courtyard a bright flash of flames swirled from the large tent his men had made into their makeshift barracks. The orange glow lit through Fort Charles' interior and for a second Lieutenant Trenton saw a flash of the dire situation he faced. Attackers were moving along the rampart and had stormed down the far stairway and taken part of the courtyard. Their heads and faces were wrapped in black cloth. A pair were running from where the barracks tent was being consumed in flame towards the Fort's main gate.

Lieutenant Trenton scanned the courtyard for any soldier he could direct their way. No soldier stood between the pair of masked men and the front gate. *If the gate is breached, we're all dead.* The sounds of clashing steel mixed with gunfire above him on the rampart tore the lieutenant between aiding his men and sprinting back toward the gate. *If the gate is breached, we're all dead.* He wheeled himself down the stairs, moving his feet in a descent that felt almost in control. The masked pair would pass the foot of the stairs before he could intercept them.

"Stop them!" Robert screamed, pointing at the running men with his blade. Several shots sounded from the wall above the gate and dirt kicked up at the pair's feet as they ran past the base of the stairs. *We still hold part of the ramparts, all is not lost yet.* The two men disappeared into shadow as they crossed into the alcove of the wall where the gate was located. Robert's foot touched onto ground level and his pace quickened. Torchlight from the command quarters entrance bled into the alcove just enough for Robert to see one of the masked attackers heaving at the crossbar inside the gate. *If the gate is breached...* With his heart racing, Robert raised his pistol. Cocking the hammer with the hilt of his sword as he ran, he could see the two were only a moment from opening Fort Charles' front gate. His feet skittered to a halt as Robert raised his pistol, he took aim at the figure barely lit in the orange torch glow and squeezed his trigger until a flash erupted from his pistol. The man he was aiming at staggered and crumpled backwards, his companion rushing to his side.

Robert bolted back into a sprint for the gate. One masked man at the gate lay crumpled on the ground and the other stooped over him. As Robert reached within a few running strides, the stooped man snapped into a fighting stance, with sword in hand. Robert let out a scream as he swung his sword in a sideways slash at the remaining masked attacker. Their swords met in a ringing clash and the man expertly parried and wheeled around in a counter that Robert barely defended. The masked man followed with a series of aggressive slashing and lunging attacks that rocked the weary lieutenant backwards as he struggled to defend. Lieutenant Trenton defended on his heels as the masked man attacked with intensifying aggression driving him back away from the gate and into the light of the moon in the courtyard and the smoke from the burning barracks tent. The ring of steel sounded through the courtyard. To Lieutenant Trenton it was the only sound audible. His attacker's eyes became fiery embers burning a hole of rage and hatred straight through his chest. The man was skilled and aggressive, each attack was rapid. The attacker's recovery from each of Robert's defenses seemed to blend in with his next attack.

Lieutenant Trenton felt his balance shift, he wheeled to his side to avoid an overhead strike only to have the attacker spin on his footing and turn his recovery from the overhead swing into an upward slash. He dodged again, this time further off his balance. The upward swing missed his cheek and flicked the edge of the lieutenant's ear. Robert plunged his curved longsword at the masked swordsman in a desperate attempt to break the chain of attacks building against him. The masked man parried and brought his sword back across the lieutenant's forearm, opening the flesh and drawing a spurt of blood with it. Lieutenant Trenton grunted as the slicing pain shot through his arm and wrist, begging he release his grip on the sword in his hand. Smoke filled the courtyard and caught the orange glare of fires burning in several places around the interior of the fort. Lieutenant Trenton's eyes watered and stung, he struggled to see the deft movement of his opponent as the following attack came in a high diagonal arc. He brought his sword up to parry at the last possible instant. Steel rang together. The masked man then punched the hilt of his sword forward in an explosive violence that overcame Lieutenant Trenton's resistance. The sword hilt slammed into the lieutenant's brow, opening a gash over his eye. Then another follow-on attack missed a wild parry attempt and the point of the masked man's sword met Lieutenant Trenton's belly, plunging deep into his side flesh.

All wind escaped Lieutenant Trenton. He could feel a rush of warm blood running out of his side. The masked man wrenched his blade backward, pulling it out while shoving the lieutenant with a hard kick. Lieutenant Trenton stumbled backward, falling to the ground. His masked opponent walked toward him, pulling away the black fabric covering the bottom half of his face. Through the orange haze of smoke and firelight his grin beamed down at the wounded lieutenant.

"This is how it ends for you." His voice was deep, and his accent was unmistakable.

"You're an American?" the lieutenant managed while looking up into the man's eyes as firelight glistened his face.

The swordsman laughed, reversing his grip on his

weapon and grasping onto its handle in both hands. "That's right. You can let Saint Peter know I'll be sending the rest of your friends after you."

He plunged the sword down into Lieutenant Trenton's chest, driving the point so hard it dug into the ground beneath him. The lieutenant grabbed at the blade in a frantic motion to stop the inevitable, blood surging from his palms as his hands met the blade edge. The grin faded into a look of disdain and then indifference. Lieutenant Trenton struggled for air, watching as the American disappeared from view. His vision blurred. Shades of orange and yellow mixed in the night air as smoke swirled above. The stars beyond looked like eyes shining down onto the chaos around him. He closed his eyes and thought of church bells, London and a girl he fancied at home. Then his thoughts faded as the world grew dark and closed around him.

Chapter 6

'Drowned Maiden'
12 Feb 1809
21 Degrees 43' N, 68 Degrees 18' W

"Ready on the guns!" William's shout echoed through the Maiden's gun deck. A tense moment passed. Lewis' face and back glistened with sweat. He wiped his brow to avoid the perspiration from getting into his eyes. "FIRE!" The end of William's command was lost to the explosive reports of the Maiden's starboard battery. The guns roared in near unison and recoiled violently against their restraining lines. As each gun roared back the individual gun crews began a series of successive actions to prepare for a following volley. Lewis sprang into action as soon as the motion of his gun halted. Under the cramped overhead beams and boards, he scrambled to the front of the cannon carriage. He held a rod with a wet sponge on the end and in a quick motion extended the rod out of the gun port while fitting the sponge into the gun's bore. In two swipes he ran the wet sponge the length of the cannon and then withdrew it from the bore. The crewman on the other side of the cannon pushed a cylindrical bag of gunpowder into the gun's bore and Lewis rammed it home with the end of his rod opposite the sponge. The opposite crewman then placed the shot into the bore, and it rolled down onto the bag of powder. Then in a unified motion Lewis and his fellow gun crewman heaved on the gun lines, rolling the cannon carriage back into position with the muzzle extending slightly from its gun port. Once in position, Lewis pulled a thin, sharpened metal spike from a hook on the beam above his head. With the spike, Lewis pierced the powder bag inside the cannon through the touch hole, spilling some powder out of the bag and into the flash pan.

Once each gun in the battery had completed every step, the gun leader yelled to William at the foot of the stairs leading to the weather deck. "Gun four ready!"

"Gun six ready!"

"Gun two ready!"

"Gun one ready!"

These reports carried on until every gun in the battery was ready to fire. Then William examined his stopwatch and nodded with a slight grin. "Under a minute for two full broadsides, I've seen seasoned crews in the Royal Navy do worse. What say we run one more before we knock off for the evening lads?"

Shouts of approval mixed with taunts between gun crews who were in perpetual competition with one another.

"Starboard battery, ready on the guns!" William's stern face scanned over each gun crew, his eyes seemed to pierce into Lewis' soul, finding every weakness and fear in a glance. Lewis was in his position alongside his gun, eyes locked onto William's glare. His ragged shirt was soaked in perspiration and his hands were raw from handling the gun coarse gun lines through repetitive firing drills over the last half hour. The stern-faced navy man had been friendly enough to Lewis, when he had first come aboard, and William taught the newest crew members their roles on the gun deck. But during drills he was as hard and abrasive as the head splitting beams that ran overhead. The slightest delay in each task would elicit a scowl, or worse, extra duties after drills concluded. Lewis' heart skipped when William's stare locked onto him for a moment, scouring deep within him. The stern look remained, and his eyes stayed locked onto Lewis, sending the young man's blood running cold. As the navy man began to walk the battery line toward Lewis, he could feel his heart sink into his stomach, wondering what infraction he had committed. William stooped under each cross beam making his way to Lewis' gun and Lewis could feel the eyes of every pirate on the cannons lock onto him.

"Mind the carriage wheels sailor." William instructed, pointing to Lewis' foot directly behind the rear wheel. "That's a damned awful way to ruin your reload time, not to mention losing a foot."

Lewis gave William a quick nod and withdrew his foot from behind the carriage wheel. Around him, gun crews all made a point of checking their foot placement. William turned and made his way back to the aft stairs while Lewis' heart settled back to a medium quick in his chest from the racing throb in his throat. William resumed his scan over the gun deck and Lewis made a point of checking his feet one more time before the inevitable order.

"FIRE!" the thunderous roar sounded again, spewing a bright flash and smoke from the muzzles of each gun and sending them all into another round of violent recoil. Lewis sprang into action again, racing through each step to make his gun ready. Acrid smoke from the volley they had just fired drifted into the ship through the gun ports and caused the newer crew to cough and hack as they carried out their tasks, eyes watering from its pungent aroma. The first drills of the day had not gone well. Reload times were too long for the demanding navy man, a shot ball had been dropped during one of the reloads and one gun crew had failed to swab their gun before loading it with powder causing a dangerous premature firing of the gun. Luckily, the gun crew had been clear of the carriage when the unexpected firing occurred. Seasoned gunners throughout the maritime world all told stories of incidents they had either endured or witnessed where a gun carriage would maim its entire crew for lack of a bore being sufficiently swabbed.

The final reload time of the evening seemed to be satisfactory to the navy man and he made rounds of the battery, offering each pirate a "Job well done" or a congratulatory pat on the shoulder. The gun deck was a muggy mess of powder smoke and sweat as the pirates all capped their guns and heaved them back from their gun ports. Lewis lingered at his gun's port for a moment, savoring the cool breeze as it blew in off the water. The sun was setting over on the larboard side and it cast radiant hues high into the sky, streaking all the way to the eastern horizon where the dark of night was gathering. Once the gun deck was set in sailing order, the gun crews made up their hammocks for the night. Many of them made their way up onto the weather deck, to take in the evening sunset and skylark at the first stars appearing as the last glimmers of daylight disappeared.

Evenings on the weather deck were Lewis' favorite time aboard ship. The setting sun would paint a tapestry of colors ranging from bright oranges and reds fading upward into deep violets eventually fading into the night sky. The stars were Lewis' solace in his new unfamiliar nautical setting. He enjoyed listening to the experienced pirates tell the fables and legends that belonged to some of the constellations. Though it was difficult for Lewis to see the pictures they pointed out, the tales reminded him of stories his mother would tell him as a young boy. Many things about his new life at sea were uncomfortable, dangerous and unfamiliar. But despite cramped conditions, despite the unforgiving hazards all around him, he was becoming fond of his new home. For every hazard there was a story, usually accompanied by an anecdote from a sailor who had seen or heard of someone who had done so. Don't place a foot in the middle of coiled lines. Don't get between a seaward line and the ship's rail. Keep two points of contact for yourself and one for the ship in the rigging. Grab the ratlines with palms in and the rig lines with palms down. It was a tidal wave of information at first, but as Lewis' sea legs grew stronger, so did his understanding.

The beautiful pirate captain who had stayed Lewis' date with a whip was often on deck near the helm. The sight of her was intoxicating to Lewis, who adored her not only for her fierce beauty but her commanding presence aboard the ship. She was guarded at all times by either the quartermaster or another woman pirate named Trina. When the three of them were convened together the air was charge with resolution and authority. Lewis was sure in his core that not even the stern-faced navy man who ran the batteries below deck would challenge their voices, least of all Lilith's. She was firm in her tone but kind with her words, until she wasn't. When the Maiden had come alongside the Boston Autumn, Lewis had marveled at the transformation his captain underwent. She had gone from kind but firm to vengeful and violent. She was young. Beautiful. Strong and kind. But when her rage was provoked Lewis knew he did not want to be on the receiving end. The girl captain was loved by her crew, with loyal defenders never far from her side Lewis felt emboldened just by the sight of her walking the decks.

That evening as the stars came out for their brilliant send off to the last rays of dusk, Lilith was perched in one of her usual places. She stood on the starboard rail, stay line in hand, looking aloft to the stars while she conversed with the salty quartermaster and Trina. Chibs, the quartermaster, puffed great clouds of smoke from his pipe that rolled over his shoulders giving him an imposing look. Their speech was tense and even though he felt pangs of guilt, Lewis couldn't help himself but strain to hear the words they exchanged.

"If William thinks it a waste, Cap'n, why would we risk it?" Chibs asked, his eyes looking up to Lilith standing up on the rail.

"I care not for letters of marque Chibs." Lilith replied, her eyes remaining locked aloft int the stars.

"Then why send them to the governor of Nassau?" Trina asked lifting her hands in a perplexed gesture.

"The letter that was found in the captain's cabin of the Boston Autumn." She said, dropping down from the rail and pulling a pair of folded papers from one of her trouser pockets.

"I didn't know you could read." Chibs puffed at his pipe.

"I've been getting lessons from our Dr. LeMeux, he helped me read these." Lilith extended the papers toward Chibs.

Chibs raised his hands with his palms facing Lilith. "Don't look to me Cap'n. I can't read at all."

"One of these letters is from a boiling house in Port-au-Prince. It's informing the governor of Nassau that 'The Order' intends to send their traffic through his colony from now on. Since neither Jamaica nor Haiti are safe." Lilith said, giving Chibs a smile. "It seems we are making a name for ourselves. I don't expect anything from a letter of marque signed by Alton. He is only a means to get the governor of Nassau into a room, by himself."

"You mean to assassinate him." Trina exclaimed, stepping in front of Chibs and lowering her voice.

"I do." Lilith said locking her eyes with Trina's.

"How will we know if they are successful? Likely if

they are, the first notice we will get will be a cannon ball careening towards the Maiden's hull." Chibs asked, raising a brow as pipe smoke bellowed out of his nose.

"How do we know William will go through with it?" Trina added.

"He won't. Sinking slaver ships is one thing. Assassinating a colonial governor is quite another." Lilith replied. "We will need to send someone with them to do the deed. Someone we know we can trust"

"I wouldn't send his marines, nor that other officer that came aboard with him. Cap'n, send a soul that only owes allegiances to the Maiden." Chibs suggested. His teeth clamped back onto his pipe stem as he finished talking.

Lilith's gaze shifted across the deck. "Someone with a keen sense of listening to conversations that don't include them?" A chill ran up Lewis' spine as he heard the captain speak, he turned his head away and tried to look inconspicuous.

"Well. I suppose that could be helpful…" Chibs gruffed, shrugging his shoulders with a bewildered look. His eyes followed Lilith as her gaze rested onto Lewis. He could feel it on his back. The captain's steps beside him sent jolts of lightning through his nerves with each hollow clunk until a hand rested on his shoulder.

"I think we have just the sort for the job Chibs." Lilith mused toward the quartermaster before leaning into Lewis' arm. "Remind me, what's your name?"

"Lewis," he replied.

"Lewis, the Maiden demands a service." Lilith said,

giving him a mischievous smile.

Tortuga, Haiti
7 Feb 1809

Tortuga was a buzzing hive of activity unlike anything John had ever seen. Its streets were busier than Boston. Its market was an assault of the senses. Colorful clothes, flowers, fruit and food filled booths lined the streets near the harbor. Beautiful women of every size, shape and nationality stole his attention. Shouting merchants hawked their pitch to passersby while sailors either staggered or strutted along the thoroughfare. The intensity of activity only grew as he neared the shipyard until the cart he had hitched a ride on was no longer able to navigate through the swarming throngs of pedestrian traffic.

"This is where I leave you, Au revoir mon ami." The cart driver said as he pulled the team to a halt.

"Thank you." John replied while climbing down from the cart.

"The pleasure was all mine young man. I am honored to meet a man who has survived such a grisly encounter. But, I do hope you consider a new profession, your last seems not to suit you well." The man said with a blank expression before snapping his reigns and pulling away.

John watched as the cart turned on the next side street. He was surrounded by gawking strangers. John's clothes had been in tatters since he first set sail on Boston Autumn. Aboard ship he was just another sailor in ratty, stained clothes. Now, surrounded by townsfolk of Tortuga and visitors alike, he realized how pitiful he must look. Even the sailors taking in their stay in port looked better dressed than he did. The blood stains around his wounded shoulder caught attention and drew stares. The women strutting about seemed to allow John a wider swath of room than others, as if they could smell him by his look. A burly man passed him, carrying a large burlap bag over his shoulder in one arm and puffing away at a pipe with the other.

"Do you know a ship looking for able hands?" John asked as the man walked by, receiving nothing more than a blank stare. John turned and found another man who had a sailor's look, repeating his question. The reply he got was unfamiliar Spanish and hostile hand gestures.

John looked through the crowd. Passing faces seemed either not to notice him or intentionally avoided meeting his gaze so as not to get drawn in by this ragged looking stranger. French and Spanish words floated into his ears, all unfamiliar. Without a penny to his name, in torn and bloodstained clothes and no knowledge of the prevailing local languages. A swell of panic began to rise up inside John's chest. He wandered the street, glaring at the averted faces, silently begging for someone to reach out in a desperate prayer. Along the street the market stalls crowded closer together as John neared the piers. The buildings along the street stood taller. Some two stories, some three stories. Balconies above and windows ajar dotted the structures, it seemed each was unable to contain the activities within. Voices and laughter floated above him, while the incessant noise of street level conversation and the shouts of merchants flooded his ears. A sign on one of the buildings portrayed two large mugs, overflowing with froth. *A pub.* John longed for a lager to ease the edge from his sorrows. But with no money, a drink was too much to hope for.

"Those damned Brits will have it from us again at some point!" the voice from within smacked John's ears and caused him to perk his head up. "Mark my words, there's another war a-brewing with the crown and the Shark Fin will have her spoils!"

John ducked into the establishment as quick as his wobbling, fatigued legs would carry him. The light of sunset outside gave way within the pub's walls and inside it was dim and smoky. John stood near the door and scanned the room, seeing a mess of people all around engaged in hearty conversation. The table nearest him was packed and John picked up on their English exchange right away.

"I am looking for someone who can take my friend aboard their crew. He hasn't any money. But he's insistent that his business partner in America will pay his fare upon his arrival." A large dark-haired man at the table said before tipping his mug to drink.

"Is he experienced at sea?" a man across the table asked, "I need able hands at the mast, but America isn't soon in my future."

"He was terribly injured and sick with infection when he first came to stay with me. But he has grown strong again." The dark-haired man replied, his hulking shoulders and huge hands looked imposing even as he held them with open palms in front of his belly as if he were begging for something. "He has a fighter's spirit. Most men I know would have died in the condition he was in."

"Where is this friend of yours? Why isn't he here?" the sailor asked.

"He is at my home now, I can bring him to town in the morning if you wish." The large dark-haired man answered eagerly, "He asks me every day if there are Americans in port. He is eager to return home."

"Bring him and I will see for myself if we will take him aboard. Do you know where the Shark Fin is moored?" the sailor asked, digging in his pocket to pay for his next drink.

"I will, oh he will be so grateful! I will bring him and you will see, he will be a good hand."

"Pier five, we sail with the dawn tide and won't be delayed for anyone, short crew or not." The sailor said turning over his shoulder to look for a barmaid. His eyes landed on John. "What in the name of God? What happened to you son?"

John felt his face flush as the inhabitants of the table all turned to look at him. "Pirates. The ship I was on was attacked and sunk off the coast to the west of here. I am the only survivor." A tense moment passed, and John's explanation was met with blank stares. The faces around the table looked John over and exchanged glances among themselves.

"Pirates you say?" the near sailor turned in his seat, "What was their banner?"

"A skull, a skull with twisted horns on it and a trident." John answered, his heart began to race as the sailor's looks turned from disbelief to a knowing glare.

"Was there a chain on the banner?" the sailor asked with an intense stare.

"I hardly saw, they started firing on us right away, I think so, maybe." John felt his fingers go cold and his palms start to sweat at the same time. Every word seemed to draw him out of breath.

"I've been hearing tales of this pirate crew. They are captained by a Negro woman. Her crew sacked Kingston and sunk the better half of the Royal's precious Caribbean fleet. For that I'd like to shake her hand. But pirating against the peaceful trade traffic of my countrymen, that we cannot let go." The sailor crowed over shoulder to the men at the table, drawing a few hearty grunts of agreement.

"Sir. If I could. I have nowhere to go, nor anything to my name. If you would take me on as a deck hand…" John started.

"Of course sonny, of course. I can always use an able body at the mast." The sailor grumbled, putting his arm around John's neck with a smile. The weight elicited a grimace from John. "You are an able body, are you not?"

"I can carry my weight and earn my keep." John rushed his reply.

"Very well. We sail on the dawn tide, as I was telling the Spaniard there. The Shark Fin, moored along pier five and don't be late boy, or our wake will be all you'll see of us." The sailor replied extending his hand for John, "Captain Bernard."

John took the man's hand at an awkward angle, "John Tarley."

"Well, John." The captain pulled his arm off John's shoulders, "I've had as much of landsmen and their boring conversations as I can stand for an evening. It's time I be off to the ship."

With that the rest of the men at the table, all but the big dark-haired man, stood and followed Captain Bernard out of the pub.

"You mean to go with them? It sounds like he means to hunt after those pirates." The large Spanish man asked John with widened eyes.

"I do. Will your friend be joining us?" John was immediately put at ease by the large man's soft, dark eyes.

"That I don't know. It was pirates who put him in such a bad way to begin with. I'm not sure if he will want to go hunting after them. I wouldn't." The man rose to his feet, sliding a pair of coins across the table, "Here, for your troubles. Eat something, have a drink."

John was speechless. The large man walked around the table and patted his good shoulder with a huge, meaty paw.

"Revenge is a thief my friend, if you aren't careful, it will steal away everything from you."

John leaned forward and placed his hand onto the coins the Spanish man had left for him, "If revenge wants to steal away my sorrows, let it. That's all I have left to lose."

'Ranging Falcon'
16 Mar 1809
29 Degrees 30' N, 80 Degrees 35' W

A strong wind from the east held the sails of the sloop, Ranging Falcon, taut as she slid through cresting waves along the Carolina coast. With Charleston long astern, Clyde stood on the rail, leaning hard over the windward side of the vessel and gazing out over their intended course. In the wake of the sloop, two brigantines trailed along. Slower by far, the brigantines were far more cumbersome than the nimble sloop Clyde had selected as his impromptu flagship. A sloop's strength lie in her agility and superior speed, while the brigantines carried far heavier gunnery. Clyde's notion was to travel to the southern waters where his carefully laid network had crumpled into chaos. He would attempt to locate his lost transports and the slaves they held. If that failed, then he would land in Haiti or Jamaica and abduct himself new labor. At saber and pistol point if necessary. Tim Sladen had failed him. Rory Walters would surely get caught up either by the pirate crews that were the talk of every coastal pub from Boston to Trinidad or the inevitable squadron the crown had surely dispatched. Clyde had set his mind, he and he alone would ensure the success of his newfound consortium of slave owners.

The salty spray flicked up onto Clyde's face with each pitch of the sloop and though their journey had scarcely begun, he could hear green complaints aboard from several of his hired men. A cavalry man at heart, Clyde wasn't overly fond of the cramped conditions aboard ship, nor the rancid food sailors often endured. But, there were worse things than being at sea. The bow of Ranging Falcon dipped as she pitched over a rolling wave and one of his men clamped onto the rail while Clyde stood high, stay line in hand leaning into the wind.

"How are you not sick?" the man scathed before retching.

"I possess the constitution young man. I suggest you summon some within yourself, the task we sail to won't be schoolyard games. I have no patience or time to nurse along children at play." Clyde replied with disdain as the man retched again.

Out ahead, the sea stretched out like low rolling hills, capped in white froth from the winds. Scattered clouds let the day's brilliance peep through just enough to ward off shivers. Clyde grumbled to himself, "Sailors love this weather. If I'm not mistaken these bastards will be..." His grudging's were confirmed as a song broke out on deck, a shanty centered around an old dying horse and their intended uses of his worldly remains. Clyde Ritten was fond of music, but the vulgar wailings of a bunch of rotten mouthed seamen didn't land within the realm of music to Clyde's reckoning. Still, a singing crew is a happy crew and happy crews don't often throw their employers overboard as their seasick hired soldiers look on in vertigo induced impotent stupor.

Ranging Falcon's captain approached along the rail as Clyde looked out to the southern horizon. He was younger than most sea captains, with only a stubble of scruff along his jawline. Clyde suspected the man had started his maritime career in New England's whaling industry, at no older than his mid-twenties the young captain had a face full of scars and was missing his left hand. Sea life was dangerous and whaling even more so, but they often produced some of the finest seamen and navigators outside of the Royal Navy.

"You promised further explanation Mr. Ritten. We are out to sea and there will be no return to port at this point. So now I believe I am owed, what is this endeavor you are paying so handsomely for?" the captain demanded.

"We are hunting a prize Sir, a ship with valuable cargo that has been stolen." Clyde replied without returning the captain's gaze.

"Taken? Or lost? Either way, you're not likely to get it back, the sea is a greedy creature that way."

"No Captain, she was taken. Either I was betrayed by my own, or some unforeseen enemy has arisen to heckle and pester me. Either way, we will be dealing with it." Clyde stepped down to the deck and began to walk toward the bow.

"I'll search for your lost ship or cargo, but if it's pirates, you're chasing after the crew and I will have none of it. I don't get involved in those sorts of matters." The captain slashed his hand through the air in a downward chop as if to draw a line for Clyde.

Clyde stopped his gait toward the bow and shot an intense stare at him. "You have been commissioned and paid. Your hesitancy to engage against a pirate crew is of no concern to me, you will do as ordered, or watch from a sandbar as my men and I sail away on your ship. Do I make myself clear, Captain?"

A moment of tension passed as the captain weighed his response. Several of his crew were looking onto the exchange.

"Aye, the Falcon will do as she had been bid to. Captain and crew." He grumbled. Glares shifted as he turned away from Clyde to return to the quarterdeck.

Piracy was not the issue and Clyde knew it. Ranging Falcon had long been suspected of donning a black banner when doing so suited her crew. Most respectable figures in Charleston refused to do business with her captain or crew. When the Ranging Falcon wasn't privateering, or skirting that line into outright piracy, her crew often ventured into smuggling. Clyde suspected at some point during this endeavor he would have to make good on his threat. A band of seasick mercenaries would make a haphazard crew to sail the sloop. Haphazard or not, there is no value greater than loyalty for a quest as dangerous as the one Clyde had in mind.

'North Wind'
14 March 1809
30 Degrees 37' N, 73 Degrees 44' W

Admiral Torren had settled into his broad hammock. Coaxed into a deep sleep by the gentle rock and sway of North Wind, his thoughts had drifted over the vast oceans to a countryside farmhouse among rolling green hills from his youth. Images of his father, a navy man as well, returning home after a years long departure. The smell of flowerbeds in front of their quaint home tickled his nostrils and green, wet grass underfoot ushered Alistair into a peaceful and vivid image of his childhood. The sound of a church bell echoed through the crisp Sunday morning air. His father took his mother's hand and the two led on in front as Alistair followed them toward their Sunday rituals. He struggled in his dream to keep pace with the tough old sailor and his mum, falling further and further behind with each passing moment. The dream turned from a welcoming feeling of nostalgia to a fearful frustration of being left alone as a child. The cutting ring of the bell increased its frequency, faster and more urgent. The skies over the rolling green hills darkened and the bell's reverberation seemed to cut Alistair to his core. Shock and fear mixed in his blood.

"Man overboard!" the voice out on deck jarred the admiral from his dream turned nightmare. The clanging ship's bell rattled out in alarm. "Man overboard, starboard side! Flotsam and riff raff all about, looks like a shipwreck!" Alistair bolted from his hammock, ignoring the aching strain that gripped his legs and back as he shot his feet down to the cabin deck. He pulled on britches and stepped into shoes before shouldering his boat cloak over a bare chest. He opened his cabin door and stepped into the lamplight on deck under dark skies. A crowd of sailors huddled around a pair heaving on a line over the starboard rail. Admiral Torren pressed on through his aching joints to the crowd of men. As he neared them the pair heaving on the line pulled their fodder up over the rail. A sailor, soaked and shivering, gagging he flopped onto the deck boards at the admiral's feet. The collective gaze of the crowd averted from the near drowned man to the admiral's stone face.

"Don't stand around gawking lads, help the poor bastard!" the admiral snapped, sending the crowd into a scramble to haul the man to his feet and fetch blankets and dry clothing. The sailor sputtered and retched, spitting seawater and bile onto the deck.

"Looks like remains of a shipwreck out there, Sir." One of the sailors reported.

"Shipwreck my arse." The shivering man sputtered through a coughing fit.

"What vessel were you on son?" Admiral Torren asked while taking a step closer. The rescued man's British accent sent a jolt through his veins.

"H.M.S. Ambush Sir, I was aboard your scouting sloop."

"What happened?" Admiral Torren's voice cut the air.

"They came on us in the dark Sir. Last night. A frigate I think, she ranged us in with a single shot. We didn't stand a chance in hell. We got a single volley off and from what I could tell, when she came alongside, they damn bounced right off of her."

A chill ran down the admiral's spine. He turned to a sailor at his right hand, "Go tell the watch officer to douse every light aboard. No bells or whistles at all." He looked back to the half-drowned man as one of the flagship's crewmen wrapped a blanket over him. "Could you see their colors son? What flag were they flying?"

"I saw no banner Sir. They came at us from the starboard quarter off our stern. Their gunnery Sir, they ranged us with one shot from a chase gun and hit our rudder with the next. Before I realized what was happening, they pulled alongside and let fly with a broadside. We fired one in return and their next volley opened the Ambush from stem to mast along the starboard waterline. We were keel up before their wake was gone from view Sir." The sailor fought his words through chattering teeth.

Lieutenant Thatcher came alongside the admiral as the crowd listened to the rescued sailor's recount of the battle. A sideways glance from Admiral Torren prompted the lieutenant to turn his ear close where words could be passed quietly.

"I know of only one vessel that fits such a description. Get the captain up here at once. Why is he not on deck already?" The admiral hissed through his whisper.

"I believe he is still in his cabin, Sir. He had quite a few with his supper." The lieutenant replied.

"Damn the timing. Get him up here Lieutenant. Now. I don't care if he is as bare assed as the day he was born." The admiral looked around at the sailors on deck. All eyes rested on him. "Quarters lads. Quiet is the watchword, get everyone to quarters and cleared for action. If this phantom ship is still about, we need to be ready for her."

Looks between the sailors conveyed the gravity. Admiral Torren had heard of a frigate on the Atlantic which regularly repelled direct hits from her hull. She was American built, low on her keel draw and fast. The U.S.S. Constitution had created a fearsome reputation. Her hull was hard white oak, nearly two feet in thickness. The American Navy's crown gem. If she was lurking out in the dark, and ready for engagement, it could be a costly day for the admiral's squadron.

Lieutenant Thatcher returned on deck, accompanied by the North Wind's captain. Admiral Torren took note of the man's disposition, he was not drunk, but reeked of wine. His uniform was disheveled, trousers and bare feet with no shirt on beneath his uniform jacket.

"Captain. Stealth will be our watchword for the night. The wind is in our favor for now, but only if the vessel has behaved as I suspect. We should be making no assumptions however so hold course and run out the guns. No bells, no whistles, nor shouts or calls. Place watchmen to pass word and only use light to pass signal to the fleet. Wedge formation, every vessel to quarters and ready for action."

"Aye Sir. I'll have it done." The captain began to turn to his task.

"Captain." The admiral stopped him.

"Yes Sir?"

"I cannot fault you for imbibing with your meals, but you will be present and ready for action. This is the calling of an officer. Should we encounter another situation and I find myself commanding your vessel for you, you won't be commanding your vessel any longer." Admiral Torren lowered his voice so only the captain could hear.

"Yes Sir. Apologies, Sir." The captain said, his pale face beating a bright shade of red.

Admiral Torren pulled at Lieutenant Thatcher's sleeve, "Young man, it appears we are in for a long night. I will return to my cabin and dress for such. I believe a tea and some eggs are in order. Have the watch officer station lookouts and lifelines fore and aft."

"Aye Sir." Lieutenant Thatcher replied as he made for the quarterdeck to pass orders to the watch officer.

Admiral Torren returned to his cabin. He opened the door which led in from North Wind's weather deck and stood in the frame for a long moment staring into the dark interior. A long history of pressing foreign sailors into the service of the Royal Navy had garnered the ire of Americans in recent years. Wild claims of pirate insurrections in the Caribbean and the threat of Napoleon in Europe all seemed to weigh on his shoulders at once. Closing the door behind him, the Admiral moved to the rear of the cabin and pulled a set of thick drapes across the arrangement of windows. He lit a lantern and donned his uniform. As he pulled his shirt on, Lieutenant Thatcher entered the cabin with a tray of eggs and a wedge of hard cheese. He put a kettle of tea onto the small wood stove and began to stoke a fire.

"Signal has been passed Sir. The fleet is moving to a wedge formation and will run with no sound or lights for the rest of the night." The lieutenant informed as he worked at the wood stove.

"Very well. Now, to see to these eggs. If there is something that can make a cruise, a decent breakfast is certainly on the list and you do a fine job Lieutenant." The admiral said, settling into the chair at his desk.

Lieutenant Thatcher stood from where he had been tending the wood stove. "Thank you, Sir. I do try."

Admiral Torren pondered over his plate while the lieutenant went about fixing tea. His thoughts drifted back to the half-drowned sailor's account of the engagement. "What if I told you, Lieutenant, that the King's Navy is in grave peril of losing her dominance at sea?"

"You jest Sir. Surely." Lieutenant Thatcher said cracking a broad grin.

"Not at all, lad. The yanks have fielded a frigate superior to our own in every way. Thicker hull, but faster despite it. Maneuverable. Well-armed. Coupled with their dogged arrogance and crafty tactics, I believe her to be a true threat. Especially if they continue the pursuit of advancement in warfare. It is a matter of time, lad. Britain will be the old power at sea." Admiral Torren said, his voice growing morose.

"You're not serious Sir." The lieutenant looked frightened.

"As the grave, young man. What's more is, I believe the ship that sank our sloop could very well be the American's frigate. U.S.S. Constitution. The fact that they engaged a Royal Navy vessel without provocation, well, that bodes ill for all of us." The lamplight flickered against Admiral Torren's face.

Lieutenant Thatcher began to reply, "Nelson will…"

"Admiral Nelson and the like have their hands full with Napoleon. If we draw any more of the channel fleet away we leave England vulnerable to attack. Guess again lad. This struggle is in our lap for now. There will be no aid soon to come."

The shuffle of feet out on deck drew their attention for a moment as the lieutenant poured them both a steaming cup of dark tea.

"More survivors?" Lieutenant Thatcher suggested

with an eyebrow raised towards the Admiral.

"The proper thing would be to find out so you can inform me." Admiral Torren replied as he finished a bite of egg, "Not guess away in here so we both look like ignorant fools."

"Aye, Sir. Straightaway." Lieutenant Thatcher placed the kettle down onto the desk and hurried to the door. As he opened it to the deck the earliest glow of dawn was visible on the horizon. Admiral Torren kept at his breakfast awaiting his young steward's return. The eggs were good, and the young man never scorched them in the skillet. *A good cook is such a rare quality at sea.* A few long moments passed, and the cabin door remained ajar, drifting with the sway of North Wind. "Lieutenant. Did you mean to leave the damned door open?" Admiral Torren called, growing irritated. "What in the bloody? In my days at sea..." he paused, realizing that he was again at sea. *What would cause him to leave the hatch open like that?* The admiral put his utensils onto his plate and rose from the desk. With his trademark pace he walked out of the cabin onto the deck under the early morning glow. A group of sailors gathered at the starboard rail alerted Admiral Alistair Torren that something was amiss, and he walked over next to their huddle. Finding Lieutenant Thatcher, he rested his hand on the young officer's shoulder. The lieutenant looked over at him briefly and extended his arm pointing to a rippling white rectangle on the western horizon astern of the North Wind.

"Fetch my looking glass son. Be quick about it." The admiral said.

"Have a look through mine Sir." A nearby

midshipman offered.

The admiral took the kindly offered instrument and peered through the sight hole. Along the hazy waterline, on the far edge of visibility through the glass, Alistair could make out the stern of a heavy frigate. Her lines were graceful and sleek. Her hull seemed stout even through the great distance. Over her wake, hanging from the rigging on her stern flew a red and white striped banner with a circle of white stars set on a blue field in the top corner.

The admiral growled, "Damn them."

PART TWO

"FAIR WINDS"

Chapter 7

Ortega's - Near Tortuga, Haiti
8 Feb 1809

Afternoon wore on and sweltered in a muggy, clinging heat dying for a breath of wind. Sweat beaded across Tim's brow and dripped from his chest. His bandages long since removed, all that remained of his wounds were twisted white scars stretching the length of his ribs along his side and on his knees and shins. With a two-handed grip Tim swung an ax bit down onto a log section. He had spent the morning with Tomas' mule and cart hauling sections of hand sawed timber from a tree he had helped the Spaniard fell the day before. The longest of the logs were to be ripped down into planks, a painfully labor-intensive process. But the short sections that remained would serve as Tomas cooking fuel for the next several weeks. The short log split with a satisfying snap and Tim's ax buried its edge into the short round of log he was using to rest each piece on before splitting them. Through the heat of the day Tim had worked splitting and stacking wood, waiting for Tomas to return from Tortuga. His host made three trips a week into the port town, delivering lumber to his employer, a shipwright, and searching for a suitable vessel for Tim to gain passage back to the United States.

The small house where Tomas lived with his daughter sat at the top of a small hill overlooking the outskirts of Tortuga to the north and bordered by rolling hills of sugarcane fields to the west. To the south, thick Haitian forests loomed high, providing both all the timber for Tomas' employer and respite from the burning Caribbean sun under its dense canopy. Tomas' humble home had an extensive garden on its north side and two large sheds used for curing lumber along the east side of the hill. Between the two sheds Tim labored at splitting woods and stacking it along the wall of the shed nearest the house. With another swing the ax bit sent two halves of a log toppling onto the ground. Tim picked the pieces up and stacked them onto the pile before collapsing his rear onto the ground and leaning back on the wood stack. The clothes he wore were ill fitting, loose secondhand pants held up with a piece of rope and a cotton blouse of Tomas' that hung from his much smaller frame. His scarred face was covered by a scraggle of unkempt beard and his hair had become shaggy, hanging over his brow and past his ears. The burning rays of sun tingled and stung his sweat soaked arms and neck while Tim sat regaining his wind from his efforts. The first few days working with Tomas had been a pitiful embarrassment. Tim's long recovery from his wounds had devoured much of his physical strength while leaving his ego untouched. Tomas worked at a pace that seemed impossible to Tim, even after weeks of building his strength, the huge Spaniard would often have to shoulder most of the workload. Tim closed his eyes and rested, taking in a chance to relax.

"Sleeping while the sun shines?" the deep voice of Tomas shook Tim from his rest.

"Still not as stout as I was." Tim answered, annoyed that he had been interrupted.

"Thank you for your help my friend. I was only joking with you." Tomas said with a concerned look as he noticed Tim's annoyance.

"It's nothing." Tim stood with help from Tomas' massive extended hand. "Did you discover any new ships in port?"

A moment of hesitation passed, and Tim could see conflict in Tomas' face. "My friend. The ship that pursued you."

"Pirates. It was a pirate ship." Tim interrupted.

"Yes, so you said." Tomas continued, wringing his hands together. Tim could tell there was something he wanted to say but was holding back. "What did you say their banner looked like?"

"I didn't." Tim's heart skipped and he could feel a rush of heat rising in his face. "Has there been a sighting? Have they struck down another ship?"

Tomas' face wrinkled in a grimace that belied withheld information. "I don't think it wise to concern yourself with these matters my friend. It can only lead to…"

"I don't care what you think is wise. Was there a sighting?" Tim snapped, his face flushing hot red and his heart beating a race.

"Well, yes. There has been an attack off the coast. To the west of the port this morning. They sunk a merchant ship." Tomas gave up each bit of what he knew in hesitant fragments.

"What was the banner they flew?" Tim pressed.

"What?" Tomas hesitated again.

"The banner the pirates flew, damn it. Did anyone see it?" Tim's voice rose, cutting sharper with every word.

"One man survived the attack and made it into Tortuga. He described their banner…" Tomas' voice trailed off and he cocked his head to one side, peering at Tim through the corners of his eyes.

"And?" Tim coaxed, lowering his voice.

"Tim let's talk about this later. Come. We'll get something to eat and drink." Tomas motioned for Tim to follow him.

"No. Let's talk about this now. I want to know what you heard Tomas, tell me." Tim sidestepped Tomas as the bigger man started his way toward the house. Tim could feel the intensity of the sun growing hotter on his face and neck, without even a whisper of breeze to cool. Perspiration ran down his head and neck. His anger flared inside, amplifying the heat he felt.

Tomas stopped in his tracks. Tim could see conflict in his face. "There is nothing to gain by chasing revenge my friend. It's better for you to stay."

"Stay here and slave away the rest of my days cutting lumber? I don't think so. I want you to tell me what you know Tomas." Tim's voice slipped into a tone he hadn't used in months and a confused look crossed Tomas' face.

"I'm going to eat, friend. You can join me if you like. But the road that leads to town is wide open, as it always has been. The choice is yours mi amigo." Tomas replied with a sad note.

A shudder of rage gripped Tim's mind as Tomas turned his back to walk away. His heart raced and his hands felt a sudden dryness as blood exited his fingers. Tim clenched his jaw and gritted his teeth, drawing his lips tight in a grimace that had nothing to do with pain. In the same moment he was standing between lumber sheds in the humid Haitian afternoon, in his mind his body was being mercilessly raked over coral while pirates bombarded his ship with cannon fire. "Tomas. I need you to tell me what you heard."

The large Spaniard stopped for a second, "No, amigo. I don't think I will."

Tim's rage overcame him. His hands found the ax handle and he jerked it free from the log its bit was lodged in. Tomas took another step toward the house, unaware of Tim's advance behind him. With a high arcing swing Tim brought the ax down hard biting the blade deep into Tomas' shoulder. The large man fell to his knees with the impact, blood surging from the ax wound.

"Tim! Why?" he groaned, reaching up to shield himself from another blow with his weathered hands.

"It's been too long, and you've wasted enough of my time already. I have a job to do. If you won't help me Tomas, then you're in my way." Tim seethed, putting his foot on Tomas' back and wrenching the ax blade free bringing forth a rush of bright red blood.

"Just leave. Leave my home and never come back... oh mija, leave mi hija..." Tomas uttered as he writhed on the ground.

"No. I'll be paying her a visit before I leave, repaying her for her fool father's stubborn streak." Tim smiled hefting the ax handle again. Tomas writhed onto his side, blood pouring from his wound. His face twisted from agony into rage as Tim's promise cut through the pain he felt. A sudden shock of panic crossed Tim as the much larger man erupted from the ground, shoving himself headlong into Tim and driving his shoulder right into his breastbone. Tomas charged, lifting Tim from his feet and drove both of them through the plank wall of the lumber shed in a flurry of splinters and blood.

"No! No, you won't! I will kill you before you lay a hand on her!" Tomas screamed, driving Tim to the ground. Tomas put his knees on either side of Tim's torso and began to hammer down blows onto his head and face with his huge, balled fists. Tim took the brunt of the attack on his brow before his head recoiled to the ground and Tomas landed a fist along his jawline. The world shuddered around him with every impact, Tomas' hits were like being slammed with a hammer. After the third strike Tim could feel blood coming from his brow and nose, he tasted blood in his mouth and could feel it running into his throat. Tim's arms lay extended out to his side, helpless to shield him against the huge fists slamming his head to the ground. In his hand, he could feel the weight of the ax handle laying on his fingers. Another hit from Tomas landed on Tim's cheek and through his jarred vision he could see the deadly tool still in his possession.

Summoning movement in his hand, Tim's grip around the ax handle closed. He pulled the handle in close and ran his fingers up the smooth grain until he felt the metal of the bit. Tim wrapped his fingers around the ax bit as another hit slammed into his brow, dazing him for a second. Before Tomas could land another, Tim pulled the ax bit up beside his face and rolled his head to one side. The following hit was Tomas' fist crashing down onto the sharp blade of his own ax. He let out a howl of pain and rolled away from Tim, holding his bloodied hand. A pair of fingers dangled from the meaty fist where they had been separated by the blade.

"You bastard! Leave! Just leave us!" Tomas shouted as he grimaced over his mangled hand.

Tim staggered up to his feet, wiping blood from his eyes with the back of the hand he held the ax in. Feeling blood drip from his lips, Tim pushed his tongue along the bottom of his mouth noticing several shattered teeth floating freely in his mouth. He spit them out in gobs of blood and saliva and then loosed a blood curdling scream as he turned toward Tomas who was looking on with a pleading stare. Tim stood for a moment, panting in heaves of air through his blood-soaked lips and shattered teeth. He gripped the ax handle, squeezing its wooden grain between his fingers as he caught his breath. "It's too late for that now."

Tomas backed away, keeping his eyes locked onto

Tim's. "Just go. Leave us, I won't stop you. The ship you seek is off the coast, the pirates who chased and sunk your ship. There is a crew leaving in the morning to hunt them, the Shark Fin. She's moored in pier five. Now go! I've told you what I know, just go and leave me and my daughter in peace."

Tim staggered in pursuit of Tomas, following him from the shed into the sweltering heat of the sun. "It's too late for that Tomas. I'm not leaving until this is finished."

Tomas continued backing away, holding his bleeding hand while blood continued to flow from the ax wound on his shoulder. "You don't have to finish anything. It is done. You leave and never come back. I should have left you where I found you, for the coyotes and the vultures."

"Papa!" Emilia's voice cut through the dense heat and tension; Tim shot a look up to her shocked face. Tomas yelled something in Spanish and the woman bolted for the house.

"It's no use Tomas. Once I am done with you, she is next." Tim sneered, pulling his grip together on the ax handle in preparation to swing.

"I think that you will find her to be more of a fighter than you expect." Tomas said through wheezing breaths as he stopped his retreat. Tomas raised his arms with a loud cry and charged at Tim. The ax swing carried a high arc finding its biting mark into Tomas' forehead. The hulking man collapsed from the impact, falling to his knees. Tim held the ax handle, trying to free it as Tomas crumpled to the ground. Blood rolled down his face and pooled into the dirt while his eyes rolled back, and a guttural sigh of air escaped his lungs. Tim wrested the ax free from Tomas' skull and stared down at the man's giant, motionless body.

A piercing scream shot through Tim, startling him from the trance state he had entered looking over Tomas' dead body. Tim turned to see Emilia. Her black hair shining in the sun and tears running down her cheeks. She held a broad leather belt with a pistol and a sheathed sword. Her scream awoke a trembling of fear within Tim in a way Tomas' rage had failed to. As she screamed, Emilia dropped to her knees aiming her chin upwards and turning her voice to the heavens. She fell silent for a moment and Tim thought he could hear her utter something in Spanish. His blood ran cold as the young woman rose to her feet. Sunlight glinted off the blade of the sword as she withdrew it from its scabbard and in her other hand Tim could see the pistol withdraw from leather. Emilia was a frightful picture of rage embodied and she advanced toward him. Tim gripped the ax handle, rubbing his fingers along the grain. One hit with the ax would be the end of this fight, but one miss would be his end. Emilia stopped her advance. She cocked the flint of her pistol and leveled the weapon in Tim's direction. Tim shuffled his feet, unsure if he should charge the woman swinging the ax for dear life or flee. The clap of the shot sounded, sending a small cloud of smoke in front of Emilia and a zipping whiz past Tim's head. Tim's fingers slipped from the ax handle. She raised the saber over her head and began to scream again, he turned and ran. Weaponless, Tim ran for the rutty wagon road toward Tortuga as Emilia chased after him screaming for vengeance.

Tim ran over twisted dried mud and fist sized stones. Glancing over his shoulder every few steps he could see Emilia pursuing him with sword in hand as she let loose bloodcurdling screams every few minutes. He narrowly avoided losing his footing after stepping on an awkward stone which only seemed to encourage the young woman's quest for his throat. His knees ached and the wounds from Tomas' pummeling on his head throbbed as Tim raced down the road. Another scream rang through the dense afternoon heat and Tim looked over his shoulder to see that Emilia had fallen far behind him, her run given up to despair and grief over her father. He pressed on, not slowing his pace for fear of encouraging her to retake the chase. The final cries he heard echoed Spanish threats over the hills leading into Tortuga and Tim feared as he drew close to the small structures on the edge of town that he would be facing Tomas' daughter again.

Fort Charles - Kingston, Jamaica
21 Feb 1809

Dawn broke over the stone walls of Fort Charles, highlighting a column of smoke and embers rising into a fiery red haze beating away the night sky. The chaos within the fort had long died away leaving a scene of ruin and death. The crimson coats of fallen soldiers scattered the inner courtyard and lined the surrounding corridors. Townsfolk in Kingston gasped in shock as the growing daylight revealed men in white linen blouses with their heads and faces obscured by black scarves in command of the fort. As the sun rose higher into the sky sunlight bathed the fort's interior, revealing the depth of carnage that had occurred in the hours before its rising. A pair of the scarf clad raiders fashioned a noose at the end of a length of rope and hung the body of the fort's latest commander from the top of the wall.

Lieutenant Trenton's body hung against the fort's stone wall overlooking the town he had only hours ago been defending. A coastal breeze floated up from the cool sea, twisting his body in its suspended state giving his shadow along the wall and eerie movement. Two of the raiders stood on the top of the wall watching over Kingston as the townsfolk remained petrified within homes and shops.

"What now?" one of the raiders asked the other.

"There is a holding camp sitting empty. We will fill it. If Mr. Sladen returns with transport, then we carry on. If he doesn't, we will secure transport and fulfill our mandate." The other replied.

"There haven't been any company ships bringing Africans. How are we to fill the camp?"

The man shrugged his shoulders at the question, while pulling his black scarf down from his face and head. "It seems to me the island is littered with good candidates. I don't give a damn if they are old or owned. I'm being paid for delivered hands and that is what I'm going to do. Deliver. Gather the mounts we can, get the boys saddled and let's get it done. It's a full day to the camp dragging along Negroes who don't want to walk."

"We'll get going." The man said before lumbering

down the stairs.

The remaining raider stood over the hanging body of Lieutenant Trenton as it twisted in the breeze, the rope creaking with each movement. He looked down onto the hanging dead body and spit brown tobacco juice over the wall. "Sorry to leave you hanging like this. I'm sure the crows will come to keep you company." He called down. The only reply that came back was the creak of the rope and another gust of wind off the harbor. He turned and made his way down the stairs to the fort's inner courtyard.

At the bottom of the steps, two men were arming themselves with weapons off of the fallen. Muskets and swords lay strewn about amongst the dead soldiers and raiders.

"Get mounted. There's more work to be done." He growled at the pair. The two men nodded a response and left in search of horses.

As the afternoon sun shifted over the stone walls and beat down directly onto the hanging corpse of Lieutenant Trenton, a file of horsemen left through the fort's front gate. Each wore a black scarf wrapped around their head and face. They descended the road leading into Kingston. Chaos erupted in the streets. Gunfire echoed between buildings. Shrill screams of protest sounded as the riders dismounted and gathered every man and woman they deemed would pass as a slave in market. Shop owners and tradesmen protested over their lost labor only until their courage was met at gun or sword point. Building by building they swept Kingston, dragging anyone who drew breath with skin dark enough to fit their purpose out into a growing crowd. After hours of searching, the marauders made their slow withdrawal from Kingston.

'Southern Song'
21 Feb 1809
28 Degrees 5' N, 76 Degrees 26' W

The wind whipped at Rory's face while he stood atop the bow stem of the Southern Song. The constant pitch up and down, back and forth and rolling from side to side had gone from unbearable and nauseating to an almost comforting constant. The patterns of movement become more predictable as the seas calmed and eventually Rory went from merely tolerating the ship's movement to being accustomed with it even wondering how he would adjust to life on land. The Southern Song had skirted the Carolina coast, bypassing Florida and her keys to run through the strait between the southern coast of Cuba and the north coast of Haiti. Warm winds filled the ragged sails of Southern Song as she tacked her way through the Caribbean toward Jamaica.

Rory spent most of his time on deck in the open breeze and sunshine. Below deck was a mixture of foul odors from cramped space with too many bodies packed in, rotten food and poor hygiene. Tempers often flared between crew members due to the poor conditions and tight quarters. In addition, Rory noticed, overconsumption of alcohol was not limited to the captain. Most evenings aboard the Southern Song consisted of a barely edible meal followed by rum and whiskey rations. Shanties were sung while the men labored on deck. The wind carried away any foul odors and replaced them with the briny smell of saltwater. The horizon could be seen, in good weather, and the warmth of the sun felt on a man's back. Rory preferred to be on deck.

Southern Song's bow pitched upward as a wave crested sending a fine mist of seawater through the air. Rory closed his eyes and relished the breeze. Behind him, Dog's voice cut through the sound of waves breaking on the hull and interrupted his peaceful moment.

"Boy! You see land off your starboard side there?" Dog screeched at Rory across the length of the ship.

"What?" Rory asked, confused by what the old sailor was getting at.

"Do you see that point of land? Over there!" Dog shouted, getting visibly irritated while thrusting a finger toward the horizon over the starboard side.

"Oh. Yes, yes I see it." Rory answered, cocking his head slightly.

"Well, you blithering idiot! Don't you think you should call it out? Or would you prefer we sail around the Caribbean aimless like and run out of food and water?" Dog shouted throwing his hat onto the deck. Rory couldn't make out all of what followed but the phrase "Last damn land lubber I ever take aboard" and "Pitch him over for the fishes" carried through the noise on deck.

The ship shifted and heaved under a forceful turn. Sailors scurried to make adjustments in the rigging and on deck. Southern Song was a heaping horrid mess.

Her captain and crew were too often into their liquor and far too early in the day. Her sails were a tapestry of patches and mended tears. The lines in the rigging were in sorry condition and the blocks themselves looked to be old and neglected. Her guns were rusted, one of them cracked so bad that halfway from the muzzle to the breech a gunner would be able to see daylight through it. Her deck was a shin and ankle mangling field of broken and rotted boards.

Dog paced around the helm on the quarterdeck barking out commands and shaking his fist at the sluggish crewmen.

"Take the slack out of that line you retched lazy excuse for a sailor! I ought to drown the lot of you!" his face was beet red, and spittle projected from his mouth with every few words. He stomped over to the helm where the sailor manning it had a slack grip on the wheel. "Who taught you this?" he slapped away the sailor's loose grip, "one stout wave away from wrenching free of your lily fingers and sending us all sprawling onto the damned deck boards. As full of holes as they are, we're like to lose a hand or a foot. Grab hold and man the damned helm or swim to shore you slack jawed scally!"

Rory watched and listened from his post on the bow as the berating abuse continued long into the afternoon. As the sun dipped lower in the horizon, bringing shades of evening to the sky, the captain's appearance on deck promised more buffoonery. Stumbling and slurring his speech, the captain asked Dog about their position and course. In a lowered voice that Rory couldn't hear the two carried on an exchange that at first appeared cordial. Soon their hand gestures became more frantic and exaggerated. Rory snapped his attention between the landmass off the starboard side and looking over his shoulder at the escalating tension between the captain and mate. Their terse exchange soon became shouts and Rory could hear every spoken word.

"We were commissioned to deliver slaves, there are slaves in Haiti as well as Cuba. Why in hell would we sail to Jamaica? What in God's name are you thinking?" the captain's shouts punctuated his sloshing words, his footing seemed unsteady even in the low chop sea condition.

"We discussed this, the job we are tasked with is to first go to Jamaica so the young man can investigate what has occurred there. Then he will secure us a hold full of Negroes to deliver back to Charleston. We've been over this damn it, or are you too drowned into your bottle to remember?" Dog's reply shot every glance on deck towards him.

"What did you say?" the captain thundered, reaching at the hilt of his sword.

"I said you are a drunken worthless lubber with no damned honor and only half your wits..." Dog shouted defiantly. His retort was interrupted by the captain slashing at him with his broad bladed cutlass. Dog ducked under the first attack and drew his sword in time to parry a second.

"I'll gut you for this. You've run your mouth aboard my ship for the last time you dog mouthed son of a bitch!" a lunging attack followed which Dog parried and countered, missing the captain's neck by inches as the intoxicated commander withdrew himself in the nick of time. "Even drunk I'm out of your class Dog! Drop your sword. This be your last warning!"

Dog stepped forward with a high arcing attack that landed against the captain's blade with a piercing ring. The captain skittered his blade along while reaching up to Dog's wrist with his off hand. He brought up a swift kick that caught Dog on the side of his knee sending the man down onto the deck. Dog rolled to one side and raised his blade in defense as the captain sent another attack at him, their steel again sent a high ring and clatter with each impact. Dog managed to score a slicing swing against the captain's thigh, and he scrambled back to his feet while the captain examined the depth of his own wound.

"What's your course now Dog? Do you think my crew is going to let you get away with this?" the captain sneered with a rum infused smile. "Or were you planning to fight them all one by one?"

Dog's expression changed as the captain's point settled in. The crew on deck who had initially been nonchalantly observing the exchange on deck were now beginning to close in a circle around the pair.

"Captain, we won't collect payment if we don't deliver exactly what Mr. Ritten demands." Dog tried to reason as he grew visibly bothered by his deteriorating situation.

"And who would you say is going to tell him we didn't do exactly as he demanded. Once I drown that fool and we pick up a load of Negroes in Haiti? They're just as black as the ones in Jamaica I promise you that." The captain snarled, drawing a laugh from the crewmen around him and sending a bolt of lightning through Rory's veins.

"It makes no difference to me what you do with the whelp, but we're not finished…" Dog cut off his reply with a swinging attack which the captain parried and sidestepped with ease. A sailor stepped to Dog's side as he recovered from the parry, with a rail pin in hand he brought it high overhead and swung the heavy pin down hard onto the back of Dog's head.

The salty old hand crumpled onto the deck, blood spilled from a wound behind his ear and his remaining teeth clattered out onto the wooden planks of the deck. A silent tension followed as the onlooking crew watched for their captain's reaction. The captain had regained his footing and turned to see his opponent laying in a growing pool of blood with the sailor who had struck him standing over the body.

"Did I ask you to intervene?" the captain scathed raising his sword blade level with the man's neck.

"No Sir, but we've no love for him, Cap'n. I thought…" the sailor began a pleading reply but was cut short as the captain thrust his cutlass into the center of his belly.

"You thought wrong boy." The captain seethed, shoving the dying sailor down onto the deck next to where Dog lay bleeding. "And the rest of you, back to work!"

Rory averted his eyes as if looking at the captain would remind him of the plan he had just announced to the crew. The heat of the sun took on an overwhelming intensity. He felt as if every man aboard had abruptly become his enemy. The waves washing along the hull seemed less adventurous and inviting and more like prison walls. The expanse of water between the Southern Song and the land far away became impossibly vast. His imagination took over and he could feel the shocking chill of the water. He thought of the creatures of the deep that would inevitably chase him as he struggled to swim for shore. The violent and merciless strike of a shark and the frenzy that would ensue afterward. He imagined the slow descent into the dark abyss of the ocean's depths as his lungs filled with water and his body was crumpled by the immense pressure and cold.

Peering over his shoulder, Rory could see that the crew had returned to their tasks. A pair of sailors began the unpleasant business of dealing with the corpses laying on deck. The simple sound of a splash into the sea followed by another as Southern Song made headway westward on her course was all the ceremony that marked the occasion of two departed souls from the crew. Rory's heart raced and every passing moment he waited for the inevitable realization from one of the crewmen that he was the man the captain had suggested killing in order to collect their payment from Mr. Ritten with as little hassle as possible.

A flurry of activity on the quarterdeck caught Rory's eye as he tried to make himself scarce. A gang of sailors made their way forward and began fanning out across the deck near the main mast. Rory averted his glance as if it would somehow stay his inevitable fate. He pondered the cold water below again, his heart raced. Before he could make his move to the bulwark

Rory felt a strong hand take him by the shoulder. In a swift motion he was spun around to face the group of sailors and their crooked, rotten smiles.

"Here he is!" the man who spun him called out.

The stroke that hit him next came too quick for Rory to see, much less defend. It wasn't a rail pin, but the handle end of a pistol swung like a club. It crashed down onto the crown of his skull and slammed darkness over his vision. He didn't even feel the impact of his body slumping onto the deck.

'Drowned Maiden'
16 Feb 1809
24 Degrees 48' N, 73 Degrees 33' W

Lilith brought her cutlass around in a wide slash where it met steel with a clashing ring. She withdrew her attack and immediately followed with another ending in the same result. Frustrated, she sidestepped and brought her sword down into a low ready position. Trina stood across from her on the bow of the Maiden, the pair locked in a dance of footwork and swordplay.

"You've improved girl. But, there's still more to learn." Trina said before feinting a thrust and then bringing her sword around in a quick arc, stopping inches from Lilith's neck.

"Damn it, Trina. Why is it that I miss that every time?" Lilith fumed, sheathing her sword and picking up a leather drinking skin of water. She took a deep drink.

"I've told you love. You keep looking at my eyes.

Watch my shoulders, I can make my eyes lie to you but my body tells the truth." Trina replied with a smile. "Every day you get better. I wouldn't want to cross with you in a fight."

"Not so long as I have you and Chibs with me." Lilith said before taking another drink from the skin. "You have both been my strength."

Trina paused for a moment, shooting a sideways look at her young captain. "What of the lieutenant? What is your plan for him in all this?"

"Lieutenant Pike is a good man. I've learned a lot from him. How navy sailors think, how they act. But he has to accompany the governor into Nassau. I know the position that puts him in, but I don't see another way." Lilith said turning back to look over the deck of the Maiden. She could see Omibwe, gingerly standing on the wooden prosthetic Dr. LeMeux had fashioned as he manned the helm in the sunshine. "The ship we scuttled, with her crew aboard…" her voice trailed off.

"The 'Boston Autumn'?" Trina said.

"I found a letter in her cabin and Dr. LeMeux helped me read it." Lilith said picking at a stay line with her fingers. "It was addressed to the initials C.R., Dr. LeMeux thinks it's a message from a spy of sorts or one of the members of The Order. Whoever wrote it specifically said the governor of Nassau would harbor their traffic since Jamaica isn't safe." She turned back to Trina, "We haven't stopped them. We haven't stopped a damn thing and they are going to keep stealing people to make slaves."

"The letter of marque?" Trina pressed raising a brow.

"A ploy. We have to get the governor of Nassau in a room with one of us. You or I would never make for a companion of a rich old governor. But to be accompanied by a naval officer, I think that could do the trick." Lilith said with a grin. She grabbed the stay line she had been picking at in her hand and hoisted herself up onto the rail, leaning out over the spraying waves as they broke along the Maiden's bow.

"And Lieutenant Pike, does he know the true nature of this errand? He seemed to object to the letter of marque." Trina stepped close to the rail, looking up at her captain while holding her hat against the wind.

"No dear. I don't think Lieutenant Pike would go through with what needs to be done. But we will be sending one of the crew with him. One I can trust." She pulled up from her lean over the side and hopped back down to the deck. "Lieutenant Pike is a good man. I hope nothing happens to him. But the Maiden has her course, and she demands we sail it." Lilith said, her smile fading as she saw Lieutenant Pike appear from below deck through the weather hatch. He wore his uniform jacket, which he had spent the morning mending and cleaning. Even without his hat, the young officer in uniform held her stare for a long moment.

"If things go awry in Nassau. If he is captured and they discover he aided us girl, you know what they will do to him?" Trina said over Lilith's shoulder in a hushed voice as they both looked on toward Lieutenant Pike.

"I do." Lilith replied, her voice seemed to lose its edge. Lilith could feel a sadness creeping over her, climbing her spine and wrapping around her ribs as if to squeeze away her breath. A keen awareness took her senses. The smell of the sea lingered in her nostrils. Spray from the waves misted her face, cooling the kiss of the sun which flashed in her eyes as rigging and sail obscured it with the rock and pitch of the deck. Lilith could almost feel the course texture of the rigging ropes as they creaked with the motion of the ship, strained by the wind.

"If he is discovered by them?" Trina pressed in her lowered tone.

"We will do what we must. Nothing is without risk, you know that." Lilith answered. She felt the nagging dread of what could happen slip away. Like casting off lines to set sail. "Whatever comes. We'll face it head on."

"I'm with you either way girl. You know this. That man saved my life. So, if the worst should happen..." Trina's voice drifted as Lieutenant Pike caught the pair in his sight.

"We will do what we must." Lilith cut in as Lieutenant Pike began walking their way, "Not a word of this to him. I need him to get us to the governor."

"Well captain? What do you think?" Lieutenant Pike's hair fluttered in the breeze, and he smoothed it back, "Can I pass as an official escort for the governor?"

"You would be the better judge of that. But you look the part to my eyes." Lilith replied. "How is our governor getting along?"

"Bursting at the seams I'm afraid. But, even with ill-fitting garments, I believe it will be enough to gain audience with the governor of Nassau." Lieutenant Pike answered while leaning into a shift of the deck beneath them. "I must raise my objection again, Lilith. Your plan to have Governor Alton present a letter of marque is well intentioned, but I know it will not be as beneficial as you think."

Lilith turned away, catching a glimpse from Trina. Her eyes were pleading. The young captain glanced back over her shoulder and gave the navy man a nod, "It may not work out as you think, Lieutenant. But who is to say it won't work out as I planned it? You will take him to meet the Nassau governor."

"I had never imagined I wouldn't captain. I only want you to be forewarned, the results may not be favorable." His words cut Lilith into her core. She imagined him being restrained by guards, struggling as he is drug away to a cell.

"It will be what it will be. Should we come to an undesirable outcome we'll navigate those waters when we get there." Lilith walked toward the stern, ignoring both Trina's glare and a gesture of frustration from the lieutenant as she passed them.

Behind the helm, Lilith found Omibwe dutifully watching the sails above and managing the ship's wheel. Her memory drifted to when Chibs had first instructed her on the skill set of manning the helm on ship. It had been so new and intimidating to her, but as she learned the art of reading the sails and feeling the rudder through the wheel it inspired a confidence unlike anything Lilith had experienced up to that point in her life. The Drowned Maiden had saved her from a miserable fate, given her confidence and a sense of family and destiny. Though the lieutenant and his fellow navy men had melded with the crew, they were still outsiders in Lilith's mind. They knew nothing of the struggles and pain the many freed slaves aboard had endured. Their loyalty to the Maiden remained a question in Lilith's mind day and night. But the saved ones, those the Maiden had rescued from a future of servitude and subjugation. Lilith knew where their loyalty aligned.

"Is she handling well?" Lilith asked the young man as he balanced between his good leg and a crude wooden prosthetic.

"She handles fair running before; broad reach is still hard for me." Omibwe replied, smiling a broad grin as he realized he had the captain's attention.

"It was difficult for me too. It requires a lot of arm strength and some heft to hold her steady. You're doing a fine job Omi." Lilith returned his smile and patted his shoulder. "Where is the Doctor?" she asked, regarding the French doctor that had joined the Maiden's ranks alongside Omibwe's the past fall, the two were seldom far apart.

"He is below. Helping that governor man fit into his fancy clothes." Omibwe answered with a chuckle.

"Quite a sight I am told." Lilith joined him in laughing.

"Oh, it is!" Omibwe said, looking back up to the top sails as he heard a flutter of canvas. He moved the wheel and watched as the sail went taut again.

The two continued talking and Chibs made his way up from below deck trailing a cloud of pipe smoke behind him as he moved.

"Nassau in two days' time Captain. By my reckoning anyway." Chibs informed Lilith before gesturing her away from the helm. Lilith followed him to the starboard rail where Chibs removed his pipe from his teeth and leaned into her.

"The young man is a might shaky, but he'll manage. The governor looks his part, overstuffed, but they all sort of do anyway. Is the lieutenant going to go along with this? It's likely to end badly for him." Chibs said in a hushed voice, just loud enough to be heard over the water breaking against the Maiden's hull.

"He will be fine Chibs." Lilith said while averting her gaze out over the sea.

"I'm not so sure Captain. Once it's done, if they find out he has been sailing with a pirate crew he'll be locked up in a cell. If they hear he aided us in sinking a vessel flying the King's colors, he'll be strung up." Chibs explained.

"I know this Chibs. But what else are we to do? If the governor of Nassau is left alive, The Order remains." Lilith replied, she was growing weary discussing the same matter over again.

Chibs' face softened, "Difficult choices my dear. I'm sorry, I didn't consider the weight of it I suppose. You've done so well as a captain. Sometimes, I forget your youth."

"Captain James lived to free us and he died fighting to free more. I won't abandon that cause, not for one man." Lilith looked up toward the bow again seeing Lieutenant Pike and Trina visiting near the bowsprit.

"As it should be miss, forgive me, I only want you to understand where this course leads us." Chibs said, following her gaze up to the pair on the bow. "And don't you worry, Captain. Trina would slit his throat a hundred times over for you, if ever you asked her to."

"I don't doubt her loyalties Chibs, or yours for that matter. But I wonder about the navy men." Lilith replied breaking her stare back to the bearded old sailor.

Chibs clamped his pipe back into his teeth and looked forward at the lieutenant, "As do I Captain. As do I."

London, England
10 Feb 1809

Lord Admiral Becker stepped from the drizzling rain into an unassuming black carriage. The inside was nice enough, padded seats and black lace shades. He felt as if the transport belonged in a funeral procession. Outside, the London sky was a bleak picture of early spring. Gray, dreary and rainy. Winds from the northwest brought more cold and rain, making every venture outside unpleasant. The tasks he left his office for were an unpleasant necessity though and the dreadful weather fit with his task, mood and also his transport.

"The huntsman inn, without delay." He ordered the driver without so much as a look.

London's streets were busy, and the driver had to negotiate between other carriages and pedestrians, much to Becker's annoyance. The ride was comfortable, and Becker enjoyed a burning pinch of tobacco snuff as he peered out at the people on the street. Market booths and fish sellers intermingled with trade warehouses and the streets were a chaotic bumble of activity for the first half hour of his ride. When the outlying areas of London were on display outside his window, Becker relaxed and enjoyed the green fields and rolling hills. The huntsman was a massive masonry structure with ornate windows and fixtures. A society club more than an inn, the dining was touted to be some of the best in England. Perfectly manicured lawns and hedges lined the drive leading up to its grand entrance and as the carriage pulled to a stop a doorman and a valet were ready to meet the admiral.

"The Lords Umbridge and Black are inside awaiting your arrival Lord Admiral. Lord Wellerby and Lord Stockton have not yet arrived. They are in the parlor by the library." The doorman greeted in monotone.

"Good. Please see to it they find their way to us then." Becker said removing his hat.

The parlor by the library sat on the western end of the large structure, with tall windows and ornate curtains. Paintings of military figures and fox hunts adorned every space on the walls not occupied by windows and the dark hard wood floors were polished to a high shine. Liquor was already poured for Becker as he entered the room and closed the doors behind him.

"What in God's name has happened?" Becker pressed the two men who were present.

"We were hoping you could shed some light on that for us." Lord Black replied in a quip, "After all, this entire scheme was born of your doings."

"My doings? If I'm not mistaken, it was the lords in ownership who approached me! I merely facilitated the enterprise. It seems now, to my own undoing. Do you have any idea what this will mean if the royals catch wind of this? Or Parliament? This could be construed as treason!" Becker hissed, his voice rising louder than he intended.

"Shhhh. Enough of that." Lord Umbridge held a finger to his lips, hoping to calm both parties involved. "We have a setback here. Nothing more."

"A setback! One of my most senior admirals has been informed that Kingston has fallen to a slave revolt, or a pirate attack or some such nonsense. It was the governor of Jamaica those yanks were using, was it not?" Becker's face had gone red, his irritation and fear too intense to obscure.

"It was. But what is far more dangerous than a few escaped slaves with tall tales no one will believe?" Lord Black said, removing the top from a decanter and hoisting the bottle to give the liquor a smell.

"I don't know what you're getting at." Becker answered easing himself into one of the chairs.

"The admiral. The admiral you dispatched is a liability. As well as the governor, should he still be alive. Our partners in America have no idea we aren't working at the behest of the crown. They certainly won't want to draw further ire, that would only complicate things for them."

"If the Royals even get a whiff of this…" Becker lamented looking out the window at the green hills.

"They won't. Not if we deal with this now." Umbridge interrupted. "The company still commands one of the largest armed navies in the world. The Monarch is too consumed with Napoleon at the moment to fret over a small island in the new world. We will restore order ourselves and carry on with our plans."

Becker felt the flushing red drain from his face. "You intend to keep moving slaves? After all of this?"

"There is still profit to be made. Is there not? We are businessmen Lord Becker." Black sneered as he poured more liquor from another decanter into a pair of glasses. He walked over to Becker and handed him a glass of the dark golden drink. "We will continue our pursuits. With or without the Americans, the crown, the French. It makes no difference. As long as the American agricultural system demands labor, we will supply them and continue to reap the profits."

Becker took a long pause, staring out the window. He felt the flush returning to his face. The men in this room had largely been responsible for his meteoric rise through the ranks of the naval structure. Their constant influence, coupled with his family name, had catapulted him through the officer ranks with little sea experience and almost no combat on his record. The creeping feeling that he had been groomed and placed by these men so they might further exert their influence gripped his spine. "Did you say the French were involved?"

"It's far too late to be playing coy, Lord Becker." Umbridge scoffed from behind the seat Becker sat in. "You couldn't possibly have been unaware of our dealings with the French. How do you think we arranged the initial investment?"

Lord Becker shot up from his seat with his pulse beating into his temples. Every word spoken by these men had been coated in condescension and malice. "I had assumed that the opulently wealthy Lords in ownership of the East India Company had used their own funding!"

"Don't be ridiculous!" Umbridge cut back with a laugh, "Why on earth would I use my own funds when I can get some other fool to risk his? I swear you sound more like a commoner every time you open your damned mouth. You might try listening instead of talking for a change, there is plenty you could learn."

"I think I've learned enough about how to commit high crimes against the crown, thank you. If that is all gentlemen, I'll be on my way." Lord Becker uttered as he turned to head for the door of the parlor to find Lords Wellerby and Stockton standing in his way.

"Lord Becker. You disappoint me. Leaving as we arrive? Have a seat, get comfortable. We are going to be here until there is a plan to remedy this, situation." Lord Stockton said as he strutted into the room. Of the men present, Lord Stockton was by far the wealthiest and the largest shareholder in the East India Company. He had a tall, slender frame and jet-black hair bordered by gray above his temples. His face belied his age and for a moment Becker thought of Admiral Torren. His easy demeanor faded as Becker hesitated, "Sit!" he ordered while pointing at the chair Becker had just vacated.

"This is more than I thought it was. This is treason, this is corroborating with an enemy of the crown. For profits! How did I not see?" Becker said aloud as the

Lords around him all focused in on him.

"It's almost unbelievable that you didn't know the true nature and extent of what has occurred. So unbelievable, in fact that I don't think denying prior knowledge will stay the royal hand, should it come to that." Lord Stockton retorted. "But we needn't be too hasty, Lord Becker. All is not lost. In fact, we need little more from you than reporting events to the Crown in the proper way. A way which will not get us all hung from the neck. Now sit. Have another drink and we will lay out a plan for you. You will report certain findings to the King, should he summon you. And we will all move on."

For the first time in his dealings with the Lords holding ownership of the East India Company, Lord Becker felt trapped. He had been lured into aiding their venture. He was now a party to a treasonous plot, flagrantly disregarding the laws of parliament and collaborating efforts with an enemy of the crown. If he crossed these Lords now, they could use him as a scapegoat. If he continued with their efforts, they could all be discovered and hang together. It would only take one slip. One misdealing. One of the King's spies in the wrong place at the wrong time, overhearing the wrong conversation. Becker's head spun and his stomach knotted. The smell of the liquor and tobacco in the room worsened his nausea. "What would you have me do?" he asked the group.

Lord Stockton let a sickening smile spread across his face, "For now. Nothing. You will play the part. Nothing is amiss beside the report of an uprising in Jamaica. You have already responded in an appropriate manner. Dispatching the admiral. I'll need the names of the ships he has in his fleet."

"For what purpose?" Becker asked, feeling another wave of nausea building.

"Not to worry son. We will clean this up." Stockton turned grabbing a sheet of paper and ink quill. "Here you are. The names of those ships, as legibly as you can."

Lord Becker set his drink on a slab table near the windows and stooped over to scrawl the names of the ships that had accompanied Admiral Torren to the Caribbean. His head woozed and felt heavy as he wrote down the ship names each one becoming harder to recollect as he added to the list. When he started to write the name of the last ship, Admiral Torren's flagship North Wind, his vision began to double.

"I'm not feeling well at all…" he uttered and stood upright.

"I would imagine not." Lord Stockton replied with another sick smile. He stepped over and grabbed the paper away from Lord Becker.

Becker's face felt hot and swollen, his head spun, and his insides felt like they were full of broken glass and being squeezed in a vise. His breath came in ragged pants and as the room turned around him uncontrollably, he fell to his knees. The Lords that stood around him broke their gathering and went back to their seats or to the windows, still looking down on him as he struggled with every breath.

"What… what did you do to me?" Becker wheezed.

"A very rare toxin. Though I didn't expect it would take quite this long, you have a stouter disposition than we expected." Lord Black sneered while looking down from his seat in the chair Becker had been seated in earlier.

"Why?" Becker choked out before collapsing further onto his hands and knees.

"You know too much son and your idealistic loyalty to the damned Royals puts us all at risk. A shame, really. You had such potential."

Becker's limbs gave out, sending his body crumpling onto the hardwood. His throat felt as if it were on fire and with each labored attempt at breath, he could only squeak precious little air in. His mouth foamed and drooled a thick saliva that felt like glue under his tongue. Lying on the floor, his vision faded as the Lords continued talking among themselves. Lord Stockton was reading the list of ships. "North Wind, that was Admiral Nelson's flag at one time. Admiral Torren will be on that one…"

Chapter 8

'Shark Fin'
8 Feb 1809
Tortuga Harbor, Haiti

Along the creaking boards of pier five in the Tortuga harbor, Shark Fin bobbled next to the wooden docks as her crew loaded supplies in a haste under the first glow of dawn in the eastern skies. John Tarley arrived on the pier just as the crew were about to load the last of their dry goods. He waved to the captain who stood alongside the ship's railing.

"I'm here Captain. If you will still take another hand." John said as the crew loading goods gave him scornful stares.

"Almost too late. I figured you had better judgment than to lope about the Caribbean with the likes of us. Climb aboard son. We'll take you." The captain replied. "Where did you spend the rest of your evening?"

"I slept in the stables behind the inn, just up the road there." John reported, pointing back over his shoulder.

"Did you happen across anyone else on the pier looking for the Shark Fin?" the captain jutted out his jaw and squinted as he asked, rubbing the scruff under his chin.

"No, Sir. No, it was quiet the whole way here." John answered with a shrug.

"Perhaps that Spaniard's friend has more sense than you. No matter. Give the boys a hand loading those crates and come on aboard. We'll put you to good use."

John had a wooden crate thrust into his arms and was shooed up the gangplank before he could formulate a 'thank you' to the captain, who had already turned his attention elsewhere. On deck, the crew milled about working on tasks to prepare their vessel for sailing. Sailors were climbing the ratlines aloft while the gangplank was hauled in and dock lines were cast away. A commotion off the dockside rail caught John's attention and he joined a growing number of the crew as they gathered along the side.

"Wait! Please, wait! I was told you are taking able hands!" the voice of a haggard man called as he waved an arm overhead to catch the attention of anyone aboard.

John could see the captain's demeanor shift as he stood at the rail, he looked down at the man who had hurried onto the pier. "I was. But now I am putting to sea. I need able bodies that show up on time, by the look of it, you're neither."

"Please, I need to make my way to Charleston. I have urgent business there and I can get you paid handsomely for my passage!" the ragged man huffed as he doubled over.

"Charleston isn't the course I have set, sorry." The captain dismissed, turning inboard.

"You're hunting after a pirate crew? Am I right?"

"Aye, we are. And what in hell would you know about it?" the captain snapped back to the rail, his attention captured by the man on the pier.

"I was aboard a ship they targeted. I am the only survivor." The panting man stood up straight.

"Hold that line!" the captain called forward to the bow, "Lower that gangplank down again and get this man aboard!"

"Thank you!" the ragged stranger called back.

"You were a friend of that Spaniard? The one who works for the shipwright?" the captain inquired, with renewed interest in his newest crew member.

"I was... Am. Yes, Tomas you mean?" the man answered as he watched the gangplank drop down to the dock where he stood.

"I don't know his name. It makes no difference. Climb aboard man! We are off to chase down those rogues and see justice done!" a few sailors near the captain offered shouts of approval. "That Spaniard told me you were all mended from your encounter, what in blazes happened to you?"

The stranger hesitated for a moment. "I had a misunderstanding. It's resolved now."

"I'd say. I should hate to see the other half of your 'misunderstanding', if he looks anything like you it was probably one hell of a fight." The captain gave an uneasy smile, "Is the constable looking for you?"

"No, no. It ended just between us. You have my

word." The stranger replied as he made his way to the top of the gangplank.

"I'll have to take you at your word. Not that I care. I've set sail from more than a few ports with the town hot on my heels." The captain grumbled in reply, then he turned to the hands on deck, "Alright, set to your task. We haven't a moment to lose!"

John was ushered by one of the crew to the base of the ratlines.

"Up we go boy, get going! Those sails aren't going to loose themselves." The sailor growled.

John hesitated, looking up into the rigging gave him a chill as he remembered tumbling from the tops of Boston Autumn. The bite of the rope wound still aching his shoulder, John reached for the coarse grip on the lines and hefted himself upward. The first few steps found his heart fluttering and his breath seizing in his throat but as he progressed his way up each step and hand hold came with greater ease and a sense of confidence began building within him. Scurrying his way across the yard John assisted the crew with setting the main and top sail. Shark Fin eased away from the wooden pier with the land breeze. The aromas of Tortuga blended with sea air and John's heart felt lighter as land slipped away from Shark Fin's stern. The brilliant beauty of sunrise faded into a piercing blue as the sun rose higher into the sky and the waters of the Caribbean took on an almost jewel like quality in John's eyes. The blue green ripples of waves sparkled under the shine of the sun while birds circled overhead. Below him, the captain shouted some commands and then followed with a shrill statement for the crew to hear, "We're chasing after damned pirates boys! It's going to be foul seas and hard fighting for all, any man who has second thoughts should have stayed on shore!"

'Southern Song'
8 Mar 1809
19 Degrees 4' N, 75 Degrees 32' W

A loud clanging rang through Rory's ears, jarring him into the conscious world and alerting him to splitting pain emanating from his scalp down through the base of his skull. His surroundings were dark and blurry, opening his eyes only revealed a vague outline of a man to his front. The clanging resumed and Rory attempted to lift his gaze from the wooden floor in front of him, only to be rewarded with another wave of pulsing, shooting pains through his head.

"Awake and arise fish food!" the blurry form slurred.

Rory attempted a response, only to produce a grumbling cough through his chapped lips. His shoulders felt like they were being pulled from his torso. Rory's awareness rose in a slow progression, and he realized he could not feel his hands or fingers. Panic flooded his mind, and he struggled to lift his head to look around. Everything was a blur. He tried to move his fingers and realized that his hands were suspended above his head. His entire weight was pulling down on his shoulders. Managing to drag his feet beneath him, Rory attempted to stand and relieve the pressure from his shoulders. A wave of lightheaded nausea enveloped him and the effort it took to stand up failed the first time. Breathing required deliberate labor and Rory became aware that the voice which taunted him had left. Another attempt to stand yielded the reward of easing tension from his shoulders and allowing him a sweet deep breath unencumbered by the strain in his chest. The deck under his feet shuddered and heaved, reminding Rory that he was still in fact at sea. His mind traced through the events that had led to him being manacled below deck. The captain's fight with Dog. His murder of the sailor who had intervened in the fight. Rory's head throbbed harder as he recalled the details and the captain's plan to harvest slaves for Mr. Ritten without investigating matters in Jamaica.

He said he was going to kill me. Rory thought to himself. *Then why am I still alive? Why hasn't he killed me yet?* The deck shifted again almost causing Rory to lose his footing. Another rush of panic enveloped his mind as Rory tried to think of a way to free himself. His wrists burned with hot pangs of pain, emanating into his forearms. Dried blood felt sticky on the backs of his hands and his wrists. Another pitch of the deck forced Rory to shift his weight or risk losing his footing again.

"You couldn't wiggle free of those shackles if you had a month to, so you might as well give up." A voice came from the dark blur surrounding him.

"Who is that? Where are you?" Rory wheezed through his pain wracked chest, "Show yourself!"

A form stepped into his vision. Blurred at first, but Rory found his focus in the dim lantern light below deck. The captain of the Southern Song stood in front of him, an expressionless stare on his face. He reeked of alcohol and his voice was rougher than a wooden hull on gravel. "Where is the slaver camp in Jamaica?"

"Why would I divulge anything to you? You intend to kill me." Rory's voice drug out with each word as painful as the last.

"Your employer wants for you to sail to the camp and collect slaves from the island, feeding the markets in America. In turn, myself and my ship get a share of the profits. I am assuming you will get a share as well. Let's increase our end by leaving Mr. Ritten out of things. There are plenty of slave markets throughout the Americas and beyond. We could gain ourselves a tidy sum." The captain's words slurred and ran together with each other. Rory could smell the spirits on his breath with each syllable he announced.

Rory laughed. He laughed despite the pain wracking his ribs and shoulders, radiating into his arms. He laughed until he coughed and then coughed until he almost retched. "You have no idea what you are talking about."

"Enlighten me then." The drunken captain demanded.

"You intend to cross The Order? Steal away something they have determined is theirs? It's a fool's errand." Rory's laugh ceased as the taste of blood from his coughing fit entered his mouth.

"The Order?" The captain looked confused, "What the hell are you talking about?"

"Mr. Ritten is not supplying the slave markets of America solely for his own gain, although that would be enough for him to. The operation is sponsored by

The Order, they provided assistance and money to fund the endeavor once the Brit Parliament outlawed the slave trade." Rory explained, watching as realization dawned on the captain's face.

"So they are British?" The captain leaned in, further offending Rory's nostrils with his foul mixture of booze and years of neglecting the wash basin.

"Yes, some of them are British. But then some of them are French and some are Spanish, they are as far scattered as they are elusive. If you cross them, you will never recognize the one they send to kill you. I am a pawn, Mr. Ritten is a pawn and the world is their game board. You have no idea what you have gotten yourself into. If you cross us, if you cross THEM you are as good as dead." Rory's words came with a vigor he could feel pulsating through his body, it energized him to threaten this drunk who was in control of him at the moment. But it faded quickly.

The captain took a step backward, his eyes sunk to the deck. He appeared to be considering his options. "If you won't tell me where the camp is willingly, I'll drag it out of you. You can keep your fairy tales and grand threats; they won't work aboard this ship."

Rory rolled his eyes as the captain spoke. "Ship, right. More like a rotted out old tub!"

The punch that came in reply landed on Rory's right cheek, reeling his head around and sending a lightning flash across his vision. The next came and smashed his nose, sending a spurt of blood down his face and covering his mouth. A third strike hit him in the jaw and dropped Rory's world again into darkness.

'North Wind'
18 Mar 1809
28 Degrees 51' N, 76 Degrees 37' W

North Wind crested through a large rolling Atlantic wave on her southern course. With full taut sails, she was making remarkable speed for a ship in her class. Since the loss of H.M.S. Ambush, the crew aboard North Wind had all become experts on the political intricacies between Britain and the United States. Consensus among the crew was that after dealing with Napoleon, Britain would turn its attention to the rogues occupying the former colonies and bring them to heel. In the solitude of his cabin, Admiral Alistair Torren knew a very different truth. Britain's naval supremacy was already in question and her land armies undoubtedly outmatched by the strength of France under Bonaparte's regime. The channel fleet was all that prevented Napoleon from subjugating the United Kingdoms under his rule. In addition, the loss of the colonies was still a sore spot to the monarch and their growing military prowess made any hope of bringing the rebels back into the fold more and more remote with each passing year. The American's advances in naval construction and tactical refinement made them a real threat on the high seas and while they did not yet command the large fleet sizes of the British Navy, ships like the U.S.S. Constitution could outmatch comparable adversaries in battle. The French and Spanish were employing larger numbers of privateers while also investing in their own naval fleets. Britain long relied on expanding her power by using the East India Trading Company and the West African Trading vessels to augment her fleets in time of need, those days had passed and neither fleet commanded the numbers they once had.

Days had passed as Alistair delved into the global implications of his suspicions. The British Navy had used the press gang at home and at sea for generations. Recently, the Americans had been a regular target for impressment at sea. Both because of their proximity to British trade lines and as a form of retaliation for the long and costly war they waged for their independence. Which was lost in large part due to France's growing naval prowess. Alistair endured in his routine walks every morning, but instead of making small talk with the crew on deck he kept to himself. Afterward he would retire to his cabin for the remainder of the day, only emerging in the early hours the next morning for his walk. Lieutenant Thatcher was his sole companion, delivering his reports and fixing his meals while ensuring the admiral's orders were delivered in a timely and precise fashion. He still managed to visit with the lieutenant, inquiring about certain things aboard or if orders had been relayed or acknowledged. He still took the moment whenever the opportunity presented itself, to give the lieutenant a note or two on things like seamanship or leadership. But the admiral's more amiable nature seemed to have slipped beneath the waves along with H.M.S. Ambush and the souls lost aboard her.

The seas were high, and Alistair had just concluded his walk. The weather had warmed in the few days since the loss of H.M.S. Ambush, but the old admiral still wore his heavy boat cloak, which he removed as he entered his cabin. Lieutenant Thatcher was fixing the admiral's breakfast, a pork steak and a pair of eggs.

"The deck seems in good order Lieutenant. She's sailing nicely. How is the spirit amongst the crew? I'm afraid I've kept to myself of late." The admiral inquired as he pulled up his seat at his desk.

"Mostly in good spirit Sir. Though there are always some detractors, losing the Ambush seems to have solidified their resolve rather than inducing fear as I thought it would." Lieutenant Thatcher answered while laying the admiral's breakfast in front of him. He shifted to pour tea, holding the cup in his off hand to compensate for the roll of the ship.

"You'll find that the case more often than not lad. Especially when the men aboard weren't even afforded the opportunity to fire a shot in anger. Now if we had traded broadsides with her, it would be a different matter." The admiral said, cutting into his seasoned pork. "Action always brings them tighter together, especially if there are losses sustained. There is always an edge of fear, don't misunderstand that. Deep down, they are afraid, but they won't openly admit it."

Lieutenant Thatcher put back the kettle and turned to the admiral, "Sir. If I could press a question."

"What is it?" the admiral said after swallowing his first bite.

"The American vessel we saw. To my mind, it is obvious they engaged and sank the Ambush. Why would we not engage in turn?" the lieutenant looked hesitant to ask, like he was awaiting the admiral's wrath for questioning his command decisions.

Admiral Torren cracked a smile, "Are the lads on deck thinking I've gone soft? Or perhaps there's rumors of the old admiral being an American conspirator?"

"Well, no Sir. Not that. But I have heard some of the men ask why we didn't. To be completely honest Sir, I was wondering the same thing." Lieutenant Thatcher took up a stool beside the admiral's desk so he could sit facing him.

"Why do you think I ordered us to keep course son?" the admiral said before taking a fork of egg into his mouth.

"As best I can reason Sir, you must judge our tasking to be more urgent." The lieutenant answered with a thoughtful stare.

"Hogwash. Nothing is more important than engaging an enemy vessel that has sunk one of ours. Guess again." Admiral Torren put a hand next to his tea to prevent it from sliding along the desk as the ship rolled with a wave. He took another bite of his eggs with his other hand and looked up to the lieutenant who was deep in thought.

"Do you have some notion of a larger American fleet? Or is there a spy aboard her? Honestly Sir, I feel at a loss. I can't think of any more reasons we wouldn't engage." The lieutenant scratched his head in frustration.

"No. Neither of those are the case. But those are good considerations." The admiral put his fork down, "That American ship, I suspect, was the U.S.S. Constitution. She represents the dawn of a new era in sea power lad. In England, I read a report from a privateer she engaged off the Maine coast. They fired a broadside of twelve pounders at her and not a single shot penetrated. The cannonballs hit her hull and fell into the water. She is designed differently, her hull is thicker, but her draw is shallow. She is said to be ungodly fast, maneuverable as a damned sloop but carries the firepower of a heavy frigate. Beyond that. The Americans are aggressive to a fault. I'm sure it will be their own undoing someday, but the bloody buggers will attack at any provocation." Admiral Torren sipped his tea for a second, letting his words sink in with the young officer.

"You think she could've bested us Sir?" the lieutenant asked looking concerned.

"No. Not all of us at least. No, had we engaged her, we would have won the day. But, at what cost son? She certainly would have dragged at least one of our ships down with her, likely two. If there were any survivors of the encounter, not likely this far from shore but possible, we would most certainly start another war with the Americans. At a time when we grapple with Napoleon and deal with uprisings in the Caribbean, the end results could be catastrophic." The admiral paused for a moment, "But there is another reason as well. It has nothing to do with spies or a big American fleet. And you already know it, you just don't want to say it aloud."

Lieutenant Thatcher's eyes lowered for a moment as he thought, "We didn't actually witness the American engage anything."

"Right you are young man. Now suppose H.M.S. Ambush was engaged by a Frenchy, who unlike the

Americans, we are currently at war with. And suppose we mistakenly engaged an American frigate, losing God knows how many souls and how many ships and starting an entirely new conflict. We would be judged as fools in history, blundering idiots with no sense or discipline." Admiral Torren stood from his chair, turning to look out the window array behind him. "It's not for lack of want to avenge our lost, son. That I promise you."

"I understand Sir. Thank you for the explanation. Do you think it would be beneficial for me to share that explanation with the crew?" Lieutenant Thatcher asked.

"Absolutely not lad. No, these men must carry on as if Britain were invincible. The knowledge that our situation is so precarious would only endanger morale, encourage desertion or worse, mutiny. No, let them talk amongst each other as they will. It's the natural way of sailors anyhow. We will carry on with the knowledge we have and keep it to ourselves." Admiral Torren turned back to the lieutenant as he spoke, locking eyes with him in an intense stare.

"Aye Sir, I'll keep it to myself." The lieutenant managed, looking a bit uncomfortable.

"Alright Lieutenant, now, what of our heading? We should be seeing Nassau soon if I am not mistaken." Admiral Torren softened his tone, taking his seat again.

"Yes Sir. By my reckoning and judging by conversation with the sailing master, we should be seeing Nassau by morning tomorrow. Do you have orders for me to relay to the squadron Sir?"

"Yes, actually. I want a shore party organized. I will

be paying the governor a visit, as well as the garrison commander. Have a party of marines and an officer from each ship ready to accompany, including yourself. Captains and their crews are to remain aboard their vessels until I give further orders." Admiral Torren cracked a wry half smile, "You will be the accompanying officer for North Wind's marine complement."

This took Lieutenant Thatcher by surprise and his expression betrayed him. Hesitancy mixed with excitement, followed by the realization that the crew's reaction would not be so favorable. "Sir, maybe a more senior lieutenant would be better…"

"Admiral Torren held up a hand, "No. I've spoken my orders. You will be a fine commander for the shore detachment and I'm sure having land under your legs will be a welcome change for a day."

"Aye Sir, it will." Lieutenant Thatcher replied, biting at his lower lip.

The admiral ignored Lieutenant Thatcher's reluctance, instead pulling a chart across his deck and peering through a magnifying glass. "The shoals around Nassau are no amateur navigation exercise. Do pay close attention to the sailing master and helmsman as we approach. You're likely to learn a few things about precise sailing in tight quarters."

"Yes Sir, I will be sure to." The lieutenant replied, still visibly bothered by the prospect of overseeing a shore detachment.

Nassau, Bahamas
18 Mar 1809

Will watched the outline of the Drowned Maiden grew smaller into the fading evening as Lewis pulled the oars of the small rowboat, propelling them toward the docks of Nassau. Lilith had elected to anchor to the south, away from the dangerous shoals and reefs which guarded the Nassau harbor. Those same shoals and reefs that could deter an enemy force from approaching undetected could also prevent the Maiden from making a hasty escape if needed. The longer row meant William and Lewis would have to endure the governor's company all the longer. The governor squirmed uncomfortably in his ill-fitting attire, voicing his complaints at a frequency that drove William mad. The beauty of the Caribbean sunset was lost to gripes about the rocking of the boat and the slow pace of progress toward the docks.

"Really, have you been that far removed from the cane fields boy? Put some of your back into it, I thought we would be there by now!" Governor Alton huffed, pawing his brow with a kerchief.

"Check your tongue Governor. You would do well to remember yourself and your current situation. I only have so much patience for your drivel, and it has run dry." William snapped cutting the governor a scolding look. He turned to Lewis, "I would assist you, but if anyone is watching."

"I'm fine. I'll make it." Lewis said between straining pulls at the oars in his hands.

The lantern lights of Nassau grew brighter as Lewis

continued his toiling pulls propelling their small craft toward the docks. Orange and purple hues had faded away like melting fingers as the inky blackness of the night sky set in revealing the gems of the heavens in crystal clear detail. With the moon already high overhead Will and Lewis pulled the rowboat in next to a wooden dock and steadied the craft while Governor Alton managed his way up onto the wood planks of the dock on unsteady legs.

The three men gathered themselves for a moment where the boat was tied to the dock. At the head of the pier a registrar kept vigil at his small booth, flanked by two red coated sentries he waited to record names and collect payment for each vessel using the pier. William led the way up the pier followed by Governor Alton and Lewis trailing along behind him. The registrar gave a forced smile to the trio as they approached.

"A good evening to you Lieutenant." The thin aged registrar offered.

"Good evening to you as well Sir. I have in my company Governor Geor Alton of the Jamaica colonies and his servant Lewis. My name is Lieutenant William Pike and I am the governor's personal escort from H.M.S. Endurance, we are here to seek an audience with Nassau's governor for urgent matters." William's voice found its commanding tone again.

"I can waive the boat fee for a representative of the Crown and have one of my sentries here show you fine gentlemen the way to the governor's mansion. Be forewarned though, he will not allow that to enter inside." The registrar pointed to Lewis, "We just dealt with another uprising a week ago. All the other

Negroes on the island are required to be shackled."

The registrar's disdain was plainly visible through the yellow lamplight flickering over his hard features. "We do appreciate your consideration for a representative of the Crown and for a guest of the governor." Governor Geor Alton's self-important tone interrupted Will as he was opening his mouth to respond. "I am sure the governor won't deny an old man of my station the necessity of my servant. I need him quite often, my knees aren't what they once were though my pride is still intact as ever and I just can't bring myself to ask another gentleman for help up stairs."

Will fought his surprise, trying to keep his face from revealing the shock of what he had just heard. An awkward pause passed while the registrar digested the information. He nodded over his shoulder at one of the sentries, "Show these fine gentlemen the way. Do send my regards to the governor and pass along Governor Alton's need to keep his servant at his side." The registrar turned back to address Governor Alton directly, "My apologies Governor Alton, typically a visiting official allows some forewarning. I have no transportation arranged, but you will find the walk to the governor's mansion very attainable, less than a mile Sir. Again, my apologies."

"Hmmmph. No need no need. I should like to stretch my legs anyhow." Governor Alton huffed, lifting his chin high and turning to the near sentry, "Lead on son. We've pressing business."

The soldier led the way with Governor Alton and William following closely behind and Lewis bringing up the rear. The late evening was cool, but the streets of Nassau were still busy with people. Local merchants peddled their wares while haggling sailors and traders attempted to edge out a deal on whatever goods were available. Noise from the taverns and brothels spilled into the street and the aroma of cooking food and liquor mixed with the fruits and flowers of the island into an intoxicating blend. Will looked over his shoulder at Lewis, half expecting the young man to have wandered off in the overwhelming street filled with bright colored fruits and tempting smells and sights. Lewis' eyes locked onto his, filled with a determined flame. Lilith had sent him along for a purpose, though Will himself was unsure what end the young man would serve, his suspicion was that a drastic surprise awaited him.

The governor's mansion was large, though not as large as Geor's had been in Kingston. It was two stories, with a grand front entrance guarded by tall columns. Lamps flanked the front door and even though the hour was late, light emanated from the front facing windows in several rooms of the large manor. The soldier escorting the trio stopped at the base of the stairs leading up to the front entrance.

"Here you are gentlemen." He gave a curt nod to the governor and gave Lieutenant Pike a crisp salute.

"Well done lad, thank you and pass my compliments to the garrison commander." Will replied, returning the soldier's salute.

Governor Alton proceeded up the stairs and gave the knocker a pair of polite taps. After a moment the front door edged its way open, revealing a formally clad valet. Lieutenant Pike recited his introductions and requested their formal meeting with the Nassau governor. The valet ushered them inside, giving Lewis a scornful and suspicious look before leaving to inform the governor of his visitors. The foyer of the home was grand, Will noted the ornate carpets and curved staircase leading to the second floor. High overhead were two large pieces of artwork depicting majestic ships of the line under full sail. Near the base of the curved staircase a towering grandfather clock clicked away seconds and William thought back to his meeting with the Admiralty board. Standing in the hallway under the constant stare from portraits of notable admirals before the disastrous events that had led him to this very moment. He felt the familiar prickle of heat rising beneath the collar of his uniform jacket, though this foyer was nowhere as stuffy and uncomfortable as the hallway had been.

"Gentlemen! Governor Alton! What circumstances bring this pleasant surprise?" the Nassau governor exclaimed as he entered the foyer from the hallway. He was a large man, not quite as round as Governor Alton but a full foot taller. He has full large lips and a round nose. Even in the late hour of their calling, he was still dressed formally and wearing a long-curled wig that reached past his shoulders.

He strutted over to his visitors, "Governor Alton, I am very surprised to see you. We have been hearing disturbing news of Kingston! The harbor inaccessible, rumors of a slave revolt or a pirate raid? We all feared the worst for you."

"As you can see, I am quite alright though Kingston

is in shambles. I am here to discuss some urgent matters to rectify that." Geor paused looking around. "Do you have somewhere we can talk, perhaps a bit more comfortably?"

"Yes, my study should do. Will they be joining us?" the governor gestured to Will and Lewis.

"Yes, yes Lieutenant Pike here has important information which is pertinent, and my servant scarcely leaves my side. That is if you don't mind indulging." Geor answered, looking back at Will and Lewis with a pause.

"I don't make a habit of allowing Negroes into my home, but I will make an exception for you. We have had several slave uprisings as of late, the most recent was quite severe in fact. But it has been dealt with, the offending parties are still hanging near the docks. You may have seen them on your way up." The governor turned and looked at Will. "Governor Benjamin Culbertson," he extended a hand toward Will, who took it in a firm shake.

"Lieutenant William Pike," Will returned the introduction.

"Your uniform is out of sorts Lieutenant. I'm not quite sure what to make of it." Governor Culbertson said with blunt affect.

"These few months have been trying Sir, do forgive me. I haven't had an opportunity to visit a tailor and the mending is quite beyond my skill." Will replied before gritting his jaw and hoping the governor would not press the matter. It was highly irregular for a naval officer to present himself in such a manner, regardless of circumstances.

"Well, in any case, mad times these are. Come along, we will sort out what we can tonight." Governor Culbertson motioned them to follow and turned up the hallway walking along the corridor until he came to a doorway flanked by bronze busts Will couldn't recognize the likeness of.

The study was a small room, with a fireplace positioned directly behind a large desk. Bookshelves lined the inner and side walls, and the opposite wall held a bank of ceiling to waist high windows, tinted by fog from the humid air of the evening. Governor Culbertson motioned for his guests to sit in a pair of wooden ladder-back chairs as he skirted the edge of his desk to take his seat on the opposite side in a large, padded chair.

"You'll have to forgive me if I seem out of sorts gentlemen. I just concluded a dinner party and meeting, I was not expecting further company this evening." Governor Culbertson said, scooting himself in closer to his desk, "Now please, do tell me how I can be of assistance."

"Kingston has indeed fallen as you have been told. Though not to a slave uprising or a pirate attack. Kingston was attacked by a group of mercenaries attempting to continue the slave trade, covertly. I have come to deliver a letter of marque that I issued to a privateer crew, hoping they can escort me while I recruit assistance to retake Kingston." Governor Alton began to explain. Will watched Governor Culbertson carefully, measuring his reaction.

"This is troubling news, Geor." Governor Culbertson said after a long pause. "Perhaps it is even more troubling to be hearing you share the news so freely."

Will felt a chill grab hold of his spine as the Nassau governor's tone changed. He fought against betraying his thoughts through his facial expressions.

"What do you mean Benjamin? I don't understand." Geor asked, looking genuinely confused.

"I am making an assumption here, but you knew these mercenaries were trafficking slaves. In fact, you were assisting them. But correct me if I am wrong here, The Order demanded your silence as well as your cooperation. If Kingston was attacked by the men you are saying, then you must have breached these terms Geor." Governor Culbertson lowered his brow as he spoke. "You weren't the only man to strike a deal with them, but it seems you are the only one who has managed to foul the way for us all. What on earth could have happened?"

Will gritted his teeth, clamping his fingers into the arms of the chair. His heart raced, pounding through his temples and ears.

"My residence was attacked by an agent of The Order, yes. But if you are involved with these men, Benjamin, I must warn you..." Governor Alton's voice cut off. He seemed out of breath, with a puzzled look on his face he looked down at his chest. He let a gasp loose before drawing a ragged breath in labored spurts. Blood soaked the front of his blouse, growing in a dark red splotch. Governor Alton slumped forward a little, slowly at first and then tumbled from his chair onto the floor revealing the blade base and handle of a dagger protruding from his back.

Will's eyes darted from the dagger to Lewis, who

was standing immediately behind the fallen governor's chair. Lewis pulled a pistol concealed in his waistband and cocked the hammer. Lewis paused for a breath and pulled the trigger erupting the pistol into a bark and sending a stream of smoke from its muzzle. Will's unbelieving stare snapped to Governor Culbertson as he collapsed backwards, toppling his chair over into the base of the fireplace behind it. A splatter of blood spurted from his throat spattering across Will's face.

"Lewis! What have you done? What... Why?" Will shouted.

"The Maiden demanded their death." Lewis replied, his face was a stone expression of determination. "We have to go lieutenant; they will be coming for us."

Will felt like he was frozen in place as he watched Lewis rip a drawer from the desk where and use it to smash the glass window to their side. Lewis pulled the ladder-back chair Governor Alton had been seated in to the base of the window. He stepped onto the seat and then the window frame, turning back to wave Will onward. Voices in the hallway snapped Will from his shock. Shouts echoed through the hallway and Will could hear running footfalls approaching. He bolted from his seat, dragging his chair to the study door and wedging its frame against the door as best he could before following Lewis through the window and into the night.

Chapter 9

'Drowned Maiden'
19 Mar 1809
Near Nassau, Bahamas

High in the Maiden's rigging with the hues of evening painting the sky Lilith had watched the departing rowboat until it rounded a sandy point and left her sight. She stayed aloft for nearly an hour afterward, watching as the stars revealed themselves against the inky backdrop of the night sky. Memories of the evening she had spent on the quarterdeck with the Maiden's previous captain, James, flooded over her. Her heart rose as she remembered the tales he had told her of the constellations. Then visions of the battle aboard H.M.S. Endurance flashed through her mind. She remembered James standing tall on deck, a sword in each hand. He had held back attacks from the sailors on board until they circled him, hesitant to engage the skilled pirate and fall the way their shipmates had. Lilith tried to shake the memory, but her mind lingered, replaying the scene and remembering the sequence of events until her hands were shaking. She watched as Johnathan fell to an attack from behind, could smell the blood and gunpowder hanging in the air as she rushed to come to his aid only to stand vigil over his dead body. Lilith killed many sailors that night, but she could not save James and it haunted her in moments of stillness.

When Lilith climbed down from the Maiden's rigging Chibs awaited her at the rail. A look of tense concern on the old sailor's face gave Lilith a moment's hesitation and for a brief flash she thought of climbing back aloft.

"They've made it to Nassau by now Cap'n. We should know their outcome by dawn." Chibs stated, looking up as Lilith stood on the bulwark.

"Lewis won't fail me Chibs." Lilith replied knowing where the conversation would go next.

"He will surely succeed, but will he survive? Will either of them survive? Or have we sent them off to their deaths on a suicide mission?" Chibs asked, his voice was insistent, demanding action from his captain.

"What would you have me do Chibs? Send more of the crew? Do we not trust that they can manage their task?" Lilith's response was quick but measured. She loved and respected Chibs but was growing tired of the challenging questions.

"The lieutenant could only have guessed at your true intentions sending them to meet the governor. He may be taken by such a surprise that we lose his allegiance." Chibs continued as Lilith balanced her way up the rail past the foot of the ratlines.

"Did we ever truly have the lieutenant's allegiance?"

Lilith shot Chibs a hard glance from the sides of her eyes.

"He has served the Maiden loyally for months now Captain. All the navy men we took on have. Without them we wouldn't have escaped the mutineers aboard their ship." Chibs replied, his voice begging the young pirate to reason with him.

"It was my maneuver that put them into the reef." Lilith cut back as she hopped down to the deck and met Chibs' stare.

"And it was their gunnery that did her in." Chibs added. "Like it or not Captain, we do owe them credit. I understand the task had to be done. But we should have warned Lieutenant Pike."

"He wouldn't have followed through." Lilith said, turning to head back to her cabin.

"And what do we tell the rest of his navy men aboard, when he doesn't make it back? Or perhaps he does and he is furious that we basically set him up?"

"I'll deal with it Chibs." Lilith began to reply, her voice interrupted by a distant clattering of bells. "It's done. They've done it."

The ringing bells continued with a furious urgency that could only be townsfolk raising an alarm. Lilith clung to the wooden railing on the Maiden's larboard side staring at the dark figure of the island under the half moon. Shouts and cries floated in the night air. Reports of gunfire cut through a moment of stillness and Trina ran up to Lilith's side.

"What are your orders Captain?" she urged Lilith.

"Have the crew ready the guns. I want every available hand on deck and armed, we will wait for their return until dawn threatens to break and then we must make sail. If they have not returned, we will show Nassau the gunnery skills Lieutenant Pike has given us." Lilith replied, "We will give them every chance we can. But we cannot risk the entire ship."

"Aye Captain." Chibs said, heading to ready the crew.

Trina lingered a moment, her face betrayed a hesitation to speak before she finally let her thoughts be heard. "Captain, I know this is hard for you. But…" her voice trailed for a moment, "It's what Johnathan would have done. I'm with you, however this ends."

Lilith's eyes flooded and blurred. The tension and dissent she had perceived had been welling within her until this moment. "I hope they make it Trina, but, if they don't…"

"We will carry on without them Captain. The Maiden demanded their service and they have fulfilled their duties. That is all it is." Trina interrupted to finish her sentence.

"Doesn't it feel like a betrayal? To leave if they don't return?" Lilith asked, lowering her voice so no other ears would hear her voice her doubts.

"It would be a betrayal to the Maiden for us to lead her into capture while The Order still poses a threat. The lives of two men mean nothing compared to the ship and her mission. Come dawn, Captain Lilith, you give us a heading and we will sail." Trina said in a resolute tone, grabbing Lilith's shoulder.

"Aye, ready the crew then Trina. The morning may bring fury with it." Lilith said, wiping her face and pulling her hat lower over her brow.

Revenge of the Drowned Maiden

The Maiden's crew made quick work of being ready, running the cannons out on both sides as quietly as wooden wheels would allow. An orange glow lit the silhouette of Nassau far too early for dawn and more shots were heard slicing through the night. Bells sounded again, ringing with a fervor more vigorous than before and a cloud of smoke emanated from the island town, hanging low over the falling tide. Lilith scoured the sea between the Maiden and the island with her eyes, searching for any sign of her crewmen returning. Nothing appeared as she gritted her jaw and willed them to peep out from the sandy finger of land guarding Nassau harbor.

"Sails on the horizon!" a lookout called from up in the Maiden's rigging, "a whole mess of them, and under full sail, headed this way!" Lilith's heart jumped. She scrambled to the ratlines and raced her way upward, hand over hand and footfall after footfall she topped the small platform atop the main sail yard. In the moonlight beyond the dark silhouette of the island ghostly white rectangles bobbed and pitched in motion from the wind and sea. Her eyes shifted back to the expanse of water separating her ship from the island. Only a dark expanse of bobbling waves met her eyes. The time had come for hard decisions.

"Let fly with main and top sails, cut away that anchor and come about hard to starboard!" Lilith called down to the deck. Lilith moved to the ratlines and began a mad descent to the deck. As she reached about halfway Chibs appeared in her sight at the base of the webbing.

"Captain, how many are there?" He called up.

"At least four. Too many to fight and maybe too fast to outrun, I couldn't make out their hulls but at least three of them have three masts!" Lilith replied as her feet found the solid deck again.

"Aye, we'll make all haste then." Chibs replied, turning to help the crew on deck adjust lines.

In moments the Drowned Maiden was making a hard turn under taut canvas, her rigging and masts creaking and groaning under the sudden increased strain.

"Get those bow chasers moved back to the stern and start bringing up shot. Once daylight breaks, we're going to be using them." Lilith's order caused a flurry of the crew on deck to adjust their pace.

As the Drowned Maiden made her wheeling turn through dark waters under a pre-dawn shimmer the orange glow of fire grew into a furious bright flame above Nassau. Gunshots and bells continued in a symphony of panic and chaos. Lilith's eyes flitted between the sandy coast of the island and the point on the horizon she expected to see the approaching sails appear. As the Maiden turned, Lilith walked along the rail, her stare set on the expanse of beach and sea where she hoped to see a rowboat and dreaded to see the approaching ships. A thunderclap explosion sent a flame spiking above the tree line that obscured Nassau from her view, its report shuddered through the air and Lilith could feel the concussion in her bones. The bells died away, leaving a column of smoke and a growing glow emanating from the town.

"What has happened?" Lilith said aloud as she reached the stern, where Chibs was stood watching the cannons Lilith had ordered to be moved being set in place.

"I'm guessing Lewis and the lieutenant had a run in with the garrison. They didn't surrender quietly by the sounds of things." Chibs replied clamping his pipe into his teeth and letting a big puff of smoke roll.

"Do you think they could have survived?" Lilith asked Chibs as they watched the orange glow fading below the tree line while hues of morning took hold of the sky.

"It's possible. Hard to say really. If they succeeded in killing the governor, I'd say it's not likely they're breathing right now though." Chibs' flat tone did little to comfort Lilith's mind.

In the orange pink haze of dawn the silhouettes of the approaching ships began to protrude from the edge of the island, revealing them to the Maiden and her to them.

"Fly the black Chibs." Lilith ordered.

"But Captain, maybe we ought to…"

"I want them all to know exactly who is responsible. Fly the black banner." Lilith interrupted.

"Aye Captain." Chibs replied, holding his palms out. "I'll fly her high for the world to see."

Daylight broke over the horizon and Lilith watched over the stern as the squadron of ships drew nearer. Above her head she could hear the banner flapping and unfurling in the wind as Chibs hoisted it high above the deck. That horned skull and trident were known in these waters. The broken chain beneath them was Lilith's promise, her duty to fulfill.

"If they were wondering what was going on at

first…" Trina said stepping up beside Lilith as they glared through the bright sunrise at the approaching ships.

"They will certainly know now." Lilith cut in.

"It looks like one of them is taking up pursuit Captain." Trina shielded her eyes from the sun's gleam off the water to get a better look.

"Good." Lilith replied, looking over to a pair of her crew readying one of the stern guns. "Is she ready for firing?"

"Almost Captain. We've just got her brace ropes in place. I'll need to load her and it will take a round or two to get her ranged." One of the pirates answered.

"Be quick about it. We haven't much of a gap." Lilith peered over her shoulder and looked aloft to ensure the sails were taut. The Maiden lurched forward under a gust of wind and the banner over Lilith's head flapped in the change. One of the approaching ships did not alter course for the harbor and Lilith raised her looking glass to inspect the engaging vessel. On the bow a uniformed officer mirrored her action, looking at the Maiden through his glass.

"Is that cannon ready yet?" Lilith urged while the pirates at her side hurried.

"Almost, Captain. Loading powder and shot now." One of them replied as he rammed down the bag.

Across the gap of sea between the vessels Lilith heard the oncoming ship's deck bell begin ringing furiously, followed shortly by a rattling drum roll as the navy crew aboard her beat to their battle quarters.

Lilith lowered her looking glass and looked over at the gun crew by her side, "They've seen the banner.

Fire when ready!"

Nassau, Bahamas
19 Mar 1809

Urgent pounding sounded on the door. "Governor! Sir are you all right? Sir, open the door." A muffled voice on the other side cried in panic. Will looked through the window frame to see Lewis extending his hand toward him in a gesture to help him with the step up.

"We have to go Lieutenant! Hurry!" Lewis said with pleading eyes.

Will took his hand and hoisted himself through the window frame. Outside the governor's mansion was a small expanse of low shrubs before the dense forest. In the moonlight, the darkness ahead was a formidable and eerie unknown. As his foot hit the soft soil below the window, Will could hear the voice on the other side of the door was growing more frantic by the second. Before Will's second step landed the man was kicking at the door trying to force his way into the study. Will propelled himself behind Lewis and the two men ran for the tree line. The sound of breaking wood split through the broken window frame behind them, and shouts and cries echoed behind the pair as they vanished into the tree line.

Will's uniform shirt and jacket soaked through in perspiration as he followed Lewis through the thick woods. Lights from Nassau intermittently pierced the dark spaces between trees, flashing in his eyes as they ran. Noises from the town streets floated on the air, barely audible of the racing heartbeat in Will's ears. His veins pulsated with adrenaline. His heat seemed as if it were going to beat its way out of his chest. His ribs hurt and soon his legs ached from the mad sprint. Lewis' feet skittered to a halt causing Will to almost collide with him in the darkness. Will doubled over, trying to catch his breath from the shock and exertion. His head spun and he felt faint. Lewis' sweaty hand firmly clasped onto the back of Will's neck and Will looked up into his companion's face. Lewis held a finger up to his mouth in a quieting gesture. Ahead of them, the streets of Nassau appeared to be completely unalert to the crimes that had just occurred.

"We have to make it to the docks Lieutenant." Lewis whispered.

"We cannot be seen on the streets. The garrison will be sounding an alarm any moment now and soldiers will be out looking for us." Will huffed between stifled breaths.

"To go around Nassau will take us too long Lieutenant. We must go, now. You should take off your navy coat and maybe we won't be noticed." Lewis' voice was urgent.

Will hesitated, giving Lewis a scornful look of doubt, "We won't make it through town without being discovered. But, perhaps we can get enough of a lead on them to outrun their pursuit." He shifted his officer's coat off of his shoulders and discarded it into the darkness. Will thought about discarding his sword also, thinking it may draw more attention but decided to keep it. "Should we be confronted, I'd rather be armed." He said, shifting his scabbard slightly.

"I think it will slow you if we have to run." Lewis looked back to the street. "Let's go."

Lewis stood in the shadows and walked through the remaining trees out into the sporadically lit street. The night was late, but Nassau was still lively with traffic between taverns and bawdy houses. Merchants had gone from peddling their wares to drinking away their worries and the sounds of revelry echoed from open doors and windows lining the street. As Will made his way onto the rough cobbled street he fussed at his blouse, trying his best not to appear as disheveled as he felt. He felt the eyes of every stranger passing by sizing him up. His heart skipped with every eye contact he made, and his thoughts were a flurried mess of paranoia and urgent escape. Lewis weaved his way between pedestrians and soon Will was long stepping at his heels to keep up. Then the teeth rattling clang of bells began. Women cried out. Music within the taverns ceased and all forms of people spilled to the street to see what the alarm was being raised for.

"Lewis. Run! Run, we must go, now!" Will bolted into a sprint while calling to his companion over his shoulder.

Lewis seemed to be disoriented for a moment. Cries echoed from the far end of the street behind them, near the governor's mansion. Will reached back and grabbed Lewis' arm dragging him along behind as he ran towards the docks. The garrison lay ahead of them, along the side of the street just a few hundred yards from the docks where their means of escape to the Maiden was tied up.

"There they are! Stop them!" a soldier cried out from

behind them.

Will kept pulling on Lewis' arm until the young man's strides exceeded his own. Shots rang out, sizzling over their heads through the lamp lit night air. More people cried out and all along the streets the foot traffic scurried for the safety of indoors. Will glanced back over his shoulder to see a small group of soldiers from the governor's mansion was in chase. Another volley of shots echoed through the night and Will could feel as shots whizzed by him. Ahead, Lewis stumbled on the cobble losing his pace for a split second. The garrison doors opened spilling light from within out onto the street as a complement of red coated soldiers rushed into a line formation. Will reached to pull Lewis back, looking for a side alley they could duck into. Alongside a blacksmith shop between them and the formation of soldiers a narrow alleyway opened in between buildings. Giving Lewis an encouraging push Will drew his sword with his other hand, "The alleyway Lewis, there!" The two dashed toward the darkened gap between shops, missing a volley of shots as they careened off the walls in hisses and pops. It was a narrow space, dark except for light spilling through intermittent curtained windows.

"You there! Stop!" a voice shouted from the alleyway entrance as Will and Lewis scurried their way through the narrow passage. A shot cried out, singing its whine as it slipped past Will and buried itself into the wooden wall behind him.

"Go Lewis! Go!" he shouted, hearing soldiers piling their way into the alley's entrance.

Up ahead, Will could see another lamp lit street, the dim lamp glow offered an opening from their cramped dark passage and revealed no signs of hostile soldiers as far as Will could see. Lewis stumbled into the street first with Will right behind him. The voices of soldiers funneled through the narrow alleyway behind them.

"This way Lewis, this way!" Will shouted to his companion, running in the direction of the docks. "We can still make it!" Ahead of them Will spied an oil lantern hanging from a post outside of a shop. The stable two buildings down caught his eye next. Will drew his sword at a full run and while passing the lantern, hooked its handle with the tip of his blade. The lantern came free and slid down to Will's waiting off hand. In an arcing throw, Will slung the lantern at the open stable. Oil sloshed inside of the lantern as it flew toward a pile of dry straw and the flame engulfed the space inside of the caged glass globe. On its impact the glass shattered sending fingers of flame racing outward, engulfing the straw and licking along the wooden walls of the structure.

Will's lungs burned from the sprint, and he could feel fatigue taking its hold of his legs. Lewis made a sudden turn as the street came to a tee intersection and for a brief moment exited Will's view. Digging deep for strength to continue his pace Will took a deliberately deep breath and urged his legs on faster rounding the corner. As he came around the corner, he saw Lewis come to a stop. Will tried to slow himself, his boots scraping on the rough street to avoid colliding with Lewis, but he slid right into his companion's back, toppling them both to the ground in an unceremonious heap.

"Lewis, what in God's name?" Will shouted as he struggled to pick himself up.

"Soldiers." Was all Lewis could manage.

Will's heart dropped as he looked up to see a line of soldiers to their front, advancing with their muskets at the ready.

"This way Lewis, hurry, we must go." Will struggled to his feet and pulled Lewis' arm to help him up. A single shot rang through the street singing off the cobble near Will's feet. At his side, Will could see Lewis stumble in a jerking motion.

"My leg, Lieutenant. Agggh…" Lewis groaned, falling back to the cobble. "That shot hit me, Lieutenant, go, go and leave me."

Will looked up toward the approaching soldiers, then in the opposite direction. Another line of red coats had formed and began approaching from that direction also. Looking back down at Lewis, Will could see his leg was opened just above his knee. Dark blood poured onto the cobbled street below him, pooling in the crevices between stones.

"You there! Stop! Don't move or we will open fire again!" a voice called from the closest formation of soldiers.

Lewis' eyes met Will's, "Run. You can't let them take you."

"No. I won't be running." Will stooped to apply pressure to Lewis' leg wound, letting his sword clatter to the ground as the soldiers formed a circle around them.

"You both are under arrest for the murder of

Governor Culbertson." The soldier who had ordered them to stop continued his commands, turning to the soldiers next to him. "Shackle them and get them in a cell. We will deal with them once the fire is out and order has been restored."

"Yes Sir." A burly soldier answered, stepping forward and grabbing Will's upper arm.

Will struggled against the soldier's grasp, "He is wounded and cannot walk. He needs pressure on that wound or he will die before you have had your chance at justice."

The lead soldier appeared annoyed, "I care if the Negro dies?" he turned to the soldier trying to grab Will, "Get him restrained and get him into a cell damn it."

Will looked at Lewis with a mournful glare. They young man's eyes were clear, he understood what was going to happen and he was ready to face it. "I am sorry." The soldiers hauled Will to his feet, instantly loosing another rush of blood from Lewis' leg. Another pair of soldiers grabbed Lewis and bearing most of his weight hauled him up as well. Will resisted their grip at first, trying to pull free until a musket stock was slammed square between his shoulder blades.

The forced march to the garrison was a parade of misery. Will tried every few steps to wrest himself free from the soldiers holding him, desperately wanting to aid Lewis as his life faded with every step. At first the young man was able to hold his head up and respond to Will's cries but after only a few minutes of walking Lewis' head hung limp, bobbing while the soldiers drug him alongside their quick gait. Will screamed, pleading with their captors to let him help Lewis. Their stone disposition was unflinching, unmoved by his pleas. Smoke fogged the street, stinging Will's eyes and burning his lungs, causing his voice to go hoarse amid his screaming pleas. The fire from the stables had spread to another building. Embers floated on the breeze through thick clouds of smoke and ash. Will could feel the heat from the fire he had set soaking his skin as it emanated from the blaze.

The explosion came as the party escorting Will and Lewis was nearing the garrison entrance. It rocked the street, throwing debris and flames high into the air and toppling the soldiers over as the concussion wave pelted their bodies. Will's ear rang with a pitched whine as debris fell all around him. Ash and smoke hung in the air, sticking to Will's sweat soaked face and blouse. He reached out and pulled himself in a crawl towards Lewis. The young man had been shocked to consciousness by the force of the explosion and his wheezing pants told Will that his shipmate was in dire distress. As Will pulled himself the last few feet toward Lewis he could see his officer sword laying on the ground. Will grabbed the handle and using the point against the rocky paved road pushed himself up to his feet. The soldiers lying about began to move, checking themselves for wounds and staggering to their feet. Will stood over Lewis, swaying from shock and fatigue he turned and faced the soldiers as they recovered from the blast.

"You won't lay another hand on him, so help me. I'll run every last one of you through." Will said between ragged wheezing. "Do your worst."

The first soldier to challenge Will came at him with a fixed bayonet, lunging in the typical fashion soldiers were trained to. Will parried, losing a bit of balance before recovering enough to counter by running his blade edge across the young soldier's neck, sending a spray of crimson from the wound. The next came with a sword similar to Will's, a back hand slash that Will defended but only just in time. The following attack was defended earlier, and Will countered by running his blade point first into the soldier's chest, dropping the man to his knees where Will pushed his blade free. He raised the point of his sword back into a ready position, waiting for the next soldier to engage him only to find that the remaining men were standing in a hesitant half circle around him. Will darted his eyes between each man, sizing up who would be the next attacker. The crashing impact on the back of his head came with a blinding lightning bolt of pain. Will dropped to his knees and fell forward onto his face his sword slipping from his clutch as the world around him went dark.

'North Wind'
20 Mar 1809
Near Nassau, Bahamas

An eerie orange glow flickered from Nassau as North Wind eased her way near the harbor. Reports of a fire and gunshots had been enough to coax Admiral Torren up to the bow. He scoured the coastline through his looking glass, tracing the rocky shore up to the edge of Nassau for any sign of hostile parties.

"Sail Ho! Making a hard turn southward, she's south of the island!" a lookout up in the rigging called down.

Admiral Torren didn't wait for the watch officer, "What colors is she flying sailor?"

The lookout, high aloft the foremast was looking through a looking glass himself, though smaller. He pulled the brass tube down from his eye and held it up in frustration, "I can't see that she is flying any colors Sir."

"Keep watching her." Admiral Torren replied, then turning to Lieutenant Thatcher by his side, "Signal the Longsword to make pursuit of that vessel. Inform Captain Landreth to send his full complement of marines ashore and assist the garrison."

"Aye Sir. Did you still want me to accompany them Sir?" Lieutenant Thatcher asked with a slight grimace.

"Damn your coward's heart Lieutenant. Just do as I have instructed. I ought to send you just to temper your nerves, but I am not." Admiral Torren snapped, his typically amiable nature fading.

"Yes, Sir. Right away." Lieutenant Thatcher grimaced a little at the admiral's scolding and departed to relay his commands.

Admiral Torren kept his stare locked onto the silhouette of Nassau. Whatever chaos was consuming the town had not died down, more gunshots floated through the night. He traced his looking glass over the tops of the buildings, seeing the column of thick smoke rising, illuminated a bright orange by what he knew must have been a raging fire. Embers and ash floated in the air, swirling in the heated wind. The admiral let down his looking glass, squinting to restore his eyes' focus. An explosion split the darkness, thundering through the night air and sending a jolt of flame soaring high above the building tops. The concussion rolled from the coast, landing on the North Wind in a gentle wave the admiral could feel on his face. Hands across the deck went still for a moment, looking at the source of the explosion.

"What are you looking at? Back to work!" a petty officer howled at the idle deck hands.

Admiral Torren snapped around, walking at an urgent pace towards the quarterdeck. Mid way through his jaunt, Lieutenant Thatcher caught him as the young officer was on his way back to rejoin the admiral where he had been at the bow.

"I've relayed your orders Sir. Everything is being executed now." The lieutenant turned to match his commander's stride.

"Change in plans lad. We will be joining the landing party. Signal to the fleet, have the Taurus and the Destiny send a complement of marines ashore along with us as well. Whatever chaos reigns in Nassau, we will bring it to heel and establish some order. I'll not have another of our colonies fall to anarchy." The admiral rattled out without breaking stride at all. "And I said US lad, you will be joining me with the lads ashore and I won't hear a squabble about it." Admiral Torren turned to the watch officer near the helm, "Beat to quarters."

The admiral left the deck into his cabin, leaving the lieutenant on deck to deal with his changes and adjust to his new task under the moonlight as deck hands readied for action around him and a drum rattled on its signal.

Inside his cabin, Admiral Torren opened a chest of his personal belongings. He found a broad leather belt with a scabbard loop and a pair of leather thongs to attach a brace of pistols. Flag officers traditionally don't participate in combat, rather they lead and make the strategic decisions that set the conditions for the success of their junior officers. The admiral buckled the belt around his middle and drew his officer sword down from its resting place on his cabin wall. He held the blade up to the lantern light. It had been ages since it had been wielded against an enemy. After inspecting the edge and finding it to his satisfaction Admiral Torren sheathed the blade in its scabbard and attached it to the belt. Digging into the chest, he found a pair of ornate pistols. After inspecting these in the same manner he tucked them into his belt and made his way back on deck.

Each oar stroke propelled the longboat through the low chop of the falling tide. Admiral Torren sat among the marines in the bow, giving encouragement to each man and regaling Lieutenant Thatcher with tales of landing parties he had led long ago.

"I shored H.M.S. Red Fin in Egypt more than a decade ago. We were hunting for survivors of a Barbary pirate crew after we sunk their vessel off the coast. It was hotter than hell there, dreadful place. We shored a full complement of marines from three different line ships and tore through Alexandria in search of those buggers. Unsuccessfully. But, you will find no better soldier than a Royal Navy Marine, son. They are enthusiastic and competent, if not a touch too aggressive. I count that from being penned up aboard ship without an enemy in striking range for such long stretches, when the bastards do get to ply their trade, it's usually boarding warfare, some of the nastiest business you could imagine." Admiral Torren looked over his shoulder at the marines behind him, "You boys can sort this little mess out in a hurry I'm sure of it."

"Right we will Sir." One of the marines replied, "Lads, fix bayonets and check your loads, we'll be ashore in minutes. Expect anything and keep the admiral safe.

"I'll handle myself lad." The admiral scorned, "Bring Nassau under control and report to me at the garrison."

Gravel and sand crunched beneath the wooden hull of the longboat and the marines piled their way out, rushing ashore to accomplish their task. Admiral Torren patiently let the marines ashore before he stood and as dignified as he could, stepped ashore onto the soft sand. Lieutenant Thatcher remained glued to his side and a pair of marines remained with him as his personal security detail. Four more longboats landed as the admiral looked on, two from the Taurus and two from the Destiny. The marines quickly formed into three columns at the edge of Nassau and marched inland.

The admiral walked with two marines at his side and Lieutenant Thatcher hot on his heels. The admiral smiled in a dry half grin as he heard the marines shouting orders at local residents up the street. Smoke wafted from the remains of the structure that had burned while beams and timbers still smoldered in a slight breeze. The early coolness of dawn was setting in over the island and glowing rods of light began to radiate from the eastern horizon illuminating the town under it. Turning up the street toward the garrison, the admiral was delighted to find clear streets with marines posting themselves on each corner and a formation moving inland to secure the governor's mansion. As he approached the entrance to the garrison Admiral Torren greeted the pair of soldiers flanking the entrance.

"Fear not. His majesty's naval service is here to restore order. Is the post commander about? I should like to visit with him." Admiral Torren smiled at his own verbal jab; the soldiers looked weary.

"Colonel Bighton is in his quarters, Sir. I will send for him." One of the soldiers replied, his face was drawn and tired and he let out a deep sigh as he turned to pass word to his commander.

"Pass along my compliments as well, son. I was only jesting about your rescue." The admiral added, patting the tired soldier on his sunken shoulder.

"It's not far from the truth Sir. With the assassination of the governor and the fire, we've been wondering what would come next." The remaining soldier said through a dry cracking throat.

Admiral Torren's grin faded, and he furrowed his brow. "The governor of Nassau has been assassinated? When did this happen?"

"Last night Sir. That's what started all of this." The soldier answered, wiping his forehead underneath his hat with his sleeve.

"Was the assassin caught? Do you have him here?" the admiral pressed with an urgent tone.

"Yes, Sir. It was a pair of them actually. One of them was shot in the leg, he's likely dead by now." The soldier replied. "The other is a pirate, we believe. He's shackled in a cell. He killed two men when we were subduing them."

"I see. I shall want to see this man as soon as is possible." Admiral Torren said through a sigh before turning to Lieutenant Thatcher, "Signal the fleet to form a defensive line around the harbor. And get me word on the Longsword as well. I want to know if she is still visible and if she has relayed anything back to the fleet."

The admiral sent his marine with his lieutenant to relay his orders and messages. *I want him concentrating on the damned signal flags, not looking over his shoulder the whole time.* Once inside the garrison, Admiral Torren was greeted by Colonel Bighton.

"Alistair. It's been forever, in fact, the last time we spoke I believe you were still a captain. Congratulations are in order." The colonel said with an exuberance that Admiral Torren found to be inappropriate, annoying even, given the circumstances.

"Perhaps another time Colonel, I think it would be more fitting to dispense with the pleasantries and report your situation. Everything in its proper turn, am I right Colonel?" The admiral replied with a snap, not even attempting to disguise his irritation.

"Of course, of course. Well, as I'm sure the gossips I posted to the gate have informed you, our Governor Culbertson was the victim of an assassination plot last night. I am still gathering the details of how exactly it unfolded myself. But we do have the assassins in custody. Pirates, I believe. One of them is a damned Negro, he was shot in the leg last night and probably won't live out the day. I'm surprised he is alive now to be honest." Colonel Bighton rubbed his fingers on his mustache and then folded his arms across his big belly. "The other one, he's another matter entirely. He killed two of my men when they were taking him into custody, with this."

The colonel pulled up a sword off a wooden table in the courtyard and extended the handle end to Admiral Torren. A cold chill gripped the admiral through his ribs, sending goosebumps up his spine and down his arms and legs. The sword was a Royal Navy officer sword.

"You said you believe him to be a pirate?" Admiral Torren inquired, raising his brow while looking at the colonel. Several things seemed off and the colonel's temperament was suspicious.

"There has been talk, Admiral. I've heard from merchantmen and whalers. There is a pirate crew of blacks roaming the Caribbean, freed slaves taking their revenge on the civilized world." The colonel held out his hands with his palms extended upward, "They could have taken that sword from any navy ship."

"If you have been hearing these things, then why is this the first I am being made aware of it. The governor in Barbados was the first and only report we have received in London, despite being more distant than this colony. Why is that Colonel? Why would you hear these things and not share these details?" The admiral had gone from annoyed to accusatory, his tone terser by the minute.

"Well, I, I thought the governor had sent a communique. He advised that he was sending for additional reinforcements for the garrison and sea power to investigate the rumors." Colonel Bighton guffed, visibly embarrassed by the admiral dressing him down in front of his troops.

"Right. You thought he had. What exactly are you doing down here, that a civilian would be left to request reinforcements for you. It appears that you know how and where to procure rations. That part you have nailed down. But reporting and requesting reinforcements seems to have eluded you somehow. My question is how you are still in command of a garrison at all, Colonel." The admiral scathed, "And all of these shortcomings have created such a deficiency with your garrison that you have somehow allowed the governor of your colony to be assassinated by a pair of renegades. Colonel. With honor so wounded, please, return to your quarters. You are hereby relieved of your command."

Colonel Bighton's face flushed a hot red. He turned his gaze to the ground and then back up to the admiral. "The prisoners are being held in the cells by our arms room. You can find them there."

The admiral's face turned from disdain to disbelief, "A fine place to house a prisoner, don't you think? Next to your armory you say? Please, Colonel, leave me."

As the colonel slunk off in shame toward his quarters, Lieutenant Thatcher and his accompanying marine burst into the garrison front gate. "Admiral! Admiral, the Longsword has signaled back to the fleet! The vessel they are pursuing is flying black colors!"

'Shark Fin'
19 Mar 1809
24 Degrees 56' N, 77 Degrees 18' W

Nighttime aboard ship was John's favorite. Busy work ceased, only the tasks related to keep the ship upright and on course were in the ship master's mind. On moonlit nights, when he climbed up high into the rigging he could look out over the waters and watch as they shimmered in the moon's glow. Night also brought cool relief from the Caribbean sun which was relentless even in the early spring months. But when the gap of nightfall after the last fiery fingers of sunset burned away and before the moon rose her way up was John's pinnacle. He could be found high aloft looking up into the heavens, marveling at the blanket of stars. Out at sea, with no competing light, no mountains or building or trees or hillsides blocking their glory, the stars would reveal their secrets to him. The stars could sing glorious harmonies, beginning their song as the sun slipped away. The rising wonders would serenade him under their glow, brilliant jewels of light splayed out into an endless sea of inky black. The milky way weaving its path across the sky was like a rising crescendo, which would build its summit as the moon edged her way over the eastern horizon to steal the show.

The moon. She intrigued John, as she did many of

the sailors. Her gravitational field controlled the tides, which sailors set the pace of their lives to. Her relative distance to many constellations was a good indicator of time and the light she reflected down in her fuller states made deck work at night almost pleasant. The moon's crater scarred face inspired many sailors' imagination, claiming they could make out an image of this thing or that person. Some would say they saw a man's face; others would claim to be able to see a beautiful woman the debate among sailors was universal, and never ending.

John had climbed the foremast rigging as high as his recently frayed nerves would allow and was gazing into the nature's tapestry in the heavens. Bells sounded for the watch to change and the faint silvery glow of the moon rising crept over the horizon. His eyes locked upwards, John didn't even notice the man climbing up into the rigging to take over his post.

"Did you not hear the bells?" the man grumbled, "Or do you hate sleeping below deck as much as I do?"

"No, no I heard them. I'm… just…" John's voice trailed as he traced his eyes over the formation of Orion the hunter. The streak of a meteor flashed in a sudden brilliant glow as it streaked its way past Orion in the direction of Taurus the bull. "What are the chances of that? It's almost as if Orion were loosing his arrows at the beast!" John exclaimed pointing to the figures above.

"What in the hell are you talking about?" the man growled with a confounded stare. John could detect a note of irritability in his voice but ignored it.

"The constellations, the magnificent show overhead

every night. How can you not enjoy it?" he asked, finally dropping his gaze down to the man beside him. It was the man who had scrambled aboard right after John in Tortuga. His face was still marred by cuts and bruises, but the disfiguring swelling had waned to the point where he would be recognizable.

"I quit skylarking when I was a boy. I've no time or interest anymore." The man guffed, tilting his head away in annoyance.

"The stars hold many secrets and are still the keys of navigation to a master sailor. I take pleasure in gazing and spotting constellations. One of the few things aboard ship that can be a pleasure." John replied, dismissing the man's curmudgeonly demeanor.

"Well, I would agree with you on that, there are far too few comforts or pleasures on a ship." The man said with a change in tone, "Are you going below, I am here to relieve you. It's awfully rude to dismiss my discomfort of missing sleep by remaining here while one of us could be resting. Preferably me."

"I don't believe we have met, properly." John ignored the man's complaint and extended his hand, "My name is John Tarley."

"Tim Sladen." Tim took John's hand, suddenly seeming to take interest in the conversation. "Say there. Are you the sailor who survived the attack of those pirates?"

John's stomach turned and he felt a wave of heat rush up into his face. "Yes, I am. But I'd rather not talk about it."

"Well. I'd rather not sit on a yard high enough to kill a man with a fall listening to child's talk about starlight. But here I am." Tim's voice was antagonizing and sarcastic. "We have something in common, you and I."

"What's that?" John looked back at the man, perplexed.

"We have both survived an encounter with pirates. Maybe, we have both survived the same crew. But you don't want to talk about it. I understand." Tim said, his voice was coarse, but his words baited John.

"How would we know, if it was the same crew?" John asked, feeling a knot forming in his stomach. Revisiting the sequence of the last attack was not a pleasant task and John would have preferred to spend his time gazing high into the heavens.

"What did their banner look like?" Tim pressed, his voice gained a demanding tone and his stare locked onto John.

"Well, it was a black field, with a wretched looking skull. Like a devil skull, with twisting horns." John said recalling the large flag as it billowed over the stern of the pirates' ship through the fog of that morning.

"Yes, and what else?" Tim said, urging him on.

"There was a spear as well. Behind the skull, canted like, at an angle." John continued, hoping to satiate Tim's interest.

"Was there a chain? A broken chain, across the bottom of the field?" Tim kept on.

"Well, yes. Now that I think of it, there was. Was it the same crew who attacked you?" John asked realizing the interest that Tim felt.

"Indeed, it was. Now, this is important. Because I've only seen the crew from afar and heard what rumors tell. The captain of this ship. Tell me, did you see the pirates' captain?" Tim edged his way a bit closer along the yard.

John began, "I did. She was…"

"She?" Tim interrupted, "They are led by a damned woman?"

"A girl more like. I would put her younger than I, to be honest. She's a black girl too, mixed maybe. Beautiful, but the things she did to the captain…"

"You mean she wasn't the captain? I'm not interested in your savage crush boy; I want to know who commands the pirates." Tim snapped, causing John to lean back in surprise.

"No. She killed my ship's captain! Tied the mate to a mast, threw me overboard and drowned the entire crew as she sunk the ship! She is beautiful like I said, but that girl is after blood. And her crew…" John's voice slipped away for a moment. His scabbed shoulder injury throbbed as he mentally writhed over the images his mind conjured of the crew slowly slipping beneath the waves. Struggling against their bondage to the mast.

"What about her crew boy?" Tim kept pressing.

"They are a mix of blacks and white men. But mostly blacks, men and women." John said, he took a stay line in hand and rose to make his climb down. The night had been pleasant while it lasted, but this Tim fellow wouldn't allow him to enjoy it any longer.

"What would you say if I told you it was that same crew that sunk the vessel I was on?" Tim quipped, looking up at the young man attempting to leave.

"What? When?" John felt an urge to plant his seat

back onto the yard.

"It was last fall. I was aboard a navy vessel; we were hunting the pirates after they sacked Kingston and killed the governor there. We pursued her for days. She sunk several of the ships in our party, including a line ship of the Royal Navy. They led us to the mouth of a cove, and the captain on our vessel took the bait and ran us right into a reef. Those pirates opened fire on us while we were lodged on the coral formation. I barely escaped with my life." Tim's words flowed, each phrase grabbing John's attention a little more at a time.

John was hooked in now, "How on earth did you escape with your life?"

"I bailed over the side as the ship was breaking up. The tide rolled me into the coral, shredded my body, but it couldn't break my will. I made it ashore and walked until Tomas found me. He brought me back into good health and arranged my passage on this ship. So I might have my revenge for all those lost shipmates." Tim replied. His eyes locked onto John's. "I will see that ship and every last one of her pirate horde dip beneath the waves and sink to the depths."

John perched in a squat on the yard, holding a stay line in one hand. "When I first came ashore in Haiti, I was picked up by a French merchantman. He told me the pirates were hunting slave runners."

"Was your vessel smuggling slaves?" Tim inquired, raising his eyebrow.

"Well. Yes, we were, among some other cargo." John answered, looking down to the deck. The moonlight had unleashed her glow on the water's surface, bathing everything in a silvery pale hue. The deck looked to be miles away beneath them. The eastern horizon was forming in a glowing line far away as the sun sent its first rays to herald its arrival.

"What was to be your next destination? Were you made aware of it?" Tim pried, snapping John from his hypnotic appreciation of the moon's intoxicating light show.

"I did hear the captain and the mate arguing about it. We were going to make sail for Nassau and then Charleston." John scratched at his head, wondering what difference it made where his sunken former vessel was destined.

Tim cracked a wide smile and mumbled something John couldn't hear. Off in the distant darkness, beyond the visibility from moonlight a deep thud echoed through the night air. Both men snapped their eyes forward, to the north, straining to make out where the sound could be coming from.

"Was that a cannon shot?" Tim's voice was suddenly snapping, almost hostile.

"I can't say. It sounded like it could be. Can you see anything out there?" John asked as he squinted, trying to find anything in the darkness to make sense of the noise they had heard. Another thud echoed, barely audible over the constant whisper of wind and the creak of rope and wood. Voices filtered up through the rigging from on deck. The chop of waves against the ship's hull sounded in a steady succession. The space between noises grabbed John and Tim's ears, holding their attention. Another thud sounded, followed by a faint whistle. The two men looked at each other in a shock state.

"Shots! Cannon fire out ahead!" John called down.

John saw the men on deck freeze as they heard his alarmed shout. The sailors in the bow exchanged looks, one of them turned up to where John and Tim sat perched aloft the foremast yard.

"Cannon fire? Are you sure?" he called up.

"Yes. Yes I heard it once, I just heard it again. A thump, the last one followed by a slight whistle." John called back down. He looked over to Tim, who remained silent through the exchange. Only offering a nod of approval to reinforce John's appraisal of the sound they had heard.

The men on deck hurried to the rail, several of them taking up a perch near the bowsprit and scanning the horizon.

"Can you see anything? A sail? Flashes?" the sailor who called back up.

"No. But I know it was cannon fire. Go roust the captain!" John replied, pushing down a tinge of panic that threatened his nerves. He felt an urge to get himself down, out of the rigging and off the foremast yard. Memories of his crashing plunge beneath the water's surface cascaded through his mind.

"There. There it is!" Tim said pointing out to the horizon.

John's mind seemed to blur a little, he felt a dizzy wave grab him as he was looking down. The webbed ratlines were calling to him, begging him to run for safety below. "Where?"

"North of us, on the edge of the dawn's light." Tim shook his arms to emphasize where he was looking.

John looked up, breaking his longing gaze at the ratlines. Far in the distance, at the edge of the growing light of dawn a dark set of silhouettes caught his eye. A low-lying dark spot, long and barely above the horizon showed an island ahead. Scanning just to the east of it, two dark forms were visible. A flash erupted between them, followed by the faint thud they had heard earlier.

John cupped his hand around his mouth to amplify his voice, his heart beat hard in his chest, and he had to force himself to gather air in order to call down, "Sails on the horizon. Land spotted too! Looks like there's a pair of ships about to get to it!"

Chapter 10

20 Mar 1809
Nassau, Bahamas

Will awoke to the shock of cold water being thrown on him. He wheezed and coughed as a hand grabbed his hair, lifting his face upward. Another splash of water hit him, soaking him and covering his torso in chill.

"This is the man?" a voice asked. The voice was familiar to Will.

"This is him." Another voice confirmed.

"He looks familiar to me. But damned if I can't quite place it." The first voice said, "What is your name?"

Will shook his head to try and clear his eyes. His vision remained bleary and distorted. His hands and wrists ached, and he pulled at them, realizing he was bound at each wrist, holding his arms in tension out to his sides and above his head. Will couched more. His head throbbing with a splitting pain that spiked with every cough.

"Your name, damn you. What is your name? Or

have they cut your tongue out?" the familiar voice demanded.

Will pushed himself up from his knees, standing to relieve the strain from his arms. "My name is William Pike."

"Lieutenant Pike. Lieutenant William Pike? Of the Royal Naval service? You stood in front of me not even a year ago for a promotion review Lieutenant! What in God's name has happened to you?" the voice snapped. Will knew the voice. It was Admiral Torren.

"Quite a lot Sir. None of it good." Will replied, biting his lower lip from the pain he felt at the back of his head.

"I should say so Lieutenant. Do you realize the implications of your situation? Murder? Treason?" the admiral scorned, his face finally becoming clear in Will's sight.

"Yes, Sir. I do. But, if I may, Sir. All is not what it would seem." Will said, his head spinning and throbbing.

"I should hope not. Although, I don't know quite how you could explain away obviously being involved in an assassination plot!" the admiral seethed, his face was hard as stone and beet red.

"I cannot explain it away, Sir. Only offer you my recounting of the events that have led me here." Will offered, squinting as a wave of throbbing pain enveloped his skull.

"I dearly wish you would Lieutenant." The admiral's tone softened, but only slightly. He turned and looked to one of the marines at his side, "Get me a chair if you would and something to drink." Leaning on his cane he looked back at Will. "Alright Lieutenant, get to it."

"You assigned me to the Valor as her First Lieutenant. I took that post and we sailed for the Caribbean. On our arrival here we were ordered by Governor Geor Alton of Kingston to conduct a search for a missing trade vessel, to no avail. When the search proved fruitless, Captain Grimes ordered us to make sail for Kingston with all haste." Will paused to take a breath as a chair was brought in for the admiral and he sat. "We were caught in a terrible storm in route to Kingston. As the storm waned, we spotted a pair of hostile vessels off our stern with the weather gauge on us. We made for the Jamaican coat to evade them…"

"Captain Grimes evading engagement? That would be the first I have ever heard of." The admiral interrupted, giving Will a scowl marking his disbelief.

"Valor had sustained some damage during the night, Sir. From the storm. We were a bit out of sorts to be engaging two vessels." Will continued, "As we approached the coast, we spotted the fleet with Admiral Sharpe's flagship, weathering the storm in a cove. Captain Grimes elected to turn off outside of the cove and engage the approaching vessels in order to divert them from bottling the fleet inside the cove."

"That's more Captain Grimes' speed." Admiral Torren said, shooting a look to the marine by the door.

"Yes Sir, we engaged the vessels as they made their approach and effectively drew them off from the mouth of the cove. Their return fire exacted a terrible cost, they killed several aboard, wounded the captain and myself as well as many more. In the aftermath, Admiral Sharpe visited as we made repairs. He outlined a suspicion he had that the governor of Jamaica was involved in some illicit plot and after we were able to make way, we departed for Kingston." Will grimaced again as he was overcome by a coughing fit, sending pangs of hot pain radiating from the back of his head. The taste of ash and blood dried his mouth, further aggravating his cough.

"Get him some water." The admiral said without breaking his glare on Will. "You mean to tell me that the King's governor of Jamaica was involved in some kind of conspiracy?"

Will was offered water from a cup held by one of the admiral's marines and he drank as deeply as he could before it was removed from his lips. "Yes Sir. Something to do with the slave trade. When we arrived in Kingston to accompany Admiral Sharpe as he confronted the governor, we were attacked by an organized force of mercenaries. They murdered Admiral Sharpe, fired on the fleet from Fort Charles sinking the Hunter and the Bayonet."

Admiral Torren held up a hand at Will. "That's quite enough. A fantastic tale, insulting that you would think I would believe as much. Also, it still doesn't explain how you have come to be here, away from your assigned duties, suspected of a murder and treason against the nation you have sworn yourself to serve. I have heard enough Lieutenant. You will be brought aboard my flagship, where I can legally try you for your crimes."

Will's heart sank. As the admiral spoke he imagined Captain Grimes' face in the final moments Will saw him alive. He remembered the fleet in Kingston harbor, helpless under the battery of Fort Charles as the guns were turned against them. Images of the admiral's body crumpling after the American had shot him flashed in his mind. Anger rose inside Will, flashing like a fire getting a sudden burst of wind.

"You can deny what I've told you admiral. But the truth will be revealed! The Crown has betrayed its subjects. The Order carries on with the slave trade and you are its puppet! Hang me if you wish, but you will be known in history as the coward who stood amongst the traitors of mankind!" Will screamed, ignoring the pain in his head, and rattling against his restraints.

The admiral stood as Will shouted his reply. His face remained unchanged, a stone expression of disappointment and loathing. "Hang you? Oh no. A simple hanging does not fit the crimes you are accused of. As far as I can tell, you are responsible for the murder of two governors. Not to mention Admiral Sharpe, who was a dear old friend of mine. And Captain Grimes? Was he grievously wounded by a daring pirate attack? Or was he murdered by his second in command so a young lieutenant who prematurely thought he deserved a captaincy could go play at anarchy? I've heard enough. You will stand trial aboard North Wind. Default will be at noon tomorrow. May God have mercy on your soul son."

The admiral turned to leave, looking back as he walked through the door to shoot another scornful look toward Will, shaking his head. Will was left in the barren cell. Unable to sit if he so much as knelt then his arms were suspended painfully overhead. His heart pounded in his chest. For the first time since leaving the Maiden he'd had a moment to consider what had occurred. Though Will had suspected something larger at play, Lilith never explicitly told him what she had intended to have done in their visit ashore. He felt another wave of anger. Betrayal. Will had served the Maiden loyally for months. He and Lieutenant Shelton had instructed their crew on all manner of seamanship, gunnery, and navigation. Will wondered if this hadn't been a planned disposal of him. A final use for the useful navy man. A square of daylight from the barred window marked hours of the day as it played its way across the floor. Will watched it work its way across his cell, tolling away his final hours.

Night brought a chill. The marine sentry standing guard outside of his cell entered in the waning hours of daylight and removed his shackles.

"Admiral Torren bids you rest well tonight. You will be standing trial tomorrow." The marine said as he released Will's restraints.

"Rest well. For you won't live out the day tomorrow." Will scoffed sarcasm. The marine regarded him with the same disdain the admiral had. *A fair trial it will be, I'm sure.* As the marine left Will watched with longing through the door, peering out to the courtyard of the garrison for some sign of hope. A pair of soldiers carrying Lewis' limp body out through the gates was all that met his eyes.

Dawn's light peered through the barred window, its arrival was being announced by every manner of singing bird outside. Will's eyes opened slowly. The sound of his cell door being unlocked clinked and rattled, echoing through the small room and the courtyard outside. Two marines stepped in. Wasting no time, they moved to Will and took hold of his arms, lifting him to his feet. Will was marched outside, where a formation of marines stood alert and ready. His two escorts took him to an anvil near the staircase leading to the upper ramparts. They watched as a smithy applied a set of wrist-bound shackles and chains to him, and then a set around his ankles as well. Once the restraints were in place, they took hold of Will again and marched him to the center of the formation. Will struggled to see his surroundings. Everything around him seemed to be moving in a blur. The garrison, the shackles, being marched in a formation out of the gate and onto the streets, it all seemed surreal. Like it was happening to someone else.

The streets of Nassau were lined by local citizens. Tradesmen and merchants, women and children all lined up along the route to the docks to catch their glimpse of the criminal who had murdered their governor and stolen their peace. As the column turned out of the garrison gate the townsfolk erupted into a chorus of shouted insults.

"Traitor!"

"Pirate scum!"

The roar of shouts muddled in Will's ears; he could only make out the loudest of individual shouts.

"Hang him here for all of us to watch!"

Will's heart beat harder and harder in his chest, making his head spin. The column marched its way through Nassau and turned at the street lining the dockyards. Will spotted the aging registrar he had met the evening of his arrival. The old man shook his head as the column passed and clunked its way down the wooden pier.

The procession ended where a set of longboats were all tied to the docks. Admiral Torren stood with his entourage at the moored boats.

The admiral looked over the formation as it stopped, he didn't even spare a glance toward Will. "Take the prisoner aboard and deliver him to North Wind. My longboat will follow. The fleet is covering your movement, men, there will be no rescue of this man today."

'Drowned Maiden'
21 Mar 1809
24 Degrees 40' N, 76 Degrees 44' W

"Unfurl those gallants and set auxiliary sails! She is gaining on us and fast!" Chibs called aloft, sending a lightning bolt through the crew of the Maiden. Pirates were working furiously to evade the pursuing ship. Lilith remained on the stern, watching as the distance closed and sizing up her opponent. The sun was edging its way over the eastern horizon, giving the wind a renewed vigor. Trina helped the stern gun crews reload as they fired intermittent shots to ward off the impending ship.

"Port side gun ready!" She called out.

"Fire." Lilith replied, holding up her looking glass to study the effectiveness of their gunnery.

The cannon roared, sending a nine-pound ball at the enemy ship with a screaming shriek. In the humid morning it left a slight vapor trail as the ball exited a cloud of gun smoke from the barrel of its cannon. A plume of water cascaded the bow of their pursuing ship. Lilith watched, waiting to see if they would alter course, slack their sails, anything indicating their fire was discouraging pursuit. Nothing. Her eye remained focused on the prow of the warship as waves broke along her bow lines. A sudden cloud of smoke emitted from the railing high on her bow near the bowsprit. A shriek whined through the air and Lilith turned over her shoulder, "Returning Fire!" The Maiden's crew braced for impact. The shot whistled nearby but impacted harmlessly into the sea, sending a skittering shower of water spraying high into the air.

"They have us in range now Captain! What are your orders?" Chibs called to Lilith.

A moment passed. Lilith's expression belied no fear, only deep concentration. "What are our odds against her? Can you make out her class Chibs?"

"She's a heavy warship Cap'n, our odds are, well, not good, at best." Chibs replied with a sobering look. Lilith could tell his concern was only growing.

"Then bend ever sail we have and pray the wind stays in our favor. Keep firing on her bow, maybe we can discourage them in the meantime." Lilith's stomach knotted as she spoke. She could feel the eyes of the crew upon her, looking to her to guide them. As she looked toward the helm, dutiful Omibwe with his awkward wooden leg and bright-eyed disposition was waving at her, urging her to come near. Lilith knew the young man had eyes for her. He was always striking up conversation and he lit up whenever she came near.

But this was a different urgency, Omibwe wanted something in a desperate way as he waved her over. Lilith walked her way over to the helm, stutter stepping as the Maiden lurched under new speed from the sails Chibs had ordered to be set.

"Captain Lilith, the doctor and I talked about a plan for something like this." Omibwe was beside himself, he made careful adjustments, watching the sails above as he spoke to Lilith, breaking his gaze only for a quick glance at his captain as he spoke.

"Sails on the horizon! A point off starboard bow, headed our way Captain!" a lookout aloft called down.

"Damn the luck! Hold on Omi, I will be back." Lilith clasped the handle of her cutlass at her side, biting her lower lip as her stomach turned harder. She made her way toward the bow, where a group of her crew was already forming along the rail, trying to see the new threat. Lilith extended her sight glass, raising it up to her eye as she approached to Maiden's bowsprit. Her eye took a moment to focus but, on the horizon, she could make out the form of sails and a hull. Not as big as the warship trailing her, but still a threat she must weigh in her maneuvers. Lilith bounded back toward the stern as she heard Trina's gun crew let another shot loose with a roar. A moment later the thumping report of return fire sounded, and another shriek sounded as the shot whizzed by the Maiden, closer than the last, but still missing. As she passed Omibwe on her way to the stern, Lilith held up her hand as the young man beckoned her to return. "In a moment Omi, I have to see to check on the gun crews."

"Did we hit them?" Lilith asked Trina when she

arrived back at the stern.

"No, Captain. But we were close. Closer than our last." Trina replied, hurrying to prime the powder bag that had just been loaded into the cannon. "We should score a hit this time, unless they slack their speed."

"It doesn't look like they intend anything of the sort." Lilith remarked, looking through her sight glass again. She felt like a bystander as a storm developed around her. A whiff of pipe smoke announced Chib's presence.

"What we need here is a stroke of damned luck. This standoff business won't last, especially with another ship in the mix now. We need something to give." Chibs' gravel voice usually brought Lilith a measure of comfort, regardless of what he had to say. Lilith appreciated his steady demeanor and experience.

"What would you suggest we do Chibs? I'm afraid I'm rapidly running out of my depth here." Lilith quieted her voice so only Chibs would hear her duress.

"Ah. It's simple Cap'n, try not to get us all killed." Chibs' teeth clamped onto his pipe stem.

Lilith pulled her eye from the sight glass, looking over at the bearded pirate as he smiled with a broad grin at his own quip. "I'm being serious Chibs. What do we do? We cannot turn and fight, especially with another ship approaching the bow. If they throw in against us also, likely since we are flying black colors, we won't live out the day."

"There's a young man at the helm. I just got done speaking with him, he's been waiting to talk to you. I think you should go talk to him." Chibs replied, grinning even wider as he did.

"Chibs, we don't have time for a chat. I need to make a decision!" Lilith was growing angry as Chibs continued to smile. "And I don't see how any of this is funny! Have you gone mad?"

"Long ago Cap'n, all the same. You should go visit with the boy. I think you'll find your solution." Chibs let a cloud of pipe smoke roll over his shoulder as he turned and walked away, taking the stairs down below deck.

"He's gone mad! Just when I need him most, my quartermaster has lost his mind." Lilith said aloud. Her eye lingered where Chibs had taken the stairs below deck, at the rear of the quarterdeck just behind the helm. Omibwe turned, catching Lilith's gaze, he waved her over just as urgently as before.

Turning back to Trina, Lilith patted her mentor on the shoulder, "Keep firing. I'll come up with something."

"Aye Captain." Trina said, while making an elevation adjustment.

Lilith walked to the helm, where Omibwe had been joined by Doctor LeMeux. "Ok, Omi. What is it that could not wait? We are in a bad spot here."

"Exactly, Captain. I have an idea I think can help us." Omibwe replied with a broad grin covering his face.

Lilith was growing tired of everyone finding such good humor in their plight. "What is your plan? What can get us out of this mess?"

"We need to sink that warship." Omibwe's smile grew as he looked over for a moment at Lilith.

A flush of anger rose in Lilith's cheeks, "I know that

Omi. We all know we need to sink her. We can't turn and fight now, especially with another ship coming our way!"

Doctor LeMeux raised his hand to interject, "If you will allow me Captain. I think what Omi is trying to impart here is that he has come up with a way for us to sink that ship. With some further development by yours truly, but the idea is fully to his credit."

Lilith squeezed the handle of her cutlass, grasping and flexing her fingers as her temper rose, hotter and hotter. "Doctor, out with it." Her eyes narrowed and her gaze fell solely on his face, Lilith could tell he was beginning to grow uncomfortable with her stare.

"A keg of powder, treated in tar and wrapped in a chain. We lower it over the side and run it back in a rope web attached to a line. Along with a lengthy fuse, once she gets close enough, we could blow a hole in her hull large enough to sink that damned tub and rid you of half your problem." LeMeux stuttered as he tried to get his whole thought out at once.

Lilith felt her anger soften and her curiosity rise. "We will have to draw her in closer then?"

"Oh surely. We could not do it at this distance." LeMeux answered, "We will surely need to draw her within range of her cannon fire. It is a plan, not a plan without risk Captain."

Lilith shifted her eyes between Omibwe and LeMeux, rolling over the idea in her mind. "What is to keep the fuse burning once the barrel is lowered over the side?"

"We treat the fuse by running it through some grease mixed with gunpowder and then covering it in wax.

That should hold the water out long enough for what we need." LeMeux offered.

"How will you know how much fuse you need?" Lilith asked as her doubts began to subside, a slow grin coming to her face as she realized what Chibs and Omibwe had known.

"I think, if we drop a similar sized barrel overboard, we could range the approaching ship in the same way we would a cannon. We drop the barrel over and time its float until it comes in line with the enemy ship's hull. Then we would burn a length of the fuse and mathematics will handle the rest." LeMeux beamed with pride at the plan.

"How much gunpowder will we need?" Lilith pressed swapping her gaze between LeMeux and Chibs as he reappeared at the stairs, coming up from below deck.

"A considerable amount, Captain. If we want to blow a hole in her hull, we need to create a very forceful explosion." LeMeux answered, following Lilith's stare over to Chibs who led the way for a pair of the crew who hefted a large barrel, wrapped in chain.

"We still have enough to swap rounds with a few ships, Captain. But I think this will prove to be of good use. Hell, we would go through this much powder trying to sink her with broadsides. This way should save us damage on the old girl and blood from the crew. I think it's a winning idea Captain." Chibs pulled his pipe from his mouth, waving it in Omibwe's direction, "The boy is starting to get the hang of this sailing thing. With good solid thinking like that, he could make for a fine captain someday."

"Or Quartermaster." Omibwe piped in.

"That too." Chibs replied, turning to Lilith, "What do you think Cap'n, should we give it a go?"

Lilith stepped up on the rail, grabbing a stay line and looking aft toward the approaching warship. They were gaining. "Aye Chibs. Make ready with our barrel bomb. Trina's gunnery doesn't seem to be discouraging them. Maybe a hole blown in her hull will give them something else to worry about."

'North Wind'
21 Mar 1809
24 degrees 51' N, 77 Degrees 5' W

Cool morning air had given away as the sun rode high into the noon position, beating down onto the deck of North Wind and prickling at Will's skin. A day breeze kept the temperature moderate, but the sun's rays were unrelenting. Will stood awaiting his fate, flanked by a marine sentry on either side and with his wrists and ankles shackled his hopes of escape seemed futile. On deck, hands were busy preparing for his emergency tribunal. A table and chair were set for the admiral, all hands seemed to be present and in an orderly formation. Will's legs ached as he stood waiting. *If this is to be my end, let's get on with it already.* He looked aloft, gulls flew in circles high above screeching and cawing, looking for an easy meal. The piercing blue sky belied no promise of foul weather. A fine day to put to sea.

A commotion erupted on the quarterdeck; sailors

began flurrying about the deck as if they were just given a new set of urgent orders. The table was taken away, followed by the chair. The admiral came out from his cabin, still clutching his cane. He paused in the doorway for a moment, looking over the deck of his flagship. Will could see a signal flagman begin flagging out orders to the other vessels in the fleet. He made out the word 'sighting' and 'pirate' before Admiral Torren stepped in front of him.

"Fate has granted you reprieve. Though I am not sure for how long, I could conduct your trial underway, but you may prove to be useful to me. For now. Consider every drawn breath a gift of my benevolent nature and begin coming to terms with being the embodiment of cooperation. It may be your salvation." Admiral Torren's glare was locked into Will's as he spoke, he moved his head slightly sideways and changed his tone for the marine sentries. "Take the prisoner to a cell in the hold. Do not remove his restraints. He is to be under constant guard. Am I clear?"

"Yes Sir." The marine at Will's left arm replied as they began to pull him across the deck to the stairs below. Will peered in the direction of the flagman again, trying to make out another signal. 'Missing'. His heart skipped. Was it the Maiden that was missing? Had Lilith evaded their pursuit? Or perhaps she'd turned to fight and left one of the admiral's ships along the bottom. His mind raced. As they walked to the stairs Will could hear the snap of canvas being set and felt the lurch of the great flagship beneath his feet. A petty officer growled at the sailors on deck, "Extra lookouts fore and aft! Another man for the crow's nest and make the deck guns ready!" Will's stomach knotted. Something drastic had occurred which he was unaware of. The marine sentries moved him along the deck, apathetic to the painful digging shackles that slowed Will's steps. As he descended the stairs Will took in the full measure of the warship. She was formidable, three decks of guns gave her the firepower to stand and exchange broadsides with anything floating. Will imagined her lining up against the Maiden and his heart sank. He hoped Lilith had the wits to avoid this seaborne behemoth.

Deep in the hold, Will was introduced to his cell in the dim yellow flicker of a lantern. A bucket in the corner to relieve himself and a small pile of damp straw to sleep on were all the cell contained. It seemed as though even the rats aboard were above his new living quarters. The marines opened the door, shoved Will inside and swung the door closed. Damp darkness enveloped him. The only light that entered his cell was the flicker of the lantern from out in the passageway shining in through the small, barred window in the door. The cell seemed so dark that the dim light couldn't penetrate, its meager rays retreating at the threshold of the door. Will felt utterly alone within the confines of the small cell. *This must be what Governor Alton felt.* A sudden wave of guilt wracked him as he thought of Governor Alton. The shocked look of pain and surprise as Lewis plunged his dagger through his back.

Will's head jumbled with a mix of emotions and thoughts. He felt betrayed by the pirates he had helped and a traitor to the nation he owed his allegiance to. He felt wronged by the system he had been a part of and grievously guilty for the wrongs that system was responsible for. Admiral Torren was disgusted by his predicament without fully understanding the circumstances which had led Will to be in that position to begin with.

A shift in the hull alerted Will that North Wind was making a hard turn. Above, he could hear footfalls and movement but only guess what was actually going on. Will crumpled onto the pile of damp straw and found that the rats indeed were not above occupying his cell as one scurried out of the straw as he sprawled onto it. Rattling drums signaling North Wind's crew to clear for action sprung Will to his feet. Instinctively he bolted to the door of his cell, looking out into the passageway. The dull lantern flame sputtered in its sooty, stained, glass globe, barely illuminating the corridor of the hold where his cell was located. Outside the door, a pair of sentries stood watch, conversing amongst themselves.

"What is going on?" Will asked, "Do you know what happened?"

"One of the marines huffed, turning to Will with an annoyed look, "Someone called the crew to beat to quarters."

"I know that. Why are they beating to quarters?" Will pressed as he tried to peer up the passageway, desperate to find out anything about what was occurring.

"Makes no difference to us. We're stuck here, guarding you." The sentry replied, then looking over to the other sentry, "I suppose you think you'd like to run on deck, dashing about with an officer's sword and barking out orders, eh?" The pair of them laughed.

"Yeah, I'm sure the admiral will call you up to lead a boarding party!" the other said as they laughed harder.

Will could feel his face flushing as a wave of anger rushed up to grip him. He was the butt of the sentries' jests, but their jokes were painful because they were pointing out truth and Will knew it. He knotted his fists tighter and tighter as the sentries outside his cell continued their prodding.

"Maybe the admiral will be turning over command of the ship to him next!" Raucous laughter followed. Will returned to the misery of his straw pile. His hands quaked in rage as the pair outside his door continued their onslaught.

'Southern Song'
24 Mar 1809
17 Degrees 44' N, 72 Degrees 14' W

A queasy feeling engulfed Rory, who awoke in the darkness of Southern Song's hold. Seawater sloshed at his feet in the cramped cell. For a moment he panicked, thinking the ship was in some form of peril. Voices above him carried on in the casual manner of the haphazard crew that manned the ship he was now a prisoner of. Rory winced from the painful throbbing through his head. It seemed to come in waves from the front of his skull and radiated along his scalp, penetrating deep down to his eye sockets and creeping into his neck. His arms still hung in short chains shackled to his wrists, which were raw from the unforgiving iron against his skin. As Rory gathered his bearings, he noted an odd movement of the ship. Or rather a lack of movement. Southern Song was gently yawing side to side without the heave of forward motion that came with being in the open seas under power of sail. Footsteps overhead grabbed his attention and Rory strained his ears to make out what they were saying. Another set of foot falls thumped overhead, these ones were softer than the others, followed by hostile shouts.

Rory tried to imagine what was occurring on deck. He pictured the crew revolting against their drunkard captain. That couldn't be it. There were no sounds of a battle, no guns firing, no sword clashes. Rory imagined they were being boarded by the Royal Navy or maybe the Americans. But the foot falls seemed too cluttered all around the deck above to be an orderly search of the vessel. When the weather hatch creaked its way open, Rory's heart fluttered with the realm of unknown possibilities. A swaying yellow light worked its way down the stairs to the hold. It shone from a soot-stained lantern globe in the hands of one of the Southern Song's crewmen. The sailor made his way down the steps, dragging along one dead leg in a painful gait. Rory craned his neck to see, holding back a grunt from the pain radiating from his head and the searing spike that came from any movement he made. Behind the lantern bearer, a line of figures descended the steps, their footwork hobbled by chains binding them.

Through the clanking of chains Rory tried to listen to

the sailor guiding them below deck. Another member of the Southern Song's crew brought up the rear of the line, giving the last of the prisoners a shove as they stepped from the stairs.

"Do we put them in a cell?" the lantern bearer asked turning to the sailor behind the line.

The sailor shook his head, "No room. Not with the prisoner we already have. Let's just leave them chained and keep them down in the hold. We can post a watch on the weather hatch to make sure they don't come rousing us in our sleep later, eh?"

The sailor holding the lantern lifted the dim light to shoulder height. "Well. What do you know? Looks like our fine friend has awakened. Awoke. He woke up!" the sailor stumbled over his words, stammering, and stuttering as he spoke.

His companion drew near to Rory's cell, dim yellow light washing over half of his face. Rory could see blood from a fresh wound on the man's face. "How about that? He thinks the old Southern Song is a tub! At least that's what he told the captain!" the wounded sailor looked at Rory hanging by his arms in the cell. "I'll bet the captain corrected that thinking, didn't he?"

Rory started to open his mouth to speak, but a jagged pain shot through his jaw, bringing a fresh wave roiling through the rest of his skull. He squeezed his mouth tight, feeling his lips against each other. They were swollen and cracked, and his bite didn't seem to line up correctly.

The sailor with the lantern looked at his friend and guffawed in a big wet belly laugh. "Looks like the captain knocked him speechless!" he turned to Rory.

"That'll show you. Talking about her like that. After all we've done for you. Not throwing you over for the sharks and all. We brought you some company."

His friend took a few strides forward, lurching around the chained prisoners in the murky hold. "Where are we going to fit em all? The captain's wanting to take on more you know!"

Rory's eyes traced over the faces of the prisoners. Their dark brown skin gleamed under the dancing light of the sailor's swaying lantern. Their faces looked sullen and defeated, eyes locked onto the wooden planks under their feet except for an occasional glance at Rory or their captors. One of them looked at Rory and for a moment their eyes met. It was a silent exchange. Rory felt a streak of compassion looking at their shackled wrists and ankles.

The sailors continued their angry debate. "Well, we can't just leave them loose in the hold! What if they get the notion to wander about? Maybe come up on deck and strangle us in our sleep?" the sailor with the lantern growled.

"Like I said! We'll post a watch on the hatch! Now come on! The captain will be after us for taking too long, there's more to stow aboard you know!" The two sailors made their way to the ladder well, only sparing a scornful passing glance at Rory along the way. The lantern bearer paused for a moment at the base of the stairs and shot a scouring look back over the prisoners. "Don't you be getting any ideas about storming the deck neither. We'll cut the whole lot of you down and toss you over for the sharks. You hear?"

A shout from the deck above caught the sailor's

attention and he turned up the stairs, climbing each step in a painstaking hobble.

Chapter 11

'Drowned Maiden'
21 Mar 1809
24 Degrees 37' N, 76 Degrees 44' W

The thunderous report of a cannon shot echoed across the shrinking sea gap separating the Drowned Maiden from her pursuer. The whistle of the shot was ear piercing. The navy ship, hot on their stern and beating closer by the minute was narrowing their aim from their bow guns. The last two shots had come dangerously close, and Lilith was growing impatient.

"Chibs! It's now or never, if she gets any closer, they're like to take out our rudder!" She called to the quartermaster as he made the final preparations on their improvised weapon.

"Just another minute or two Cap'n, we don't want to get this wrong!" Chibs called back. He was missing his trademark pipe and already his temper was suffering for it. "If it blows too soon, we will look like a bunch of dandy swinging lubbers. Give me a damned minute!"

On the quarterdeck, Doctor LeMeux was fussing

over the fuse. The test string he had burned was inconsistent, part of it burning quite rapid while other sections burned slower.

"I think we need to start over with the fuse Chibs, I really do." LeMeux insisted.

The salty quartermaster reached his hand back behind his head, balling it into a fist for a moment before opening his palm and rubbing the back of his head. "Doctor, then you go tell her that. You're welcome to whatever treatment you get, I promise it won't be pleasant." Chibs ran his hand around his jaw and stroked the graying chin of his beard. "Sometimes you just have to jump in with both feet and hold your breath. This would be one of those times."

"Chibs, I still don't think…" LeMeux began to voice another disagreement.

"Chibs! Are you waiting until they blow a hole in our ship?" Lilith shouted as another shot boomed from the warship. This one whistled loudest of all and punched a hole in their top sail, snapping a rigging line on its way through.

"Ready Captain! Let's get her lowered over the side and hope to God the boy's plan works!" Chibs leaned over LeMeux tugging hard on the rope webbing that wrapped around their hopeful ship killer. "Both feet Doctor and hold your damn breath!"

Chibs and four pirates heaved the barrel up, walking it to the rail where they gingerly lowered it down to the water's surface. The sea took it and in moments it was trailing away toward the pursuing ship's hull. When the barrel bobbed about half a cable length away from the Maiden's stern LeMeux held up a wick to the end of the fuse trailing its way back to the barrel. A pop and a hiss sounded as the fuse began to burn spewing smoke and sparks. The first few inches burned at an even, steady rate until the flames hit a section that almost seemed to combust all at once for several feet.

Doctor LeMeux's face went red, "Damned fuse! Chibs, I tried to…"

"Hold your breath Doctor! What about that did you not understand? Let's see how she does." Chibs cut in through gritted teeth.

The fuse burned in a furious vigor sending flames and sparks sizzling and dancing on the water's choppy surface. Lilith watched as Chibs let the rope slip uncoil from the deck, its fibers running along the edge of the stern rail in an increasing hum. The barrel drifted sideways, veering off its intended course.

Lilith turned to Omibwe at the helm, "Omi, a point starboard!"

Omibwe diligently adjusted the ship's wheel, "There Captain?"

Lilith watched as the barrel corrected in its trajectory. There was a lag between wheel adjustment and the barrel changing its course, but it was right in line with the warship's bow. "There, hold her steady!" she called back to Omibwe.

The barrel bobbed its way back, while the crew of the Maiden watched. Every soul aboard stared with an intense hush falling over the deck. As the barrel neared the approaching hull of the warship, Lilith's blood ran cold when the smoke trail from its fuse disappeared.

"Chibs!" Lilith said without moving her eyes from

the last spot she had seen the fuse smoke.

"Aye Cap'n I seen it. Give it a minute, she may still be burning." Chibs said taking grip of the rail in each hand, his pipe lodged between clenched teeth.

Another moment passed. Lilith could feel a burning in her chest as she realized she was holding her breath. She released air from her lungs in a long slow exhale, feeling the weight of the warship behind them press on her shoulders. The barrel bobbed into the rush of water being pushed apart by the warship's hull.

"Hold that line!" Lilith ordered to the pirates that had been letting it out as fast as the barrel had floated away. "Chibs, how can we set it off? Is there some way to ignite it without the fuse?"

Chibs pulled his pipe from his teeth, rubbing at his bald head with his other hand. "She's a ways out of musket range Cap'n. A direct hit from the guns would do it, but, that's a damn small target. She'd be a once in a lifetime shot."

"Captain! Look!" LeMeux cried from the opposite side of the stern.

Lilith turned her eyes back to the barrel just in time to see a sparking, smoking crackle of flame work its way the last few inches to its destination. A massive eruption thundered as a ball of flame and smoke engulfed the bow of their pursuer's ship. Debris flew and flames grabbed hold of splintered timbers. Smoke cleared in the cross wind and Lilith watched as a gaping, massive hole was revealed in the warship's bow. The ship lurched, turning hard toward her wound as the sea invaded her hull.

"She's breached beneath her waterline Captain!"

Trina gave an excited shout sending an echoing cheer from the Maiden's crew high aloft on the wind.

Lilith remained silent as everyone around her lifted their voices in celebration. Her mind turned only to the next threat, a vessel sailing towards the Maiden's bow. She turned and walked away to the bow, with Chibs following right behind her. Together the two walked onto the forecastle and got their bearings on the approaching ship.

"How long to get the guns from the stern up here?" Lilith asked Chibs before extending her sight glass and focusing her eye on the distant ship.

"Half a turn at least Cap'n. But we should have that before they are in range." Chibs replied, while repacking his pipe from a leather pouch he kept tucked away in his belt.

"Let's get them to it then." Lilith said, withdrawing her eye for a moment and giving Chibs a smile. "Unless you and Omibwe are holding back some plan to destroy this ship as well."

"No, no Cap'n. Just one brilliant for today. Omi's idea too, don't forget." Chibs answered.

"Oh, I won't forget it. His bright streak likely saved us quite a bit of blood and heartache." Lilith stole a glance back over the deck of the Maiden, watching her crew celebrate as a plume of dark smoke rose from the ship behind them. "Is there any chance they will save her?" she asked Chibs. As she spoke a flash of flame erupted carrying upward through shattered deck boards.

"Doubtful. But in any case, she's in no condition to carry on against us." Chibs replied, rubbing at his grayed beard.

Lilith turned and focused back onto the vessel ahead of her. She watched as the ship nosed its bow in her direction. Lilith took note of her size, two masts protruding upward from her deck. She could not count gun ports through the distance, but the vessel was definitely smaller than the Maiden and with only two masts, likely didn't have more than a single gun deck. The sound of waves breaking along the Maiden's hull in her ears and with wind caressing the side of her face, Lilith watched in a diligent vigil. Around her, the crew set up their bow guns, lacing lines around the bow rail and through each gun carriage. Trina had taken on the role of gunnery, filling the void left when Lieutenant Pike did not return from Nassau.

"Just a few more minutes here Captain and we'll be ready to range her." Trina said, standing up from where she had been crouched next to the larboard chaser gun. "Have they altered course?"

Lilith looked again; her eyes easily found the ship running its way toward Drowned Maiden. "No, they are hell bent toward us deary. It looks like you will have another chance to practice your aim."

Trina scrunched her face and put her hand up to shade her eyes from the sun. "Not much longer and she will be close enough to range Captain. We'll be ready. I'll have the gun crews below deck ready their guns and run them out on both sides."

A distant rumble sounded, and a puff of smoke drifted from the bow of the vessel, followed by a plume of sea water from an impact between the two ships.

"It seems they have the same idea, Trina. Get us ranged and score some hits as they close with us." Lilith said resting her hand on the hilt of her sword.

"Aye Captain. It'll be a fight then for sure. We'll be ready." Trina said, slipping away to ready the gun crews below deck.

Lilith focused in on her new target ship. Below deck Trina's voice carried up as she called out commands to the gun crews. Lilith listened as gun ports clunked open one by one and felt the rumble of the wheels as the crews heaved their pieces into place for the opening salvo. Another shot reported over the distance, followed by another harmless impact into the seas ahead of the Maiden. Lilith felt a tap on her shoulder. She turned to find Lieutenant Shelton, one of the navy men that had been brought aboard after the Maiden's battle with the Endurance the previous fall.

"If I could have a moment, Captain. I need to speak with you." The officer's manner had endured through all these months of sailing with a pirate crew and to Lilith's memory, this was the first time she had interacted directly with him.

"Say what you need to." Lilith said, giving him a cautious look.

"Lieutenant Pike, miss. He went ashore in Nassau but did not return. The vessel you just blew a hole in, that is a ship of his majesty's navy. It is likely that the Lieutenant…" Lieutenant Shelton's voice drifted as Chibs approached them.

"It is likely that he is dead, Lieutenant. I sent Lewis ashore with them, with a pistol and dagger to murder Governor Alton and the governor of Nassau. Your navy ship was not alone, the rest likely made port in Nassau and Lieutenant Pike is most likely dead." Lilith's tone had a grievous note.

"While it is a possibility. Captain. Even if he was captured, Lieutenant Pike would be afforded a trial. He could still be alive." The lieutenant replied, shifting his eyes nervously between Lilith and Chibs while he spoke.

"Even so boy. What are we going to do about it now? A rescue attempt would cost us lives and we aren't interested in exchanging half the crew for a chance rescue of one man. One man we don't even know still lives." Chibs' voice growled in a puff of smoke as he withdrew the stem from his teeth with a meaty fist. "Don't forget your place. And don't forget that our captain let you aboard. Against her better judgment."

Lilith lifted her hand from the hilt of her cutlass and held it in front of Chibs' chest. "Hold on a second Chibs. Let's hear him for a moment." She turned to Shelton, replacing her hand onto her sword hilt. "If Lieutenant Pike is alive, what would be done with him?"

Trina stood from behind her gun on the bow, "That will have to wait Captain! She's coming into range!"

'Shark Fin'
21 Mar 1809
24 Degrees 36' N, 76 Degrees 44' W

Tim lingered at the rail, near the Shark Fin's Captain as he sized up the ship they were sailing toward. The captain seemed to be a confident man and no stranger to sea borne confrontations. On deck, the men of the Shark Fin were readying themselves for a fight. Weapons were being distributed, swivel guns were loaded, and marksmen had climbed aloft to take their positions. An awkward blend of tension and excitement floated on the deck. Young hands, eager to prove themselves in the heat of battle and experienced sailors dreading the fight to come. Tim stole a glance upward to the pirate ship as he was deliberately taking his time coiling a line at the larboard rail. She looked like the ship he had encountered before. Though he couldn't see her black flag all that well, he noticed as the wind shifted slightly, that skull with its twisted horns. It was her. That was the ship which had sunk the Valor beneath him. Thrown him into the coral with the surf slamming his body against its sharp edges, slicing him near to death. Tim's stomach knotted and his mouth went dry as he overheard the captain talking about the plume of smoke rising high into the air behind the pirate ship.

"It looks like we've caught her in the act! Just sunk one of her victims and still flying her banner for all the world to see!" the captain crowed loud enough for deck hands around him to hear. Several men on deck looked up from their preparations to steal a glimpse of their nearing opponents.

"You're mistaken if you think this will be an easy fight, Captain." Tim said, standing from the line he had taken entirely too long working on.

The captain shot him a hard sideways glance before raising his sight glass back up to his eye. "Combat at sea is never an easy fight. Just when you think you have your opponent fixed, they can turn the tables on you in a heartbeat. But you would know about that, wouldn't you?"

"I think they are the ship you are looking for, and I think that is the same crew that sunk me and left me for dead." Tim replied, ignoring the captain's banter.

"Generally, Mr. Sladen, when someone blows a hole in a ship, or runs her aground in a pursuit, the intent is to kill everyone aboard. Leaving you for dead was the whole purpose. The fact that you survived is a testament to your will." The captain paused for a moment and then lowered his sight glass, turning toward Tim. "You'll have your chance to prove your mettle again."

A shot erupted from the Shark Fin's bow guns. Causing Tim an involuntary jump in his surprise. The captain stood stock still, a smile stretching across his face before he turned to take note of where the shot impacted relative to the pirate ship.

"Was that max elevation?" the captain asked his bow gun crew.

"No, Sir, three quarters. Do you want me to run it all the way up?" a crewman said as the rest of his crew worked at reloading.

"No, no. Range her at three quarters elevation. I'll tell you when to give your turns boys." The captain's growl preceded a distant thump as the opposing ship let fly with a shot from one of their bow chasers. A shriek cried through the air, sending Tim sprawling to the deck for cover. Embarrassment rushed into Tim's face as sailors on deck laughed and lobbed jests at him.

"We aren't in range yet, get up!" the captain snapped, "You are embarrassing yourself."

Tim rushed back to his feet, "You don't understand how treacherous this adversary is. Don't underestimate them. They sank a crew of seasoned sailors, ran us aground on a reef and fired their guns with devastating effect into the wrecked hulk before the crew could do anything to escape their plight."

The captain sneered at Tim's warning, "It sounds like a well thought out attack by a skilled commander against a haphazard crew of landsmen well out of their depth. That won't be the case with us Mr. Sladen, I can promise you that."

Tim felt another hot wave rush into his face as laughter erupted on deck again. His eyes searched over the faces on deck. Anger welled up inside him. The sailors were laughing off his warnings as the ships drew nearer. Another thump echoed across the gap of sea separating the two ships followed by a piercing whistle.

"She's getting her range now Captain! You want that we should run them up and have another round at her?" one of the gun crew called over.

"Aye, let her fly boys!" the captain shouted back in reply, "Hold fast boys! She's ours now!" followed by a cheer from the crew on deck.

The bow gun crew made their final adjustments and checked the gun's alignment with the enemy ship. Tim peered over the rail as the crew let their shot go with a thundering report, sending a cloud of smoke and a flash of light erupting from the end of the cannon. Every eye aboard the Shark Fin fixed onto the ship they were firing on, searching for a sign of impact. A tense moment passed until a plume of seawater splashed skyward beyond the approaching ship and just slightly to the side.

"That would have scored a hit on her hull if you had waited for the proper alignment! Damn it, reload the damned cannon! What are you waiting for?" the captain screamed at his bow gun crew, kicking a wooden pail the gunners had been using for their bore swab. His face flushed as he shot a look to Tim and then back over the rail toward the pirate crew.

As Tim fixed his eyes back onto the pirate ship, he noted their sails being adjusted. "She's turning! Captain, she's turning into the wind!"

"They're bringing her close reach on the bow. Damn it. I want to land the first hit." The captain seethed which each word, getting sharper with each syllable. "Marksmen, fire at will! Keep their heads down and cowering!"

"There's no cowards on that ship." John said in a low voice over Tim's shoulder. "But I think this captain isn't going to figure that out until it is too late."

"Right." Tim replied, lowering his voice to match John's, "And we are along for the outcome."

The two exchanged a glance. John's face was painted in fear.

"You're not so keen on revenge now that you're confronted with the awful business of it, eh?" Tim said, taunting the younger man a little before another shot erupted from the Shark Fin's bow guns.

"I thought the crew a bit more capable when the captain introduced himself as a pirate hunter. That seems to be a bit of an exaggeration. What do we do now?" John's voice hissed.

"Let's hope our pirate hunters prove to be all they have claimed. If not, we will find a way to survive. That is all we can do." Tim replied looking away to the imposing pirate ship as its turn began to bare the open gun ports of its larboard side. The ugly sight of gun barrels protruded from their ports.

"I won't face her again. I'll die first." John wheezed as reality began to set into his mind.

"You may just get your wish," Tim raised his voice, "Hurry, come with me now!"

The captain's voice rose from the bow deck, "Cover boys! She's got a run on us and here it comes!"

One by one, the pirate's cannons roared to life in a raking pass by the Shark Fin. Hits scored along the hull and rail sending wooden shards flying. Stay lines snapped and recoiled, whirring through the air above deck and threatening life and limb in their unpredictable paths above deck.

Tim and John hunkered low, crawling toward the stern through the chaos of the impacting cannon rounds. Shouted cheers and threats floated through the air from the passing pirates, punctuated by the exchange of musket fire from marksmen in the rigging of both vessels. The intensity of fire increased. Tim felt the Shark Fin tremble as her gun crews below let loose a volley of cannon fire. Ahead of him, Tim could see the weather hatch leading to the stairs below deck. A scream cut into his ears and Tim looked aloft. One of the marksmen who had perched on the top sail yard toppled from his seat and dropped his musket. The weapon he had held in his hands fell, toppling end over end and clunking onto the deck a few feet in front of Tim and John. The marksman came next, his limp body slumped off the yard and followed the path his musket had just taken, slamming him onto the deck and erupting a spray of blood and body fluids onto Tim's face. The pirate ship had almost completely passed Shark Fin, letting one more shot loose as they passed the stern.

All along the deck of Shark Fin, the sailors were reeling from the attack. Tim looked back to see the captain, bleeding from a shard of broken deck rail lodged in his forearm but still upright. He walked the deck, shouting at sailors taking cover on deck.

"Get up you cowards! She's coming about! Do you want to die cowering? Get up and get ready to fight!"

The helmsman of Shark Fin spun the wheel, shifting a desperate look between the captain and the sails aloft, "Captain! Captain, they've shot away the rudder! She's not answering the wheel!"

Tim stood from his crouch, realizing the pirate crew had reduced the ship of supposed 'pirate hunters' to a band of helpless targets, adrift at sea. Grabbing John's sleeve he stopped his companion, staring into the younger man's face.

"Below deck isn't going to be ideal when these bastards sink this tub. We have to go over. Get off this ship." Tim hissed in a hushed voice.

"If the rest of the crew catches us, they'll kill us before the pirates get a chance!" John's reply was fraught with fear and panic.

Their debate was interrupted by a sailor standing

near the fantail, "She's coming about for another run at us!"

The captain passed in front of Tim, shooting him a sour glance as he stomped his way to the helm. As if he didn't believe his helmsman, he grabbed a hold of the wheel and gave it a turn, checking for resistance. When he felt none, he pulled on it furiously letting it spin free as he let go. He then ripped open the weather hatch and screamed below, "Starboard battery be ready to fire, she's going to come abreast of us on your side!"

Musket fire picked up again, slicing its way through the air above deck and cracking into wood all around as the shots came nearer and nearer to where Tim stood on deck. Over the starboard rail, the ship's bow slid into Tim's sight. She was close. Pirates stood high along the rail and up in the rigging, shouting insults and threats and shooting pistols and muskets. For a moment Tim froze. This was as close as he had seen the ship before, and the sight of their crew brought a gripping chill into his blood. A large black man holding a cutlass in one hand wielded a line with a grapple on it. Several more stood along the rail of the pirate ship.

The captain of the Shark Fin shouted down the weather hatch, "What are you waiting for? An invitation? Fire!" His screams were met with silence, except for the shouted taunts of the pirates, Shark Fin had fallen into a dead quiet, her sailors realizing they had been bested at sea and were about to pay a steep price for their ineptness.

The captain's face shot red when no answer came to his order. No volley opened from his battery below deck, he turned and searched the deck for a hand to send below. Tim saw the captain's gaze land upon him and inside he could feel his guts tighten.

"You there! Run below and see what's holding them up. I need that battery to open fire, now!" the captain shouted his order.

Tim hesitated for a moment, shifting his eyes back to the pirates coming into view while their ship drew alongside the Shark Fin. A grapple hook clunked onto Shark Fin's wooden deck and Tim bolted for the weather hatch, running below so quickly he lost his footing on the stairs and had to stumble the rest of the way down, struggling to hold himself up with his hands.

The scene on the gun deck was a slaughter. Tim looked over dead gun crews, strewn about the deck. The deck was slicked with blood and at first glance Tim thought none of the crew on the gun deck were alive. He waved his hand in front of his face, trying to waft away the dingy smoke impeding his vision. Shouts from above on the weather deck sifted down. Heavy footfalls and more gun shots sounded above. Tim shuffled over bodies and debris to get to a pair of gun ports which had been blown open, the bulkhead between opening shattered away in splintered shards from the pirate ship's skilled gunnery. As Tim stepped over a sailor to get to the opening, he felt a hand grab hold of his ankle.

"Where..." the sailor struggled to pull himself up to a sitting position. He looked around the gun deck, dazed and wounded. His bewildered eyes fell back onto Tim. "Where are you going?"

A shock ran through Tim's blood, and he balled a fist as the sailor's eyes put together what he had planned to do. "I came down to check on the gun crews, I didn't realize anyone had survived."

"You're trying to abandon the ship. You thought no one would see you leaving, and you thought you would make your escape." The sailor winced, looking down at a wound in his midsection as blood oozed forth.

"I've survived more than one encounter with these pirates. That's what I do. Whatever it takes to survive." Tim pushed the sailor away and began to climb his way through the hull opening. The sounds of combat echoed above as steel clattered together and pistol shots rang out through the clunky thudding of footfalls on the deck above. The pirates had boarded Shark Fin and it wouldn't be long before they made their way below deck.

The sudden grasp of a hand on Tim's shirt sent him into a boiling rage. He turned back into the hold of Shark Fin to receive a fist smashing into his cheek.

"You coward. Come here and die a coward's death!" the wounded sailor swung another punch toward Tim's face. The meaty hand impacted into Tim's nose, and he could feel blinding pangs of pain and a rush of blood as his nose crunched under the force of the huge fist. Tim fell backward against a shattered hulk of gun carriage and loose cannon barrel, the sailor pulling himself to his feet over him.

"They're boarding right now. If we go together, we can escape them!" Tim held his hands up, knowing he couldn't best the man by brute force.

"I'm not interested in bobbing along in the sea for days and dying of thirst or being eaten by sharks. We're going up there to face them with the rest of the crew." The sailor extended a hand for Tim to take, "Come on, we may even take a few of them with us."

Tim took the man's hand and was promptly pulled onto his feet. He was short, stocky and powerful. Even the wound from his side, bleeding profusely, didn't seem to steal his strength away. "I have no weapon."

"I'm sure there's plenty laying around on deck." The sailor turned and began to lead the way.

Tim's hands clasped around a nine-pound shot ball laying at his feet on deck. The cool iron felt good under his fingers, a welcome chill crept up his spine. The shot's surface had been hammered and little indentations covered it all over. Tim seized the heavy ball back over one shoulder and took a lunging step toward the sailor in front of him, smashing the shot ball with every ounce of strength he could muster into the man's head. The sailor toppled, letting a ghastly sigh of guttural exhale go. Tim chanced nothing and dashed on top of his limp victim, slamming the shot again into the man's caving skull until a dark red spray of blood emitted from a gaping wound encompassing the back of the sailor's skull. Blood and brain matter ran onto the deck as Tim stood, dropping the shot round through his blood-soaked hands in a loud clunk on the deck.

Above, the sounds of combat still raged. Clashes of steel and gunshots told Tim the victor hadn't yet been decided. He scanned the gun deck for any further sign of survivors. Smoke filled the space, spilling out of the breech in the hull. "It's now or never. Damn. This again." Tim climbed his way through the twisted hole in Shark Fin's hull, tearing his shirt and impaling him between his ribs. With a final heave, Tim managed himself through the hole and fell away to splash into the sea.

'North Wind'
22 Mar 1809
24 Degrees 42' N, 76 Degrees 44' W

Smoke lingered on the breeze as Admiral Torren looked down at the waters rippling behind North Wind. Nassau grew smaller on the horizon behind them, and the admiral took in the sounds of his flagship putting to sea. Only a day in port had not been sufficient time to restock their hold, they would need to return before continuing their journey to Jamaica. Admiral Torren's heart felt a heaviness that he hadn't experienced outside of a major loss at sea. The lieutenant imprisoned within his hold promised to be a major problem. The service demanded that he deal with the young officer in a swift and harsh justice for the Crown. Hangings were always a nasty business, especially when it was a fellow of the Royal Naval Service, but with an officer it would prove to be even more demoralizing. Admiral Torren played through the young officer's wild claims in his mind. It just didn't make sense. There was no disputing that corruption existed, especially in these remote outposts of the empire. But the level of lawlessness insinuated by Lieutenant Pike would have been laughable had the accusations against him not been so dire. A twinge of anger welled inside the admiral's chest as he thought over his conversation with the young man.

Lieutenant Thatcher approached on the aft castle stairs, "Sir, the lookouts are reporting sightings of flotsam and debris, but no sign of Longsword."

The admiral's gaze remained set on the water swirling behind North Wind's wake. "Is the ship they went in pursuit of in sight?"

"No, Sir." The lieutenant replied with a grimace.

"Very well then. Leave me." The admiral replied, placing his hands wide along the stern rail.

North Wind sloshed through choppy waves with every hand on deck scouring the debris for any sign of Longsword while Admiral Torren maintained his place on the stern, scowling at the passing waves. The sun's rays did little to improve his foul mood.

"Man overboard! Get a line out there, we've found one alive lads! Let's go!" a haggard voice shouted from the bow.

Admiral Torren snapped out of his melancholy and turned to see the sailors of North Wind scrambling a lifeline over the rail.

"Reach for it man! We'll haul you up!" another sailor shouted overboard.

In a moment they were hauling on the line, hand over hand until a sputtering man came up to the rail. Coughing and gagging, he retched a belly full of seawater onto the deck. Admiral Torren made his way over to the man at his dignified pace. Standing well out of range of the man's retching until heaves produced nothing but guttural gasps.

"You are most fortunate to be alive, though you are very obviously not of the King's navy. Do tell me. What vessel do you belong to sailor?" Admiral Torren demanded. "The last report I received from the frigate I sent in pursuit of a sighted vessel told of a ship flying a black banner. You wouldn't be a pirate from that ship, would you?"

The coughing man still half drowned looked up from where he was on all fours on the wooden deck. He coughed again, producing more seawater. "No. I was aboard an American privateer. Hunting the pirate crew, you speak of."

"A fine job they did with you. Where is this American ship, this privateer you speak of? I should like to have a word with your commander." The admiral's voice was devoid of sympathy, demanding, accusatory.

"The Shark Fin lies beneath us. They blew away the guns, blew away the rudder and set her afire with all hands aboard. I barely escaped with my life." The man managed through ragged breaths; his head turned downward at the deck.

"And what of the frigate that sailed this way? H.M.S. Longsword. She would have been pursuing the same vessel you claim had sunk yours." Admiral Torren inquired while pulling his cane up under one arm.

"They sunk her. She was beneath the waves before we were close enough to offer aid." The man replied before a powerful hacking fit rendered him face down on the wooden deck boards beneath him again.

The admiral turned to his aid, Lieutenant Thatcher with a grim expression. "I have no reason to distrust his claims. Nor do I have reason to take them at face value. See to it that he is clapped into irons and placed in a cell below until we can make sense of what has occurred here these last few days. Double the night watch as well, on all vessels, if there is a pirate crew about, I won't have them catching me by surprise."

"Aye Sir." Lieutenant Thatcher turned and gestured to a pair of waiting marines, who promptly began executing the admiral's orders.

Admiral Torren walked to the rail as the half-drowned man was forcefully stood to his feet. He looked down at the debris field bobbing in the water. "What is your name sailor?" he turned and asked before the marines began to march him off.

"Tim, Sir. Tim Sladen. Of Southern Carolina." The man answered, his face begging for some change of course away from his current destination.

"South Carolina is a notorious stomping ground and safe harbor for pirate crews, dating back over a hundred years. If you were going to lie, that would have been your opportunity." The admiral said in a scalding tone. "You were out here to hunt down a pirate crew? Or you were part of a pirate crew yourself."

"They are targeting slavers." Tim said as the marines began to drag him away.

"Hold him there!" Admiral Torren snapped, freezing the pair of marines in place. "What did you just say?"

"The pirates you seek are targeting slaver vessels. The ship is crewed by a motley of freed slaves and pirates." Tim's reply was frantic as if he couldn't spit out the words quick enough.

"That's the second time I have been told about the illicit slave trade. In two days. No matter, we will get to the bottom of it." He turned from Tim and gave the marines a nod, "Go ahead, lock him away. We will question him further when I have the patience for that sort of thing."

Admiral Torren turned back to the rail and looked over the debris field. Lieutenant Thatcher stood for an awkward moment at his side. "A tea Sir?"

"Not now Lieutenant. Bring me the letter recovered from Governor Culbertson's office as well. I should like to read over it again."

Alistair Torren placed his hands on the rail, leaning hard onto them he squinted his eyes at the sun glittering off the water's surface. His fleet made a zig zag pattern throughout the debris, searching for any confirmation that Longsword had indeed gone down with all hands. It wasn't the first ship the admiral had lost under his command, but that did little to numb the biting edge of loss and regret. Something was eluding him. There was a truth behind what Lieutenant Pike had told him and now after hearing the same information from another source something must be done. Alone at the rail, looking out over the water the aging admiral mumbled to himself, "Did he truly believe he was still acting in honor?" He pondered for a moment before shaking off the notion. In his mind he pictured Captain Grimes, the last time the two men had spoken. It was a shame to lose such a fine commander, which only made dealing with the aftermath that much more difficult. Admiral Elliot Sharpe was a personal friend of Alistair's, that loss grieved him as well. In Alistair's mind, when he had assigned Valor to report to the Caribbean fleet the pair of them would have created a team that would have been insurmountable. A brash captain with sound, battle tested experience and a bit of a rogue streak paired with an approachable strategist with a gift for bringing out the best of his command. But all indications told the admiral his well thought out team was no more. Admiral Torren realized he had been clenching his jaw, tighter and tighter as he was deep in thought. It ached from the tension. Lieutenant Thatcher approached with the letter from Governor Culbertson's desk in hand. The parchment still had stains along one side from flecks of the governor's blood. He could tell that handling the letter made Lieutenant Thatcher uncomfortable and in his already perturbed mood the inclination of a naval officer being dismayed by a bit of blood further irritated him.

"I want you to read it aloud and try not to look so disgusted by a bit of blood. My guess is you will be seeing quite a bit more than that before this whole mess is put to rest Lieutenant, you might as well get used to it." The admiral quipped, before turning back outboard.

"Yes, Sir. It reads: Governor Culbertson, exchange in Jamaica is no longer an option. Nassau needs to be secure against threat of piracy before the delivery of any tea shipments. French tea traders must be welcomed to Nassau." The lieutenant lowered the letter as he finished. "That is all it says Sir."

"I've read it over. It just makes no sense, unless I apply the reasoning that I've been given by a traitor.

This is madness, son. Never would I have thought to lived long enough to see such a day." Admiral Torren turned to the lieutenant and relived him of the blood-stained letter. "We have some digging to do, and you need to understand something before we go below to talk to Lieutenant Pike. He is guilty of treason; he is guilty of murder. He will die for those crimes. No matter what the reasoning was, no matter how he tries to justify it. That man will be held accountable for his crimes. If you find him gaining your sympathies, remember that."

"I'll try to, Sir." Lieutenant Thatcher mumbled as the admiral strode past him toward the stairs.

"Watch officer." Admiral Torren called out as he crossed the quarterdeck, beckoning a young lieutenant to report in a rigid form. "Pass my compliments to the captain and have him join me below deck. I will be having a visit with our incarcerated officer. Also, your helmsman ought to be using both of the hands God gave him, eh? A slip at the helm can be catastrophic. See to it."

"Aye aye Sir!" the watch officer snapped a crisp salute and turned to his tasks, addressing the helmsman before Admiral Torren descended the stairs below deck. "Both hands on the wheel sailor. A shift in wind could rip it right out of your grip as you are now."

The admiral started to grin, turning the corners of his mouth upward for a moment before the absence of open air returned his mind to the task at hand. He took each step down the stairs in painful succession, his arthritic ankles and knees screamed in creaks and groans of pain. Biting his lip as he descended, the admiral's pride managed to fuel his movement at a pace that no sailor would scoff his advanced age aboard a warship. Descending three sets of stairs brought him down to the hold, where the only light permeating the dark belly of the ship was from a pair of flickering lanterns at either end of a long corridor through the middle. On either side of the narrow walkway were stacks of supplies. Barrels, bags, wooden crates and cases lined the walls from deck to overhead. Every few feet he passed a crossbeam that required him to stoop down, bringing another dull ache into his back and neck. As he neared the end of the corridor, Admiral Torren could hear an exchange of commotion coming from the cells ahead of him. The marine sentries were batting at a pair of arms that protruded from the barred port in the heavy cell door leading to the passageway.

"Murderer! That man is a killer!" the arms darted outward from the cell, one of them balling into a fist at the end that slammed into the wooden door beneath. "Let me into his cell, I'll kill him with my bare fists! Let me out!"

"If you don't shut your mouth, I'll be coming into your cell! How's that?" one of the sentries taunted, slapping at the arms protruding into the corridor.

"Enough!" Admiral Torren snapped, loud enough to interrupt the exchange. He looked into the cell as Lieutenant Pike withdrew from the door. "What is the meaning of this?"

Lieutenant Pike's eyes looked crazed in a wide, bewildered expression of rage, "Sir. That is the man who killed Admiral Sharpe in Kingston!"

United States Capitol Building
Washington D.C.
18 March 1809

Humidity pressed the windows of the United States Capital building, rising in a wave as cloud banks retreated westward and the sun rose into its high arc of midday. John Gaillard was returning to his office from a meeting of his fellow southern senators. The topics of the day revolved around a growing liberal sentiment that favored abolishing the import of slaves from Africa and South America. It promised to be a contentious issue. Among the proponents were conservative northern merchants whose vessels were being targeted by British warships under the false pretense of enforcing their parliamentary ban of the slave trade. The merchant ships, when boarded, were then often subject to having their crews pressed into the service of the Royal Navy as well as their cargoes being either ransacked or pilfered. It was piracy disguised. A blatant disregard for American sovereignty and growing threat to a nation still in its infancy. John's footstep echoes mixed with others in the hallways, and he maintained a brisk stride toward his office. He maintained a manner of politeness, acknowledging fellow senators and familiar aides as they passed. But John's mind was wholly consumed with the struggle he was trying to balance while the nation he called home was teetering on the edge of another war.

Arriving at his office, John opened the door. The room sweltered in muggy warmth and John stepped in to remove his jacket. At first glance, he did not notice the man sitting in his chair behind the desk at the far end of the room. John pulled his jacket off and removed his wig, turning toward a washbasin in the office corner. Emptying a pitcher into the basin, John wet his face and neck.

"You've taken quite an anti-war stance as of late Senator." A voice behind him startled John and he jerked, knocking the stool the washbasin sat on. The basin tumbled onto the floor, spilling water and splashing John's shoes and ankles as he turned in alarm.

"Who are you? What are you doing in here?" John snapped as his eyes fixed on the man sitting at his desk.

The stranger seemed unmoved by John's challenge. "I am a representative of sorts myself. My name is not important, but I can assure you, Sir, you would do well to heed my warnings."

"You've come to deliver a warning?" John's voice lowered and a sudden chill came to his neck despite the swampy heat of afternoon.

"I most certainly have. You have been a vocal opponent to the growing sentiments within this building. Your constituents grow tired of the Royal overstep of foreign sovereigns, and yet you remain steadfastly opposed. Why?" the stranger stood from John's desk, moving around its edge in graceful steps with his gaze locked onto the Senator.

"I don't want another war. What is that to you? Who

are you?" John regained some assertiveness in his tone.

The strange man lifted a hand, inspecting his fingers. "I am an associate of one of your constituents. I am a representative in league with some very powerful and wealthy benefactors who wish to remain anonymous and, well, detached. But I can assure you, Senator, you want to listen to my heeding. You need to."

"But I don't even know who you are! Why would I hear anything from a man I know nothing about!" John's voice began to elevate back to a shout until the tall stranger held a single finger in front of his lips. His other hand pulled a small pistol from behind his back.

"I will educate you Senator. But first, you need to understand that I am not alone. In fact, I operate in league with a number of distinguished representatives in this very building. So understand when I tell you this, to ignore my warning today means your certain death. Do you understand me, Senator?" a wry smile spread across the stranger's face while he waited for John's answer.

"I do." John felt his shoulders slump.

The stranger tucked his hand with the pistol back behind his back, "Very good. Now, you need to know only a few things for the time being. There will be a war with the United Kingdoms. If you get on board, you will be rewarded with financial resources well beyond your current means. In addition, you will be using your voice within these halls to shift sentiments toward repealing the abolition of the slave trade in the United States."

"I already support repealing that. But how does war with the United Kingdoms accomplish anything?"

John's voice leveled though his hands began to tremble as he spoke. The strange man's calm, authoritative demeanor had the Senator in a state of shock.

"War with the British Empire means chaos. Chaos means opportunities. Napoleon challenges them in Europe, at sea their power wanes as it is stretched thin. The American Navy proves to be a small challenge to slave smuggling, but if it is busy harassing British warships…" the man's voice trailed, and he turned to look out of the windows arrayed along the side of the office where he stood.

"You are in league with slave smugglers." John felt his stomach tighten.

The man turned back to him displaying a tight grin for a moment, "I assure you, Senator. Slave smuggling is only a small piece of the pie. Joining my benefactors means you will be in some of the most elite company in the world. One could almost say, holy."

Chapter 12

'Ranging Falcon'
24 Mar 1809
Eastern Shoreline of Jamaica

Water lapped at the edges of the small rowboat, splashing Clyde's fingers as he held onto the sidewall. The surrounding cove opened as they passed a narrow finger of land that separated a small inner bay from the larger body of the inlet. Once past the outcropping finger of land, the water lightened and stilled, taking on a light blue green color and an almost gem like sheen under the brilliance of the afternoon sunshine. Clyde's eyes traced over the shoreline, inspecting the sandy edges, and penetrating the floor of the forests within. According to the correspondences he had with his employee, the camp that had been used for holding slaves between exchanges from East India ships and the American smugglers they were using should be just inland. Clyde looked back to the man pulling on the oars and held a hand up, beckoning him to pause their progress.

"Hold here for a minute. Let's watch the shoreline for a bit and see if we can make out the trail head to the camp. I'd rather not spend all day combing the forest looking for it." Clyde said while pulling his hat from his head and wiping sweat from his brow with his sleeve. "As much as I would enjoy getting out of this sun."

As Clyde scanned along the shoreline, his eyes caught focus of a figure stepping out from under the shade of dense overhead canopy. A man with a slung musket stepped into the glaring sunlight and held up hand in a simple waving gesture.

"Over there. Let's make landfall and be looking out as we draw near. I've no idea what awaits us." Clyde said, his chest felt full of anticipation. He was ready to set things back on their intended course. Stealing back what was his, without hindrance of European overlords to take away his profits and dictate his terms. The small rowboat drew near to the sandy shore and the man on the beach unslung his musket and called over the water.

"Who are you? What business do you have here?" the lone man called out.

Clyde stood in the rowboat, bracing himself against the shoulder of one of the men sitting next to him. "My name is Clyde Ritten. I am looking for Tim Sladen. Is he up in the camp?"

The man on shore, slung his musket back over his shoulder, his expression changing, and he stepped down into the water's edge to receive the rowboat. "My apologies, Mr. Ritten. We were expecting Tim would be back at some point. No, he's not here. He's been gone for months. We thought he would either be dead or off trying to secure new transport means."

"That is unfortunate for him. I expect, given the way things appear to be developing, he is probably dead. Am I to assume then, if you are waiting for transport, that you still have slaves waiting for shipment?" Clyde asked, stepping down to the edge of wet sand as the rowboat made landfall.

"Yes Sir. We have a full camp; I sure hope you brought more than that little rowboat." The gunman quipped as he fell in behind Clyde's pace inland.

"Don't you worry about transport son. We have enough hold space for half the damned island. Can you fill the camp again?" Clyde said as he made his way out of the sand and into the grass and brush of the forest floor.

The man stopped following for a moment, "Will the company ships not be delivering? We filled the camp this time. We could maybe do it again, but there's no telling how long that would work. Jamaica is our domain for now, but when the Brits arrive…"

"We will be continuing our operations without the aide or interference of any of the old-world powers." Clyde cut off the gunman's objection, "We may need to reconstruct how we obtain slaves, but our profits will be all the greater. Trust me on this, it is a smart move."

The man remained still as Clyde took a few more steps into the tree line. "Sir. I believe it was you that warned me of the extensive reach of The Order in the first place. Is this wise?"

Clyde could see the trail head deeper in the thick undergrowth, he paused his stride and turned toward his hired mercenary, "You're being paid to do a job. You've done it as well as I could ask you to. But I am not paying you to question my decisions, much less make them for me. We will gather what we can from Jamaica. When that proves too difficult, perhaps we move on to Haiti or Brazil. The opportunities are there, we just have to be daring enough to reach out and take them."

The gunman shrugged and nodded, "The camp is up this trail a ways. I can show you the way."

Clyde kept a brisk pace up the trail, his head buzzing with an anxious excitement as he could see the shattered pieces of his plan coming back together into a new formation. Muggy heat sweltered under the forest canopy in visible vapors highlighted by columns of sunlight that penetrated the thick vegetation. The trail wound its way to a steep hillside and Clyde had to slow his pace. His face and neck dripped with beads of sweat, soaking through his blouse while also failing to cool him in the slightest measure. The mercenary put his hands on his hips, bending forward to catch his breath.

"It's just at the top of the hill Sir. The trail flattens and there is an opening in the jungle. It's a miserable walk, but Tim didn't want anyone just stumbling upon it." The man huffed, taking a big step and leaning his weight uphill.

Clyde shook his head after wiping his brow with an already soaked shirt sleeve. "It seems Tim should have put more effort into concealing the damned camp or guarding it. Probably both. Whoever discovered it should never have lived to tell the tale."

The mercenary grimaced after taking a long drink from his canteen and handing it to Clyde. "Tim killed him. I watched him do it. Shot him right on the steps of the governor's mansion in Kingston. We blew away half the soldiers they had and sank all but one of the ships they'd sailed into harbor. Tim sailed in pursuit of the surviving ship."

Clyde handed the man his canteen back after taking a long drink himself, "They were Royal Navy then?"

"Without a doubt, Sir. The man Tim killed at the governor's mansion was an admiral. He'd brought his fleet into the cove and scouted around, found the camp. The old man sailed right into Kingston harbor to confront the governor Tim had his thumb on. It didn't work the way they had planned." The mercenary squinted his eyes toward Clyde as he described the series of events.

"Damn blunder after blunder." Clyde mumbled.

"Excuse me Sir. But we did all that could be done." The man objected, turning to look further up the steep trail.

"No, son. None of this is your doing. I warned Tim about that damned governor. Nassau would have been better, but Tim insisted it would be frequented by the fleet far too often to use as an exchange point. Can't say I would argue against it. But from what I understand…" Clyde took a cumbersome step uphill and resumed their arduous climb, "Nassau is on a flat island."

'Drowned Maiden'
21 Mar 1809
24 Degrees 36' N, 76 Degrees 44' W

A strong wind carried the Drowned Maiden through rolling waves that broke on the bow and sprayed mist along her decks. The crew gathered at the quarterdeck as sunset blazed its way lower along the Maiden's starboard rail. Two men with hands bound behind their backs and nooses around their necks balanced themselves in a precarious position along the aft castle rail overlooking the weather deck while the pirates shouted and chanted at them below. Lilith paced the aft castle, cutlass in hand, watching the pair squirm as they tried to keep their feet beneath them in the pitching and heaving of the ship. Far behind them a formation of white sails dotted the northern horizon. Lilith caught them in her gaze and looked to Trina and Chibs who stood along the quarterdeck rail.

"One of you, I recognize. One of you has met my crew before!" Lilith called out for the entire crew to hear. A fury of shouts followed, threats ranging from gutting each man to skinning them alive and feeding them to the sharks. Lilith placed her sword point between the shoulder blades of the man she recognized. "I spared you to warn others. I offered you reprieve, and you have repaid my generous act with treachery!" Silence fell over the deck of the Maiden as Lilith leapt up on the rail between the two men. She placed a hand on the shoulder of the younger man. "How do we repay our kindness being rebuffed?"

Another chorus of shouts erupted from the crew.

"Cut off his hands and throw him overboard!" a pirate shouted.

"Gut him!" cried another.

Lilith lifted the point of her cutlass to the young man's abdomen and the pirates below cheered in a wild frenzy. She drew the point across his shirt, opening a small hole in the fabric where she inserted her blade before pulling its edge through the fabric in a swift slash. The front of the man's shirt fell open.

"Please, please, no." He pleaded, as Lilith turned her cutlass edge against his bare skin.

Lilith brought her face close to the man's ear, so he could hear her whisper, "I warned you and you crossed me. Now you will be my warning boy!" She pressed her blade against the soft flesh of his belly, sending an ooze of blood dripping from its edge. Lilith let the edge of her sword dig into his belly, slowly biting deeper until the young man's face dripped with tears of fear and pain. She pulled on the blade, slicing through the muscle and fat guarding internal organs from the outside world. As the young man's insides bared to open air and blood rushed down his trousers Lilith gave his shoulder a hard shove sending him swinging by his neck over the crowd of cheering pirates. The young man's legs kicked in a flurry of panic and agony, thrashing blood as he bucked and writhed against the rope dangling him over the deck. His body twisted and spun, swaying with the motion of Drowned Maiden as she battered her way through wind and waves.

"And what of this one?" Lilith asked wielding her

sword into her opposite hand and stepping over to the remaining man as he managed his balancing act. "Should I gut this one too? Or just let him swing?" The uproar of shouts made each voice indistinguishable from the next. "He was the captain! Should we send him overboard to join his ship?"

The remaining man trembled as Lilith brought her sword up to his torso, clamping his eyes shut in a hard wince. Lilith looked over her shoulder at the sails on the northern horizon. They were without a doubt sailing in pursuit of the Maiden. Lilith counted three ships, from what she could see. A full engagement with the last warship would have been costly, but winnable. A confrontation with three warships would be disastrous. Lilith turned her attention back to the trembling captain as he feebly balanced on the wooden rail underfoot.

"Captain. They are surely sailing for us!" Chibs called over to her as the shouts from the crew died down.

"Aye, they are. Suppose we send them a message Chibs?" Lilith replied, lowering her sword from the shaking captain's chest.

"Like, in a bottle Captain?" Chibs asked with a bewildered look flashing across his face.

Lilith flexed her grip on her sword for a moment, thinking over her intentions. "No. Not a message in a bottle. That would be too easily missed. Get a barrel, anything that floats."

Chibs' eyes darted to the trembling man standing next to Lilith on the rail. "Aye Cap'n, a barrel it is."

Lilith pulled back her sword and swung it hard,

lopping the line of rope off just above its noose knot. "Don't make the same mistake your young friend did. You are a poor captain and a worse pirate hunter. You tell them I will see every slaver ship to the bottom of the sea and only death awaits those who stand against me." Lilith stepped down from the rail, dragging the terrified captain with her toward the stern rail. She turned to see Chibs and Dr. LeMeux carrying a barrel up onto the aft castle deck. Lilith shoved the captain to the rail, lifting her sword and running the point over the rope knotted around his wrists. In a snap, the line binding the pirate hunter's hands gave way and Lilith grabbed what remained of the noose knot around his neck.

"You can keep this, a gift from the Maiden." Lilith gave the rope a slight tug, forcing the man to stand up straight before she plunged a kick square into his lower back toppling him over the rail. The pirate hunter yelped as he fell overboard, slapping into the water on his belly.

Chibs and LeMeux tossed the barrel over after him, "Here's something else for you. No need for thanks you sniveling coward!"

A line of pirates joined them at the stern, watching and hurling insults as the bobbling man swam in a desperate rush toward his barrel. Lilith's gaze locked onto three sets of sails off in the northern distance.

"They are coming for us Captain." Trina said over her shoulder. Lilith's attention turned to Trina. Her eyes were locked onto the sails in the distance.

"I don't suppose we have enough powder to load up another barrel. Do we?" Lilith asked hoping to be wrong.

Trina shook her head, "No. We do have powder left, but not near enough for that. I don't believe they are interested in a chase anyways. They will pursue us, maneuver against us with their other ships and then blow the Maiden into slivers and bits."

"We have a lead. Could we outrun them?" Lilith asked, her mind already working at a solution.

"Nightfall is coming. The moon has been shrinking for a week now, in darkness we stand a chance at losing them." Trina paused for a moment, looking at Chibs as he caught interest in their conversation, "But sailing for evasion at night is a risk. We need to make a drastic course change as soon as they lose sight of us and run without any light or noise. The slightest mistake could give us away."

"Not to mention the shoals and reefs out here. This part of the Caribbean can be cruel to a sailor at night, deadly even. If you want to lose them Cap'n, that's the way to do it. But there is a risk we could run the Maiden aground." Chibs added as he pulled his pipe from its leather pouch on his waist.

"I'm afraid it's our only option Chibs. We don't stand a chance against three at once." Lilith said, backing away from the crowd against the stern rail. "But if we can evade them. If we can separate them. Then maybe there is hope for us."

Chibs expression changed his eyebrows lifted and his eyes widened in warning, "Cap'n, the Valor, that was one thing. This is different. These are warships, they are crewed and commanded. They are here to hunt us."

Lilith thought on the warning for a moment, holding back her first reply as she could see several of the crew turned to hear what the quartermaster had to say. "Let's discuss this further in private Chibs. I agree that we cannot engage them head on. But if we can outwit the bastards, I don't see why we wouldn't."

"Aye, Cap'n so long as you don't plan on lining up with them." Chibs nodded, biting on his pipe stem.

From the crowd of pirates at the stern, Lieutenant Shelton approached Lilith as she made her way to the stairs leading down to the weather deck. "Captain. Could I speak with you?"

Casting a hesitant glance over her shoulder, Lilith answered. "That depends on what you want to speak of."

Lieutenant Shelton followed her down the stairs, with Trina falling in right behind him. "It's Lieutenant Pike, miss. I believe if he was taken prisoner, he could be held aboard one of those ships."

"And what do you want from me? We can't know for sure what has become of our friend. Sad as it is, it won't stay my hand if I have a chance to sink them." Lilith's reply cut the lieutenant off before he could finish. She shot the lieutenant a cold stare, daring him to challenge her. "He is gone."

Lilith departed from the deck, closing her cabin door behind her. For a moment she relished its dark space. The smell of timbers mixed with sea air and the faint lingering of Chibs' pipe. Tears welled in her eyes, blurring what little she could make out in the darkness. Her eyes traced over the large chest that had belonged to Captain James, the Maiden's former commander. In moments of loneliness Lilith had opened the chest before, smelling and feeling the fabric of an old shirt that had belonged to James. It smelled of him. A musky smell, with notes of gunpowder and leather. Lilith thought of locking her cabin door and opening the chest. Her heart beat quickened as she thought of James, followed by an icy chill of pain as she remembered the fight that had stolen him from her.

A knock at the door jarred Lilith from her painful memory.

Lilith wiped away a tear from her cheek, "Who is it?"

"Quartermaster." Chibs' voice carried through the door, muffled but unmistakable.

"Just a moment." Lilith answered, gathering herself and wiping her face again. She opened the door, letting Chibs enter the cabin before closing it right behind him.

"They're gaining Cap'n, but we should be able to stay well out of their reach until nightfall." Chibs looked around the cabin for a moment before making eye contact with Lilith. "Are you alright dear?"

"Yes." Lilith tried to put on a brave front for a moment, but her eyes met Chibs' and she could tell he knew something was wrong. "No, Chibs. No, I'm not. I knew sending him was wrong. I knew they could both be captured or killed. It had to be done. But why do I feel so terrible now? I didn't even like him all that much." Lilith's eyes welled with tears again.

Chibs held out his arms, wrapping Lilith in a bear hug. She buried her face in his chest beneath his graying beard. "It's the price of being the captain my dear. But, you are handling it so well. In all fairness, it shouldn't have been put on you. But who better to lead these people to freedom than a girl who secured hers for herself?"

Lilith wished for a moment that Chibs' comforting gesture wouldn't end, but the big pirate released his hug and took a step back. "How do we do this Chibs?" She asked.

"I suggest making a course adjustment eastward in the waning daylight Cap'n, then when the light of day fades entirely we should make a drastic course change. Westward say, until dawn." Chibs replied, pulling his pipe out of its pouch at his hip. "With any luck, and running quiet and with no lights, we could possibly make the Cuban coast. Plenty of inlets and shoals to run them afoul out there. You'll have your revenge deary."

Lilith smiled, "Not giving up on me yet Chibs?"

The big pirate pulled a wick from his pouch, stealing flame from the lone lantern in the cabin he lit his pipe and took a big puff of smoke, "Never Cap'n. Never."

Lilith took a deep breath, feeling a burn from Chibs' smoke, she opened the cabin door and paced her way out toward the helm.

"Omibwe."

"Yes Captain?" the young African boy answered.

Lilith took a deep breath of sea air and noted the dying light of day shining on Maiden's sails. "Come about larboard. Hard, but don't lose the wind."

'North Wind'
22 Mar 1809
24 Degrees 32' N, 76 Degrees 41' W

"She's tacking over larboard!" the voice of a lookout aloft on the foremast floated down through the evening breeze. North Wind's watch officer extended his telescopic sight glass and verified the report before looking at Admiral Torren, who was standing at the bow.

"Would you like a look for yourself Sir?" the watch officer offered his sight glass.

Admiral Torren had been deep in thought, only paying vague attention to the events on deck. "Yes, yes I would lad. Thank you." He took the expanding tube and held it up for his eye to gain focus on the ship ahead of them. She was a three masted frigate, heavy enough to do some real damage if well handled. Her larboard stern quarter was visible beneath a billowing black flag with indistinguishable white markings on it. The last rays of evening sun were painting her sails orange and pink hues. Her sails were taut or appeared to be through the distance. Pursuit beyond nightfall came with inherent risk. His target could heave over to another course entirely and slip through his fingers. He could fly more canvas and try to close further with her, but that carried the risk of being run into a shoal of sand or rock or even a reef. Admiral Torren clamped his jaw a few times over this new dilemma. In the back of his mind, he was still digesting the conversation he'd had with Lieutenant Pike below deck. When the admiral had finally gotten him to stop his wild yelling.

Within the bowels of his flagship, Admiral Torren held two men, both accusing the other of a list of crimes as wild and far-fetched as the imagination could roam. Treason and murder on the lieutenant's part were a bygone conclusion. The American prisoner, accused of murdering Admiral Sharpe by Lieutenant Pike, charged that the lieutenant had aided the very pirate crew North Wind pursued in sinking H.M.S. Valor, something the lieutenant had not yet divulged. Admiral Torren lowered the sight glass from his eye, handing it back to the watch officer with a nod.

"Relay your findings to your captain and get me Lieutenant Thatcher. I need to relay orders for the fleet." The admiral remained at the bowsprit; his gaze locked forward onto the ship in the distance. All of the pieces that lay before him, like a maddening puzzle of treacheries. When he considered them all, as a whole, the larger picture that displayed was a shocking conspiracy almost too far-fetched to believe. But the American's involvement lent credibility to what Lieutenant Pike had claimed. What remained was a mess. Two of the King's governors dead. One colony still in an unknown state of upheaval. A pirate ship roaming the Caribbean unchecked. "We'll deal with her first. Once she lies below the waves, then Kingston. Damn the madness before me." The admiral grumbled aloud to himself. North Wind's Captain Landreth came onto the forecastle with Lieutenant Thatcher at his side.

"She's made a course change with the last light of day. My guess is Captain, she won't be holding that course through the night. There will be only a sliver of moonlight tonight and not until quite late. Check over your charts and do everything feasible to close the gap while she remains visible." Admiral Torren turned to Lieutenant Thatcher, "Relay to the fleet to maintain an open formation. We have less chance of her slipping by us undetected that way. Signal the fleet to sail at visual range, keeping running lights lit. Perhaps we can discourage her from making maneuvers in darkness by keeping a full pursuit."

"Aye Sir." Captain Landreth replied, snapping a salute before turning to give his orders to the crew. Lieutenant Thatcher remained on the forecastle for a moment, his eyes following the admiral's stare out to the ship on the horizon.

"Would she turn to engage Sir? At night?" the lieutenant asked.

Admiral Torren felt an annoyance, it seemed every concern the young officer had related to his personal safety. "It's possible lad. The type of rogue who takes up a black banner on their ship is usually prone to making rash decisions. But with three men of war in pursuit, it would be folly. Let's hope they do. So we can end this chase and continue on to secure Kingston for the King's peace."

"I'll go see to the signal flags Sir." The lieutenant said, taking his leave.

Admiral Torren turned back outboard, watching as North Wind closed the sea gap while light faded from the world. With the sun dipping below the western skyline all that remained of the day's light was a lingering curtain of reds and violets punctured by starlight. Day was done and all he could do was run on in blind pursuit and searching cannon fire. The bow gun crews were already preparing their pieces for firing.

A thought crossed the admiral's mind. If Lieutenant Pike had been aboard the pirate ship, he may have knowledge of their port of refuge. The admiral looked out over the dark waters. Her sails on the horizon were only faintly visible in the afterglow of dusk. She could make a course change and slip past his squadron with ease once the last glow from day had gone.

"Watch Officer." Admiral Torren called over his shoulder.

A midshipman on watch hurried to report to the admiral, "Yes Sir?"

"Bring the prisoner up on deck. The lieutenant. Have the master at arms and a pair of marines to accompany him." The admiral paused for a moment and raised a finger to the young man, "I want a line rigged from the outboard mainsail yard block to the capstan as well. And have Lieutenant Thatcher bring me a tea."

"Aye Sir." The watch officer snapped a sharp salute before taking his leave, pacing away with purpose. Admiral Torren smiled for a flash as the young man began turning orders to carry out his task. *Young men like that are the hope for us all.* The smile faded as he thought of Lieutenant Pike. It wasn't long ago he had looked on the lieutenant with the same thoughts. *That's hogwash Alistair, you can't go around looking at every junior officer through a lens cracked by one traitor.*

A bow cannon roared to life in a great flash that sent a cloud of smoke shooting out of its bore. The admiral glare over the sea gap didn't shift. Even though visibility had dropped, and he could no longer make out the shape of sails through the darkness, he stared into the blackness where he last saw them.

"Lieutenant McGillis reporting, Sir. I have the traitor here, as you commanded Admiral." The master at arms' voice cut through the sounds of the bow gun crew reloading for another shot.

"Very well Lieutenant. Bind his hands and rig him to the line on the mainsail yard block," Admiral Torren ordered without so much as a look back. "Let me know when it is done."

"Aye Sir. The line on the mainsail yard block." Lieutenant McGillis replied, turning to and gesturing to the marines at either side of Lieutenant Pike. "You heard him boys, let's get to it. Get him rigged onto that line, I'll go get a crew from the deck watch to heave on the line."

Admiral Torren's thought swirled in his head. The assassination of two governors. Losing one of his ships to a vessel he believed to be the American U.S.S. Constitution. His dear friend Elliot Sharpe and the fresh revelation of his passing. The man he held below, accused to be responsible for that killing and the man on deck who was responsible for the deaths of both governors. He felt his jaw throbbing and he realized as his thoughts consumed him, he had been clenching it, grinding his back teeth. If there were two colonial governors involved in a conspiracy to continue the shipment of slaves, how many others were involved?

How deep did this go?

"We've got the prisoner all rigged up Sir. They're at the larboard rail at midship awaiting your orders." A sailor informed him.

Admiral Torren still faced over the bow, his eyes searching the darkness for any sign of the elusive prize he hunted. "Very well. They will wait on until I've had my tea."

"Aye Sir." The sailor stepped away, hurrying as if he could catch the admiral's wrath and have it directed at him at any moment.

He will tell me what I want to know. Admiral Torren made a deliberately slow walk back to where the master at arms had his prisoner in a precarious tension along the larboard rail. The lieutenant's wrists were bound together over his head and attached to a line running up to a block on the far end of the main sail yard, overhanging the sea. Lieutenant Thatcher arrived on deck with a steaming cup of tea and brought it over to the admiral.

"Ah, thank you, young man." The admiral said, taking the cup and blowing on the liquid's surface for a moment. He looked over Lieutenant Pike with a scowl and had his first sip of the hot tea. "I haven't the inclination to play at games with you lad. So, we will do this the way I learned early on. The way I saw it done as a young midshipman. I'm going to ask you a question and you will answer me, or you will writhe in the sea until you either tell me what I want to know or until you drown."

Lieutenant Pike struggled against the tension holding his hands overhead, grunting as the sailors heaved at the line bringing him onto his toes and pulling his upper body out of balance over the wooden rail. Admiral Torren stepped in close.

"Where does that pirate crew make berth?" he asked.

The lieutenant's breaths came in ragged heaves as he tried to keep his toes on deck. "She has no home port Admiral. None that I know of."

Admiral Torren shrugged his shoulders and raised his teacup, "That won't do Lieutenant." He looked back over his shoulder to the crew of sailors manning the line and gave them a nod. The men hauled at the line with vigor, lifting Lieutenant Pike off the deck and swinging him out over the sea as it rushed past North Wind's hull. "I'll ask you again, young man. Tell me where she makes berth, and I will spare you this unpleasantness."

Lieutenant Pike's body twisted in the passing wind; his neck craned to look at the inky water below him. "I don't know, please Sir, you must believe me!"

"I do not." Admiral Torren waved his hand at the line crew. They counted in unison and let the line go dropping their prisoner into the water below. A splash echoed up the side of North Wind and Admiral Torren peered over the rail. The line led down into the water where Lieutenant Pike thrashed in a cloud of bubbles until the motion of the ship drew the line taut, dragging him along just beneath the wavy surface. The admiral took another sip from his teacup finishing the last of the brew and handed the empty cup back to Lieutenant Thatcher whose eyes were as wide as the saucer under the delicate cup. "Haul away." The admiral called to the line crew. They grabbed hold of the taut line and began dragging it in hand over hand until Lieutenant Pike broke above the surface. The line crew continued pulling until their prisoner was twisting in the wind, hanging level with the larboard rail where Admiral Torren stood. He gagged and sputtered, spitting out sea water and laboring to draw breath.

"We can end this now Lieutenant. You can end this, just tell me where the pirates go for refuge. Tell me now and I will spare you any more of this." Admiral Torren called over the rail as Lieutenant Pike twisted in the breeze, coughing, and gasping for breath.

"I've told you what I know!" Lieutenant Pike rasped.

Admiral Torren held his hand up in the direction of the line crew, "I can watch you go through this far longer than you can endure it, I promise you that son." He dropped his hand, and the line crew released the rope after another unison count. Lieutenant Pike dropped into the sea again, writhing to break through the surface until the line holding him went taut dragging him along and only allowing him to the surface in brief jaunts between waves.

A bow cannon roared again, plugging out a shot into the dark curtain of night. Admiral Torren looked forward as the cloud of gun smoke drifted off to North Wind's larboard side. His eyes scanned back over the deck and locked onto the watch officer. The wind had shifted. A wave-soaked cry from Lieutenant Pike grabbed the admiral's attention back. "Haul him up." He ordered the line crew, who started pulling right away. Admiral Torren turned and found Lieutenant Thatcher, "Get the watch officer and find out why he has not adjusted for the wind shift, flapping sails is sloppy ship handling, snap to!"

"Admiral! Admiral! I think we've scored a hit on her! Look! She's burning!" the watch officer shouted across the deck, pointing in a frantic motion toward the horizon.

"Wha…?" the admiral uttered in disbelief as he looked forward and saw a spot of orange flame dancing in the wind. He turned back to Lieutenant Thatcher, "The odds of us scoring a hit at this range, in darkness, nonetheless. Maybe the master at arms is right about the luck of the Irish he is always drolling about. Get that watch officer back here to the helm where he ought to be and trim these sails. If she's aflame, now is the time to press our advantage."

London, England
16 Feb 1809

Drab gray clouds lined the sky, a stark contrast to the green of the English countryside. Lord Stockton departed his estate in a carriage drawn by a team of fine horses. Rattling up the road, he enjoyed the cool morning of early summer and took in the sights on his way toward the Huntsman Inn. Horse hoofs clopped along in a steady progression and the carriage jostled over the road as the team and driver led on through rolling hills. Hedgerows and tree lines passed by his window and Lord Stockton indulged in a pinch of snuff as the carriage rounded a turn onto an adjoining road. He took a piece of paper with half legible scrawling on it. The list of ship names provided by the late Lord Admiral Becker. Lord Stockton smiled. He hated loose ends. Beyond that, he hated social aspirants. There were classes of society for a reason. Those born to it were meant to be where they were. It was not a ladder. The last ship listed, H.M.S. North Wind. The last word was a messy scribble with all but the W indecipherable, but there was no doubt in Lord Stockton's mind. Admiral Torren would be aboard her, taking the finest and most powerful as his flagship. Lord Stockton knew of the Admiral by reputation only. He would have been as famous a name as Lord Admiral Nelson, had he not been implicated in the strategic disaster of being plugged against the American coast by the French under Admiral Cornwallis. All the better for what Lord Stockton had planned.

A pair of valets met the carriage as it pulled up to the front entrance. They opened the carriage door and placed a dark wooden step beneath the carriages built in steps.

"Good morning and welcome, Lord Stockton. There is a table in the parlor prepared for you and your guests." The valet said gesturing with his free hand to the front of the building while opening the carriage door with his other.

"Have any of them arrived yet?" Lord Stockton asked in a flat tone without making eye contact to either valet.

"No. None of your usual company is here. Though there is a stranger staying with us who has been asking about you. He checked in after your departure yesterday." The valet's response caught Lord Stockton off guard. He stopped mid step and turned to look at the valet who gave him the information.

"A stranger you say. What name did he give?" Lord Stockton's typical icy reserve broke under a wave of sudden concern.

The valet stumbled for a second, hesitating to give an answer. "He kept his name to himself, Lord. All I have been told of him is that he was asking about you. He is in the study now, if you would like I could show you to him."

Lord Stockton shot a sneering look toward the valet before scoffing, "I know my way."

An icy chill of the unknown crept up the English Lord's spine as he ascended the stairs and entered through the grand front doors. Inside the atrium, another valet waited to take the Lord's coat. Lord Stockton waved the man off and continued his urgent pace into a hallway lined in artwork and lit in the soft glow of oil lamps with sooty globes. Lord Stockton passed the open doors of a dining room with a low din of conversation emanating out into the hallway and then paused at the next doorway leading to the study. The large dark wooden door glistened as yellow flickering lamplight cast its hues against the finish. Lord Stockton stood for a moment, hesitating to enter. He questioned the intentions of this stranger, who he was and where he was from. Was he here to inquire after the sudden passing of Lord Admiral Becker? Taking a deep breath, Lord Stockton reached for the door handle and opened the door in an abrupt motion.

Inside the study a man sat in an overstuffed chair,

staring out the very window Lord Stockton had stood next to while watching Lord Admiral Becker struggle for breath in the last moments of his life.

Lord Stockton walked around the side of the chair, casting his gaze for a long moment out the window to the rolling green hills and hedgerows. "I've been told you were inquiring about me? I am Lord Stockton." He turned and looked over the stranger. The man sitting in the chair was younger than Lord Stockton by at least twenty years. He had a stout build and round face with dark eyes and a light complexion.

"Good morning, Lord Stockton. Please, have a seat and take a moment to share a few words with me." The stranger looked up from his stare for a moment before letting his eyes drift back to the scenic view. "There are a few matters I must discuss and relay to you before your other guests arrive."

Lord Stockton was taken aback for a moment before a swell of anger rose from his belly, "Who are you?"

"Have a seat, Lord Stockton, and keep your voice down. There are matters for us to discuss which need privacy and discretion. If you draw unnecessary attention, we will have to have this meeting elsewhere and not at your convenience."

Lord Stockton's throat locked before he could utter another objection. He stepped over to a chair next to the stranger and sank into it.

"Very good Sir. Now. I have it from reliable sources that the operation in Jamaica is in ruins. Can you confirm this?" The stranger's voice held an indistinguishable accent Lord Stockton couldn't quite place. He was certainly not from England, notes of

Spanish and French tendrils lingered around the edges of his word, but it wasn't distinctly either of those.

"It is. The governor who was brought into the fold in Kingston seems to have betrayed us or lost control of the island. It is unclear which." Lord Stockton was deliberate with each word choice. Incompetence was not dealt with lightly within The Order, but treachery was worse still.

"That's right. From what we have been told it seems a bit of both occurred. You dispatched a fleet? Or rather your pet admiral did, am I correct?" Lord Stockton fought off a look of shock from his face and his eyes met with the stranger's. "Oh come now, you didn't think there were any secrets, did you? In fact, the message that was brought from the Caribbean was months late and wildly incorrect. The insurrection in Kingston was not the work of pirates or slaves. It was one of ours. Taking charge of a situation before things got too out of hand. If I could meet that man I would shake his hand. But from everything we have been told he went aboard a vessel that has not been seen again."

"How do you know all of this?" Lord Stockton couldn't fight his shock and confusion any longer. "I have been receiving regular dispatches…"

Lord Stockton was cut off by the stranger holding up a hand in a dismissive gesture. "Our network extends far and wide. French spies, Spanish merchants, Dutch whalers, and every last missionary across the world. This situation is not unique, I just dealt with a similar ordeal on an island in the Pacific. The opium trade is far too profitable to be left in the hands of the locals. But that's another matter. You promised us ships and safe harbor for exchange to smugglers. Has there been a change of heart? Or are you just unable to live up to your end of the contract?"

"It is a problem, that is all. I have people working on it. We will resume at full capacity soon." Lord Stockton said with a low voice.

The stranger raised an eyebrow. "That half dead old admiral? He is your solution? Is he, within the fold?"

"No. No absolutely not. I have another man, in the American south, he is handling the problem, I assure you." Lord Stockton looked over his shoulder, nervous that anyone he knew would hear him in this position, speaking this way.

"I didn't take you for a dullard Lord Stockton. Mr. Clyde Ritten murdered your envoy, that isn't a sign of his good faith and cooperation. It was a mistake, trusting a man so dependent on the product and not the income it provides. You see, Lord Stockton, slaves, like opium, are far too profitable to be trusted to the locals." The stranger stood, picking up a pair of glasses from the dark wood table by the window. He hefted a decanter and removed the stopper, pouring a generous portion of a light gold whiskey into each glass. He turned and held one out for Lord Stockton.

"No thank you." Lord Stockton felt his face flush and mouth go dry at the offer.

"Relax Lord Stockton," the man lifted both glasses, taking a sip from each. "If I wanted to kill you, I would shove a dagger into your ear. Have the drink."

Lord Stockton reached out and took the glass, fighting a tremble in his hand. "What do you suggest I do then? As far as the East India Company is concerned?"

"Lord Stockton, arrangements have been made. I am here to ensure you understand your future role in this. We supplied ample upfront payment and have received nothing yet in return. The East India Company will supply its ships, its manpower and every means available to it to ensure this endeavor succeeds. I'm not here to relay threats, but if you fail us again…" the stranger looked out of the window and let his voice trail off as he lifted his glass and took a drink.

"I won't. We won't." Lord Stockton answered, lifting his own glass for a sip with a quiver in his fingers.

"That's very good. Good news." The stranger turned, holding out his glass as if to toast Lord Stockton's renewed commitment. "Our solution will take care of the whole lot. That decrepit old admiral, the pirate threat, your rogue plantation owner. We will establish a new exchange point and relay that to you. Nassau is too small and frequented by your warships too often. Expect a messenger within a month. We will expect our recurring payments the month after."

"I'm sure that won't be a problem. How might I ask are you setting everything back in your favor so surely?" Lord Stockton leaned forward as he asked.

"Things have already been set in motion. You need not concern yourself with it. That is all, Lord Stockton. You should excuse yourself to the parlor where your guests will be arriving soon." The stranger gave Lord Stockton a small wave as if to shoo him away.

The English Lord spun with wounded pride. His face flushed a beet red and his brow beaded with a line of sweat. His mouth hung open for a moment as he contemplated making another statement. The notion passed him, and he stood, giving the man a nod and walked away trying to regain his composure. As he passed back into the dim hallway, Lord Stockton gave his vest a tug smoothing out the front. He looked to his left and could see the door to the parlor was open with light from the room flooding into the hall. Lord Stockton took a few tentative steps toward the parlor door. Familiar voices floated from within the room. Lord Stockton could hear the Lords Ownership discussing their predicament. He edged his way toward the door.

"It is an unfortunate bit of business. But we must break ties with this whole endeavor. It has cost us dearly already. I have been complicit until now, but we all stand to be implicated in crimes ranging from murder to treason. Not to mention the ships and men we have likely lost. I say enough is enough. If the Royals find out this scheme, we will all hang." The voice ranted.

Lord Stockton's face radiated in hot anger while his hands trembled in a combination of fear and disbelief. He fought the urge to barge in and confront the dissenting voice with a violent ending. A deep breath calmed his nerves. He looked over his shoulder to the study door he had exited moments ago, then back to the daylight pouring in through the parlor entry. Another deep breath and Lord Stockton regained his composure. He stepped into the doorway silencing the voices within the room.

PART THREE
"ACTA NON VERBA"

Chapter 13

'Drowned Maiden'
22 Mar 1809
24 Degrees 30' N, 76 Degrees 44' W

Lilith watched as flames licked higher into the dark night sky. The longboat Chibs and Dr. LeMeux had set adrift contained split wood, old rags of sailcloth soaked in lantern oil and much to Chibs' chagrin, a barrel of rum. The Drowned Maiden eased away from the burning light and slipped into total darkness as the flames grew higher. Just as Dr. LeMeux had predicted, the lantern lights from their pursuing ships began to vector their way toward the ball of flame bobbing along on the ocean's waves. With no lights and as little sound as possible, the Maiden would hopefully be able to slip by her pursuers undetected. As Lilith watched the ships draw nearer to the burning decoy her heart sank. Fleeing felt like defeat. In her mind, she worked through the possibilities of firing on the warships as they became silhouetted by the fire of the decoy. The smell of pipe smoke announced Chibs' presence behind her, and Lilith smiled in the dark.

"Trying to figure a way to sink them?" Chibs' rough voice asked.

Lilith turned toward Chibs, giving him a shrug. "What's to say we couldn't Chibs?"

"Near forty guns on two of those ships, and likely a hundred guns on the flagship. We be blasted to slivers before we could reload." Chibs pulled a long breath of smoke from his pipe, exhaling through his nose. "We've already sunk one of their fleet miss. They aren't chasing us around to board the ship and bring us in for a trial and hanging. Whoever is in command of that fleet wants to see us to the bottom with every soul aboard."

Lilith shifted her gaze back out to the fire light of their burning decoy boat. "What do you suggest we do Chibs?"

"Well, Cap'n. We can't run forever, so at some point we will have to face them." Chibs' stare followed Lilith's out to the wave tossed boat as it burned away, drawing in their adversaries. "Why face them all at once?"

"I'm not sure what you mean." Lilith said reaching out toward the stern rail and leaning against it.

Chibs took another draw from his pipe and pulled it from his teeth, smacking the side of the bowl against the wooden rail to knock the ash and residue out. "Well, Cap'n, if we can manage to separate them somehow, we would stand a far better chance against each one on its own. But that flagship will be a problem. She's not like the one Captain James attacked.

This one is far bigger, and she will have more guns and more men aboard her than we could ever hope to battle."

"Suppose we run her into a reef somewhere?" Lilith suggested, grinning at Chibs while reminding him of their clever victory over H.M.S. Valor.

Chibs shrugged his shoulders and shook his head, "We were lucky with that. This ship is going to have seasoned sailors and very skilled navigators aboard her. We could try it, but the chances they will fall for that one are slim my deary."

Lilith thought in silence for a long moment. The shrinking light of their burning trick glimmered against her eyes. Chibs mentioning Captain James had stirred up memories and she felt her nose tickling while her eyes began to well with tears. "We need to look over the charts we have Chibs. Come sunrise, I want to have a plan to separate them."

"Aye Cap'n. I'll see what we have for charts." Chibs left the aft castle to head below, passing Lieutenant Shelton who was on his way up to see Captain Lilith.

"A well-done maneuver Captain Lilith. It appears we have slipped from the grasp of the fleet. For now." The lieutenant offered as he walked along the rail.

Lilith felt a clash within her. She did not want to engage in another discussion over the fate of Lieutenant Pike. "I've managed a few good decisions. It was Dr. LeMeux's idea really. He is a clever man."

"Aye, a clever man indeed. But it takes a bold commander to entertain clever ideas. You've done well." The lieutenant stopped alongside Lilith at the rail, turning aft watch through the dark gap of night as the burning debris in the longboat slipped further and further away.

"What is it you want Lieutenant Shelton? Are you here to continue trying to convince me that Lieutenant Pike is alive?" Lilith was not in the mood to entertain small talk.

"Well, Captain Lilith. If he is alive, he was probably taken as a prisoner on the flagship. But that is another matter entirely. I believe if we run now, we would be missing an opportunity." Lieutenant Shelton paused for a moment to see if he still had Lilith's attention. "We are beating close haul and have been since you set your fire adrift. Which was a brilliant plan. The fleet has converged around your decoy, and we now stand upwind with several hours of darkness left."

"Are you suggesting we turn and fight?" Lilith raised her eyebrows, scrunching her forehead a little. At first instinct she was skeptical of the plan. The firepower amassed around their decoy was enough to out gun the Maiden ten times over.

"Not necessarily turn and fight. We could turn and keep the wind, broad reach, fire a volley and then tack back over to close haul. They will surely pursue us, but in darkness and beating against the wind we will retain enough of an advantage that I believe we can do some real damage before slipping away yet again." The lieutenant's eyes were wide with the possibility. "Our batteries must be performing at their absolute best and the deck crew will need to make very sharp sail changes. But I believe we are capable of it, Captain."

Lilith looked through the darkness. The glow of light

given off by their decoy still glimmered bright enough that she could make out the full silhouette of the large flag ship, the bow of one and the larboard hull wall of another. She let a long moment of silence elapse and thought over the lieutenant's plan. Running close haul to the west would be slow, turning northwest and running broad reach would be much quicker, but it would lead back toward Nassau. Lilith's thoughts landed on Lieutenant Pike for a fleeting moment and her heart sank. He had trained her gun crews. They were capable of reloading quickly enough to execute Lieutenant Shelton's plan. "Get me Chibs and get the gun crews below deck, run them out and be ready."

"Aye Captain." Lieutenant Shelton cracked a smile as he departed company from Lilith, scurrying below deck as quick as his feet would take him.

'North Wind'
22 Mar 1809
24 Degrees 32' N, 76 Degrees 41' W

All hands were ready for action as North Wind slipped through low choppy seas in the darkness toward the burning hulk. Admiral Torren stood near the bowsprit looking over the water and scanning for flotsam that would accompany a sinking ship. A single pile of burning refuse was all he could make out as they drew nearer, and anger welled inside of him. Again, he turned his eyes over the seas beneath him, scouring for any sign of a sunken vessel.

"It appears they have already surrendered to the deep, Sir." Lieutenant Thatcher noted in a joyful tone as he stood alongside the bow rail next to the admiral.

"No, lad. We've been duped." The admiral retorted, shaking his head in disgust with himself.

Lieutenant Thatcher shifted his gaze from the burning debris up to Admiral Torren's sullen face. "Pardon Sir?"

"Tell me what you see in the water, son. What do you see floating on the water's surface?" the admiral asked while flexing his jaw and tamping the tip of his cane on deck.

"Part of their ship, Sir. Burning." The lieutenant pointed out at the burning debris.

"No. You're seeing what they wanted you to see. What they wanted us to see. A shot from that distance, in dark, scoring a hit that would do enough damage to sink them? I should have known better. Boyish optimism has put us in a very precarious position. My better instincts disbelieved this and now they have been confirmed. This was a blunder." Admiral Torren turned inboard looking over the sailors on deck. "Watch officer?"

A young lieutenant promptly reported in front of the admiral, "Yes Sir."

A distant rumble sounded stealing Admiral Torren's next words from him. With the glint of light from the flames dancing through the rigging and glowing against the sails a series of flashes showed through the darkness. Then a sailor's scream cut through the night, "Get down!" the last note of his voice was drowned out by the scream of incoming shot. North Wind shuddered as iron crashed into wood. The admiral stood, unmoved by the furious scream of incoming rounds and impacts. The deck trembled beneath his feet, but it did not heave or pitch. In a moment the chaos faded, replaced by shouts of sailors and petty officers.

"They'll have to do much better than that. A clever trick though." Admiral Torren said, looking over at Lieutenant Thatcher who had taken cover behind wooden bulwark. "Get up lad. We've business to attend to."

"Aye, Sir." Lieutenant Thatcher replied as he rose from the deck boards, a hesitant grimace on his face.

"Get a damage report for me at once." Admiral Torren's sharp tone betrayed his annoyance. He turned and looked over the deck of North Wind. From where he stood, he could see a single stay line had been severed. There were a few sailors on the aft castle that lay on deck, wounded. He searched for North Wind's captain on deck. At first glance, not seeing the vessel's commanding officer, Admiral Torren felt his face flush with irritation. He stepped his way toward the quarterdeck, leaning forward in an urgent march without the aid of his cane. "Watch officer!" he called out, scanning the deck as he walked.

A lieutenant rushed down from the quarterdeck, "Yes Sir!" His uniform had smears of dark blood on the front.

"Where is Captain Landreth? We were just fired on, why are we not maneuvering?" the admiral asked in a stern voice.

"He was on the aft castle as we took the incoming Sir. I'm afraid he is wounded, Sir." The lieutenant looked flustered.

"Oh." Admiral Torren's tone changed, "Very well. See to it that he is brought to the surgeon at once. Where might his first lieutenant be?"

The young officer hesitated for a beat, "He is wounded as well, Sir. They were in conversation when we took fire."

Admiral Torren knew before he spoke, "You are the second lieutenant, aren't you, young man?"

"I am Sir." The reply came with a burdened sigh.

"Not to fear Son. I have the ship. Have the helm bring her about larboard adjust for broad reach and run larboard battery out. We've wasted time already so snap to lad." The admiral rattled his orders as if it came as natural as drawing breath. "I will have my aid deal with the wounded. You handle the crew; I will handle the enemy."

"Yes Sir." The lieutenant gave a sharp reply before turning to the quarter deck. "All hands! Prepare mainsail for broad reach, helm four points to larboard and hold! Run out larboard battery and clear for action!"

Another rumble sounded in the dark distance. Admiral Torren jaunted as quickly as his legs would allow, grabbing an intact stay line and leaning over the rail to try and catch a muzzle flash in sight. The whizzing screamed overhead, sending sailors scrambling to the deck. North Wind shook from a pair of impacts on her stern railing and another sailor who had gone to aid the wounded rose his voice in a blistering scream of agony. Admiral Torren looked aloft, there were several holes in North Wind's sails. Whoever was in control of this pirate ship's gunnery was skilled. "They are aiming for the masts and the rudder. They want to cripple us." He mumbled to himself.

On deck, North Wind's crew sprang into action, adjusting sail and preparing their batteries to return fire on their enemy.

"Lieutenant!" a voice called out from the quarterdeck. Admiral Torren's attention was stolen by another set of cannon reports in the dark, the incoming fire whirred and whistled but in a softer pitch. The admiral rushed to North Wind's starboard rail, opposite from where he had just been standing. The sound of crunching and cracking wood, screams and shouts sounded from H.M.S. Destiny drifted in over the water separating them.

"Lieutenant!" the voice from the quarterdeck sounded again. "The steering, Sir. She's not answering!"

Admiral Torren lowered his eyes to the murky black surface of the Caribbean below, his shoulders weighing heavier with each further development. "Damn."

'Southern Song'
26 Mar 1809
17 Degrees 48' N, 73 Degrees 52' W

Darkness filled the hold of Southern Song as the ship sloshed its way forward. Rory had no notion of their course other than that eventually the crew intended to bring their cargo of slaves to the American south in hopes of netting some profit. Since their boarding, the space below deck had become increasingly more inhospitable by the hour. Several of the captive slaves had become seasick, the results of which filled the cramped space with a pungent odor. It was damp and crowded. Outside of Rory's cell, which scarcely allowed him room, the slaves were crammed together with their cramped bodies constantly in contact with one another. Rory's lamentations for his own condition faded while he listened to the misery surrounding himself amplify. He heard the voices of the strong comforting those whose nerves were frayed. He listened while a young man consoled another. Nearest to his cell a voice whispered.

"Mister!" it was a young black man, with a French slant to his accent. "How long have you been in here?"

Rory let a long silence pass. "Days. Weeks. I'm not sure."

The young man's voice slipped through the darkness. "Where are they taking us?"

"I don't know exactly. I would wager you will wind up in the cotton fields of Georgia." Rory pulled against the shackles restraining his hands. "But they could have any destination in mind. New Orleans, Chesapeake, there's no telling really."

"I think the pirate lady will come. I think she will free us and kill this crew." The voice came again. A quiet settled through the cabin.

Rory thought for a moment. Southern Song's captain knew of the pirate threat, he wanted to avoid it, at least, that's why he claimed he killed Dog. "Where were you when they took you aboard?"

"We were taken from our bunkhouse. In Haiti. We all worked in a sugar house." The voice cut through dark silence. Rory knew every ear in the hold was listening.

"Haiti. I didn't think the captain was that foolish. He is trying to avoid the pirates." Rory said aloud, mostly to himself.

"I heard the pirates are led by a woman." Another voice came in across the dark hold. "A slave woman who wouldn't be a slave anymore."

The fouled air of the hold gave Rory a shudder. He had heard of the pirate crew; had heard they were raiding slave smugglers and gave no quarter to those that they caught in their clasp. But Rory hadn't heard they were captained by a woman. Much less an escaped slave woman. "Hell hath no fury, the saying goes…" His voice trailed into the dark.

"She raided the cane plantations in Haiti. The harvest suffered for it, that's why we are being sold. Now she will catch this ship and free us!" the first voice exclaimed, growing in volume until he was shushed by a pair of scornful whisperers.

"The whole island is changing. The masters, they are fearful of this woman. Some have sold their slaves, sold their crop fields. They fear us, for the first time ever, they are afraid." The first voice chimed again.

Rory felt a lurch in Southern Song's hull. She was in the open sea and running with the wind for sure. The prisoners in her hold were not as accustomed to the motion as Rory had become and with the growing intensity of her rocking and heaving more of them became ill. The smell made Rory nauseas. Shuddering wave rolled from the back of his neck up through his throat. He retched onto the floor. Another wave rolled through his body, induced by the smell permeating the confines of the hold. His stomach heaved but nothing came forth. He strained against the shackles on his wrists, opening the raw skin where the iron met his flesh. The voices of the captured continued to talk amongst themselves while Rory was consumed by his own agony. They faded in and out with his consciousness, only allowing him to comprehend snippets.

"She will come..." a voice floated through the dark, more words were said but were muffled out by Rory's pounding pulse in his ears. He shifted his weight as Southern Song lurched into a wave.

The voice returned to his ears. "If they find us, will they rescue him too?"

The question lingered in Rory's mind. Floating in and out with his awareness was a lingering sense that the rescue of these captured slaves would also be the seal of his fate. Rory grappled in his mind, fought through the liquid exhaustion that threatened to steal him back into unconscious drifting. If he could convince the prisoners below deck that he was somehow a fallen champion of their freedom, perhaps they would insist he be spared. Footfalls on the deck above wrested his mind back into the present. His wrists ached and throbbed against the iron restraints holding him suspended within his filthy confines.

Muffled shouts filtered through the noise of the hold. The imprisoned outside of Rory's cell hushed all at once. Southern Song shifted in a hard turn that pulled Rory's weight against his arms. The steps above them were rapid, almost running. The volume and intensity of the shouts above grew before they faded beneath the rumble of cannon carriages being rolled into their firing positions. It was happening. Something was going on that threatened the Southern Song's crew. Rory's imagination raced. He pictured the fearsome band of pirates coming over Southern Song's bulwark, slashing her crew to ribbons and liberating the slaves from their dismal prison below deck. His mind wheeled, thoughts buzzing through faster than he could process. If it was the pirates, what would they do with him? Would he be held as a prisoner again? Could he convince them that he was somehow aligned with their cause? What if Southern Song wasn't reacting to pirates? Could it be the Royal Navy or the American Navy? Rory tried to concoct a solution for every eventuality.

The roar of a cannon shook Southern Song and reverberated through the hold. Rory's pulse raced in his chest while his wrists and ears throbbed and pounded with every beat. The voices in the hold started their chattering again. They exclaimed some of the same questions that spun through Rory's mind. Another cannon fired above on the gun deck, trembling the ship. A flurry of voices followed the explosive shot and footsteps rushed above them in a frantic dance of panic. A faint whistle pierced through the noise of the hold and Rory tightened every fiber of his body for what came next.

Revenge of the Drowned Maiden

Ortega's - Near Tortuga, Haiti
10 Feb 1809

Tiny craters littered the dust at Emilia's feet. She stood at the foot of a large grave, staring with tear blurred vision at the rough wooden marker she had placed. Tears streamed down her cheeks, dropping from her jawline and landing in the dirt. A few of the men who worked with her father had helped with the burial. She had no money for a coffin. Her father hadn't been wealthy or influential. The friends he had were laborers for the shipwright, dockworkers, or sailors. Men who were struggling themselves to provide for their own families. A small bundle of wildflowers Emilia had gathered fluttered in the breeze as she stood in the afternoon heat of the Haitian sun staring down at the fresh mound of dirt. Her eyes were a glaze. She felt the weight of loss and grief laying across her shoulders, clasping its fingers around her ribs and squeezing her until it felt difficult to draw breath.

As the sun dipped low, Emilia's despair waned beneath a rising tide of anger. The man her father had taken in, the man she had helped nurse back to health, had betrayed them in the worst possible way. To the north, lights and smoke began to announce the festivities of evening in Tortuga. Beyond the huddled buildings and dirt roads of town, the sea expanded across the horizon. Under the light of the setting sun, its radiant blue called to her.

In the days since his murder, Emilia was haunted by the memories of her father and an overwhelming sense of regret that she did not take her revenge when the opportunity was before her. Her father had taught her how to wield the cutlass he had kept as a holdover from his seafaring days. He had taught her how to aim and fire his pistol. She had been face to face with the man who killed her father and yet unable to do anything about it. The walls of her home closed in tighter around her every evening and each night she spent tossing and turning, restless with visions of regret and fantasies of revenge. Her father's voice would enter her mind, but they were not words she wanted to hear.

"Anger is a poison, mija. Let it go." She could hear it as if he were next to her. "Revenge doesn't serve you, it consumes you. Killing him won't satisfy it."

"I know it papa, but I have to. I cannot stay here, and I cannot let it go." Emilia whispered into the darkness of her home. "You were a sailor. You had your adventures, so will I."

Emilia would not be haunted through another restless night without sleep, a few steps behind her in the grass lay a leather pack with the clothes, tools and supplies Emilia had packed from her home. On top of the pack, a belt with her father's scabbarded cutlass and pistol sat waiting for her to begin her journey. Emilia wiped away her tears, silently pushing down her emotions.

"It's time for me to go Papa. Goodbye." She said aloud to the wooden marker. Emilia turned to pick up her things, rushing to outrun the wave of guilt and sadness building within her. To the south, the forest loomed in the dying light of day. Emilia took a deep breath as she stepped onto the trail her father had used in search of large straight trees for timbers. The urge to look over her shoulder at the home she had been raised in tugged at Emilia's mind. It belonged to the shipwright, she reminded herself, no matter how much he had valued her father's skill and labor for all those years, eventually he would want to house another of his employees there.

Evening faded and the cool of night began to settle in. The trail twisted and turned through the jungle and Emilia had to fight back tears when she would see her father's mark on trees of various sizes. Enough moonlight filtered through the canopy above to light her way forward until she came to the far edge of the forest. Plodding her way out of the jungle she walked into a field of freshly harvested sugarcane. The night sky opened up as she made her way out from under the canopy, and it seemed as if millions of stars were visible while moonlight lit the fields in front of her under its soft white glow.

Emilia forged ahead, letting the moonlight guide her way. She was careful to avoid roads, sticking to the recently harvested cane fields and those that weren't at maturity yet. The countryside was littered with hills and intersected by natural streams and irrigation ditches. She continued her way southward until she came across the road where her father had found Tim on that fateful night so many months ago. Crossing the road, her eyes flitted back and forth. The spot where Tim had lay next to the ditch glared at her from just up the hill. It mocked her and waved her father's death at her in contempt. Emilia shook away the feelings of doubt and sadness. Her father was a kind man, to his core. He had died being the man he was, at the hands of an animal who would take advantage of anyone. Emilia thought of Tim for a moment. She thought of how easy it would have been to drive her father's sword through his chest as he lay in bed, wounded and dying from a fever. If only she had aimed her pistol shot more carefully.

The long hours of night dwindled away as Emilia plodded along, her father's sword swaying in its scabbard at her side. Her feet ached and her back longed to be rid of the leather pack she carried. Daylight began its calling off in the east just as she crested a long, steep hill. Golden pink tones beat away the inky dark skies and stirred a breeze that carried a slight chill across her light brown skin. The sea was close again, she could smell its salty tang in the air. Her suspicions were confirmed, as Emilia walked over the highest ridge of the hill, she could see the Caribbean stretching out in front of her. Dark blue for now, with high choppy waves that washed out with the tide. Staying high on the ridge, Emilia made her way westward. She was careful about her footing; the hillside was steep and as she made her way westward, she began to suspect the hillside ended in a sheer drop to the sea. Off to the north Emilia noted the tree line of forest was again visible, it slanted from its east-to-west orientation southward up ahead of her and disappeared behind rolling hills. Emilia continued westward as the ridge she walked rose higher in front of her. The breeze stiffened, tugging at her shirt and making her eyes water. The ridge grew steeper still and to her right she could see the grade falling away down toward a small cove lined by white sands and bordered by the tall canopy of forest. Emilia's breath became short and labored as she took the last few strides to the top of the ridge.

The view was spectacular. The ridge she stood on fell away in a steep drop to a pocket of cove below. White caps topped the Caribbean waves as far as she could see. The sun's first direct rays of daylight poured over the landscape and glinted off the sea. Stepping toward the ledge in front of her, Emilia looked down to the water as it roiled through the narrow opening of the cove. Through the shadows, Emilia laid her eyes on a sight that made her heart skip. The wooden hull of a ship laying on its side. Battered by waves but unmoving all the same, the ship was lodged hard onto the coral reef below. Its deck was a splintered mess of twisted and buckled timbers, its masts were shattered and lines hung limp into the sea. Tim had not lied about the band of pirates, nor about the shipwreck. Emilia's stare locked onto wooden hulk. Whoever had battled that ship had been the victor of their fight. Emilia had found what she was searching for.

Chapter 14

'Southern Song'
26 Mar 1809
17 Degrees 48' N, 73 Degrees 52' W

The crack and groan of twisting timbers drowned all other noise in Southern Song's hold. Her hull trembled and seawater gushed in through a breach. Rory closed his eyes, fighting back his panic. His wrists screamed with the pain of raw flesh under constant tension as he tried to wriggle himself free from the constraining shackles. Outside of his cell, the captured slaves bound together and stood little chance of escaping the water. Inside, Rory was a rat in a cage. Even once he wrested himself free of the chained shackles, if he could, he would still be locked in his cell. He could feel the ship listing to one side, water began to collect around his ankles. Rory pulled at his shackles, ignoring the burning pain that shot up his arms he twisted and writhed against the iron restraints. He gritted his teeth, setting his strength against his right wrist and pulling with every ounce of his waning strength. A trickle of blood oozed from the back of Rory's hand, working its way down his forearm while water began to lap at his shins.

A scream of pain escaped from Rory's clenched teeth. His wrist came free from the clenches of the iron shackle. A wave of nausea washed over him as he immediately shifted focus to his other wrist. Footsteps ran in frantic jaunts on the deck overhead. Loud concussions sounded as Southern Song's crew returned fire against their aggressors. Outside of his cell, Rory hardly noticed the captured slaves frozen in panic. His sole focus centered around freeing his remaining wrist from the iron shackle. He leaned his weight down, pulling and twisting, rubbing the raw flesh into an open wound that tore and bled. He bunched his fingers all into a point, trying to make his hand smaller. He lifted his weight and then twisted his hand, pulling again to try and extricate himself from the shackle. The seawater had risen to knee level and forced the slaves in the hold who were sitting to their feet. Rory could feel their panic. It mixed with his own. He lifted himself onto his toes, pushing his bound hand as high as he could and then dropped his weight down, pulling with everything he had against his wrist. The pain was excruciating. His first attempt moved the shackle up his wrist and over the base of his hand. He repeated his maneuver, letting out a scream in anticipation of the jolt of pain. The shackle slipped. His wrist came free in a spray of blood with a ribbon of torn flesh that remained gripped by the iron ring. Rory fell into the rising seawater in a daze of shock and pain. It had risen to his mid-thigh while he struggled to free himself from the last of his restraints. As he fell free, the cool water surrounded him, it drowned out the chaos of the hold, smothered the noise. Rory's awareness faded, drifting with the motion of Southern Song.

A pair of hands grabbed his shirt and hauled him above the water's surface. Dark skinned faces with wide eyes looked on as a pair of them hoisted Rory's head above the water. He coughed and sputtered, spitting seawater out. The woven flat iron door that had enclosed his cell lay slanted, leaning against the opposite wall of the hold.

"How did you?" Rory coughed, looking around at the eyes of the captured slaves. "Why?"

An explosion shattered through Southern Song's hull sending shards of wood and iron flying through the hold. The ship shuddered and pitched from the force of impacting rounds. A storm of muskets fired above, and Rory could hear the thudding of bodies collapsing to the deck under the withering fire.

"Come on! Move already!" a voice urged, spurning Rory into motion.

The clatter of steel against steel rang through the air and more gun shots could be heard while Rory moved through the rising water in the hold toward the stairs. He paused at the bottom, looking back over the faces following him. They didn't know him, yet they had gone to the effort of freeing him from his cell. Voices called Rory's attention back to the deck overhead. The voices weren't from Southern Song's crew.

"Where is the captain?" one shouted in a thick French accent.

A brief pause elapsed. Rory held a finger up toward the captives waiting for him to continue moving up the stairs. "Bugger off frog! This is an American vessel, you have no…" A single gunshot cut off the reply.

Rory's blood turned to ice in his veins. His mind reeled with the possibilities that awaited him above deck. The clattering of swords had died away, the only reminder that anything had gone awry was the gradually building amount of seawater in the hold. Behind him, one of the captives began to press against Rory's back. Above him, the weather hatch flew open. Rory was greeted by the sight of a pair of sailors training pistols downward at him. They shouted urgent orders in French, which Rory did not speak nor understand. He raised his hands in a gesture of surrender.

"I mean you no hostile intent." Rory shouted, hoping one of them could understand English. "I have been wrongfully imprisoned by these slavers!"

The pair of sailors exchanged a glance, one of them stepped forward onto the next plank of the stairs. "Would you be the man under the employ of a Mr. Clyde Ritten?" his heavy French accent made his words difficult for Rory to decipher, but the name, Clyde Ritten, rang through unmistakably.

"Yes. Yes, I work for Mr. Ritten!" Rory shook his upraised hands in excitement, feeling he had been saved from his string of bad luck.

"I am sorry for your luck then. But we are here to deliver a message from your employer's partners in Europe." The French sailor smiled beneath his thick mustache. He trained the muzzle of his pistol onto

Rory and squeezed the trigger.

'North Wind'
22 Mar 1809
24 Degrees 32' N, 76 Degrees 41' W

Dawn found H.M.S. North Wind bobbing adrift at sea. Her crew was hard at work to repair damage sustained the night before. Admiral Torren stood over the stern rail, looking down as a pair of sailors hanging from lines worked at repairing her rudder. Lieutenant Thatcher approached the admiral holding a steaming cup of tea. Admiral Torren took the beverage, giving his aid a small nod before turning his attention back over the side.

"Lines and sail will be replaced within an hour Sir. I spoke with the surgeon, and he has done what he can for our wounded for now." Lieutenant Thatcher reported, looking aloft over his shoulder as sailors replaced the tattered main and top sail on the main mast.

"Very good. Once the rudder is in working condition again, we will be on our way." Admiral Torren said before blowing on the surface of his tea sending little wisps of vapor outward from the cup.

"Nassau then Sir?" the lieutenant asked.

Admiral Torren shot him a sour glare. "We won't be returning to a port lad."

Lieutenant Thatcher looked confused for a moment,

"Sir, the wounded..."

"The wounded are in the King's service. Our present situation demands that we press an attack against our adversary. If that means that some of them do not survive, they will have died an honorable death in service to King and country." Admiral Torren interrupted his aid before the young officer could complete his thought.

"Right Sir. Very well. I will notify you as soon as the sails and rigging are back in good order." Lieutenant Thatcher stiffened as he gave his reply. He snapped a salute before departing the aft castle.

The admiral brooded. His stare lifted from the sailors dangling off North Wind's stern out to the horizon. It had been such a rudimentary ruse. A simple ploy to gain the wind against him, but it had worked. He had bitten into the bait before taking a moment to consider every angle of his circumstances. North Wind and Destiny had sustained the most damage. Though Destiny was still fit for sailing. As early as the sea was visible Admiral Torren had ordered signal flags raised directing the two ships still fit to sail to pursue a search pattern after the pirate crew. An angry regret grabbed at his insides as he looked over the horizon. Both Destiny and Taurus were beating a course upwind in search of the pirates. The admiral hoped his boldness would not prove to be another rash step directly into the pirate captain's hands.

"Watch officer." Admiral Torren summoned a young midshipman over to himself. He was very young, with a fresh face and bright eyes.

"Yes, Sir?" the midshipman replied, standing in rigid

attention in front of the admiral.

A smile crossed the admiral's face, the young midshipman before him was a familiar face. "Midshipman Brant, isn't it?"

The young man returned the admiral's smile, "Yes, Sir. Yes, it is."

"I thought so. No doubt you have heard the rumors of your father's command. How are you holding up son?" the admiral asked in a softer voice than normal, lowering his volume so none but Midshipman Brant would hear.

"I am ready for action Sir. If it proves out true, he died valiantly while doing his duty. I will not shame him by shying away from mine." Midshipman Brant replied as the smile faded from his composure.

"No doubt your father would be proud. No doubt at all. I want you to have the master at arms bring me up the prisoner." Admiral Torren's tone slipped back into a formal bearing.

"Which prisoner do you intend to speak with Sir?" Midshipman Brant asked.

Admiral Torren finished his tea, though it had gone cold. "The traitor. I have no use for the American."

"Aye Sir, I'll have him brought to you at once." Midshipman Brant rendered a sharp salute before departing.

Warm winds from the southwest were picking up as the sun rose higher in the eastern sky. Dark spots on the horizon revealed that land was close, and Admiral Torren began to consider if North Wind would need to put out longboats and tow themselves into an anchorage to complete repairs. As the thought crossed his mind, one of the sailors over the stern began to hoist himself up to the rail. The admiral leaned over, giving the sailor and inquisitive look.

"All finished Sir. We've got her fixed up as good as we can out at sea." The sailor reported as he took in line hand over hand, lifting himself toward the deck.

"I plan on making sail in pursuit of those pirates. Will it hold?" the admiral asked, raising an eyebrow at the carpenter's mate.

"It's not my best work Sir. But it will hold through storm and swell well enough. I'd recommend replacing it when we get the opportunity." The sailor answered as he crested over the top of the bulwark.

"Well, enough then. Good work the both of you, an extra tot of rum for each tonight." The admiral smiled, clapping the first sailor up on his shoulder.

"Thank you, Sir." The sailors said almost in unison as the first one up helped the second onto the deck.

Admiral Torren caught sight of the master at arms, accompanied by a pair of marines, escorting Lieutenant Pike up onto the aft castle.

"Mr. Pike," the admiral began, drawing a long reluctant breath. "It seems I have run out of time and therefore patience. Your uncooperative attitude thus far has forced me to measures which I do not want to take." He looked forward over the prisoner's shoulder tracing over North Wind's rigging. "I need to know where that pirate crew makes port. Be it an established port, an anchorage somewhere remote a damn native village or a Jesuit mission. Wherever they seek respite, I will be there waiting for them when they return next. Either that, or I will have you hanging from the highest yard as I scour the Caribbean in search of them."

Lieutenant Thatcher made his way up onto the aft castle, peering around from behind one of the marines. "North Wind is rigged and ready to sail, Sir."

Admiral Torren shifted his gaze to his aid. "Very well, young man. Full canvas, bring her about close haul to the wind. Have the quartermaster run a line under keel."

Lieutenant Thatcher's eyes went wide, and he shot a look over to the prisoner, standing in his tattered uniform with his hands and ankles in shackles. "Aye Sir, full canvas and close haul. Run a line." He repeated, rendering a salute slower than normal while trying not to look at the pitiful sight of the prisoner.

Admiral Torren turned back to Lieutenant Pike with a grim look. "Tell me Mr. Pike. Have you ever witnessed or heard tales of a keelhauling?"

'H.M.S. Taurus'
10 Apr 1809
19 Degrees 53' N, 72 Degrees 33' W

Afternoon sun cast its light against H.M.S Taurus' taut sails, her canvas basking in its rays in stark contrast to the piercing blue sky. The Caribbean lapped against her hull as she slid through its gentle swell, varying shades of sea from teal blue to an almost emerald played along beneath the surface as varying depths ran under her keel. Off her larboard rail, a white sand shoreline bordered the overhanging forest of the Haitian coast. Her crew milled about the ship, busy with the work of sailing and navigating while lookouts scoured the horizons and coastline for any sign of the ship that had thus far eluded their search.

"Eight fathoms, sandy bottom." A leadsman on the larboard bow called back toward Taurus' quarterdeck.

"Aye, eight fathoms." The watch officer replied before turning to the helm, "Take her one point over to starboard, toward deeper water."

A sailor manning the helm adjusted the ship's wheel, watching closely as she responded. He let out a deep sigh, realizing he had been breathing in short, shallow breaths. There was a tension on deck, as tight as the stay lines holding onto the main yard in a storm. The vessel they were searching after had made a group of the Royal Navy's most senior commanders look like children at play the other night and every man aboard the three-ship squadron had as exposed as fish washed ashore. Taurus still wore battle scars on her hull from the rounds she received after they had charged in like fools only to find a burning decoy.

Captain Wilford Hemshire, commander of H.M.S. Taurus watched with an intense scrutiny while each sailor went about his task. With Admiral Torren's flagship, North Wind, still disabled as she repaired her rudder, the rest of the squadron was in a precarious ordeal. The admiral had raised signal flags at dawn the morning after the attack for the Destiny and Taurus to conduct a three-day search pattern in hopes of finding the offending ship and bringing her brigand crew of savages to heel. Thus far there had been no sign of her. Gossip floated amongst the crew on deck. Stories either heard or completely fabricated were exchanged amplifying the crew's tension. Captain Hemshire had overheard varying accounts of the pirates they were hunting. Everything from rumors of cannibalism and a crew of heathen witchcraft practitioners to the pirates being a band of escaped slaves. The captain gave each account a smug chuckle as he overheard. Most of these sailors hadn't had any contact with anyone but their shipmates since Taurus left England. The marines who had returned from Admiral Torren's landing party had brought some rumors, but those had since taken on a life of their own. Sailors at sea could thread together some tall tales with nothing more than a snippet of hearsay and some imagination.

A wind shift prompted the sailing master to call for a sail adjustment. Captain Hemshire turned his focus upward and watched while his sailors aloft performed their duties. On deck, a group of men let slack in line on one side of a line while on the opposite rail another heaved tension for their adjustment. It all took place in a matter of minutes, keeping Taurus' sails taut and her hull gliding along through the water at an even pace. The coastline to Taurus' south was edging in closer and Captain Hemshire turned his eyes back to its beach line, which had gone from inviting looking white sands intermixed with washed up sea grasses to a cobbled mix of sand and rocks.

"Watch officer." He called across the quarterdeck, "Another point starboard."

"Aye, Sir." the watch officer repeated, "Helm. Another point a-starboard."

The captain kept a close eye on his sails as the minor course adjustment was executed and gave a curt nod of satisfaction to the watch officer. The Haitian coast loomed higher off the port rail as the low-lying beach became bordered by taller and taller trees and hills which eventually were dwarfed by a rocky outcropping of tall bluffs. Crewmen aboard the Taurus scanned the horizon seaward. Their high state of alert wore thin as the lowering sun stretched shadows seaward from the coastline bluffs. Intently scanning eyes became casual glances amid hands sharing sea stories as sailors tended each course change. Captain Hemshire's mind even began to wander as his stomach reminded him that breakfast had come before dawn and had been a rushed affair at that. As he looked on deck for a hand to have summon his steward a shrill cry split through the warm breeze filling Taurus' sails.

"Sail! Sail! One point off the larboard bow! She's flying that black flag!" the lookout cried down. Captain Hemshire felt a chill wrap its fingers around his neck and he scrambled in manic steps down the aft stairs to the weather deck. Ahead of Taurus and lying in the shadow of the bluffs he could faintly make out the form of the ship. For a moment a hysterical fear set over the captain. He did not run across the pirate ship by chance, and as her sails unfurled and snapped taut as they filled with wind Captain Hemshire could only manage one thought. The Taurus had stumbled into a trap.

The pirate ship's dark silhouette emerged from shadow into the daylight and a single shot erupted from one of her cannons facing the Taurus. Deck boards trembled beneath Captain Hemshire's feet and before he could utter a word directing his crew the pirates followed their ranging shot with a full volley.

Taurus' deck erupted into a hell of snapping lines and shattering wood sending recoiling rope dancing in wild arcs and jagged shards of wooden shrapnel flying. A sharp pain bit into Captain Hemshire's side just beneath his arm, with an impact that sent him reeling into the bulwark before collapsing onto Taurus' deck. Smoke and dust hung over the deck and an eerie moment of silence passed before the cries of wounded sailors entered the captain's ears. His gaze shifted fore and aft for a moment as he sized up the damage already done. Jags of pain raced through his ribs with each ragged breath he drew. Captain Hemshire looked down at his torso to find his uniform coat soaked in blood. The warm liquid pooled around where he lay, spreading in a slow progression as his life drained out of his body.

Another series of shots sounded. The crew of the Taurus raced for whatever cover they could find, but a series of falling bodies and screams let Captain Hemshire know that their evasion was of little value.

"We're taking fire from the bluffs! We need to get her out to sea!" a panicked voice near the captain shouted.

A shouted reply came from the bow, "We can't! She's already tacked to our starboard side! Overboard boys! She's going to loose a broadside on us when she pulls abreast!"

Captain Hemshire drifted into a nauseated disconnection with what was occurring around him. The only thread tying him to consciousness was the searing pain of drawing breath. Musket fire crackled through the air, splintering even more of the Taurus' once immaculate woodwork. As darkness overcame his vision, the captain's parting image was grappling hooks bouncing onto the blood-soaked deck before being drawn back biting their hooks into the Taurus' bulwark and rail. He faded away, drifting, and spinning through a sea of noises processed only by his subconscious until another jagged pain from his ribs jolted his eyes open.

A young woman, beautiful, with high angled cheek bones and eyes a shade darker than her skin, held Captain Hemshire's chin upward with one hand as she knelt next to him.

"The ship's captain?" asked the young woman. Shots rang out around them. Captain Hemshire could hear the ghastly heave of guttural air escaping someone as they were run through with a blade. He closed his eyes for a moment before staring up at the young woman and nodding a silent gesture of assent. The woman stood and turned over her shoulder, "Here is their captain! Be sure he gets strung up the highest!" She turned back toward Captain Hemshire and gave him an icy stare, narrowing her eyes before lifting a cutlass with both hands and driving it into his chest. Pain branched through Captain Hemshire's torso stealing away the air in his lungs. Spasms pulsed through his entire body as he tried to recover his breath, his stomach and chest heaving against the pressure of the rigid steel blade but unable to pull in air. Captain Hemshire looked upward at the young woman, desperate for a new breath of air. She placed a boot on his chest and gave her saber a firm tug, wrenching the blade free. Captain Hemshire felt no relief until darkness came over him for the last time.

'North Wind'
22 Mar 1809
24 Degrees 32' N, 76 Degrees 41' W

William Pike's stomach twisted into knots when he heard the admiral order a line be rigged under North Wind's keel. His mouth had been swollen and dry since he had been strung from the main yard and dragged through the sea. Dehydrated, exhausted and malnourished, as Will heard the order given, he had to fight back against tears welling in his eyes. Admiral Torren's demeanor seemed to be made of stone. Unflinching. Dispassionate.

Forward of where Will stood facing the admiral the crew worked with swift efficiency to string a heavy line cross deck beneath the keel. Admiral Torren kept his eyes locked onto Will's in an intense, unflinching stare.

"I take no pleasure in this. But you have what I need. I would rather have you hung as a traitor and give you a swift and merciful end. You have forced this upon yourself young man." Admiral Torren said in a low voice.

A petty officer called back to the gathering of marines and ship officers in a crackle of voice rough from shouting orders all day, "We've got this line all strung and I've got a crew of backs to haul against it Sir."

Admiral Torren raised an eyebrow while his eyes remained locked on Will. "Last chance Lieutenant. Tell me where she runs to and I will spare you this."

Will's heart was in his throat. His stomach twisted and roiled in knots sending pangs of pain through his abdomen. He could only manage rapid, shallow breaths while his heart raced in fear and dread. "I know of no port or anchorage she would run to Sir."

Admiral Torren's face flushed red. His neutral expression, normally unchanging, morphed into a disgusted grimace. "You leave me no choice then, Mr. Pike. In the name of our King and within the sight of God, I hereby strip you of your rank and sentence you to death." Admiral Torren turned to face aft again, disdain plaguing his face and body posture, "Quartermaster, rig him up and run him under."

Will felt an urge to resist, to fight against the marines pulling on his arms and shoulders, but his body would not obey. A shock state of denial had set in, and he could not believe what was happening. He felt weak, like a frail old man unable to defend himself. Will stumbled over his ankle shackles as he was led down from the aft stairs to the weather deck, but the marines marched onward, dragging him by his arms while his feet skittered helpless to bear any of his weight. The marines stopped at the larboard rail near the main mast, hoisting Will's hands high overhead where his wrist shackles were tied onto the line.

The quartermaster watched as a sailor tied off a knot in the center of Will's wrist shackles. A malicious grin crossed his face and he looked directly at Will while shouting his order to the line crew. "Haul him up!"

A violent jerk pulled Will's feet off the deck, and he dangled from his wrists. The iron shackles bit into the flesh of his hands, stretching the skin beneath while a sailor took his time fixing a line to the chain between Will's ankle shackles. The quartermaster kept his gaze affixed to Will, mocking his pain with a feigned whimper before breaking into a laugh interrupted by a coughing fit. The quartermaster spit overboard before shouting, "Hoist him higher and then haul slack boys!"

Will's wrists burned and ached as the line crew drew him higher off the deck. He could feel an ooze of blood creep down his forearms even before the line to his ankles was drawn tight. Air came to his lungs only through labored wheezing effort when he was drawn under tension. Will looked down onto the ship's deck, his eyes flitting amongst the sailors hauling at the line suspending him. Admiral Torren strolled to the rail, patting the quartermaster on his shoulder as he passed.

"You needn't suffer this way young man. What you are feeling now is only a fraction of the pain you will endure in a moment. Tell me where I can find the pirates and you will be spared." The admiral called up to Will, narrowing his eyes from the sun as he looked up.

A moment passed and Will drew in a breath. His mouth was open, an image of the cove on the west Haitian coast setting in the front of his mind. He exhaled, dropping his chin down to his chest. Beneath him, the water lapped at North Wind's hull. Ripples of waves bounced off the wooden structure as she plowed her way through them. The sun felt warm on his back and for a moment he closed his eyes, thinking of that first morning after he had assisted the pirates in sinking H.M.S. Valor. The warm kiss of sunshine on his face. A low fog hanging over brilliant blue and green water mixed with gun smoke in the cool of the morning.

"Haul away." Admiral Torren shouted in an abrupt outburst; his face hardened into a stern scowl.

The line holding Will came to life with a tug of intense pressure, bringing fresh pain into his wrists and ankles sending him toward the water's surface in jerks of two or three feet at a time. Will's heart raced faster as his feet entered the cool sea. He struggled to take in as much breath as he could before he was submerged completely. His final breath was cut short by a rolling swell. Water rushed past him, tugging at his ragged clothes. Another tug of movement dragged him along the hull. The wooden surface of the hull was clean and smooth here and Will tried to concentrate on holding his breath while the rushing seawater battered his face and entered his nose. Another heave of the line brought him further down and angled his legs along the curvature of the hull. Will felt the rough sharpness of barnacles digging into the tops of his feet, his shins and knees. The line jaunted again, and Will could feel the skin of his legs being torn and cut by the jagged barnacles. They bit his skin with sharp edges and remained unforgiving as his body dragged across them. From his feet, his shins, knees, thighs, groin and belly he could feet gouges and incisions opening with every haul at the line holding him. Every inch of movement brought another wave of agonizing pain. His lungs pulsed and throbbed in a base desire to exhale. The unrelenting seawater battered him against the hull, rushing past and adding lateral tension to his already taxed frame. Will could feel warm spots of blood escaping his skin, washed away by the sea and the torturous line dragging along the gauntlet of barnacles stabbing at his skin like miniature knives. His ankles shot with pain as the line hauled him in another sudden jaunt, Will tried to hold his face away from the hull while a steak of blinding pain from his ribs forced a water muffled scream from his lungs. Seawater invaded Will's mouth and throat while also pouring into his nose. He could feel his lungs contract and his abdomen spasm.

His body's reaction to the entrance of the sea only caused him to allow more of the salty brine in. He gagged and his stomach cramped. Will felt consciousness beginning to slip through his fingers as his legs made the bend around the curvature of the hull again signaling his ascent from the sea. His feet broke the surface in another jerk of the line while his mind spun in darkness. Incoherent thoughts flitted through his mind. Will thought of Captain Grimes and the treachery of Cobb. The water's surface broke around his upper body and his head cleared away from its oppressive grasp. Water poured from Will's lungs, and he retched. He tried to fetch a breath but air hitting his throat only caused him to retch harder. He opened his eyes to a distorted view of the sea frothing below him. Vomit drifted away on the surface. The dark blue of the depths stared back up at him and he hung inverted, seizing every bit of air he could manage into his chest. The line pulled at his ankles again and Will was hauled up, face to face with Admiral Torren standing at the rail.

"Welcome back, Mr. Pike. Now, are you ready to divulge what you know?"

Chapter 15

'Ranging Falcon'
28 Mar 1809
Eastern Shoreline of Jamaica

Gulls cawed overhead, dipping into low glides off of the Ranging Falcon's bow. They circled just beyond the reach of the mast, playing mindless circles and droning on in an incessantly replaying song of screeches. Clyde leaned far over the rail, craning his neck to watch the small squadron of brigantines as wind caught their sails and propelled them onward. Their holds were full of the quarry he came to Jamaica seeking. Labor for the fields and homes of those willing to pay. A smile stretched across his face, the cool shadows of the Jamaican coast covering them from the scorching rays of the sun as it dipped lower into the sky. Evening was approaching and after the stifling humidity he had endured all day at the prison camp and in the sheltered cove while the slaves were marched down and loaded, he relished the breeze. Evening coolness would envelope them soon. Clyde closed his eyes. His success was intoxicating. He had beaten them. His victory was as sure as the waves lapping along Ranging Falcon's sides. He had instructed the sloop's captain to plot a northern course, looping around the western coast of Cuba before jaunting east toward the Florida straits then it would be a swift trip north toward the Carolinas. He could almost smell the sweet air. Harvest would be coming and with a fresh crop of labor his profits would be immense.

Thoughts of his commitments to The Order only frilled the edges of his mind. Let the old world stay in the old world. Out here, a man could forge his own destiny. Blaze his own path. The King of Britain be damned, Napoleon be damned, the Prussians, the Spaniards, all of them. Clyde opened his eyes and looked forward to the north where the shadows of the Jamaican coast were receding and golden hues of the long rays of a setting sun reached across low chopping waves. Exuberance filled him. The joy of accomplishment and independence. He beamed as he stepped down from the rail and walked his way forward to the bow. The sloop's nose dipped and rose in a steady, gentle arc as the western winds propelled them along toward the sunshine. Clyde thought it would be nice to have a drink as he watched the sunset off the larboard rail while the sloop slipped its way north.

Sailors milled about the deck, making adjustments as they prepared to move out of the lee of Jamaica and into the full force of the open sea. Stay lines were adjusted. Sheets were cinched tight, and lines dressed, all called out by the ship's quartermaster who combed the rigging with a keen eye for anything out of place. Clyde felt as full as the sails overhead, smiling at each sailor who passed him and breaking a laugh as they started chiming out a shanty.

Heave them up and heave away, we sail hoping ladies someday say.
Come home Johnny come home.
Black of hair and blue in eyes, French girls holding fresh baked pies.
Come home Johnny come home.
Salted pork and watered rum, bread full of rot right down to the crumb.
Come home Johnny come home.
I'm stealing away at the next port we make.
Come home Johnny come home.
To that girl from France for my own soul's sake.
Come home Johnny come home.
No cannon roar, no chest of gold.
Come home Johnny come home.
Could keep a sailor away when the nights turn so cold.
Come home Johnny come home.
Spray of the sea and sails so full.
Come home Johnny come home.
It'll drive you mad, it'll drive you dull.
Come home Johnny come home.
Every salted sailor knows.
Come home Johnny come home.
While you're out to sea she's at home, but rarely alone!
Now you're home, Johnny go on!

The sailor's shanties were nails on his nerves during

their voyage south to Jamaica. But now, with his quarry in hand and nothing standing in his way, Clyde caught himself humming along to the last few lines. He had heard the song so repetitively he could lead with the words himself. It was one of only four or five the crew repeated while working on deck, enough to drive a man insane under normal conditions, let alone when he was surrounded by seawater and baking in the sun all day. When the crew's vocals faded, Clyde could feel it more than he heard it. The repetitive line after spray of the sea and sails so full, fell empty. A lap of the waves against Ranging Falcon's hull was all that met his ears. Clyde scanned back toward the helm, searching for the unrest that had broken the crew's melody.

Warm sunlight cascaded over Ranging Falcon's sails, finally falling on Clyde's shoulders. He scanned the faces of the sailors near him, trying to figure out what was wrong. They all faced to the larboard bow quarter, eyes suddenly weary, faces drawn. Clyde followed their gaze. His jaw slacked into an open gape. His fingers went numb, and his chest drew tight. Sunset's brilliant rays shot golden fingers around a trio of ships, their masts and sails silhouetted but also obscured by the angled reflection off the water's surface. Clyde shot a hand up to shield his eyes from the blinding sun and squinted to make out who lay in wait for them. As shapes became visible through shadow, Clyde strained his eyes. Ranging Falcon was beyond the cover of Jamaican coast and laid bare for the waiting vessels. They were each bigger than the sloop, bigger than the brigantines that followed. Clyde wasn't an expert but to his eye they looked like war ships. Frigates, if not heavy frigates. The vessels flustered into a buzz of activity and began to make a steep turn northward, shadowing the Ranging Falcon's course. Their gun ports were open. Their cannons run out. Clyde was frozen. Words raced to his mind. Order the captain should have been giving, course changes, a warning to the following ships. Ranging Falcon's crew all seemed petrified just as he was. As the nearest ship laid her broadside of cannons to bare against them, Clyde's eye caught on her banner of colors flying high above the stern.

"The damned French." His uttering was drowned by the thunderous roar of fire and cannon smoke as a broadside let fly.

'H.M.S. Destiny'
14 Apr 1809
20 Degrees 54' N, 72 Degrees 14' W

Distant sounds of cannon fire had alerted the crew of H.M.S. Destiny that a battle ensued to the south. At first it had been only the faintest noise, making the lookouts aloft strain their ears for confirmation. But when a plume of black smoke rose from the coastline to their south all doubt was erased. Captain Harrison Gray ordered the ship to turn south and investigate. The long fingers of evening shadow played over the long faces of hesitant sailors as they made their way south to an unknown fate. The elusive pirate crew had made a mockery of them all in the previous engagement and disabled their flagship while the two accompanying vessels watched in helpless frustration. Captain Gray knew his sailor's hesitation, he felt it himself. If they came upon a victorious H.M.S. Taurus, their worries would be over. But there was a chance that the Destiny would arrive to the south and find a flotilla of debris and bodies in the wake of the pirate vessel. That is, if the pirates were not lying in wait to spring an ambush on them. The tension of the unknown was palpable. It was heard in the voices of petty officers as they ordered sail adjustments. Sailors were curter with each other. The captain could feel his crew's reluctance to charge headlong into battle with a ship that had already outfoxed a commander vastly more apt than he was.

The warm wind held steady, coming from the west as the sunset painted streaks of purple and orange high into the Caribbean skies. The failing light of day illuminated along the southern horizon sketching the silhouette of the Haitian shore. A normally boisterous crew grew quieter as Destiny pushed along her southerly course in search of Taurus, each sailor contemplating for himself what lay ahead of them.

"Man overboard!" the cry from a forward lookout cut through the soul of every man aboard. The first sighting was not of their sister ship, but a body floating near the shore in the last few glimmers of daylight. Captain Gray's heels clunked along the wooden deck as he strode forward under dire urgency. Sailors gathered on the bow, outstretching arms to point at the debris field that lay bobbing in the sea along the coast in front of them. A pair of petty officers noticed the captain's arrival and cleared a path for him. Captain

Gray extended a sight glass and scanned the water ahead. Barrels, bodies, sailcloth and timbers floated on the surface. The sheen of a small slick from lamp oil was visible as well.

"It's the Taurus! Those rogues have done her in!" a sailor lamented, drawing the ire of several sailors near him.

Captain Gray felt a rush of anger send his face to a flush. He lowered the sight glass and scolded the sailor, "It could very well be those rogues bobbing in the waves as well. Perhaps Taurus has made them fish food and carried on about it like another Sunday at sea. It would do you well to see the work of sailors with some fortitude."

The man shied from his commander's sneer, lowering his eyes to the deck. "Right you are Sir."

Captain Gray turned to the rest of the sailors on the bow, "In any case, whether it be friend or foe that lay in the surf before us, let them not find our hands idle and unprepared. Quarters, and bring her about west by south, scanning the shores as we go."

Destiny's crew fell into a frenzy of activity as Captain Gray resumed his diligent scan of the shoreline. Amid the shouted orders and calls of acknowledgment and reply a voice filtered down from one of the lookouts above. His words were lost in the mix at first, failing to garner any more attention than a call between sailors not intended for other ears. The sailor called again as Destiny's drew nearer to the floating debris, still raising no heads aloft to his cries.

"Sail ho! Ship flying a black banner!" the lookout's cry finally met Captain Gray's ears. The captain turned his attention to the southwest, where the last glowing of the disappeared sun gave only the stark outline of the Haitian coast.

Captain Gray looked aloft to the lookout who sounded the alarm. "Where do you see a sail? There's nothing but ocean and island to my eye!"

A quiet settled over the Destiny's deck and a sailor sprinted to the bow rail by where Captain Gray stood. The sailor's face was wrenched into a fearful grimace while his arm was outstretched over the water toward the coast. "There Sir! There she is!"

The last notes of evening light silhouetted a bowsprit as it protruded from behind an outcropping finger of rock. The suns glow faded to nothing, and the hull of the predatory vessel was lost to the darkness of night. A flash appeared, followed by the echoing report of a cannon. The low whistle grew in intensity as the crew of the Destiny leapt and scrambled to find what cover they could before a resounding impact shook the ship to its core. Another thunderous boom reported and another. The impacts slammed into Destiny's bow sending lines whipping in frenzy and hunks of wood rocketing through the air.

Captain Gray pulled himself up from the deck. Rage filled his veins. He extended his sight glass and took a quick gauge on the pirate vessel's course. He shouted back toward the helm, "Bring her about, two points starboard, larboard battery, make ready!"

The Destiny lurched in a dogged turn, bringing her cannons to bear against their foe off in the darkness. A still moment elapsed. Sailors on deck began to wonder if their Captain had lost his nerve when out of the darkness his wild shout resounded, "Fire!"

The guns of the larboard battery sounded in unison, roaring to life with flashes and smoke. The Destiny lurched and shuddered under the recoil of the guns. Captain Gray bolted to the larboard rail, scouring the darkness for any sign of effect on his target. The satisfying sound of iron crashing into timbers met his ears and brought a smile to his face. He turned to one of his lieutenants on deck, "Bring her up close haul and make ready to board!"

'North Wind'
22 Mar 1809
24 Degrees 32' N, 76 Degrees 41' W

A cold anger laced Admiral Torren, wrapping around his head and filling his mind with thoughts of his old friend Elliot Sharpe and the promising Captain Grimes. In the admiral's mind, their deaths lay solely on Lieutenant Pike. He was a traitor. He had mutinied against Captain Grimes. He had led a revolt in Jamaica and murdered not only an admiral of the King's Navy but the governors of two colonies. The depths this young man had sunk to knew no bounds. All to run about the Caribbean and play at pirates with a band of mutineers and escaped slaves.

The lieutenant was hoisted up to the starboard rail where Admiral Torren stood waiting. He watched. Coughing and gagging, ragged breaths and regurgitated seawater left the disgraced officer as he hung inverted. His eyes were level with the admiral's. Lieutenant Pike opened his eyes.

"Welcome back Mr. Pike. Are you ready to divulge what you know?" Admiral Torren kept an even tone. The sea was his shout of anger. The wrath of the hull provided his punctuation. The prisoner would hear him loud and clear, even if it killed him in the process.

Lieutenant Pike struggled against the tension holding his shackles, straining his limbs while blood dripped from scores of wounds across his body. "I know of no port or anchorage where the Maiden would seek refuge."

Admiral Torren furrowed his brows into a deep frown. He couldn't help but lower his eyes away from the disgrace in front of him. "Have you no scrap of honor left in your body son? Would you so completely betray us that you will further obstruct the King's justice? Save yourself the wretched fate of being torn apart and drowned beneath the keel young man. Tell us where she will run to. Tell me and I will end this."

The lieutenant's eyes wobbled over the sailors and officers standing near the admiral. His breaths were ragged and short. Sharp inhalations punctuated by painful grimaces on his face. It was agony just to watch. He made no effort to speak. Admiral Torren turned over his shoulder looking to the crew holding tension on the lines. He raised a hand, pointing a finger skyward and holding it still for a moment. He used the finger to draw an invisible circle, signaling the crew on deck to rotate the prisoner around. Several sailors moved to the rail, turning Lieutenant Pike around to face outboard towards the horizon. Their faces were a mixture of disgust and hesitation, their hands bloodied by the wounds of the half drowned, half shredded body that hung from their rigging.

Admiral Torren took a step closer to his prisoner, speaking low as they both faced outboard. "If your belly isn't enough then perhaps your back will do. If that doesn't work, then we'll haul out the cat of nine and have a go in between trips under the keel. I will learn the location of their refuge, or I will watch you die holding their secret."

Lieutenant Pike let a long sharp breath go, spitting seawater and blood dripping from his body away from his mouth. A pause of silence elapsed. Admiral Torren's stare burned oblique to the hanging prisoner and for a moment connected with a flitting glance from the corner of his eye. The lieutenant averted his eyes from the demanding glare. Admiral Torren looked skyward, tracing the wispy thin clouds high overhead. They punctuated the sheer blue skies, promising fair winds for the time being. His attention settled back to the prisoner hanging inverted before him, facing away and awaiting his fate. "Damn you for forcing my hand." The admiral said before turning back to the line crew. "Haul away."

The sailors of the line crew pulled against the tension holding their prisoner aloft, sending him down towards the waves sloshing against North Wind's hull. Lieutenant Pike pulled against the tension of the lines, writhing his body as the timbers of the hull scratched and scraped his back. After the line crew made a few pulls Admiral Torren watched as his prisoner disappeared beneath the waves. His skin crawled as he imagined the awful fate that awaited the man below. Though his contempt for the disgraced officer clashed with his hesitancy, Admiral Torren was steadfast in his mind. He would hear what he wanted. He would learn where the pirates escaped to.

Early in Admiral Torren's career, as a young midshipman, he had been told by a salty old sea hand about the excruciating process of keelhauling. It was a deadly combination of the rough timbers and a collection of barnacles along the hull that flayed its victims flesh open. In addition, the time spent below the surface along with enduring the staggering amounts of pain suffered from incisions ensured the subject would most definitely inhale seawater. If the punishment was administered while under sail, as it was being done, an additional torture awaited the unlucky recipient as he would be repeatedly slammed into the hull by the force of water rushing past his body. It was a fate feared and despised by all seafaring men. Admiral Torren had witnessed it only once. While serving aboard a line ship in his youth, Midshipman Torren had watched a lieutenant who had plotted a mutiny against his captain receive four passes beneath the keel. What the young would-be admiral witnessed was a body that was torn and mutilated with each pass. The end result was a drowned corpse, torn to ribbons and unrecognizable, devoid of life after the final haul beneath the waves.

A putrid sounding froth of coughs and retching announced the lieutenant's emergence from the water. Admiral Torren strutted across the deck, lifting his cane from the deck, and tucking it under his arm. As he approached the larboard rail, the line crew halted their pulls when Lieutenant Pike was above the bulwark rail. Still facing outward, his back was visible to the crew on deck. It was a wretched mess of gashes. Some superficial, some were deep enough that rib bone was visible through oozing blood and torn flesh. His coughs and gags were interspersed by grunts of agony and surrender.

Admiral Torren whirled his cane from under his arm and slammed its side down onto the wooden rail next to where his prisoner was suspended. He looked aft to find the quartermaster. "Have the master at arms bring a cat of nine tails."

An awkward silence passed. Horrified expressions crept over the faces of sailors on deck. Admiral Torren scanned over them and then landed his gaze back on the quartermaster. "Have the master at arms bring the cat of nine tails, before I have to repeat myself again, preferably." The admiral could feel a wave of anger building in his guts. He wanted to end this. He turned back to Lieutenant Pike, motioning for the sailors near him to rotate the tattered man so he could look into his face. A series of seawater producing coughs and agonized grunts accompanied the movement.

"Mr. Pike." The admiral's tone was low and hostile. "The master at arms is on his way with a cat of nine tails. I will have you flogged until his arm gives out before your next haul beneath the keel, if you force me to that."

Lieutenant Pike's face was broken and battered. His scalp had lacerations that dripped blood mixed with seawater down over his face. His lips were cut and swollen, and his eyes were surrounded by gashes and swollen nearly shut. At first the admiral felt a streak of pity, but as his prisoner opened his mouth, he formed no words only a retch of seawater that landed on the deck at Admiral Torren's feet. The admiral's face flushed red, and he turned to see the master at arms arriving on deck with his whip in hand. He looked at Lieutenant Pike, announcing through gritted teeth. "This is of your own doing. All of it." The admiral motioned for the master at arms to ply his instrument.

"Haiti!" Lieutenant Pike's voice erupted from his swollen mouth. The word was barely understandable, but it caused Admiral Torren to halt his master at arms with an upraised hand.

"If I get you a chart, you can show me?" the admiral inquired, raising his brows in hope.

William Pike remained silent for a long moment, blood, saliva, and seawater dripping from his cut and swollen mouth. He nodded his head. "Yes."

'Drowned Maiden'
20 Mar 1809
19 Degrees 53' N, 72 Degrees 33' W

The force of the impact had rocked the Drowned Maiden, sending all hands aboard off their feet in a violent tumble onto the deck. Lilith felt the grain of deck boards under her skin, a tremble from the hull shivered up and into her. The Maiden was wounded.

"Make ready! She's coming about to close with!" Chibs growled over the deck as he lurched back to his feet. Lilith could see in the drawing light of evening a flash of concern in his eyes. He scanned over the deck and then paused when his gaze landed on her. Chibs took a couple steps and offered over his calloused hand to help her up.

"Thank you." Lilith said as she rose to her feet. The two of them moved to the starboard rail.

"They got us with their first volley, damn the luck!" Chibs exclaimed looking over the deck again, as the Drowned Maiden's crew recovered from the impact, Lilith noticed that there were several not rising back to their feet.

She glanced out to the warship making her turn inward to close the gap. "Have all hands make ready. Another broadside before she comes along. We'll board her and leave none alive."

Chibs paused, he scanned back over the deck. Lilith followed his eyes again. It seemed each time she looked over the deck there were more bodies not rising to recover. "Captain. We struck a good blow. It may be time to turn and run. I'm afraid we may not have the numbers to win if we're boarded."

Lilith clenched her jaw, growing impatient. "Well, if we struck such a good blow, then maybe they have as many wounded. We could still…"

"Maybe." Chibs interrupted, "But only by a margin. Is that the victory you want? There's still another warship out there hunting us."

Lilith turned back, looking outward as the warship beat closer. "Fire a volley. Then fly all canvas in haste for the cove."

"Aye, Cap'n. We'll regroup and come back at em!" Chibs exuded agreement, turning toward the weather hatch. "Starboard battery, fire!"

The cannons roared to life again sending a volley

screaming toward the approaching warship. Impacts echoed through the cloud of smoke as it wafted, dissipating in the breeze. Lilith looked on to judge their effect. There were gashes in her hull. Railing blown away. Snapped stay lines swayed in the wind, but her gait through the water belied no listing from taking on water. Lilith gritted her teeth. Chibs barked orders and the Maiden shifted her course away from the approach of the warship. They were still distant enough to evade, but only by a hair and only if they handled the Maiden with tight precision.

Lilith walked the rail as the Drowned Maiden made her turn, watching the warship as it approached. She gave Omibwe a nod as she passed the helm. "Don't let a single knot slip away from us Omi, we need all the speed she'll offer us."

"Aye Captain!" Omi replied with an enthusiastic grin.

The Drowned Maiden reeled through her turn and collected speed as Lilith's pirate crew coaxed every bit of slack from their sails. Chibs paced the deck, issuing orders to every available hand. Trina gathered the wounded for Dr. LeMeux to treat. A small crew began deploying one of the Maiden's nine pounder deck cannons onto the stern. The Maiden wouldn't be giving up without a fight.

Above the Maiden's stern flew her black banner. Lilith looked aloft as the wind fluttered through it, floating it in ripples and waves like the sea surrounding them. The menacing skull with its twisted horns, the trident, an homage to Poseidon, angled in the back. Lilith traced her eyes over the length of broken chain at the bottom. Her heart fluttered with a wave of pride. The approaching warship fired a chase gun and drew Lilith's gaze away from her banner. Chibs joined her at the stern, still huffing from his hasty orders to change the Maiden's course.

"They think they will have us Chibs." Lilith said without breaking her eyes from the warship.

Chibs put a hand on the rail as he stood next to her. "I'm sure they do Cap'n. But only because they haven't crossed us before now."

"You have that much faith in us?" Lilith asked, looking over to Chibs.

Chibs grinned, hauling out his pipe. "I'll bet the crew aboard the Valor thought they had us too. You showed them for damned fools."

Lilith smiled, turning back to the warship. Their captain stood on the prow, unmistakable in a large bicorne hat. "You're right Chibs. We did."

Evening wonder painted the horizon as the Drowned Maiden held her course along the Haitian coast. Intermittent shots were exchanged between the bow guns of the British warship and Lilith's chase gun on the stern of the Maiden. The first few exchanges had come very close causing Lilith's pirates to take cover. But as the Maiden broadened the gap between ships it became apparent that the warship's fire would be nothing more than a threatening nuisance. Noise preventing sleep and encouraging them to keep their sails taut and full.

"How long until we make the round toward our cove Chibs?" Lilith asked, keeping a close watch on the pursuing warship.

The grizzled pirate was puffing on his pipe, watching the gun crew prepare to fire another warning round. "I'd venture to say by morning, maybe just before dawn. We'll want to keep well wide of Tortuga, but so will they."

"If we keep gaining distance on them, we may lose them." Lilith offered, sounding more like a question than a statement.

Chibs shrugged, rolling smoke from his nostrils. "Hard to say Cap'n. We might. We'd be better off."

Lilith kept her eyes locked on the shadow of the warship in the fading light. "No, Chibs. Let's keep them in sight. I don't want them getting away."

The old sailor coughed; his eyes widened. "Cap'n, that's the idea when we turned to sail away. We want to lose them so we can…"

"We lost crew to their broadside. Our brothers and sisters. I'm not going to start a habit of letting that sort go unanswered. Keep them in sight quartermaster." Lilith retorted.

Chibs clamped his teeth back onto his pipe stem, "Aye Cap'n."

Chapter 16

'North Wind'
22 Mar 1809
24 Degrees 32' N, 76 Degrees 41' W

Will collapsed into a heap on the floor of his cell, still coughing spurts of seawater and bleeding from a litany of wounds inflicted by North Wind's hull. His thoughts were a jumble. He was only slightly cognizant of his surroundings. The smell of wooden timbers and smoke mixed into his nostrils as his escorts had brought him below deck. For a moment it was an almost pleasant smell, until they descended another deck and brought him to his cell, deep in the hold. A mildew scent mixed with the smell of dried urine, wafted up into his nose and mouth as they had crossed into the area of the hold where his cell was located. The marines who had brought him tossed his body onto the floor as if they were disposing trash overboard. The thick wooden door slammed behind him, only allowing the wavering light of a lantern in through a small, barred window.

Will lay motionless on the floor, his wounds discouraging any movement as blood seeped from them onto the wooden deck. His body was wracked by pain. Every inch of his flesh ached. The movement of North Wind coursed through the timbers of the hull, sending waves of pain through his body with each shift of her motion. After hours of slipping in and out of consciousness, Will became vaguely aware of himself. He reached a hand up to his face and felt his swollen eyes. Deep cuts in his brow and forehead singed with pain as he ran his fingers over them, feeling thick sticky blood at his fingertips. His arm ached in throbbing pain with each movement as he adjusted himself to try and assess the wounds on his abdomen. More deep gashes laced his ribs and belly, each of them oozing bore blood as he checked himself. Will pushed his torn arm against the deck, trying to sit himself up. A gasp escaped his lips, followed by a series of coughs that brought a salty sting into the back of his throat and sent his head spinning until he collapsed back onto the wooden timbers beneath him. A voice jolted him out of his spiral toward darkness.

"You'd gone quiet so long. I thought you were dead." The voice drawled. "They must have done quite a job, working you over."

Will only grunted in response. The voice belonged to Tim Sladen, the American mercenary whose actions had precipitated all of the events leading Will to his current state. He drew another ragged breath, straining against bolts of pain through his chest.

"I was wondering. Did you give him what he wanted? The admiral that is. I am assuming he wanted something from you, but perhaps I am wrong. Maybe he hauled you up to be flogged for your transgressions against the Crown?" Tim's voice taunted. "Either way, it's just as well for me. Let them flog you and forget me."

Will's body seethed with rage. Tim's voice sending fresh pain into his wounds. Wounds Tim was responsible for. "Your hour before the admiral is coming." Will's voice was weak and broke with each word as he struggled to speak.

A moment of silence passed. "Oh, I don't doubt that is the good admiral's intention. We shall see."

Will's hearing occluded with a ringing in his ears as North Wind shifted from the force of a turn, sending a throbbing pain through his neck and head. He struggled for another deep breath. Through the timbers of the hull, Will could feel the waves outside slipping by in an increasing pace. The pitching and heaving of the deck grew in speed and frequency. Deep in the hold, with no point of reference Will could not make out what direction they were sailing, only that North Wind was pushing for her heading in desperate urgency. While he could not decipher their current heading, Will knew their destination. The admiral was racing for a cove in the bay of the western Haitian coast.

'Drowned Maiden'
18 Apr 1809
19 Degrees 35' N, 73 Degrees 28' W

The shining brightness of dawn sifted through a cloud of cannon smoke. It lit the warship pursuing Drowned Maiden and displayed to Lilith the toll they had inflicted during the night hours. Just before dawn had broken, they had rounded the northwest corner of the island of Haiti and made their turn southeast. The sun shone in a favorable direction, blinding their enemy, and displaying the results of their gunnery over the course of the hours preceding day break. The Maiden's banner floated sideways in the breeze, fluttering, and snapping as the crisp air of dawn drove into their sails.

Lilith paced the stern, her hand resting on the hilt of her cutlass. The damage they had inflicted through the night did little to slow the burgeoning warship. It would take a larger volley to put her under. Her eyes ached with fatigue. The marathon pursuit would be ending soon, she told herself, she could rest then. Chibs appeared on deck, climbing up through the weather hatch with a steaming mug in one hand and a fist sized chuck of bread in the other. He made his way over to Lilith and held the offering out to her.

"You haven't slept Cap'n. At least have something to eat." Chibs' eyes were red and long. He hadn't slept himself.

Lilith took the cup and bread, thankful for her quartermaster and his fatherly instincts. She took a deep drink of the hot coffee; it warmed her chest and flooded her nose with its strong aroma. She nodded toward the warship approaching behind them. "Our cannon fire doesn't seem to be discouraging them."

"No. It looks like we've scored some hits, but there's little to show for it." Chibs stroked the gray shock of beard under his chin as he spoke, narrowing his eyes at the enemy ship. "It's going to take a well-placed volley to put her under."

"What about a reef?" Lilith raised her eyebrows as she looked over to Chibs for his reaction.

Chibs drew a deep breath, digging into a leather pouch he kept his pipe in. "Captain, if you're planning to run them into the reef at the mouth of the cove, they're going to see the hulk of the Valor." He packed a pinch of tobacco into the bowl of his pipe. "I'm afraid that plan won't work this time around."

Lilith pulled a bite of bread off and stuck it into her mouth. She chewed a few times before narrowing her eyes. "Suppose we tack wide at the mouth of the cove? We could come around with the wind and volley her with nowhere to run."

Chibs pulled a wick from his pouch and stole some flame from a brazier that rested along the Maiden's rail. "We've only powder left for a few volleys. If they are well placed, we could do some damage to her hull. I don't know if we could amass fire enough to sink her though deary."

Lilith drained the last of the coffee from the mug and set it on the rail, wiping the corner of her mouth with the back of her hand before leaping up onto the rail and grasping onto a stay line. She leaned herself outboard and looked forward along the coast as rocky bluffs rose up in the distance. They would be approaching the cove in a matter of hours. Lilith hoisted herself upright on the wooden rail and looked down at Chibs with a smile. "With the powder we have. Could you manage to set her adrift?"

Chibs hesitated, drawing a big breath of smoke from his pipe. He winced his eyes, drawing somewhere in his thoughts. "The surest way would be to take out her rudder. No easy task, but, doable. If we could take down one of their masts, that would have similar effects."

Lilith turned and scanned the horizons, letting her gaze settle back onto the following ship. Dawn to the east was bright and beautiful but a bank of dark clouds was gathering across the southern sky, curving around far to the west. "How many volleys can we fire, with the powder we have?"

"Three at most, and the third may not even be every gun of the battery." Chibs answered, smoke rolling from his beard as he spoke.

Lilith dropped to the deck, her smile faded as she set her plan in motion. "Very well then. Quartermaster, see to it our best gun crews are manning the starboard battery. We will cross the mouth of the cove and come about across the wind. We cannot stall mid turn or they will have us dead to rights. Once we come about I want all fire concentrated on her rudder. Musket fire on her helmsman as well."

"Aye Captain. It's a good plan. Let's just hope they don't get a return volley in too quickly." Chibs began to walk toward the stairs leading below deck.

Lilith patted his shoulder, "Trina will fix that. I'll

have her up in the rigging, she will see to it their helmsman is unable to maintain a steady course."

A smile spread across Chibs' face, his red sun kissed cheeks squinted his eyes. "That'll do Cap'n, she'll keep 'em at bay."

Chibs scurried below deck, his voice echoing through the wooden cavern below as he set about preparing the gun crews for Lilith's plan. Lilith moved forward on deck toward the bow, where Trina was watching for the mouth of the cove. Lilith shared her plan, telling Trina her critical part to play. Trina took a deep breath, realizing the fate of the Maiden's crew rest on her shoulders. She slung a set of muskets around her neck and a couple more over her shoulder before making the climb aloft.

18 Apr 1809
Pirate Cove, Haiti

The rays of late morning kissed Emilia's skin, warming her while the cool sea breeze pulled at her loose shirt. Her eyes scanned the horizon all around, scouring every bit where the skyline met the sea. It had become her daily routine. She arose from the makeshift camp she had made near the sandy beach on the cove far below at dawn, would eat a bite or two of breakfast and then spend her day combing the nearby forest for signs of inhabitance by the pirate crew she had heard of. When she wasn't searching the thick jungle surrounding the cove, Emilia would climb to the high bluff that bordered the sea, searching for any sign of an approaching sail. The shipwreck at the mouth of the cove was evidence that the story she heard was true. But after days of waiting and watching, Emilia began to wonder if this hadn't been another fabrication of the man that had murdered her father.

After several hours of watching, Emilia spotted a glimpse of white sailcloth on the western edge of visible sea. Her heart fluttered and raced, sending images of pirates scooping her from the cove and adding her into their ranks running through her mind. She watched closely, with a lungful of anticipation and anxiety held until she almost became dizzy. The ship pitched and rolled, its sails angled to harness the stout winds from the south. Every moment a new question sprang into Emilia's mind. What if the pirates were hostile towards her? She had her fears, but there was something that told her if she shared the fate of her late father with them, they would sympathize with her. After all, weren't they the reason Tim had come to Haiti in the first place? She began to wonder, questioning all the thing the treacherous man had told her father.

When the ship drew near enough for Emilia to make out any detail, she saw it for the first time. It was exactly as Tim had described, only seeing it for herself Emilia didn't get the same terrible feeling she had when she'd first heard of it. The black banner that flew over the ship's stern. In its center, a menacing skull with twisted horns and piercing voids for eyes. Behind it sat a canted trident. Emilia watched the banner flutter and then become obscured by sails as the ship drew nearer. Her eyes caught another set of sails following along behind the pirate ship. She wondered if they had overtaken a crew and made themselves a fleet. That thought faded as a distant thump of cannon fire met her ears. She held her breath, her heart pounding inside her ribs. She was about to witness a sea battle.

The pirate ship sailed nearer, plowing through waves with her sails taut in the wind. As they approached the mouth of the cove, the pirates made a sharp turn at an angle away from the coastline. At first, she held southeast, her sails angled expertly. Emilia could see figures on deck, scrambling to adjust lines while pirates up in the rigging made their sail adjustments. She could see the figure of a dark-skinned woman, several muskets slung over her shoulder, sitting high up near the top of the mast. The towering bluffs allowed Emilia a downward angle on the action, higher in elevation even than the woman in her perch by the mast. The pirate ship made another sharp angled turn, the crew on deck scrambling to adjust sails. It only took seconds, their sails snapped full of wind propelling them along on their new course. Emilia was enamored. She could feel adrenaline coursing through her veins as she watched the events below unfolding. Voices of shouted commands and responses floated up to her spot on the bluff through the wind. The pursuing ship drew alongside the mouth of the cove.

A single shot sounded. Its report came as a pop, almost lost to Emilia straining ears in the wind. It was happening! These two ships were about to engage in a battle. She felt herself hoping for the pirates to emerge victorious. The deck of the trailing ship was its own hive of activity. She could hear shouts and cursing, whistles and a drum rattling. Another pop sounded through the wind and Emilia squinted to focus her eyes on the woman high aloft on the pirate ship's mast. A faint whisper of smoke escaped in the wind from the woman's position and Emilia could see her scrambling to shoulder another musket. The warship at the mouth of the cove faltered off course for a moment, followed by coarse screams and shouts on her deck. Another pop followed. Emilia couldn't shift her eyes fast enough to take in everything happening all at once. Her heart fluttered in her chest. Her breath came in anxious bursts as she realized she was holding it through the anticipation of what unfolded below her.

The dark bank of clouds from the south was pushing its way toward the cove, threatening to drown everything in its path under a deluge of rain and wind. Emilia glanced southward for only a fleeting moment as a bolt of lightning streaked through the sky. She looked back, not registering what she saw, not wanting to miss any of the action unfolding beneath her. But as her eyes landed back onto the pirate ship, she immediately turned back toward the southern horizon. Under the darkened skies of the approaching storm, she could make out white rectangles. Another ship was pushing along northward, a very large ship Emilia judged by the size of her sails through the distance. She was riding the edge of the storm, her sails full and her massive hull pitching against waves. Another pop sounded. The ship near the mouth of the cove continued to falter, her bow angling in toward the cove entrance. Emilia shifted her eyes between the three ships as lightning split the southern skies again. Then in a thunderous roar a volley of cannon fire was loosed, sending a massive cloud of smoke billowing out over the water.

Chapter 17

'Drowned Maiden'
18 Apr 1809
19 Degrees 35' N, 73 Degrees 9' W

Cannon smoke drifted across Drowned Maiden's deck obscuring Lilith's view. Their volley had fired in such close succession that the tremble had nearly knocked her from her feet. As the wind pushed away smoke, the warship Maiden had just fired on became visible. The stern was tattered in broken timbers and smashed railing. A sailor's body hung limp from the edge of her aft castle, the side of his torso torn to shreds by the flying secondary shrapnel of cannon fire. The Drowned Maiden careened past, slipping through the chopping sea with ease under the strong wind. When the warship's stern came into full view, a roar of cheers erupted from the pirates aboard as her smashed rudder was bared for all of them to see. The warship was powerlessly adrift, unable to correct the force of wind and wave against her hull and sails. The crashing of wood against wood met Lilith's ears and another cheer erupted from the deck of the Maiden. The warship jarred with impact, listing under the force of the wind leveraging her hull against that of the long-defeated Valor. The splintering cry of wood crashing into sharp coral pierced the air. Lilith's heart soared at the prospect of another victory.

"Sail! Sail to the south of us Captain!" Trina's voice carried down from aloft. Lilith looked up to her friend. Trina's arm extended southward over the sea. Her face was wracked by a grimace of disbelief and fear. Lilith raced across the Maiden's deck, grabbing onto the larboard rail to stop herself from piling overboard. A bank of dark clouds was pushing its way northward, obscuring the seas beneath in an ominous shadow broken by a few columns of sunlight streaking through breaks in the cloud cover. A haze of heavy rain hung beneath the clouds. Lilith scanned along the shadows, searching for what had Trina in a visible panic.

"I don't see it." Lilith said aloud, she turned, looking around the deck for another pair of eyes. Chibs lifted himself up onto the main deck from the stairs leading below, his eyes met Lilith's and then averted to the horizon behind her.

"Holy mother of God." Chibs uttered, extending his arm toward the horizon.

Lilith turned back outboard, squinting to focus on what both of her most trusted companions had seen. Mists of rain cleared under a strong gust of wind. A massive set of full white sails came into view. The hull of the ship beneath them was enormous. Their Union Jack banner whipped in the growing intensity of the wind propelling the massive ship toward the Drowned

Maiden.

A spike of panic ran through Lilith's veins, threatening to paralyze her in its grip. Her ribs tightened. Her finger went cold with terror. Lilith set her jaw. She lowered her brow and drew in a deep breath. "I will not go quietly." She whispered.

In a bound, Lilith jumped onto the larboard rail, gripping a stay line in one hand while drawing her cutlass with the other. "All hands, hard to starboard! Make for the cove! Ready the batteries and arm yourselves!"

The Drowned Maiden heaved, making a lumbering turn toward the mouth of the cove. Her masts listed under the force of the wind while her crew frenzied to ready themselves and their ship for the coming engagement.

"Brace yourselves!" Chibs called over the deck as the Maiden sailed past the warship still smashing itself to pieces against the hulk of the Valor and the reef below its hull. Bodies of sailors, alive and dead collided with the Maiden's hull as she slipped by with only a narrow gap of sea between her and the dying ship. Screams of agony and screams of anger floated through the wind from a crew that fought a hopeless battle to salvage themselves and rescue their ship. As they passed, Lilith spotted their captain in his uniform coat and hat. He held a curved sword, pointed at Lilith in a gesture of defiance, his face emanated a crimson fury. Lilith drew her pistol, leveled it at the officer and squeezed off her shot, crumpling his body to the deck and tossing his hat to the wind.

Chibs came to Lilith's side. "Cap'n, they don't have

to follow us to finish this. Those guns will lay the Maiden bare for the sea."

"I know Chibs. But we can't outrun her." Lilith replied without looking over to him. Her eyes were locked on the towering warship approaching the mouth of the cove. "We'll turn for the starboard battery. Once we've fired whatever we have at them, abandon ship."

Chibs eyes went wide. "Cap'n…"

"Just damn do it Chibs!" Lilith interrupted his protest. The huge warship outside the cove began a cumbersome turn, heaving its side toward the Maiden and revealing two rows of gun ports opening in rapid succession.

"Captain!" Trina's voice called from above. Lilith looked up to see the panic painted across Trina's face.

"Helm! Hard to starboard!" Lilith cried, her grip on the stay line tightened, biting the coarse rope into her palm. She felt the deck shift beneath her. The Maiden's agile turn pulled her weight against her hand squeezing the stay. Lilith dropped down to the deck and ran to the starboard rail, her heart raced, she expected the massive warship to release their broadside at any second. "Ready on the starboard battery!" she called.

"Starboard battery ready and waiting!" a voice from below echoed. It was Lieutenant Shelton.

Lilith paused. The wind blustered her face and floated her curly hair. The front of rains had caught them and it poured hard, splattering big droplets on the deck and creating a haze just above the water's surface. A moment passed and time seemed to stand still for Lilith. Outside the towering bluff walls of the cove her adversary sat, positioned to rain hellfire and misery over her and her crew. There was nowhere to run, no chance of evasion and escape. Lilith drew a deep breath. She looked up at Trina in the rigging, Omibwe at the helm and then to Chibs just over her shoulder. Chibs eyes met hers. He gave her that knowing smile, the smile of a father that had just witnessed his daughter giving the world hell. Lilith turned back to look at the warship and rose her voice so everyone aboard could hear. "Fire!"

'North Wind'
18 Apr 1809
19 Degrees 34' N, 73 Degrees 0' W

Rain poured in relentless torrents, dripping from North Wind's rigging and soaking her sails. Admiral Torren stood high on the aft castle, overlooking the sea gap between his flag ship and the cove opening where he had successfully trapped his quarry. H.M.S Destiny was breaking apart, battered by the wind and waves into what remained of the Valor's hull and a reef beneath the surface. They were clever creatures, these pirates. Not only had they managed to coax the Valor's crew into running her aground, they had used the reef as a weapon again after disabling the Destiny's rudder in a heavy wind. Rainwater dripped from the admiral's hat, soaking into his heavy wool boat cloak. Flashes of lightning punctuated the dark skies, illuminating his enemy across the stretch of haze created by the hard rain splattering onto the water's surface. They had turned to, bringing their cannons to bear against North Wind. Admiral Torren smiled. It was a brash move, a defiant move. This girl pirate Pike had told him about was a fire pot. No matter. Daring or not, she had been bested and Admiral Torren would see her ship blown into bits and shards while he sipped his tea.

Lieutenant Thatcher came to his side, shielding a steaming cup from the rain with his off hand. He handed it over to the admiral. "Larboard battery has run out the guns. They are ready and waiting Sir."

Admiral Torren held the delicate cup to his lips and gave it a blow, sending wisps of steam forward. He took a small sip and nodded. "Right then. One gun to range her, then volley until there is nothing left." The admiral paused for a moment, dropping his teacup to chest level. "Bring up our prisoner, Pike. I should like for him to watch his fellows while they squalor under our guns."

The admiral's orders were interrupted by a partial broadside fired by the pirates. Through the wind their cannons made a low thump, several guns firing in near succession. The shots careened through the air, a high, hollow whistle announcing their approach. Above North Wind's deck the main sail danced as a pair of shots passed through tearing the canvas and snapping a few lines. Near the bow a shot collided with wood, smashing pieces of rail and hull inward. Several other hissed past the warship, landing far beyond them into the sea.

"Fury and defiance. I suppose I should have rather liked to have met this girl. She has brass." Admiral Torren mumbled over his tea. He turned back to

Lieutenant Thatcher, "Carry on lad."

Lieutenant Thatcher departed with urgent steps. He passed the admiral's orders to several officers waiting on the weather deck. Admiral Torren watched as they all scurried to their tasks. His gaze shifted out over the water, landing on the frigate inside the cove. Their black flag whipped in the rising gale of wind. Waves crashed over the wooden hulks of Destiny and Valor while rains battered everything in sight. The admiral thought of his friend, Admiral Elliot Sharpe with a slight smile creeping at the edges of his mouth. He thought of the promising young Captain Grimes and Captain Brant. All those lives, wasted to this abhorrent crew of brigands and traitors. Admiral Torren's smile faded and he set his jaw, he grew impatient for the battery to unleash their payload.

"Well?" Admiral Torren craned his neck, shouting across the deck and through the wind at the officers gathered near the helm. "I don't give orders for my health. Fire the damned batteries already!"

Midshipman Brant snapped to, scrambling toward the stairs, his full cheeks reddened by the admiral's tone. He disappeared below deck and in another moment a voice trailed up from the gun decks, "Fire!"

A deafening roar erupted from North Wind's larboard batteries, sending bright flashes and barreling clouds of gun smoke hurling over the water. Admiral Torren shook his head. The scatter of impacts landed in a haphazard mix all around the pirate vessel, only a few found their target.

"Powder is not a commodity to be wasted, lads. Range her with a single gun and then fire the batteries in unison for god's sake." The admiral snapped, his voice carrying through the wind. Another fresh-faced officer departed the deck to head below and relay the admiral's order.

Moments later a pair of marines escorted William Pike and Lieutenant Thatcher up to the deck next to where Admiral Torren stood observing his target. "As you requested Sir. Mr. Pike." Lieutenant Thatcher looked pleased with himself.

Admiral Torren handed the lieutenant his empty teacup. "It seems your comprehension is challenged as of late. I wanted Mr. Pike first, the enemy vessel ranged by a single gun next and then a full volley once those were completed. Clean your ears out and focus yourself young man, or the next time you'll be heaving at line and scrubbing deck board for the rest of our voyage."

Lieutenant Thatcher looked shocked and then ashamed, his eyes lowered to the deck. "Aye Sir. It won't happen again."

Admiral Torren gave a scathing glare to Will, "You will watch as I deliver the King's justice to your cohorts. Then we will sail to Kingston, where you will hang by your neck overlooking the harbor where you first betrayed your countrymen while I restore order from the chaos you have created."

A single cannon shot sounded. The sea just in front of the pirate ship erupted into a plume of water blowing high over their deck. A voice below deck called out the firing adjustment. Moments passed. Admiral Torren scowled at William while he wavered on unsteady legs. The volley fired in near perfect unison, rattling North Wind from the massive recoil of her guns. William dropped to his knees, letting a gasp escape from his gashed, swollen lips. He raised his voice calling out through a cracking voice, "Lilith!"

'Drowned Maiden'
18 Apr 1809
Pirate Cove, Haiti

Lilith looked on in terror as the volley from Drowned Maiden's battery sliced over the deck of the warship outside the cove. A pair of impacts near the bow did little damage while the rest of their shot zipped through rigging and sails. Time seemed to pause. Her heart pounded the inside of her chest as if it were trying to escape. She knew what was coming next. Somewhere through her racing pulse her ears detected Chibs yelling to her.

"Cap'n, Cap'n we have to go!" his voice seemed muffled, as if he were shouting to her through a thick wooden bulkhead. "Abandon ship!"

Lilith turned inboard and scanned over the deck. Her crew scurried all around her, making their way to the rails and fleeing for their lives. Dr. LeMeux held out an extended hand to Omibwe, hoisting the one-legged helmsman up onto the wooden rail. Chibs with his bald head and graying beard helped Jilhal up the stairs from below deck. Lilith looked aloft. Trina remained high in the rigging, perched above topsail by the mast. For a moment their gaze met. Her heart slowed. It felt as if it would stop in her chest, dragging on in slow motion as everything around her seemed to carry on. She filled with despair. A hopeless void of failure and regret.

"Lilith!" the coarse voice was familiar. Lilith turned to see Chibs pointing behind her.

A cloud of smoke burst forth from the side of the great warship squared off just beyond the mouth of the cove. Lilith's eyes just barely caught the flashes as they died into the cloud of white smoke that signaled the Maiden's sure destruction. The roar that followed permeated everything, rolling along the surface of the sea and shaking the Maiden's decks. It reverberated through the wooden planks, climbing through Lilith's feet and traveling up until she could feel the sick rumble in her stomach. The howling shriek followed. An ear-piercing cry, the first notes of the Maiden's death song.

Lilith felt a hand grab her upper arm. Everything seemed a blur. The terrible shrieks of cannon shot whistling and ending in the crunching maw of twisted and cracking timbers. One impact, then another. The Maiden heaved and trembled from each impact, slamming her to the deck and breaking the grip that had seized her upper arm. A moment passed; another impact came followed by another. They seemed to be never-ending and all at once. The hand that had gripped her locked onto her upper arm again. She smelled the faint wisp of tobacco smoke and leather. Chibs. His grip pulled her, her legs drug helpless over the deck. Another impact trembled the deck beneath them. Lilith twisted her neck to look up. She could see Chibs, his face pulled into a straining grimace as he hauled her to the larboard rail. Stay lines whipped in a frenzy through the air as another pair of impacts hit in quick succession. She felt Chibs' grip pull her in a violent whip before letting go. Her eyes caught the sky. Rigging. The Maiden's ripped ribbons of sails, slack lines blowing about under the fury of the wind and onslaught of the cannon fire. The black banner, snarling in the gale blew through her vision until all she could see was the surface of the water rising up to greet her.

A stinging ribbon of pain laced across Lilith's face, hands, chest and belly as the chill water surrounded her. In an instant the world had become silent. The tinkling sound of water entering her ears and bubbles escaping from her nose and mouth were all she could sense. A moment of disorientation settled over her and panic rose into her chest as she tried to find which direction was upward. Her head spun and her body ached, her fingers still stung from the shock of the impact. A rush of movement and noise beyond her head alerted Lilith to look upward. She saw nothing, just a blur of sea green and shadows of debris falling from the Maiden. Another gasp of air escaped her lungs and a cloud of bubble rose in front of her face. It rose to the surface and Lilith's eyes followed. Taking hold of the consciousness she had left, Lilith shot her arms overhead and pulled at the seawater separating her from the world above. She kicked her legs in a desperate frenzy, slicing her arms upward and pulling the sea back one drag at a time. Her lungs heaved inside her chest, her throat spasming to taste air. Lilith could feel everything around her slipping, the physical world was pulling away the same as it had the night she had nearly drowned in the Port-au-Prince harbor. Her thoughts drifted into that chilly water where she had felt her life slipping away from her. She thought of Chibs, of Captain James and then Will. She remembered the look in her mother's eyes the night before Lilith had killed Francis Gereux and she remembered the sickly gasp that exited his lips as her blade found its way into his throat. Her face broke free of the surface and Lilith sucked in a panicked breath. She thrashed the water as it pulled at her, beckoning her back into the depths. Another breath met her lungs. She opened her eyes.

The water's surface was littered with debris and bodies. Jagged, broken timbers snaked with line floated all around her. The sky was blotted by more than dark storm clouds, a thick column of dark smoke poured from the Maiden's belly. Her decks were groaning as the sea invaded her hull. Lilith clawed her way past flotsam and line to the listing hull. She put her hands up onto the rough timbers of the Maiden's, trying to sink her fingernails into the thick grain of the wood.

"NO!" she screamed as she could feel the ship trembling and breaking apart through her hands. Her eyes welled tears. Rage engulfed her. The sickening crack of wood beckoned her eyes upward and Lilith could only hold her hands aloft as a section of rail came crashing down onto her, knocking her unconscious and pulling her back into the grip of the cove.

Chapter 18

'Pirate Cove'
18 Apr 1809

Emilia's heart raced as she took in the battle. It was the most exciting thing she had ever witnessed. The ships fired at one another sending clouds of smoke pluming into the wind. With wide eyes and a knotted stomach, Emilia watched as the big navy warship had sent its first volley scattering through the cove, doing little to threaten the pirates. A single shot followed not long after. The winds howled and rain beat down hard, soaking Emilia's clothes and raising goosebumps across her arms and neck. Far below, in the narrow neck of water that led connected the cove with the sea the corpses of two warships clattered together cracking their wooden planks. Emilia took in the brief pause as the two ships appeared to be waiting for something. The pirate ship inside the cove was alive with movement. Emilia could see figures scrambling to leave their vessel.

It struck her as odd, to watch these figure she had

imagined as daring and brave in such a mad scramble to depart their ship while locked in battle. Emilia stood, looking around to make sure she wasn't missing some detail. What came next startled her, sending a lightning bolt of adrenaline through her blood. The warship offshore fired her batteries sending a series of resounding booms out over the water. Emilia watched their effect on the pirate ship. Each shot that landed sent a wave of wooden debris flying. Lines snapped and whipped the air above her decks slicing sail and even hitting one of the pirates on board.

It was gruesome, the destruction seemed never ending. Each round that impacted was followed by another as the warship mercilessly continued firing her guns. Emilia's stomach turned flips and knotted as she watched the carnage ensue. Her plans to leave Haiti were being blown into slivers before her eyes and the fearsome pirate crew were reduced to rats trying to escape a sinking cage.

Emilia felt a sudden rush. A panicking urge to try and help. On the far side of the pirate ship, she could see figures paddling and blustering their way toward the beach. Another shot impacted. Emilia's feet began to move. She started in a trot down the hill, carefully placing her feet to avoid slipping down the steep slope. Another cannon round struck the pirate ship. Emilia could hear a sickening crack split through the wind. Her feet moved faster and faster until she was racing downhill in reckless abandon. The pirate ship's tallest mast wavered while the sounds of cracking and twisting wood reverberated through the wind and rain. The woman Emilia had seen high up on the mast earlier toppled to the waves slapping through the surface in a splash that brought a cringe through her spine. She slipped and slid through the mud, flying downhill to the water's edge. Reaching the sands of the beach inside the cove, Emilia could see a canted plume of smoke pouring from the pirate ship. It chuffed out of the gun ports, rose from the deck openings and caught in the wind. Thick, black smoke that choked out her view of most of the upwind side of the ship.

A female voice cried out in desperation, "No!"

Emilia squinted to make out the white shirt of a dark-skinned woman, her arms were raised from where she floated next to the hull of the ship, hands clawing at the hull as if she were trying to climb back aboard. Another cannon shot impacted sending a large hulk of debris toppling over the side. Emilia grimaced as the debris fell, slamming the desperate woman beneath the surface.

Without a thought Emilia ran into the water, lifting her legs and slogging as fast as she could until she was in up to her waist. Heaving a deep breath, she plunged forward striding her arm's length by length and fluttering her feet the way her father had taught her. Beneath the surface, Emilia opened her eyes and watched as the floor of the cove eased away beneath her, growing deeper as she continued swimming toward the doomed vessel. The white shirt caught her eye. It was a blur through the depth of the cove, but Emilia knew from where it was located it could only be the woman, she had watched get drug beneath the waves. Pulling her face above the surface, Emilia took in a big breath before diving downward and kicking her way to the sandy bottom.

The woman was pinned beneath a length of timber with short, rounded columns attached beneath it. Emilia could feel the pressure of the depth build in her ears as she drew near. The trapped woman lay motionless with a small stream of bubbles escaping from her lips. She had a gash across her brow, from above her eyes down through her cheek and back toward the rear of her jaw. Blood clouded the water around her head. Emilia grabbed onto the debris pinning the woman and pulled. The length of wood budged, but just barely. She summoned more strength, fighting against the urge to surface and pull in a deep breath of air. Emilia planted her feet into the soft sandy bottom and pulled against the debris with all her might. Under the length of wood, Emilia could see the woman's body begin to float freely. With panic rising inside her chest, Emilia reached through the sea pressing in all around her and grabbed a fistful of the woman's shirt. She pulled her body free and let go of the debris with her other hand, kicking in a wild frenzy to return them both to the surface.

Emilia's lungs filled with a gasp of air as her head broke through the chopping waves. She pulled the woman along behind her and panted in between waves enveloping her face as she made her way toward the strip of sand along the shoreline. When her hand plunged into soft wet sand Emilia pulled herself to her feet, dragging the woman out of reach from the waves that lapped up onto the shore. Smoke poured from the pirate ship and with a loud groan it listed over onto its side, the rear of the vessel dipping below the waves. Emilia pulled her attention back to the woman she had pulled from the depths, laying her on her side and cradling her torso between her knees as she sat down on the wet sand of the beach. She was young, much younger than Emilia had first thought. The gash that curved from her brow through her eye and cheek was bleeding profusely, covering Emilia's hands and legs as she patted the woman's back trying to coax her to consciousness. With a sputtering cough that produced a lungful of seawater, the woman belched and retched over Emilia's legs, gasping for air between convulsions. Through the wind and the driving rain, her goosebumps eased for a moment as a warmth entered her body from some deep inner well. The woman heaved in a deep breath without choking out any more sea water, her eyes opened.

Thank you for reading this installment of
Treachery and Triumph
Be on the lookout for the next titles in the series.

Find my other book series, sign up for newsletter announcements including special releases and giveaways. Just scan the QR code below.

Follow along on Facebook and Instagram for cover reveals and special announcements.

If you enjoyed this title, please be sure to leave a review on Amazon or Goodreads.

Made in the USA
Coppell, TX
09 September 2024

37002801R00252